Two brand-new stories in every volume... twice a month!

Duets Vol. #91

Talented Dawn Atkins serves up not one but two delightful stories in a special Double Duets. *Wedding for One* and *Tattoo for Two* are about two bad girls—and buddies—who come home again. Mariah hooks up with the sexy Mr. Right she left at the altar eight years before. Meantime Nikki shows up with a fake fiancé whose kisses are a little too real at times! Chaos ensues as these two girls set things right.

Duets Vol. #92

Versatile Natalie Bishop returns to the series this month with the quirky *Love on Line One!* "Ms. Bishop writes with a sizzling intensity... spirit and depth," says *Romantic Times*. Completing the volume is popular Holly Jacobs and *Not Precisely Pregnant*. Bestselling author Lori Foster notes that "every Holly Jacobs book will leave you with a laugh and a happy sigh." Enjoy!

Be sure to pick up both Duets volumes today!

Love on Line One!

"I want you back on the show— pronto," Jake announced.

"You really stirred up the listeners."

"*You* really stirred up the listeners. I just sat back and took the abuse," Julie said archly.

"You didn't just sit back. I have some scars." He grinned. "And I want to talk about the coincidence of our past together."

She had trouble holding his gaze. "You mean you want to exploit the fact that we've known each other since grade school? That I hid my identity from you?"

"Maybe we could clear up a few points in your favor," Jake suggested. "I'd like to have you back on the show. Maybe you could reveal some of your techniques and I could reveal…?"

"You show me yours, I'll show you mine?" Julie asked, heat coloring her cheeks.

"Something like that."

"Tuesday."

"Tuesday it is," he said, settling back in his chair.

She wondered if there was enough red wine here to get her drunk, because she suffered from the distinct feeling that she'd just been coaxed, coerced and *had*.

For more, turn to page 9

This press conference is a disaster, thought Riley.

A class-A, number one debacle thanks to that TV reporter, Paige Montgomery. How was he supposed to get the details of the mayor's announcement with her incessant chatter?

"What, what did the mayor say? You distracted me so I missed it, and now I can't even ask a question," Riley said accusingly.

"The mayor said that the city is going to receive that big state grant for revitalizing the downtown area," Paige explained.

Riley scribbled some notes for his column. "How do you know? You were busy arguing with me."

"I don't argue. You argue. I'm just sort of the wall you toss your shots at. They tend to bounce back at you without my even trying. And I heard what he said because I'm a woman. We multitask. It all comes from being genetically programmed as the foragers and gatherers. We're forced to concentrate on many things at once. Men are genetically predisposed to be the hunters. They concentrate on one thing, and blot out everything else. I'm flattered you chose to focus on me and not the mayor."

Riley just glanced heavenward. *Oh, good grief.*

For more, turn to page 197

HARLEQUIN DUETS

ISBN 0-373-44158-4

Copyright in the collection:
Copyright © 2003 by Harlequin Books S.A.

The publisher acknowledges the copyright holder
of the individual works as follows:

LOVE ON LINE ONE!
Copyright © 2003 by Nancy Bush

NOT PRECISELY PREGNANT
Copyright © 2003 by Holly Fuhrmann

This edition published by arrangement with Harlequin Books S.A.

® and TM are trademarks of the publisher. Trademarks indicated with ® are registered in the United States Patent and Trademark Office, the Canadian Trade Marks Office and in other countries.

Visit us at www.eHarlequin.com

Printed in U.S.A.

Love on Line One!

Natalie Bishop

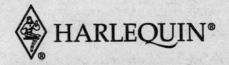

TORONTO • NEW YORK • LONDON
AMSTERDAM • PARIS • SYDNEY • HAMBURG
STOCKHOLM • ATHENS • TOKYO • MILAN • MADRID
PRAGUE • WARSAW • BUDAPEST • AUCKLAND

Dear Reader,

Thought I'd send you a recipe to explain it all.

First add Julie, our heroine. She's a psychologist,
but she just can't keep herself from "acting out"
every time she's around Jake, a longtime/sometime
friend of hers. Stir in Jake, our hero, and wow…
it's one of those baking soda/yeast kind of things.
Lots of bubbling and rising, if you know what I mean.
Except Julie and Jake are a lot like oil and water—they
simply don't mix! So to make this all work, fold in a
tablespoon or two of her baker roommate, Nora,
with a quart of Jake's job as a radio talk-show host—
a fact guaranteed to send Julie's temperature to 425
degrees—and you've got all the ingredients that
make *Love on Line One!* a confection of romance
and humor.

Enjoy.

Natalie Bishop

Books by Natalie Bishop

HARLEQUIN DUETS
51—TWO ACROSS, TWO DOWN

SILHOUETTE SPECIAL EDITION
  651—DOWNRIGHT DANGEROUS
  700—ROMANCING RACHEL
  840—A LOVE LIKE ROMEO AND JULIET
  882—THE PRINCESS OF COLDWATER FLAT
1086—VALENTINE'S CHILD

Don't miss any of our special offers. Write to us at the
following address for information on our newest releases.

Harlequin Reader Service
U.S.: 3010 Walden Ave., P.O. Box 1325, Buffalo, NY 14269
Canadian: P.O. Box 609, Fort Erie, Ont. L2A 5X3

Prologue

"LOOKS LIKE WE HAVE just enough time for one more caller," Jake Danforth said, giving DeeAnn a sign of acknowledgment as she pointed for him to pick up the line.

Hands cupping her lips, DeeAnn mouthed, "Her name's Shar. Short for Sharlene."

Punching the flashing light on line one, Jake asked, "Shar?"

"Oh, my God. I'm on the air? With *Jake Danforth?*"

She sounded as if she were about to shriek with excitement. Jake quickly said, "Yes, yes, you are definitely on the air. We've got ten minutes till nine o'clock, so jump right on in."

"You were talking about your divorce," she said. "'Cause it was final yesterday, I believe?"

Jake inwardly sighed. The price of being a public figure. Hit the news head-on and pretend like you don't care. "That's right."

"You know, you said your wife...er...ex-wife, I guess, went to that psychic? And she's the one who told your ex to divorce you?"

"Psychologist," he corrected. DeeAnn regarded him with sympathy and he shrugged lightly. Airing his dirty laundry on the air bothered him, but it was all his listeners seemed to want to talk about these days. He would just have to weather it out.

"Well, I think that's just plain mean! I think you should go to that psychic yourself and tell her a thing or two!"

"Psychologist," he corrected again. "And apparently she's a marriage counselor, too."

"Hah!" Shar sniffed in disgust. "Didn't you say she used tarot cards?"

"That's what I understand."

"Well, then, she's pretendin' to be somethin' she's not. The tarot isn't meant to be taken so literally. The tarot is merely a guide. It is not an absolute."

"Do you read the tarot, Shar?"

"I can sure pick out a charlatan, now can't I? This woman, what's her name…?"

"Julie Sommerfield."

"You think she has any idea what she's talkin' about?"

"My ex obviously believed in her."

"I'm talkin' about you, Jake. What do *you* think? I mean, *really?*"

Jake looked over at DeeAnn, who was picking up her bag and a few files from the top of her desk. She sat in on Jake's morning radio show and played devil's advocate, but today she hadn't needed to. Everybody was calling, wanting Jake to know what they thought of his ex and her celestial advisor.

"You want to know what I think?" he asked in a tone that had DeeAnn stopping cold in her tracks. She gazed at him with real worry. He ignored her. He was normally so good about keeping his feelings in check even when he'd really bitten into an issue. But right now he felt like letting it all out. "I think this Julie Sommerfield is a psychoanalyst-wanna-be. Yep.'' He nodded in self-satisfaction, ignoring Dee-Ann's wildly waving arms as she tried to gain his attention. ''Probably throws around phrases like 'control-taking' and 'self-esteem building' and 'understanding your own worth' blah, blah, blah. Then asks for payment before you've got one foot out the door. Look at what she draws inspiration from—tarot cards. I'm sure she reads the stars and tea leaves and consults with an inner voice. Does she know anything about relationships? Doubtful. Probably speaks in tongues. The kind of crackpot who shouldn't be allowed to consult with human beings at all. But hey, call me bitter, if you will. My ex not only got royally soaked by this 'marriage counselor,' she suggested I go see this nutcase myself!''

DeeAnn made a choking sound and slipped out of the room.

''I think you *should* go see her!'' Shar declared. ''You should! And tell her Shar sent you!''

The lights for all the phone lines lit up and began blinking furiously. Jake grimaced, knowing he'd taken that one step too far, the one that sent you over the edge of the cliff. But it was too late now.

''I'll think about it,'' he told her. ''But here's Zipper,'' he added with relief as his 9:00 a.m. replacement stepped inside and closed the door behind him. ''Okay, I'll be back at 6:00 a.m. sharp tomorrow. Have a good day, Portland, and keep your significant others away from pseudo-psychologists.'' He grinned to himself. ''Julie Sommerfield and your ilk, watch out. We're on to you....''

1

"I'M GOING TO HAVE TO KILL HIM," Julie Sommerfield said matter-of-factly as she turned a page of the Sunday paper. "Yep. It's going to have to be done. And it's too bad because I really don't like to think of myself as a murderer." She glanced around the paper at Nora Carlton, her best friend and roommate. "Or, would that be murder*ess?*"

"Murderess." Nora squeezed orange icing onto a cinnamon roll, forming a row of teeth in the mouth of a grinning jack-o'-lantern face.

"Murder*ess.*" Julie rolled that over in her mind. "I've dealt with Jake Danforth for more years than it's fair to count, and it's got to come to an end. A shame, really, because he is good-looking, and I used to really like him."

Nora examined her handiwork. She touched up one of the triangular eyes. "He was your Romeo."

"He was the *school's* Romeo. And he earned that nickname fair and square."

"You were in love with him."

"I was in *lust* with him," Julie corrected, snapping the paper together and tossing it onto the floor along with the rest of the scattered pages. She really hated it when Nora chose to have the last word. "You have to admit, though, he's gone too far. How could he say those things about me?"

"He doesn't know it's you," Nora reminded her, but Julie wasn't listening.

"He must be stopped. And I've got to do it."

"How?"

"Hmmm?"

"How are you going to kill him?"

"Oh..." Julie narrowed her blue eyes in serious concentration. "Something slow and torturous. Maybe some deadly poison, the kind that slowly accumulates over time, so no one would suspect it was me when he finally takes that last dose and keels over." She wrapped her hands around her own throat and made gagging sounds.

"How are you going to administer it?"

"Good question." She cocked her head. "I'd have to get it in his cough medicine, or something," she said, working it out. "Then I could sit back and wait for it to happen."

"What if somebody else drank the cough medicine?"

"He lives alone. He hates everybody. Except his dog. *I* hate his dog."

"How do you know his dog?"

"It's the same damn one his parents had! Don't you remember? It must be a hundred years old now."

"You mean—Seltzer?"

"Seltzer! Yes! What a name. And they had a cat called Alka." She gave a mock shudder. "There's something seriously wrong with that entire family."

Nora lifted a noncommittal shoulder.

Julie's sweep of chin-length brown hair swung forward and she pushed it aside impatiently. "Anyway, he would never feed the cough syrup to Seltzer. I think this plan could work."

"Where are you going to get this poison?"

"What about a garden shop? All those bottles of insect killer with skulls and crossbones on them? They're just sitting on the shelf, waiting for me."

"Do they really have skulls and crossbones on them?" Nora asked curiously.

"Well, I'm not really sure. Maybe they've got Mr. Yuck on them. Is Mr. Yuck still around? The little green guy who sticks his tongue out? They had Mr. Yuck on poisons when I was a kid."

"Wouldn't he be able to taste the insecticide? I'm pretty sure I'd be able to taste it." With that Nora squeezed icing onto her finger then sucked it off. "Hmmm...not bad."

"Let me try."

Julie climbed to her feet and crossed to the kitchen, reaching out her hand across the counter. Nora drew a circle of icing onto her index finger and as Julie tentatively tasted it with the tip of her tongue, she said, "I'm hoping to sell two thousand of them at that Halloween waterfront bazaar next Saturday. Think I'll do it?"

Nora had a tiny shop in the heart of Portland's Twenty-third Street, a narrow hallway whose glass cases were filled with her famous baked goods. She continually sold out and was in the process of hiring more help.

"How much are you charging?" Julie asked.

"An arm and a leg."

"Apropos for Halloween. But wouldn't money be easier?"

"You're so funny," Nora said, smiling. "I just hope Irving St. Cloud and his army of white-coated clones don't choose to join me."

It was Julie's turn to be noncommittal. Nora had an ongoing battle with the newest chain store phenomenon in the northwest: St. Cloud Bakeries. St. Cloud outlets were popping up at an alarming rate, and it was leaving the independents like Nora's Nut Rolls, Etc. shaking in their collective boots.

"I'm sure St. Cloud's will have a booth at Waterfront Park," Julie gently warned. "But their cinnamon rolls aren't even close to yours."

Nora's lips tightened as she bent over the jack-o'-lantern face, icing wand at the ready. Julie sighed and returned to her theme, "I'd love a slow death to make up for all the years Jake tortured me. But…I'll probably just have to shoot him. Quick and simple. A drive-by."

"You'll have to get a gun." Nora handed Julie the prototype cinnamon roll.

"And then learn how to use it. Thanks," she said looking down at the widely grinning orange face gazing up at her. She and Nora had been friends since grade school, since the time Jake Danforth and his buddies had lived within their Beaverton neighborhood and pelted them with apples and cherries whenever they walked by. Nora had always run away, ignoring and avoiding the army of boys, but Julie had stood her ground and taken the abuse. Several times she'd managed to smash Bing cherries across Jake's shirt, watching the purple-red juice stain his clothes before he could wrench free and pelt her anew.

But then they hit junior high and high school and everything had changed for the worse. Prom night senior year. Julie's date had gotten drunk with one of his pals in the bathroom and Jake's girlfriend had spent the evening crying because they were all graduating and Jake was heading back East and what was she going to do? So, Julie and Jake had ended up standing outside the function on a warm May evening where emotions ran high. It was one of those weird things that sometimes happen to the sanest people. One moment they were smiling at each other and recounting their miserable prom evenings, then they were reliving those childhood moments of mutual dislike, then they were driving to Jake's parents' home, now in a chichi neighborhood along a cliff's edge in the West Hills, and then suddenly they were entwined together, making love in the guest house with the windows open to hear the whisper of the wind through the cherry blossoms and feel it feather across their naked bodies.

Well…

It all ended when Jake's girlfriend burst into the guest house, damn near caught them in the act and let the entire school know the following Monday. To be fair, Jake tried to stop the rumors, but his soon-to-be-ex let fly with enough terrible slams to Julie's character that the last few weeks of high school were a mind-numbing blur of misery.

College erased those terrible last days. She attended the University of Washington until she ran smack into Jake Danforth one fine day. Literally ran smack into his hard flesh. He marveled at seeing her again, but Julie, sensing a strange, still unsatisfied attraction to him, transferred as fast as the admissions process would let her to the University of Oregon. Several years later, armed with a degree in psychology, a short-lived, ill-fated marriage and a whole new level of self-esteem, she returned to Portland to share offices with a psychologist specializing in marriage counseling. Julie had learned she possessed a listening ear and a fair mind, and she'd built her reputation over the past few years as a strong, sensible and caring counselor. Then last spring her partner retired and she inherited his lengthy clientele list. She was now a specialist in marriage counseling, and she'd been the reason more than a few of the couples she counseled stayed together—her ultimate goal.

Except when murder seemed like the appropriate solution.

"If this murder thing gets out, won't it affect your business?" Nora pointed out reasonably as she watched Julie nibble around the edges of the roll. "I mean, murder's kind of a last resort if you're trying to work out marriage problems, wouldn't you say?"

"Hey, Jake Danforth is the one affecting my business! I have to do something. Drastic measures are called for."

Nora arched a dark brow and wisely refrained from saying what was on her mind. In most ways, Julie Sommerfield was the consummate professional. Over the course of the past five years she had saved dozens of whacked-out marriages by her simple nononsense demeanor and advice, no easy task when the couples generally arrived with their hands wrapped around each other's throats, metaphorically speaking.

But mention the name Jake Danforth and Julie went straight back to junior high thoughts and actions. It was uncanny.

"I can't believe he's got his own radio talk show," Julie murmured for about the millionth time. She glanced at Nora who grimaced sympathetically.

"Maybe you shouldn't have advised his wife to leave him," Nora said.

Julie gazed at Nora as if she'd mortally wounded her. "I didn't advise her to leave him. She was already gone. *She* told *me* what a jerk he is, and I already knew firsthand anyway! He had no right to malign me on his show that way."

"He was a bit harsh."

"A *bit harsh!*" Nora braced herself and wasn't disappointed. In a rush Julie declared, "He *said* I read tarot cards for my inspiration. He said I was a crackpot who shouldn't be allowed to consult with human beings! He *said*—"

"He doesn't know who you are," she broke in quickly, reminding her again. "You've changed your name. He was really kind of joking."

Julie narrowed her eyes and took a massive bite out of the roll. She tried not to be influenced by Nora's reasoning. She wanted to nurse this grudge and even though she knew Jake Danforth remembered her as Juliet Adams, not Julie Sommerfield, she didn't care. He'd made those cracks on the air, and she'd been smarting from the repercussions ever since. Even Carolyn Mathers had expressed sympathy, and she was on the top of Julie's list of most unstable personalities—and that was saying something.

"These are fabulous," Julie said, reluctantly pushing aside the remains of the cinnamon roll. She wanted to groan aloud, from frustration and the bloated feeling that came from overeating on one of Nora's incredible baked goods. Nora's Nut Rolls, Etc. was a roaring success and Julie was afraid Nora might be thinking of moving out of their two-bedroom apartment into bigger and better accommodations. Though Nora only used the kitchen to dabble with recipes, she'd been grumbling about its tiny U-shape for months. It was clear that she wanted to move into a larger space, but Julie couldn't bear the thought. She liked things just the way they were. She wanted Nora to stay and she wanted Jake Danforth to evaporate. Poof! Go up in smoke, never to be seen or heard from again.

"You said yourself his comments haven't hurt your business. People are banging down your door, trying to be your client. And you know what Jake's like."

"More's the pity," she muttered grumpily.

"He doesn't sound all that upset about his wife leaving him. People keep asking him about it and he admits the relationship just ran its course. I know he went off on you, but that's kind of unusual."

Julie gave her a long look. "You sound like you're defending him. He made me sound like a gypsy fortune-teller who specializes in curses!"

"But you did read his wife's future from tarot cards."

"Oh, no, no, no, no. She read them to me! Then she showed me how to do it and we went over her cards together. She was teaching me, and it kept her from crying and sobbing over Jake. It got her focused on something besides her own hurt."

"I'm just saying, that's why he said those things on the air."

"You want to be an accessory to Jake's murder?"

"I don't think I have time," Nora said. "Remember, he doesn't know it's you."

Julie made a face. Oh, she knew Nora was right.

Jake had no way of realizing whom he was damaging. But those disparaging remarks on his morning radio show had been unfair. It had sent her simmering resentment into out-and-out fury. How dare he? Didn't he know he influenced his listeners? She should sue him for slander!

Just thinking about it made her want to groan aloud. She only refrained because she knew she was already taxing the limits of Nora's empathy. And Jake hadn't just gone off about her once. Oh, no. Those initial slurs had opened up a Pandora's box of unhappy listeners who felt they'd been had by their own therapists. They called and complained and then complained about *her,* just because she'd counseled Jake's wife! Hearing her name coupled with phrases like *psychiatric hocus-pocus* and *matchbook-cover college degrees* blasting from her Volkswagen speakers as she drove her Bug from southwest Portland through the horde of morning traffic to her office off Northwest Twenty-first Street didn't exactly start the morning off right. Sure, she had her staunch supporters, and yes, the publicity apparently hadn't really hurt her business, but Jake's comments had certainly hurt her feelings.

"I bet he *does* know it's me," she murmured now. "That would explain it."

"He doesn't know."

"What's wrong with being a psychic, anyway? I should give up psychology and turn to astrology. Half the people around here pay more attention to the stars than to their suffering self-esteem. I could probably retire in five years."

"But your kooks would suffer without you."

"They're not really kooks. Well, except for Carolyn Mathers, maybe. Most of the people I see are just locked in miserable marriages.'' Julie shook her head. ''I look at them sometimes and think 'There but for the grace of God, go I.' I could have stayed married and been just like them.''

''Heaven forbid.''

''Luckily, Kurt and I knew it wasn't going to work within the first six months. We shook hands, said *sayonara* and that was it.''

''Yeah, and he went off to find himself with an eighteen-year-old coed who possessed a seven figure bank account.''

''Maybe he'll stay lost.''

Nora snorted. ''Don't worry. He couldn't find his you-know-what from a hole in the ground.''

''Come on, Nora, tell me how you really feel.''

Nora laughed and so did Julie. Nora had been too consumed in her career to take time out for romance, but she'd been there for Julie all the way.

''He wasn't your best decision,'' Nora said softly.

''No kidding.'' She hesitated a moment, then confessed, ''He looked a lot like Jake Danforth.''

''That must be painful to admit.''

''You'll never know how much.'' Julie sighed. Kurt Sommerfield had been a dreadful mistake, but it was over now. However, her problems with Jake Danforth lived on. ''I wish I didn't despise Jake so much,'' Julie said. ''It would be nice to never, ever think about him. I didn't for a long time. I mean, not really. But then when his wife walked in…it all came back.''

''Did you tell her that you knew Jake?''

''Oh, God, no!''

''Isn't that kind of unethical?''

"I didn't have time." Julie blew her bangs out of her face. "We had one session together where she blubbered away about her soon-to-be-ex. She didn't even tell me his name until she was practically walking out the door. I just listened to her go on about what a bastard he was and I asked her what she wanted to do about it, and she said she'd already left him. Then I asked her if she wanted to have a counseling session with him, and she said, 'No way in hell.' Then she ran over it all again, and again, and again...." Julie motioned with her hand to show how protracted the session had been. "So, when she brought out the tarot cards I thought, 'Why not?' It got her mind on another track. When she wrote out the check and I saw his name, I about lost it. I asked her if she was married to Jake Danforth, the radio personality. And she said, 'No, I'm married to Jake Danforth, the s.o.b.'" Julie shrugged. "I was never really sure until he mentioned it himself on the air. That was the only time I saw her."

"Well, he'll probably stop complaining about you and your ilk soon," Nora said.

"My *ilk?*"

"All you tarot-reading, psychic, mumbo-jumbo pseudo-psychologists." She grinned hugely, giving a great impression of the orange frosting jack-o'-lanterns gracing her cookies. "So, you might not have to murder him after all."

"At least I can entertain myself with a few sinister plans."

"If you hate him so much, why do you listen to his show?"

"Masochism. Pure masochism."

THE NEXT DAY Julie rolled out of bed late, groaned at the sight of the hands on her clock, then raced through her morning ablutions, grabbing another of Nora's cinnamon rolls on the way out. She jumped in her Bug and drove like a maniac, or at least like a regular commuter, cinnamon roll caught between her teeth as she shifted gears. Thirty minutes later she was racing up Glisan as fast as the traffic lights would allow. She turned off on a side street and zigzagged toward Twenty-first. Her office was really a door at the side of a building, which led directly to a stairway that led to a second floor space, which was tucked behind a trendy nail salon that offered herbal tea and indirect lighting and occupied the entire front wall of the building. Julie never understood how the manicurists operated in those dim, somnolent surroundings but it seemed to work for them. Half of her clients came for nails and then a therapy session with their marriage counselor. None of her clients seemed to mind that she had suffered through one failed marriage herself and had no intention of repeating the experience or even looking for another mate on this planet or during this millennium.

Stepping through her door, she flicked on the air-conditioning in the outer office for the unseasonably warm day, a window banger that nearly deafened her half the time. Deluxe accommodations weren't her specialty. But then she kept her prices down for the women and men facing financial ruin over their pending divorces. Still, she was surprised by some of the wealthy clients who ferreted her out. Even the richest of the rich hated paying for marriage counseling, especially if an expensive divorce waited in the wings.

The message light was blinking on her phone. Julie touched the button and goose bumps lifted on her skin as she heard a familiar male voice waft into the room. "Hello, this is Jake Danforth. My ex-wife gave me your name as the *psychologist* who helped during our divorce." The way he stressed psychologist sent Julie's blood pressure rising anew. "Ms. Sommerfield, would you be interested in coming on my show? I would like my listeners to hear some of your advice firsthand."

She hit the skip button and sat down, pulse racing. For a moment she couldn't believe her ears. She listened to the message a second time, then a third.

I'll bet he'd like his listeners to hear my advice!

He doesn't know who you are, she reminded herself. "Ms. Sommerfield" means nothing to him. After a moment she listened to the message a final time, writing down his number. She stared at it for a long, long time, then she smiled to herself and punched out the buttons, gave her name and asked for Jake Danforth. As soon as his silky voice answered, she said in a Southern drawl quite unlike her own quick tones, "Why, I would love to discuss my methods of therapy on your mornin' show, Mistah Danforth. Even though you've been kinda hard on me, I'm an admirer of yours."

"Really?" He sounded amazed and she could hardly blame him. "How about Friday?"

"Friday would be fine. I'm lookin' forward to it."

She hung up before he could respond and collapsed on the chair, one hand over her thundering heart.

Now here was a form of murder she hadn't even considered!

2

FRIDAY MORNING dawned grim and gray, the fine weather that had followed them into late October giving way to more usual northwest conditions. Julie jumped out of bed, ran through the shower, blew-dry her straight brown hair and scoured her teeth until her gums hurt. Then she carefully applied her makeup, definitely going heavier than normal. She was heading to a radio station, not television, but it didn't matter because she was seeing Jake Danforth. She wanted to have all her armor on.

Standing back, she faced herself in the mirror. Her application of eye shadow, liner and mascara defined her blue eyes and made them more mysterious than normal. Her lips were redder. She frowned, wondering what had possessed her into making them look so kissable. Just a hint of color brushed her cheeks and she'd succeeded in completely covering the faint dusting of freckles that invariably marched across her nose. Her chin was a little too pointy, she decided. Definitely a clue to her internal stubbornness. Still, she looked damn good, if she said so herself, but unfortunately she still looked like Juliet Adams.

The thought of facing Jake Danforth suddenly turned her insides to ice. What had she been thinking? She couldn't just show up at his show and try to bluff her way through this. Good God. He'd eat her alive!

In a frenzy of fury she ripped off the red dress she'd tossed on and threw it on the floor. What had that been about? she asked herself, as she stared down at it.

I'm a complete idiot!

Scrounging through her closet she found a black oversized sweater and a long black skirt and hurriedly dragged them on. In frustration she mussed up her hair, glaring at her reflection in the bathroom mirror.

Juliet Adams still looked back at her.

Growling to herself, she yanked on a pair of black boots, zipping them up to the knee. She quickly finger-combed her hair over her face, making two peep holes. She looked like Cousin Itt from the *Addams Family,* which made her feel better. After all, she was an Adams.

But even as she smiled and relaxed her hair fell back into place. Uncombed and tangled, but her face still looked just like Juliet Adams. A shapeless Juliet Adams, but Juliet Adams all the same.

And then the idea hit her.

Grabbing her purse, she raced into the kitchen. Sure enough, there on the counter lay Nora's witch's hat, the one she planned to don when she sold her baked goods at the bazaar in Waterfront Park on Halloween.

But Nora didn't need it today....

Plunking the hat on her head, Julie cocked her head. Not a bad disguise. But then her eyes fell on a pair of wacky glasses, the kind with red and white stripes for lenses in black, horn-rimmed frames that offered a tiny peephole for sight, another piece of Nora's costume. When Julie put the glasses on she was indistinguishable. Ugly as dirt, but Juliet Adams no longer.

Cackling to herself, she grinned hugely. Let Jake Danforth figure out who she was!

''OUR SPECIAL GUEST will be here at eight o'clock,'' Jake told his listening audience as he glanced at the clock. Five till eight. She'd damn well better appear soon or she was going to be late. Guests were told to arrive an hour ahead of time in order for some ground rules to be established, but not so for Ms. Julie Sommerfield. If she had some lame story about car trouble or an emergency with one of her kids— if she had any—he wasn't going to be sympathetic. Just more grist for the mill, so to speak. After he got through murdering her character, he would let his listeners rip at the leftover carcass, and oh, could they ever be vicious.

Not that he cared one way or the other. She'd agreed to come on the show and she must know what that entailed. If he could trap her in some silliness, and score points off it, why not? He didn't owe her anything.

DeeAnn glanced at the clock too, meeting his gaze and shaking her head. They were going to be stood up.

Jake waited until two minutes to the hour. ''Well, folks,'' he drawled. ''It looks as if our guest has deigned to stand us up. I might be really hurt if it weren't for the tarot reading I had early this morning. DeeAnn, could you find it for me?'' He rustled some papers around and pretended to search, pulling out a deck of tarot cards he'd brought in that morning. "Wait a minute, wait a minute...oh, here it is. Let's see..."

DeeAnn slid one finger over the other in classic "shame on you" and shook her head. Jake grinned at her.

"Oh," he said, sounding worried. "It appears that my special guest this morning won't be here after all. She's on a trip and can't make it. No wait. She's been abducted by aliens. Is that what this spaceship on the card means, Dee?"

"I think so," she answered dryly.

Colin, one of the show's producers, opened the door and motioned to Jake, giving him the thumbs-up and stepping back to allow whoever was behind him to enter the glassed-in sound booth.

Jake said into the mike, "Wait, wait. I hear something! Is that a spaceship, Dee? That sort of stuttered, purring sound? Why, yes, I believe it is. Okay, it looks as if our guest, Ms. Julie Sommerfield, is going to make it after all. The alien spacecraft has dropped her at our door...." He swivelled in his chair to get a good hard look at her. To his amusement, the woman who slipped inside the booth was dressed head to toe in black, a witch's hat smashed down on her head nearly to her eyebrows and a pair of novelty glasses with tiny holes for viewing perched on her nose. The only parts of her face really open to viewing were her lips and chin. The chin was stubborn, the lips—full, luscious and currently sporting an obnoxious black-gray color of lipstick—were also set in a thin line. Not a happy person, he decided, giving her a raking glance from head to toe.

Ugh.

"Welcome," he said to her. "Sit down and DeeAnn will get you set up. For all of you out there who can't see our lovely guest, she's arrived in a witch's costume. I'm assuming this is for Halloween and not some kind of comment on your disposition, Julie."

DeeAnn placed a headset carefully around Julie's hat and clipped a microphone to her black shirt. Her hat lay scrunched beneath the headset. It felt tilted on her head.

"It's a little of both," she responded in her drawl. Jake half smiled. That accent was a fake. He'd bet money on it.

"So, you're a witch?"

"I have been called many things, especially by you, Mistah Danforth."

"*Touché,* Ms. Sommerfield." He itched to remove that hat, or at least those distorting glasses. He had to admit he was very curious about Julie Sommerfield, but her costume made it impossible for him to get any kind of read on her.

He glanced down at the phone lines. Lights were blinking furiously. "My listeners have a few questions for you. We're hoping you can offer them some advice about their relationships."

"Sure."

Julie swallowed. She was sweating up a storm and she'd only been here *five minutes!* And it was all Jake's fault. Did he have to look so damn attractive? From that pearly white smile to those faded blue jeans and white shirt, the sleeves rolled back from the cuffs revealing unfairly tanned forearms with a dusting of masculine hair. His hair was a bit long by today's standards; it brushed the collar of his shirt.

Oh, yes. Her downfall. And it lay smoothly on his head. His eyes were blue, a shade or two deeper than her own, and he sported those long lashes she remembered from her childhood. He had a smoothness of manner that was like a predatory cat, and no amount of her trying to deny those attributes could make them just disappear.

Everything about him was just too perfect. She longed to bring him down a peg or two.

"I actually have some questions for you, too, Mistah Danforth." She was really laying it on thick, but who cared? As long as he had no idea who she truly was, she was safe.

"Really." His lips twitched ever so faintly. "Well, let's do that first."

His attitude really ticked her off. He was getting one big laugh out of this whole masquerade. "Your wife explained to me the reasons for your divorce. Could I hear your thoughts on that, Mistah Danforth?"

"Call me Jake. I think we're past formalities."

"All right, Jake." She hesitated. "You may call me Miss Somah-field."

His brows shot up. He suddenly threw back his head and laughed. "Okay," he agreed charmingly, around a laugh, and Julie ground her teeth behind a smile. Oh, she'd forgotten how he could twist things and make himself seem like such a prize. His knack for being lovable was downright stomach-turning.

"All right, Miss Somah-field. You want to know why we got divorced? Irreconcilable differences. I often thought about reconciling, but she was just too different."

"You ah scoring points off me, I believe." Julie gave him a prim smile.

"Maybe," he agreed, undeterred. "So, you're a psychologist. And a marriage counselor."

He imbued just enough skepticism in the words to frost her cookies. "Yes, sir."

"Where are you from originally?"

"The South."

"No kidding. Could you be more specific?"

"What does that have to do with mah credentials?"

"I don't know." He stroked his chin. "You seem kind of familiar, and I was just wondering if we'd met before."

Julie's heart leapt. "Are we getting away from the subject at hand?"

"I don't know. Are we? What is the subject at hand?"

He was teasing her. Flirting, actually, and Julie could scarcely stand it. She glanced toward the clock, wondering how long this bantering was going to continue. She lived in fear that someone who truly knew her would call up and give the gig away.

"We were talkin' about your divorce."

"Look at all those phone lines. People want to talk to you about that very thing." He reached to punch a flashing button, and Julie held her breath. It was DeeAnn who saved her, shaking her head at Jake who dropped his hand. Apparently she liked the way the interview was going, just as it was. Why? Julie marveled to herself, but then was dragged back to the moment when Jake relaxed into his chair and studied her closely, saying, "You claim to be a marriage counselor, but you read the tarot cards to my wife. Do you study the stars, too? Astrological charts? Tea leaves?''

Julie dearly wanted to explain that it was Teri Danforth who'd brought out the tarot cards, but she didn't want to sound like she was making excuses. She knew he would jump all over her for that; she could sense it. ''Mostly, I listen to my client's problems and help them sort through their worries, fears and grievances. Lots of times people are just looking for a direction to take.''

''To divorce, or not to divorce, that is the question.''

''Something like that,'' she admitted. ''I have heard you say your marriage was unhappy for a long time.''

''You listen to my program?''

''If the button to your station is depressed when I'm on the road and you come on, I don't always change channels.''

He grinned again, which piqued her annoyance all over again. ''You're a fan. Admit it.''

''No.''

''I bet you turn me on before the program begins and listen to the end.''

''Your ego is enormous, Mistah Danforth.''

''Jake,'' he corrected again. ''Have you been calling in for the free coffee mugs with my picture on them. You have, haven't you?''

''I have not!''

''Ahhh…but you've never won. Oh, I see. Don't worry, Miss Somah-field, I've got one right here.'' He swept a mug from a shelf beneath his desk and handed it to Julie. It was black, with Jake's image done in white, and it listed the call number of his radio station.

"I'll try not to break it," Julie said stiffly, which earned her another huge grin. How many teeth did he have, anyway? There sure as hell looked as if there were more than thirty-two in that mouth.

"So, how do you do it?" he asked, his tone becoming more businesslike. "When your clients come in, do you sit them down, or do they lie down, like on a psychiatrist's couch, and tell you all their troubles?"

"Sometimes they sit, sometimes they stand."

"Stand?"

"And pace."

"No stretching out on the couch?" He leaned back in his chair and she was very conscious of his long, jean clad legs and flat stomach beneath the white shirt. It was hard not to look directly at his crotch, the way he was seated, so she averted her eyes. He was too damn good-looking anyway. He made her feel like a hag, and, well, she was one, she realized.

"Do you start from childhood, or just from the beginning of the marriage, or what?"

"Whatever. They talk about what they want to talk about."

"And you advise them." She nodded. "You advised my wife to leave me?"

"I believe that had already transpired. Mistah Danforth, I do not think it would be right to talk about your ex-wife."

"Okay. Fair enough. Can I ask you how many times you counseled her?"

"Once."

"Just once?" He was definitely surprised.

"Just the one time," she repeated.

"Do you ever counsel couples?"

"Yes." She nodded. "Often."

"So, could you counsel me now?"

Julie peered at him through her glasses. They really bugged her and she squinched up her nose. The hat and wig were driving her crazy, too. She wanted to rip them off and itch her scalp. "I believe you are already divorced and therefore, not a couple with your ex."

"True." He seemed to consider that. "Think I should be dating again? It's been a couple of months."

"I suppose it depends on how you feel." Her boots cramped her toes. Squirming in the seat, she tried to get a grip on herself.

It didn't help that he looked cool, calm, collected and mighty attractive. She seemed focused on his lean, muscular forearms and the vee of his shirt at his neck. His skin looked smooth and tanned and inviting. She felt her internal female warning system switch to overload.

The man had pheromones pouring out of him. What was wrong with her? Wasn't she over this high school obsession yet?

"Well, I feel that I'm ready. Why not? I've re-hashed this divorce business on air enough times. To be honest, I'm kind of sick of it. I'm ready for something new." Jake smiled at her. It really kind of ticked her off. He was pulling out all the stops trying to win her over. And the hell of it was, it was working. Against her better judgement her female antennae had picked up the message and it was thrumming along her nerves.

"What was that?" he asked.

"What?"

"You made a noise."

"I—did not," she said a bit desperately. Had she? She hoped to high heaven it hadn't been a *moan!*

"I got the feeling you disagreed with my decision."

"What decision?" Julie asked blankly.

"To date again," he said, looking at her as if she were extremely dense.

She swallowed. "Mistah Danforth, I think you must look inside yourself for that answer. We are all on different internal clocks for our emotional well-being."

"That sounds like psychological claptrap to me. Do people actually buy that? I mean, when they come to you for help?"

Julie narrowed her eyes, if he could but see them. "Are you insultin' me, Mistah Danforth?"

"Just making an observation, Ms. Sommerfield."

"It appears you invited me here just to poke fun at me. I thought it was for a more constructive purpose."

That woke him up. He suddenly leaned forward in his chair and regarded her soberly. Rarely did his guests challenge him back, even though he always seemed to be digging at them. "My divorce is final, and really, my marriage was over long before it became official. My question to you is should I begin dating again?"

"It is hard for me to answer when I have just been introduced to you."

"But Teri, my ex, must have filled you in. Can you give me a ballpark figure? I mean, should I start now? Should I wait till next spring? Have I waited too long? What?''

Julie curled her fingers into her palms. He was asking her if he should start dating for crying out loud, and for some reason that night after the prom still played in her head. Good grief! She felt like a jealous spouse! "Maybe you should...wait."

"Wait?"

"Uh-huh...you...um...you are probably still sufferin' from your divorce."

"I don't think so! Suffering?" he repeated on the verge of a laugh.

Julie said a bit desperately, "You've been laughin' about your divorce on the air but I get the feelin' that is all an elaborate act."

Jake studied her closely. She held her breath. He seemed to think that one over as he scoured her from head to toe with a dark look. "I talk about this almost every day with my listeners. If I were suffering, I wouldn't be able to even mention it."

"It sounds like you have already made your decision." She spread her hands. "Many times that is the way it happens. People, whether they know it or not, have taken steps in one direction or another long before they come to see me."

"But you suggest I wait..."

"I just think you should consider all the—emotional claptrap."

Jake relaxed. She was really a piece of work, this Julie Sommerfield. "I see..." He tapped the eraser end of a pencil against those pearly whites. "You pretty much talk in circles, don't you?"

"You asked me my opinion, I gave it to you."

"Nah..." He shook his head slowly from side to

side, those blue eyes examining her closely. She sure as hell was glad she was disguised. "You're the stereotypical therapist. Never make a real decision. If you'd told me to go out and date and I had some terrible experience, you might be liable. So, you sit back and murmur words like 'take action only when you are fully committed' and 'concentrate on positive energy.' To be honest, if I were paying you for this session, I'd feel cheated."

Julie locked her jaw until it hurt. With an effort, she separated her teeth and lips enough to say, "Then I guess it's lucky for both of us that you are not my client."

She and Jake glared at each other.

The phone buttons blinked furiously, as if the listeners were shrieking out their feelings with the rapidity of their flashing. Jake finally dragged his eyes from her face and punched a button at random. "Hello, there. You're on the air."

"Jake?"

"Yes, ma'am. Who's this?"

"This is Tracy. I just—I just wanted to say that if you want a date, I'm here, honey. I'm a six-foot one-inch love machine and my play button is set to *J-A-K-E*."

Julie stared in shock at line one as if Tracy might materialize on the spot. It never ceased to amaze her how forward complete strangers could be with celebrities, even minor, pseudo ones like Jake Danforth.

"Well, thank you, Tracy. The temperature in the booth here has hit a new low. Way, way below freezing. It's nice to have some warm thoughts."

"I'm serious, honey. Just say the word and I'm yours."

"Let me give it some thought," he said with a smile in his voice. "I've gotta take another call." His finger depressed the second line. Just as soon as he hung up line one, the button started flashing again.

"You tell that witch to get on her broomstick and skedaddle!" a voice declared indignantly.

"Looks like she forgot that mode of transportation," Jake answered, glancing around as if making certain Julie hadn't parked her broom where he couldn't see it. She clamped her fingers together until her knuckles turned white.

"Hey, I wanna ask her a question.... Lady, you think you're such a big shot, don't you know you're talking to the sexiest man on morning radio? And all you can do is insult him! You got a serious problem, honey!"

Julie wanted to crawl under the desk. This was not going well. Not at all. If she had to take on all his listeners, one by one, she was never going to survive the morning. Glancing at the clock, she realized only twenty minutes had passed.

She was doomed.

"Ms. Sommerfield?" Jake said brightly when she didn't immediately answer.

"I suppose it may sound like an insult to you..." Was it hot in here? She wanted to yank on the neck of her shirt and fan her face. Passing out wasn't that far off the chart from where she sat.

"It flat-out *is* an insult!" the woman's voice accused. "So, what are your credentials, huh? Jake's ex is a cuckoo-bird. Everybody knows it. Sorry, Jake."

"No problem. Your opinion."

"You represent the crazy half of that marriage,

honey. Jake's the sane one. Do you really have enough experience to treat 'em when they're loco?''

Julie cleared her throat. "Mrs. Danforth came for help in her divorce. She was very pleasant and professional," Julie lied, remembering Teri Danforth's uncontrollable crying.

"Now, you're lying," Jake intervened, as if reading her mind. "But, hey, at least you're protecting a client. Probably makes the rest of your clients relieved.''

Julie said tightly, "I don't reveal confidences.''

"What happened to the Southern accent?" Jake asked curiously, a smile playing along his lips.

Julie wanted to smack her palm to her own forehead. Damn the man! She was floundering, doing just what he'd hoped she would do. She needed to take control and fast. "The accent was part of my costume," she declared, smiling back with an effort. She needed to keep things light. Glancing at the clock, she wanted to turn the hands herself: it had almost been thirty minutes.

Jake's eyes followed the path hers had traveled. "Ms. Sommerfield's time is almost up, and we haven't even scratched the surface. Does someone out there have a specific question? About divorce, marriage, love gone bad…?''

DeeAnn had begun screening a few calls. She held up three fingers and Jake punched the button for line three. "Hello, there," he greeted the caller.

"Jake…?" It was a man's voice.

"Uh-huh."

"I've got a question."

"Shoot."

"Why are women all such grasping witches? When it comes to money, they suck ya dry!"

Jake threw a look at DeeAnn who looked pole-axed. Apparently that hadn't been the original question. There was a ten second delay. He could cut the caller off and start over, but Jake hesitated only a moment before turning to Julie. "Being a witch, maybe you could answer his question?"

"I'm sorry, sir," she said to the caller. "What's your name?"

"Earl."

"Well, Earl, generalizations and comments meant to hurt don't exactly translate to 'working it out' between partners," she pointed out. "Calling all women grasping witches isn't a good start to keep open communication going, if you know what I mean. Is there a specific woman you're referring to?"

"She's a witch with a capital *B!*"

"Is she your wife?"

"Not as soon as I can get rid of her! And I ain't giving her a dime!"

Julie gave Jake a long look. "Any advice for the caller?" Jake asked her, looking like he was going to burst into laughter at any moment.

Stop being a jackass? Julie couldn't really turn around and insult the man after she'd just pointed out that slurs weren't the way to go. "Earl, I think you've got a rocky road ahead of you, and depending how much time your lawyers fight it out, you could be paying them off instead of your wife."

Earl made some sputtering noises and DeeAnn cut him off before he could verbalize his feelings.

Jake said into the microphones, "Well, Portland,

it's time to let Ms. Sommerfield go. But I happen to
have some tarot cards here, and maybe we'll see
what turns up.'' He picked up the deck of cards and
plucked one from off the top. ''Oh, look at that. The
queen of cups. What does that mean?''

Julie gazed at the colorful pack of cards with
dread. She opened her mouth to tell him she didn't
read the tarot, but he cut in too quickly.

''She's looking pretty upset to me. But she's certainly attractive. Check out those cups—''

''Give those to me.'' Julie grabbed the cards from
him, her fingers brushing his. She ignored the tingle
of sensation that swept up her arm at their contact.
Danforth germs, she decided, going straight back to
grade school.

She shuffled the cards and laid them out on the
table as she'd seen his ex-wife do. She had no idea
what she was doing, but hey, he didn't know that.
And if he wanted to make an issue of the tarot cards,
fine. She was ready to roll with it.

Jake's brows lifted at her sudden capitulation. He
seemed to want to say something but Julie held up a
hand. ''Oh…'' she murmured despairingly, clucking
her tongue.

''What?'' Jake swiveled his chair around so that
he was right beside her. She could feel the heat from
his skin. She wouldn't look up into those sexy blue
eyes for all the tea in China.

''The hangman.''

''I see it. What does that mean?''

Hell if I know. Julie stroked her chin. ''In this case
it refers to your job situation.''

''What do you mean 'in this case'?''

''Umm…the way the cards are arranged. Something's going to happen to you work-wise and it won't be pretty.''

''Anything I can do about it?'' She could feel his eyes searching her face and she let her witch hair fall forward even farther, hiding her profile.

'''Fraid not. Oh, and your hair…''

''What about it?''

''Not much time left for it, I'm afraid. Male pattern baldness. Of course, you could always have a transplant, or failing that, a comb over.''

''You can tell all this from the cards?'' he said, his breath near enough to scorch her. It was minty and clean smelling, which really ticked her off. Why couldn't he have dragon breath? Or adult acne? Or some kind of physical failing so that he wasn't so damned attractive! God, she hated that about him!

''The medical problem looks like your worst one, though.''

''Medical problem? Which card tells you that?''

''The lovers.''

''The lovers? Where's that card?''

She hadn't found it yet. She wanted to yell at him to scoot back, but she concentrated on the cards, trying not to sound too much like she was flying by the seat of her pants. ''It's here. Oh…how dreadful. You've got that problem only males suffer from. But never fear, there's a pill.… It starts with a *V*. A few doses and who knows, you could be good as new.''

''Ouch,'' he said. ''Was my ex's reading as vicious, or is it just me?''

''It's just you. Oh, and someone's thinking bad thoughts about you.'' She gave him a quick, false smile. ''A woman.''

''And who would that be?'' he asked quietly.

Suddenly Julie feared she'd gone too far. DeeAnn was staring at her as if she were a vision from Hell. Daring a glance at Jake she could see he was angry behind his facade. Still, his voice did not betray him.

Julie scooped up the cards. "What do you expect from a psychologist who got her degree off the back of a matchbook?"

He had the grace to look sheepish. DeeAnn madly signaled for an end to their skirmish and Julie practically leapt from her chair as Jake signed off, assuring his listeners that there would be time the following Monday to hear all their thoughts about his lovely guest, Julie Sommerfield.

Julie didn't wait to shake hands. She was out the door with a hurried, "Thanks a lot. It was—interesting," before Jake could do more than reach up to remove his headset. Scurrying like the frightened mouse she'd become, she slammed her palm against the elevator call button.

"C'mon, c'mon, c'mon," she muttered fiercely. Damn it all. What took these contraptions so long? She could already feel regret circling around her brain, looking for a place to lie down and settle in. She wanted to kick herself for letting him get to her. She wanted to scream!

"For the love of—" she practically shouted, just as the elevator doors slid open. Just as she stepped inside the car, she glanced back. Jake appeared at the end of the hallway. Ducking inside to avoid being seen, she slammed her palm against the down button, praying the sluggish machinery would respond. Vaguely she was aware of another passenger in the car as the doors clanked, groaned and began to shut.

Thank you, God.

Julie closed her eyes and sagged against the wall. She couldn't talk to him anymore. She just wanted to go home, crawl into bed, pull the covers over her head and pretend the morning simply hadn't happened.

"Well, Jake Danforth was right," a female voice sneered from behind her. "You certainly look like a witch."

Julie whirled around. A middle-aged woman with bleached blond hair, an expensive fur carelessly tossed over her shoulder, four-inch red heels and a face-lift that made her eyes look like a Siamese cat's raked Julie with a look that could have scorched asbestos.

It was the last straw.

"Ditto," Julie muttered just as the elevator opened onto the main floor. She jumped out and beelined for the revolving doors that led to the outside parking area, knowing she'd probably pay for that snarly remark but glad she'd made it anyway.

She skidded to a halt in dismay.

Jake Danforth was waiting for her by the spinning exit to freedom, and he did not, by any stretch of the imagination, look happy.

3

"HOW DID YOU get here so fast?" Julie asked. She tried to brush past him but he didn't move so much as an iota.

"The stairs," he said.

"You must have taken them two at a time."

"Three."

Julie waited uncomfortably when he didn't elaborate further. Was she about to get dressed down, or what? She opened her mouth to offer another goodbye when disaster appeared.

Tap, tap, tap... The elevator lady minced toward them on her heels, her expression a thundercloud. A feline version of a thundercloud, actually, as her anger further heightened her resemblance to a Siamese cat.

"Hello, Jake," the woman greeted him tightly. "You certainly get the interesting characters on your show, don't you?"

Julie shrank inside her black sweater and skirt, silently thanking the heavens for her disguise. At least it gave her some protection.

"Hi, Beryl. Yes, I guess I do."

"Ask her about her remarks to me," she added in a voice Julie could only classify as snotty.

Jake looked from Beryl to Julie, perplexed. "All right."

"Excuse me..." She put her hand on Julie's shoulder as a signal that she was brushing past her toward the door, but she gave a nasty little push and Julie stumbled forward.

Jake caught her with strong hands, steadying her.

"Excuse me," Julie murmured, quickly stepping back.

"What did you say to Beryl?"

"It was more like what she said to me," Julie responded huffily, but a moment later her bravado failed her. "And then...what I said back to her." Jake lifted his brows and she said reluctantly, "She told me I looked like a witch and it wasn't in the nicest way."

"You do look like a witch."

"The point is, she meant it to be really mean," Julie insisted. "So, I just said the same thing to her."

Jake looked at Julie with a mixture of horror and admiration. "You told Beryl Hoffman that she looked like a witch, too?"

Julie just prevented herself from saying, "She started it!" Instead, she asked, "Who's Beryl Hoffman?"

"Wife of the owner of the station."

"Ohhhh...."

Jake was torn between laughter and further annoyance with her. He inclined his head toward a coffee shop in a corner of the lobby. "Let me buy you a cup of coffee."

"Oh, no. I've really got to run."

"Twenty minutes, that's all."

It was an olive branch, of sorts. She hesitated. "Ten."

"Fifteen."

Julie shot a longing glance to the revolving glass door and the sight of the parking lot beyond. Her VW Bug was out there. Freedom. But now she felt like she owed him something because of her rudeness to the station owner's wife. Inwardly berating herself for acting out—juvenile behavior she never indulged in unless Jake Danforth was in the picture!—she shrugged a "yes" and followed her enemy to the cozy little table near the back with its cozy armchairs and cozy bookshelf filled with yes, cozy books and pillows and stuff.

"Fifteen minutes," she warned.

As soon as she was seated across from him, he leaned his elbows on the table and regarded her un-smilingly. "All right, I'm sure I owe you an apology in there somewhere and you owe me one right back. So, let's get that out of the way first. I'm sorry for being a jerk." He waited. When Julie couldn't seem to get her tongue, lips and vocal cords moving fast enough, he added, "Your turn, Julie. So, why don't you take off that disguise and let's get down to it."

IT HAD BEEN a strange morning all around and Jake knew it wasn't going to get any better until he had his say with Ms. Julie Sommerfield. He sat across from her and stared into her straw-like jet black hair and googly black plastic glasses with their red and white jagged stripes radiating from a tiny hole in the center of each eye. The costume covered her up as if she were wearing a mask. The only part of her face he could see unobstructed was her mouth. She'd painted waxy black lipstick on a pair of luscious lips and her teeth were a startling white against that dark color. He wanted her to smile. He wanted her to laugh.

He wanted to see her face.

"Get down to it?" she repeated, a trifle breathlessly.

"I realize we got off on the wrong foot. I said some pretty nasty things on the air, and you retaliated. Like I said, I'm sorry. My ex-wife brings out the worst in me and you got nailed with some of the fallout."

He waited. Julie reached up and clutched her black "hair." For a moment he thought she was going to remove the wig, but no, she clung on as if afraid he was going to snatch the damn thing from her head. "I guess…I'm sorry…too…."

"The strength of your conviction awes me," he said dryly.

She was worrying her lower lip with those fantastic teeth. Something was so familiar about them. He wondered if she'd ever been in a TV commercial or print ad. He could almost swear he'd seen her before.

"So what about the wig and glasses?"

She shook her head quickly, sinking against the wooden back of the booth as if she wanted to melt right into the boards. "I think I need this armor."

"Armor?" He splayed his palms. "Am I that bad?"

"No, I…I've got to go." She glanced around. He damn near reached over and snagged the glasses, but as if reading his mind, she gave him a quick look, her mouth grim. "Goodbye, Mr. Danforth."

"Wait. Have a cup of coffee. And it's Jake."

"I don't think so."

"Julie—" He tried to reach across and touch her

hand, an automatic move to get her to stay. She yanked her hand out of reach and curled it into a fist. If he hadn't known better he would have sworn she was frightened of him.

"Don't you have work to do, or something?" she demanded, slipping from her side of the booth.

Jake got to his feet, too.

The aproned man behind the counter said, "Goody. You guys are on your feet. Ya gotta order the coffee *here*—" He pointed to the sign above his head that said Order Here—"before you sit over *there*."

"We're not having coffee," Julie stated flatly.

"Yes, we are. Two cups. One black, the other…" Jake lifted his brows at Julie.

"We aren't having coffee," she insisted.

"Leave some room for cream," Jake told the coffee guy.

"You're going to have to drink it yourself!" she snapped.

"She likes to argue. It's her nature," Jake added confidentially.

"Sheesh," the guy said, looking from one to the other as if they were both completely loony.

"I'm not staying for coffee," Julie hissed at Jake as the coffee guy poured two cups of coffee into "to go" cups.

Jake paid for the drinks and handed Julie hers. She stared into the black depths and said, "Where's the cream?" to which the coffee guy rolled his eyes and groaned as Jake gallantly pointed to an insulated pitcher at the end of the bar. He watched her pour a slurp or two of the stuff into her cup and then delicately place her lips around the rim.

"Who are you?" he asked on a note of intrigue.

She jerked abruptly. Hot coffee blurped out of the cup and onto her arms but she didn't make a peep of protest.

Jake rushed forward. "Are you okay?"

"Fine."

"Here...." He grabbed a napkin and dabbed at her skin. It was growing a dull red where the hot coffee had splashed. "I'm sorry. Again. Really—"

"No, don't...don't...." She jerked away from him.

He moved after her automatically. "Are you okay? It looks like it hurts."

"I'm fine. Fine." She glanced around to the coffee guy as if needing corroboration but the aproned fellow merely lifted his hands in surrender and shook his head.

"I'm out of this one," he said, looking relieved to help another customer.

"I'm sure I've got some ointment upstairs," Jake said. "There's a first-aid kit in the owner's office and—"

"No! No! Really. Please...." She sounded almost desperate. The more she resisted, the more intrigued Jake became. "I've really got to leave," she pleaded, one eye carefully watching the swaying brown liquid inside her cup as she turned on her heel.

"Let me at least get you a lid," Jake said. He pulled a white plastic top from the stack by the cream pitcher, took Julie's cup from her unresisting fingers, snapped the lid down on top and handed it back to her.

She gazed at him a moment through those teeny little holes in her glasses then headed toward the revolving door again and the parking lot. Jake slowly followed after her, watching her exit. He realized she drove a VW Bug and his mouth quirked. He waited for her to leave but when she climbed inside her car, nothing happened. After a few minutes he went outside to see what was up.

"Problems?" he asked, coming up to the driver's window, which was cracked open about four inches.

She jumped. She still wore the wig and glasses. Her mouth was grim. "It won't start," she admitted tersely.

"Are you out of gas?"

"No."

"Hmmm... Wanna pop the hood? I could look inside and see if—"

"No, thank you." She sounded furious.

"Do you have Triple-A or some kind of road service?"

"Look, Mr. Danforth. I really don't want your help. We got off on the wrong foot. That's okay. Let's just stay there."

Jake regarded her just as stonily as she was regarding him. He wanted to rip off her disguise. He wanted to be just as furious as she was, but he couldn't sustain his anger no matter how hard he tried. And he had the sneaking sensation that she was a casualty in the war between himself and Teri, and he knew his feelings were from guilt—guilt that another person had been drawn into his and his ex's battle. It made him feel angry and anxious, but it sure as hell wasn't Julie Sommerfield's fault.

"Look, I'm sorry. Really. I shouldn't have let Teri get to me, and I shouldn't have taken it out on you."

He smiled faintly as her funky glasses looked up at him through the crack in the window. "Okay?"

"Is that another apology?"

Realizing it was a bit lame, he shrugged. "A facsimile thereof, I guess. Can we try to be—friends?"

"Jake, you're the limit!" she muttered, surprising him. "You don't mean half the things you say!" She twisted the ignition harshly and the engine suddenly caught, sputtered and then roared back to life, surprising both Julie and Jake. The VW backfired like a couple of rifle shots, then settled down to an uneven, puttering growl.

"Sounds like water in your gas," he observed.

"You just don't get it!" she yelled.

"What? What don't I get?"

"I've never trusted you. You're—you're—untrustworthy!"

"You've never *trusted* me?" he repeated in bafflement.

With that she flapped a hand in his direction and shoved the car into reverse. Jake stepped back and watched her swing the rear end of the Beetle around and point the nose toward the gate. Idling the engine, she said flatly, "Goodbye, Mr. Danforth."

"Why don't you take off the wig and glasses and show some courage instead of hiding behind all that drama?"

"The more you talk, the more I'm convinced your wife's the smart one—*she* divorced *you!*"

"Well, that's only half the truth. I don't know what she told you, but I asked her to leave."

"That's not how she tells it."

"Did she mention her Tae Bo instructor?" Jake demanded. "The one whose moon was in the second house. And that second house was my house and it was his moon!''

For an answer she mercilessly shoved the hapless Bug into gear and jerked and wheeled out of the lot. At the gate she flung her wig out the window, quickly followed by the glasses. Jake headed in her wake, deciding to pick up the articles in case he ever felt like taking them back to her. Glancing up, he caught another movement as the Beetle tore around the corner and out of sight.

Julie Sommerfield had flipped him the rudest of rude gestures.

PULLING INTO her parking spot, Julie cut the engine and draped herself over the steering wheel. She'd shed the wig and glasses in a gesture of ''in your face, Danforth,'' but now she felt naked and vulnerable. Could the morning have gone any worse? she asked herself, hating how juvenile she felt. Groaning, she tried to pretend she hadn't acted like such a high-strung, petty, jealous junior-higher! She never, ever wanted to lay eyes on her high school Romeo again!

Shoulders weighted down, she carried her brief-case into her building and climbed the stairs to her offices. Carolyn Mathers was seated on Julie's red waiting room love seat, one leg crossed over the other, her expression blank behind her own narrow-lensed glasses, smoking a skinny, dark brown cigarette.

''There's no smoking inside the building, Carolyn,'' Julie said as she unlocked her inner office. She pointed to the sign on the wall.

''I was listening to Jake Danforth's morning show.

Not your finest hour,'' Carolyn observed, taking another drag as if Julie hadn't said anything.

"You don't know the half of it," Julie muttered.

"Is Jake really as cute as that TV ad for his station makes him look?"

"He's as ugly and deadly as a nest of snakes."

Carolyn's brows raised as she followed Julie into her office and plunked herself onto one of Julie's two armchairs arranged near the leaded glass window. The office had a homey air that Julie generally loved, but right now she wanted to just head home and bury her head in the comfy coziness of her own bed.

Ash drifted to the carpet and Julie reminded herself to buy a Dustbuster once again. Carolyn was addicted to cigarettes and bad behavior. There was no getting around it. She liked being subversive, thrived on it, as a matter of fact, and her trips to Julie's office were more a form of concession to her on-again, off-again husband than any serious desire to heal her fractured psyche. "How's Floyd?" Julie asked tiredly, thinking of Carolyn's beleaguered spouse.

"That won't get me to forget about Jake Danforth," Carolyn sing-songed, settling into the chair as if she planned to stay a millennium. "And his radio station building's right downtown. I might stop in and see him."

Julie clamped her jaw shut. "I don't think that will bode well for your troubled marriage."

Carolyn leaned forward, her eyes squinting in self-satisfaction behind her narrow lenses. "You're jealous!" she crowed in delight.

"Oh, I am not. For heaven's sake, I've—"

"Yes, yes, you are! You are!" She formed the

shape of a heart in the air with the glowing tip of her cigarette, took a final, long drag and stubbed it out on Julie's polished granite paperweight. Julie fought back the need to scream at her most troublesome client. With an effort, she pretended not to notice.

"Last time we left off, you were feeling bad about the way you were treating Floyd," she said through her teeth. "How are things going now?"

"You sound desperate," Carolyn countered, thoroughly enjoying herself. "What are you trying to hide?"

"Carolyn, don't turn my words back on me."

"Did something happen between you? Hmmm? Nobody can see you on radio."

"Do you want to waste your whole hour talking about me?"

"And good heavens, girl. What happened to your hair? It's all—smushed."

Julie desperately sought to gain control of the upper hand. What was wrong with her? At this rate she would have to turn in her credentials and find herself an assembly-line job that required no mental skills. "I was wearing a Halloween wig."

"Oh, that's right. He said so. But that getup looks like hell, honey," Carolyn added with a denigrating snort as she surveyed Julie's loose black top and skirt. "And what's that on your arm?"

"A burn. Carolyn, I don't want to talk about myself anymore."

"How did you get burned?"

"Coffee." Julie's teeth were clenched. Her whole body, in fact, felt clenched. "I spilled coffee on myself. We were having coffee and he said something objectionable and I spilled coffee on myself. Okay? Can we forget about Jake Danforth now?''

Carolyn lifted one sardonic brow, a smile flirting with the corners of her mouth. Deliberately pulling another cigarette from the pack, she slipped the filtered end between her lips. "Well, I can. But can you…?" she asked, touching the flame of her lighter to the end of the cigarette and surveying Julie through lazy, slitted eyes.

"Last time we talked you said you were thinking of leaving Floyd. You said you didn't think you loved him anymore, and you were going to go home and tally up a list of the pros and cons of your marriage. Tell me what's happening now," Julie said, watching the curl of smoke rise and dissipate.

Carolyn smiled a secret little smile. "Do you want to know what he did to me in bed last night?"

"'Did to you' doesn't sound like the kind of phrase I'd like to explore." Julie didn't want to think about bed in any sexual way, shape or form with Jake Danforth's blue eyes still imprinted on her brain. "How are you feeling about Floyd this week?"

She grinned and stretched like a panther. "Great. Especially after what he did to me in bed last night. Have you ever had a man send you straight to the moon?"

Julie gazed at her. "Depends on which house it's in," she deadpanned.

IT WASN'T MUCH BETTER later that afternoon when Julie took her mother's call. "Juliet?" she heard her mother ask cautiously. "I hated to bother you at work."

"Mom, it's Julie. Please."

"I didn't christen you Juliet to have you shorten your name just to be fashionable," she said in her "tsk-tsk" way. Julie was thirty years old and her mother still repeated the same things, in just the same manner, as she had when Julie was in elementary school.

"I know, Mom, but could you just try?"

"Honey, I don't know what's gotten into you. I heard you on the radio this morning. Isn't that that nice Jacob Danforth who used to live in our neighborhood? You remember his mother. What was her name again? Alice?"

"Alicia. Mom. Listen. I've got a client in the waiting room and I need to be professional. Could we talk later? Unless there's something particular you wanted to discuss…." The waiting room was completely empty, but Julie needed the lie.

"Didn't they have a couple of dogs with funny names?"

"It was a cat and a dog. Alka and Seltzer."

"Oh, that's right." She sounded pleased as punch to make the connection. "Why were you so militant with him this morning? And those things you said about the cards. I didn't know you knew anything about fortune-telling."

"I don't…I…I…"

"Well, Juliet, they're all going to think you know what you're talking about now. I'm sure some people feel very strongly about these things. You may have trampled on something sacred."

"We're talking about tarot cards," Julie said with extreme patience. "At least I think we are. What are we talking about, Mom?"

"Jake Danforth. You should be nicer to him. He's a famous radio personality now."

"So, that's why I should be nicer to him?"

"You know what I mean," she returned maddeningly.

"No, Mom. I don't have a clue."

"Well, that's certainly very clear!"

Julie was stumped for a response. Completely at a loss for words. It didn't matter anyway, when it came to her mother. Her convoluted thinking kept all their conversations going in circles. While her mother further cautioned her about her "less than kind words" and her "tone that was almost snippy, dear," Julie sat in silence and vaguely wondered if she should bring an ashtray into her office. Might save the granite paperweight.

"...and so that's when I told her to kick him out of the house," her mother was saying as Julie finally keyed back into the conversation.

"Kick who out of the house?"

"You're not listening, are you, dear?"

Julie gazed almost longingly at Carolyn's cigarette butts and wondered if she'd made a mistake by not taking up smoking. She could use a vice. She really could. But she was way too drug sensitive to go that route and alcohol didn't interest her much beyond an occasional glass of white wine.

Sex...sex can be a vice....

"Gotta go, Mom," she murmured, ending the conversation as her skin prickled. She'd been thinking about Jake when that thought had rippled across her mind. She'd been recalling those moments in the guest house. Prom night. Lord, what a cliché! But sometimes her recall was so sharp it had edges that cut.

She walked to the window and gazed into a darkening sky. Rain spattered as she watched, bouncing in tiny silver streaks against the pavement as it began to pour in earnest.

You take my breath away, he'd said, gazing down at her in the soft light that filtered from the moon through the guest house window. She'd soaked in the compliment, basked in the moment, delighted to run her fingers across the smooth skin of his chest and kiss his oh-so-sexy lips.

Of course, that was just before his evil exgirlfriend burst into the room and screeched about Jake's infidelity and Julie's cheap sluttiness. So embarrassing! The memory made her shudder and she hadn't realized she'd made a noise until her mother said, "Juliet? Are you all right?"

"Never been better," she answered, falsely chipper. "And it's Julie, Mom."

She drove home in a blue funk, making certain to reset the button designated for Jake's station to a country western channel. The first song wailing from the radio was a sad lament about a cowboy whose woman left him for a rodeo rider named Big John.

"Perfect," Julie muttered.

At the apartment she was glad to see Nora's white compact wagon with its black insignia, Nora's Nut Rolls, Etc. parked in the lot. Good. Now she could finally get some sympathy.

But all Nora said about Julie's morning debut was, "Interesting program," in that way she had of letting Julie know she was holding back far more than she was admitting.

Crushed, Julie sank onto a bar stool and gazed forlornly at the batch of black bat-shaped cookies with their evil little smiles. "Okay, hit me with it. Was I that bad?"

"Mmmm."

"Do they have to smile? Does everything have to smile?" Julie demanded.

Nora handed her a cookie from which she promptly bit off the little bat head. "Is the icing black enough? If you don't use gel, the black color really is just a form of dark gray."

"They're black enough."

"You sure?"

Julie gave her a long look. "They're as black as the miserable shrunken organ inside Jake Danforth's chest that was once called a heart."

"Bad day at the office," Nora observed.

"Didn't you hear the things he said to me? It was criminal!"

"He said he liked the queen of cups' cups."

"You thought that was funny?"

"It was kinda funny."

"It was sophomoric. It was base. It was low." Julie glared at Nora as she chewed up the last of the bat cookie. "Those are great, by the way."

"Thanks."

"Couldn't they be sneering though? Sneering bats would be cooler."

Nora picked up one of the cookies and frowned. "How's the murder plan going?"

"I thought I might accomplish the task today, on the air, but it didn't work quite the way I'd hoped."

"He didn't know it was you."

"No. Thanks for the wig and glasses, by the way.

I—um—owe you for a replacement set as I kind of threw them out the window in a gesture of defiance.''

"You can buy me another set for the Halloween bazaar next Saturday." At Julie's nod, she added, "Maybe you should have let him know who you were. Maybe then he'd understand a little bit more."

"Understand what?" Julie demanded, sensing Nora was stepping into Benedict Arnold mode once again.

"Why you're so—testy—about everything?"

"*What!* I'm *testy* because he called me names and cast aspersions on my professional abilities!"

Nora regarded her knowingly. "You're testy because he rings your chimes."

"Nora!"

"He's your Romeo, Juliet. He's always been your Romeo, and you can't stand it."

"I've spent all day fielding remarks just like that one. First Jake, and then Carolyn Mathers, then my mother and now you! I just don't like him. I've never liked him. I wish Teri Danforth had never crossed my threshold and waved around those stupid tarot cards!"

"I liked your reading. Very precise. Much more specific than psychics usually get."

"Is this my 'ilk' again? Is that what you're referring to?"

"You were actually very funny," Nora said. "I laughed out loud as I was serving up the customers." Her expression darkened as if a curtain had been drawn. "Until Irving St. Cloud came in."

"Irving St. Cloud came into Nora's Nut Rolls, Etc.?" Julie momentarily forgot her own problems upon hearing this bit of news. "Actually stepped foot inside your establishment?"

"Just a friendly visit to let me know St. Cloud's is opening an outlet right down the street from me."

"Oh, Nora!" Julie was horrified.

"Yes...." With that she turned toward a pan of rising dough, scooping up the plump flour-dusted mound and plopping it on a marble bread board.

"Is there anything I can do?" She watched as Nora pounded the dough as if her life depended on flattening it into a micro-thin line.

"You can get Irving's ex-wife as a client, make her take him back to court and wrest the entire line of bakeries away from him. Maybe that would stop him."

"Well, yeah...it's just that I try to *help* people work out their problems," Julie pointed out. "I don't generally advise them to take their spouses for whatever they can."

"Bummer." Nora pounded away grimly. "Murder's still in the running."

"Definitely an option."

"Drastic, but I'm liking it better and better."

Julie felt her mood lightening. "If you thought I was funny while I was on air, you should have seen me in action later." And she related the story of the run-in with the station owner's wife until Nora was laughing so hard she had to wipe tears of hilarity from her eyes.

"Why didn't I think about insulting Irving St. Cloud when I had the chance?" Nora mused, still smiling. "I could have told him he looks like a gargoyle."

"Does he?"

"No….he's…well, he's handsome, for lack of a better word."

"I hate that about men," Julie sighed.

"Me, too," Nora commiserated, and they polished off a few more smiling bats in thoughtful silence.

4

"SO, WHEN ARE YOU going to have that witch back on your program?" one of the listeners asked. "It's almost Halloween."

"I'm working on it," Jake said as he checked the clock. Some days it felt like the hands were working their way through molasses. Could he still have over two hours left?

"Didn't you say your wife wanted you to go see that psychic?"

"Psychologist," Jake corrected. "My ex-wife suggested it once, that's true."

"Well, why don't you go?"

"I have a feeling Julie Sommerfield wouldn't be interested in taking me on as a new project."

"So what? And if you're still looking for that date...?" The caller giggled and DeeAnn pointed to another phone line.

"I'll let you know," Jake said, picking up line three. "Hello, you're on the air."

"Jake?"

He sat up stiffly and gazed at DeeAnn, who shook her head and lifted her palms in a classic, "Who knew?"

"Teri?" he said, trying to remember the last time he'd actually talked to his ex-wife without a lawyer present. His mind went blank.

"I've been hearing what you've been saying about my therapist. *My* therapist."

"Oh, yeah? Does she know she's still your therapist?"

"And I think you should be dating. Get out there and make some other woman's life miserable. Am I really on the air? You're not screening this?"

"Of course we're screening it. But so far you haven't uttered any four-letter words or threatened me bodily harm so you're okay." Jake glared stonily at DeeAnn. She knew better than to put him on the spot like this.

"You leave Julie Sommerfield alone."

"Sorry, Teri. You were granted all your requests in the divorce decree."

"Jake…" Her voice warned in that way that really got his ire up.

"Well, look at the time. We only have two hours left. Sorry. Gotta go." He cut her off, put on a commercial for LeRoy's Tires and unplugged his headset. "DeeAnn," he growled.

"I knew you'd be mad. But I'm on orders to make your life a living hell."

"Whose orders?"

"Beryl Hoffman." DeeAnn started to laugh and had to bend over to keep herself from falling out of her chair. "She's really ticked at you and so when Teri happened to call in, well, I couldn't resist."

"Are you the woman who was thinking bad thoughts about me?" Jake asked blandly.

"Well, if I am, I think I'm just one of many."

Jake put his headset back on. Unfortunately, truer words were never spoken. At this rate he was going to get the entire Portland female population on his neck, starting with Julie Sommerfield.

"OH…MY…GOD…." Nora expelled through lips that barely moved. Julie, who was behind the counter at Nora's shop to cadge some of the fresh-from-the-oven nut bread currently perfuming the air and causing her mouth to water shamelessly, glanced up guiltily, certain she was in trouble. But Nora's attention was directed over the counter full of pastries to the front window where a sleek, black sedan trimmed in gold, right down to the sparkling wheels, was just pulling into a spot directly in front of Nora's Nut Rolls, Etc. Late afternoon sun slanted down on the vehicle as if directly from heaven.

"St. Cloud," she hissed.

"Ahhh…." Julie watched Nora slice off a hunk of nut bread with a wicked-looking serrated knife. Gingerly, Julie picked up her slice of bread and went back around the counter to the customer side. Nora still held the knife, her expression dark.

"How do you know it's Irving St. Cloud?" Julie asked.

"I know that car."

At that moment a silver-haired gentlemen who looked as sleek as his vehicle climbed from behind the wheel. He came around the side and Julie realized he was much younger than his prematurely gray hair would indicate. He was, well, quite handsome, too, and he smiled as he reached for the passenger handle to open the door for his companion.

"Blond, still using acne products, major breasts, legs that go on forever…."

"You know his date, too?" Julie was impressed with Nora's knowledge of her nemesis.

"Just guessing."

The door opened and Irving helped a woman in her seventies from the bucket seat. Her hair wasn't gray, it was blue, and her pink-and-lavender flowered dress was complemented by a hat with the same colored flowers adorning its straw brim. Julie fought back a smile as Nora stared in disbelief.

"Not a bad figure," Julie said. "Might have been a blonde, once. Can't tell about the acne medicine."

"Oh, all right, fine," Nora muttered crossly.

"They're coming this way...."

Nora lifted the knife as if she meant to greet her customers like a samurai. Julie flicked a look at Irving St. Cloud just as the bell tinkled as they opened the door. "Put down the knife," Julie told her. Nora didn't seem to hear. "The knife! The knife!" she whispered frantically.

"I know you're opening a shop right down the street. I heard you the first time," Nora stated coldly, the bread knife pointing toward the ceiling.

Irving St. Cloud gazed at the knife and his brows lifted. "My grandmother, Clarice St. Cloud, has admired your shop on more than one occasion and asked if we could see it."

Clarice smiled at Nora from beneath her bonnet. "I love sweet things. That's how we got started, you know. Irving takes after me. His grandfather wasn't much for anything besides a double malt and a basset hound, God rest his soul. I never could interest my children in baked goods, you know, but Irving's made up for it!" She beamed at her grandson.

Nora lowered her weapon and Julie let out a pent-up breath. Nonplused, Nora finally murmured, "I just made some nut bread. Plain, banana, or apple-cranberry."

"Is that what that lovely scent is?"

"I'd like to buy a loaf of each," Irving said. Nora snapped a suspicious look in his direction.

"Try some samples," she encouraged Clarice. With that she hacked off slices from three loaves.

Julie leaned toward her as Clarice and Irving politely moved to the other side of the room as they waited for Nora to cut off their samples. "You don't have to go about it like you're killing snakes," she said in an aside.

"Is he after my recipes? Is that it?" Nora demanded.

"Don't get paranoid. Consider it a compliment."

"Oh, sure."

Eventually she served up tastes of all three breads and Julie brought the samples to the little table where they were seated. Clarice invited Julie to sit down as soon as she learned Julie was Nora's friend. Nora glared at her from behind the counter, but Julie was happy enough in her role. She was taking a lunch break, and didn't have an appointment until one-thirty, so she'd walked the few blocks to Nora's shop for some tea, sympathy and scones, or whatever else she had on hand. An unexpected invitation to nibble on Nora's breads with the St. Clouds was an occasion she wouldn't have wanted to miss.

"Scrumptious!" Clarice declared. To Nora, she asked, "How much do we owe you, honey?"

"Nothing. They're just tastes."

"We do need to buy those loaves of bread," she

added, her hand on Irving's arm though she was still talking to Nora.

Nora took in a breath. Other people were wandering around the store or gathering nearby to see if they could get a taste for themselves. Julie worried that Nora was going to flat-out deny the St. Clouds, so she blurted out, "When are you opening your new store?"

"We're still deciding on a location," Irving answered her. Then, as if feeling Nora's eyes boring into him, he looked at her and said, "I don't steal other people's ideas."

"Did I say you would?" she demanded.

"Sometimes words aren't necessary."

Nora flushed. "I'll be right back," she said stiffly, then marched into the back room. While Julie made small talk, Nora finally returned with three loaves in clear plastic bags, Nora's Nut Rolls, Etc. printed large as life in red ink on a white label.

As Irving paid for the merchandise, Clarice leaned toward Nora. "You've got to sample the flavors of life, you know. Too much wheat bread and you forget how nice rye can be, or sourdough, or just plain white...." She smiled prettily. "Don't worry, honey. I have to remind Irving of that sometimes, too."

She toddled toward the door. Irving smiled at both Nora and Julie. "Maybe I'll stop in again sometime, if it's all right."

"I'll let you know," Nora said flatly, which earned her an amused look in St. Cloud's eyes as he let himself and his grandmother out, the tinkling bell announcing their departure.

"Was that Irving St. Cloud?" a young woman

asked, her eyes wide. "The bakery guy? He's made *millions* on St. Cloud Bakeries, hasn't he?"

"Millions," Nora agreed. "If you move quick, you can introduce yourself. It's that car right out front."

"But all their breads are wheat breads," Julie added as the woman headed for the door. "Even if they're not."

"Huh?" she asked.

"Hurry!" Nora shooed her out the door and she stumbled onto the street then just stood and gaped at the St. Clouds.

"What was that supposed to mean?" Nora wanted to know. "They're all wheat breads, even if they're not?"

Julie shrugged. "Clarice clearly thinks Irving needs to branch out, and I don't think it's all about baked goods."

"What are you talking about?"

"Well, why did you send her out there?" Julie demanded in exasperation. "He's a good-looking man who came in here to see you and now you've sicced the competition on him."

"The competition? *He's* the competition!" Nora was practically shouting. The other customers stood around with their mouths open. "His grandmother likes my nut bread, that's all! Irving St. Cloud is the enemy. Anytime a business folds—*wham!*—up goes another St. Cloud Bakery. I'm sure he'd love to close me up, too. Well, if that's his plan, he can just forget it. I'm—here—to—stay!" She emphasized this last by pointing in turn at each customer. The long-haired kid in baggy pants and suspenders gulped and said, "Well…okay. Can I have a piece of nut bread, too?"

IT WAS ALL FINE AND GOOD getting immersed in Nora's problems with Irving St. Cloud, but Julie still had a few of her own. She hurried back to her one-thirty appointment with Miles Charleston. She'd been counseling Miles about his pending divorce for nearly six months, and she'd learned in that time how anxious her client was about nearly everything in his life. It would certainly not serve him well to have his marriage counselor be missing in action when he arrived.

Hurrying to her office, Julie glanced at her watch, relieved to see she was a few minutes early after all. She walked through the outer room and stopped short. "Carolyn," she said in dismay. "We didn't have a meeting, did we?"

"Oh, no...uh-uh...." She waved that away with an unlit cigarette, searching through her purse for a lighter. "I just wanted to see you. After your radio blunder the other day, Floyd and I got to talking and it was the best conversation in years."

"Great," Julie said with no enthusiasm.

"Well, you know..." She shrugged delicately and gave Julie a sideways smile. "You didn't come off that well."

"Did you go to Jake Danforth's building?" Julie couldn't help asking.

"Heck, no. I didn't have time. Besides, I told you about how Floyd and I really connected, didn't I?"

"In vivid detail. Carolyn, I have a client due here any minute, and he's the not the kind to understand about having you here, too."

"Oh, I'll just wait. I won't be any bother." She settled into her seat and crossed her legs.

"I don't think that's such a good idea."

"I want to tell you the latest about Floyd. You're going to want to hear this."

"Carolyn—"

"Ms. Sommerfield?" Miles Charleston peeked his head inside the door to the outer office and blinked in confusion at the sight of Carolyn.

"Hi, Miles. Come on in." She turned toward the inner door and threaded her key in the lock.

"I brought candy with me."

"Oh, you didn't need to do that," Julie said, before she remembered that his wife's name was Candice. She glanced around to see a Miles clone standing beside him, only in female form. They were both thin, serious, and nervously darting looks around the room at large and Carolyn in particular. Miles had never referred to his wife as Candy before. And he'd never, ever brought her with him.

They were holding hands.

"Oh, hello, Mrs. Charleston," Julie said, stepping forward to reach out a hand.

Carolyn leaned forward, all ears. Julie shot her a quelling look.

"We heard you on the radio," Candy Charleston said in a soft, little-girl's voice. "You know, with that nice Mr. Danforth? I was worried about Miles." She glanced uncertainly at Carolyn. Julie quickly ushered the Charlestons into her inner office and closed the door with a harsh *click*.

"You were worried about your husband?" Julie said, indicating for them to take a seat. They seemed stumped by her two armchairs. Miles finally sat on one of the seats while Candy perched on his lap. Both of Candy's hands were entwined with Miles's.

"I didn't know what kind of—therapist—you were." She said the word as if it tasted bad.

"You didn't know I was a marriage counselor?"

"Well, you sounded more like someone who…" She pressed a finger to her lips as if considering. Julie had a feeling she knew exactly what she wanted to say, so she just waited, her eyes on Candy's tightened lips. "You sounded like someone who might be influenced by the wrong things."

"Candy means the psychic thing," Miles interpreted.

"Aha." Julie was beginning to wish Miles had brought real candy instead of his lovely, lovely wife.

"So, I thought I'd better see for myself." She squeezed Miles's hands then turned limpid eyes Julie's way. Julie also wished Miles had been a little more specific about why he and his wife were having marital problems. All he'd revealed during his sessions was how wonderful Candy was, how much he missed her since she'd moved out, and how he would do anything to have her back. Julie in turn had suggested ways for Miles to get on with his life while Candy sorted out whether she really wanted the marriage or not. Julie had assumed she didn't, since nothing Miles had said had indicated she gave a fig about him and their life together.

"You read the tarot cards?" Candy asked primly. Her mouth was like a little bow, all pinched in at the center with judgment.

"No."

Her eyes widened. "But you told Mr. Danforth that you did."

"He assumed I did. I let him have his assumptions."

"So, you didn't read the tarot with his ex-wife?"

"His ex read the cards. I listened to her."

Candy gazed from Julie to Miles, who was gazing right back at her as if she were the most beautiful creature on earth. Since she looked just like him, Julie considered what this said about Miles. "So, you didn't actually *do* anything?" Candy asked.

"Miles, this is your session," Julie said evenly. "Do you want to talk about me, or do you want to talk about you and Candy?"

"I want to talk about me and Candy."

That went over like the proverbial lead balloon. Candy's sweet features blackened as if a shade had been drawn. "I don't want to waste any more money," she declared. "I think maybe these sessions with Ms. Sommerfield could come to a close very soon."

"Do you mean you want to get back together?" he asked eagerly.

"Did I say that?" she snapped.

"You said you didn't want to waste any more money," he responded, confused and a little hurt by her tone. "I thought you meant *our* money."

"Your services will no longer be needed," she said to Julie curtly. "Miles, write her a check."

"But I—"

She folded her arms and looked toward the wall. Miles gazed helplessly at Julie, who knew when she'd been outmaneuvered. "We can do whatever you want to do, Miles. This can be our last session for a while. It's all right."

"Forever," Candy said, still staring at the wall.

Miles wrote out the check, bewildered. Clearly he'd expected Candy to love Julie as much as he did.

Before he handed over the check Candy gave it a long, hard look, clearly dismayed by the amount. She said succinctly, "Bill us," then kept the check and sailed into the outer room. Miles followed dutifully after her, stopping at the door as if he wanted to say something more. Before he could, Candy barked out, "Miles!" and he turned like a well-heeled dog.

Julie walked into the outer office behind them. Carolyn blew out a puff of smoke and said loudly, "Lady, you are a real pain in the butt. And I thought I was bad."

"Carolyn," Julie warned softly.

Candy turned on her heel as if someone had spun her around. She inhaled and exhaled several times. Julie watched her nostrils flare and contract in fascination. "I do not appreciate your interference, ma'am. Good day."

"Not if I ever have to see you again."

"Carolyn!" Julie repeated on a sputter.

Candy leveled her eyes on Carolyn as if they were twin laser beams. But Carolyn was impervious and simply blew a little smoke Candy's way, winking at her. Candy's face suffused with dark red color and she strode from the room, head high, Miles trotting at her heels and looking miserable.

"What," Carolyn asked, "was that?"

"Clients," Julie said shortly. "They're having— some problems—but it's not your concern."

"Oh, stop being such a tight-ass. That woman's a nightmare."

"Carolyn..." Julie said, pained. She inhaled several deep breaths of her own.

"Never mind." Carolyn waved the Charlestons away and said, "Let me tell you about Floyd. We did the wild thing last night under a black light. First time he's actually gotten out of the missionary position since before our wedding. We were on this bearskin rug and then I said, 'Hey, Big Daddy, let's have some fun.' So, I came up with this idea—"

Julie walked back into her inner office, Carolyn right behind her. "I'm not a sex counselor!"

"Oh, but you'll love this part."

"Carolyn, you only like sex so you can talk about it later. But I don't want to hear it. At all! In fact, I don't want to hear about sex ever again!"

"You're not getting any, are you?" She was sympathetic.

"Carolyn!"

"Are you?" she insisted.

"No!"

They stared at each other across Julie's desk. "Well, hey…" Carolyn said, reaching for another cigarette as she stubbed her first on Julie's granite rock. "You just need a date. How about that hunky Jake Danforth? He was asking you whether he should date? Maybe he should date you?"

Julie's eyes were on Carolyn's pack of cigarettes. She felt completely done in, as if she couldn't face another moment. She wanted a vice, something to at least feel bad about besides shooting off her mouth at inappropriate moments. She said, pointing to the pack of cigarettes, "Would it be all right if I had one of those?"

"One of these?" Carolyn was surprised.

"Yes."

"What for?"

"To smoke. I want to catch six kinds of cancer

and shorten my life. Would that be all right with you?''

"Okay."

She handed one to Julie then extended her lighter but Julie forestalled her. "I'm going to save it for later. For when I really need it."

"Have you ever thought you might need therapy?" Carolyn asked innocently.

"Constantly," Julie muttered.

"So, let me tell you about the bear rug. It was so fabulous, but it wasn't really the right texture for what I had in mind. Too furry, if you know what I mean."

"Maybe you'd better light it," Julie said and Carolyn flicked on the flame, touching it to Julie's cigarette. She hadn't smoked except for a few puffs behind the garage with a friend in high school.

At that moment there was a light knock on the inside door. "Excuse me."

The familiar male voice sent Julie jumping about three feet in the air. In horror, she glanced up to see Jake Danforth standing in the doorway to her inner office.

She gulped in horror.

Jake stared at her. "Juliet?" he asked in utter disbelief.

"Jake!" Julie gasped. She stared at him through slitted eyes and a haze of smoke. Well, at least she did until she inhaled on a gulp and started choking furiously. The cigarette rocketed out her mouth onto the floor. Carolyn calmly stomped it out as Jake clapped her hard enough on the back to nearly knock her over.

Tears streamed down her cheeks. She coughed violently a few more times then said in a squeaky voice, "So, you found me out."

He nodded slowly. "Juliet Adams," he said, giving her a thoughtful look. "It's been a long, long time...."

And Julie bent over and coughed furiously, remembering quite vividly why she'd never been able to learn to smoke.

5

JAKE WAITED while Juliet suffered through a coughing spasm. He was poleaxed. *Juliet Adams* was *Julie Sommerfield!* Juliet Adams, the one girl from his youth who still had the power to invade his thoughts with memories he cherished. Sure, she'd pelted him with Bing cherries, ruining his best shirt in the process. And sure she'd snubbed him when he'd run into her at the University of Washington. But he could still recall the sensual softness of her skin and the whisper of her soft sighs in his ear.

And here she was. As beautiful as ever and just as prickly. Blue eyes, chin-length brown hair, luscious lips. No wonder she'd seemed so familiar to him. And even though right now her skin was red and blotchy from coughing, and her eyes were watering like they'd sprung a leak, she still had power to rob him of speech.

Juliet Adams was Julie Sommerfield!

He wanted to shake his head and rub his eyes and check again. But no, this was real. Momentarily he wondered about the tall woman standing by with the amused smirk. A friend? A client? She stood by and silently smoked, gazing from Juliet to Jake and back again, as if waiting for the second act.

But Jake was too bemused at learning the identity of his nemesis to give her much thought. No wonder she had harbored such resentment against him! Not that he understood it completely, but it was a fact that Juliet had—apart from one memorable May night—pretty much treated Jake as if he suffered from the plague all through their childhood.

Juliet finally cleared her throat. The exertion had left her face with an unnatural flush and her blue eyes shimmered with faint, leftover tears. She darted him a look before turning away toward the other woman. Jake couldn't read her expression, but the other woman could and whatever she saw on Juliet's face caused her to grind out her cigarette on a granite slab on Juliet's desk. The woman tried to look contrite but fell just short of it.

There was a No Smoking sign in bold, brass letters that everyone seemed to ignore.

Juliet turned back to him and pasted a pleasant smile on her face. "So, what brings you here?"

"I have no idea," he said truthfully. "I thought I was going to ask you back on the show, and I was toying with the idea of signing up for a therapy session or two."

She looked at him in utter dismay. "What?"

"Teri suggested I come see you, and I finally decided to follow her advice," he lied, his eyes taking in every inch of her. He hadn't listened to a word his ex-wife uttered since they split up—and long before that, too, if he were completely honest.

"Well, I can't!" she said. "I won't. That's impossible…because…because…"

"Because?"

"Because we already know each other!" she burst out.

"How well do you know each other?" the woman standing next to Juliet asked curiously.

"Carolyn," she warned.

"Inquiring minds want to know."

Jake couldn't get over it. "Did Teri know who you were?"

"Of course not!" she declared a trifle huffily. "I didn't know who she was, and I don't see how she could know who I was. Until she wrote me a check and I saw the name Danforth, I didn't have a clue she was your ex-wife, and even then I wasn't completely sure."

"Did you tell her you knew me?" Jake asked.

"Not on your life! I wasn't going to bring all that up."

"All what up?" the other woman asked.

"The fact that I knew Jake Danforth from grade school," she admitted reluctantly, to which the woman in the narrow-lensed glasses said, "Ahhh," on a long note of discovery.

Jake returned his gaze to Juliet's face. Juliet Adams had been a skinny kid with a bad attitude and a tremendously accurate aim. By high school she'd grown into an attractive woman who made Jake regret all those times he'd teased and chased her. Now, she was something else again, but she'd definitely retained the bad attitude.

"But then you started maligning my character on your radio program," she added tartly. "Then I knew for certain that you were one and the same."

This garnered a "humph" from her friend. Jake looked at her and she stuck out her hand. "Carolyn Mathers."

"Nice to meet you," he said automatically.

"Since Julie seems to be suffering post-traumatic shock—or maybe it's nicotine poisoning, I'm not sure on that—" She peered hard at Juliet, who stared her down. "Well, anyway, since she hasn't asked the right question, let me. What are you doing here?"

"Like, I said…"

"No, I mean the truth," she interrupted. "The last I heard you were trying to get back into the dating scene. Well, Julie's the woman to help you. God knows she's helped me." Carolyn gave Juliet a grateful smile.

Juliet couldn't hide the look of horror that flashed across her expression, though she recovered very quickly. "I don't think it would be a good idea to see you as well as your ex, unless you were coming to me as a couple."

"You said you just saw her just one time," Jake pointed out.

"Well, yes…so far…."

Jake watched her squirm. He was starting to enjoy her discomfort a little. *Juliet Adams…imagine that.* "You don't have some kind of exclusion policy, do you?" he asked. "I mean, it's not like you're a lawyer picking sides."

"Hell, no!" Carolyn Mathers interjected. "You should have seen the fun couple that was just here. They needed tons of counseling. You could just tell."

"The point is, they came as a couple," Juliet warned Carolyn tightly.

"*She* was a particular joy to be around," Carolyn added confidentially to Jake. "The kind of woman who would make a man head straight for the priesthood, if you know what I mean. I didn't get to listen in on their session, but I've got a pretty good idea that nobody, not even the talented Ms. Julie Sommerfield here, could do anything to help her. I tried to picture what a night of romance between them might be.'' Her eyes widened and she shook her head. ''My imagination—which is pretty vivid most of the time, let me tell you—failed me completely. The thought of them getting down and dirty and doing the old bump and grind—''

''Carolyn!'' Juliet burst out.

''—was outside of my ability. But I'm sure Julie would have better luck with you.''

After that speech there was a moment of silence. Finally, Juliet began, ''Mr. Danforth, I think—''

''No, come on. Don't 'Mr. Danforth' me. We know each other better than that.''

''We do?'' Carolyn asked.

''Jake, would you mind waiting in my office a moment?'' Juliet asked through a strained smile.

''No. Sure.''

She grabbed Carolyn Mathers by the arm and dragged her into the outside room against her protests, closing the door firmly behind her. Jake could hear a whispered exchange through the door though he couldn't make out the words. It sounded rather heated, though. He smiled to himself. This just got better and better!

Crossing to the window, he gazed outside, watching brown and yellow leaves fall from the trees and twist in the wind. He was glad things had turned out as they had, even if this afternoon's meeting had been a jolt. Up to now he'd been so annoyed with Teri for spilling all to a marriage counselor who doubled as a ''seer'' that he hadn't really thought

through his feelings and actions. He'd just wanted to
stomp around and complain. And though he'd known
the tarot cards were probably Teri's doing—she'd
long been into all that psychic stuff—he'd wanted to
spread the blame to her so-called therapist just to
vent his feelings.

And he'd done it on the air.

He grimaced. Okay, that hadn't been necessary. It
hadn't even been nice. He'd opened another whole
can of worms by involving Juliet. Now he wasn't
quite sure what to think.

By the time Juliet entered he'd seated himself at
one of the chairs clumped around her desk. Having
digested the shock of her identity, he was settled in
to have a thoroughly good time.

She, on the other hand, looked less than happy.

"Let's get down to it," she said as an opening
salvo. "You wanted to poke holes in my credentials,
and you did. Now, you know who I am, so I'm sure
round two is about to start. Tell me what I can do to
get you to turn your attention elsewhere. I wouldn't
have talked to your ex-wife if I'd known who she
was, but I never mentioned to anyone anything about
that meeting. Whether you want to believe it or not,
I can sometimes act with professional conduct. And
I've purposely led you to believe I know something
about tarot cards when I don't. Actually, it was your
wife who brought them out. That may sound like an
excuse, but it's the truth."

"I know it is."

"You do." She regarded him through cool blue
eyes. She'd pulled herself back into the role of counselor and he had to admit that it was a stunning trans-
formation. Whatever she might be truly feeling at

this moment had been subverted for the sake of her job.

"Yes, I do. I know my ex. She believes all that stuff. Always has. I think it's a crock."

"A lot of people would disagree with you."

"It's one of the reasons we couldn't live together anymore."

"What are the other reasons?"

"Well, let me think…" He pretended to ponder. "How about we couldn't stand each other? Or, what about the fact that I caught her in bed with her Tae Bo instructor? And I got a clue things weren't working out when she served me with divorce papers on my birthday. I'm quick that way."

Juliet's lips had parted in either real or pretended shock, he couldn't tell which. "I didn't know," she said.

"So, it was kind of a surprise when I heard she'd gone to a marriage counselor. I thought it was all said and done at that point."

"I see…."

Did she? He doubted it. To clarify, he added, "Not that I was exactly heartbroken. From the moment my marriage commenced I asked myself what the heck I thought I was doing."

"Why did you get married?" she asked, the question popping out as if she had no control over it.

"Good question. Just kind of seemed like the right time for it. Bad reason, I know, but choices are often made from bad reasons. Being single, you probably think I'm giving you a load of bull."

"I was married. Briefly. I do have a clue about what you're talking about."

He lifted his brows, surprised how affected he was by such a simple statement.

"So, you wanted to ask me on the program? Or, ask for a therapy session. Or, maybe see your nemesis unmasked?"

"All of the above. And I—wanted to see you again."

She raised one skeptical brow.

"I have been out of the dating scene for a long time," Jake said. "And I think it's time to get back in. I guess I was kind of thinking…you and I…?"

"I don't date," she responded quickly, sitting back in her chair.

"You used to."

His subtle reminder of prom night brought a new flush to her cheeks and a frozen clamp to her jaw. "I've got clients coming, Jake. You're here during my business hours."

"If you won't date me, maybe you can find someone who will," Jake improvised. He didn't want her throwing him out of her office. He wasn't ready to leave.

"I'm not a dating service." Her voice was cold.

"How about you come on the show and we talk about dating? I promise I won't 'malign' you any further. This could work for both of us. You can restore your credibility and probably gain some new clients, and I can entertain my listeners. They love to get into my personal life," he added lightly, hiding his own feelings on that subject.

"I don't think so…."

"Come on, Juliet." He was winging it. Trying to maintain contact. Jabbing and thrusting while she was parrying with the best of them. He couldn't reach her softer side no matter how hard he tried. "You're a counselor. I've just been through a rather messy divorce. Now, I'd like to put myself back together and I'd like your help."

"I am not ready to go back on your show."

"Okay. Then how about we check out the dating scene. Say, after work tonight?"

"I'm busy tonight."

"Well, how about next Tuesday? Then I can tell my listeners that I'll be exploring the dating scene soon. If you change your mind about coming on the show, we'll do that, too. Besides, I could use some help in that field. I mean, you already turned me down. Maybe I just don't have it anymore."

"Uh-huh." The faintest smile teased her lips. "Next you'll be telling me you suffer from low self-esteem."

"I do. *Severe* low self-esteem. Very severe. Do you think there's any hope for me?"

"Go away, Jake," she said, but he knew she didn't really mean it. He was getting to her.

"How about this…you pencil me in for a therapy session. We'll just see how it goes. Then, maybe we can explore that dating scene together—strictly as patient and therapist—and talk about it on-air."

She looked at him a long, long time. Jake held his breath, hoping she didn't see through the fact that he really just wanted to be with her.

"You're so full of it," she said, but she dragged over her calendar and flipped it open to the following Tuesday.

"Name-calling," he said with a happy smile. He'd won. That's all that counted.

Her answer was a snort.

THE AIR WAS CRISP, cold, but at least rain hadn't been loosed from the low-hanging gray clouds, as yet. Saturday morning. The Halloween bazaar wound along the waterfront in an array of red-and-white striped tents and white plastic tables and chairs. Flags snapped in a wicked breeze and the scent of pumpkin spice and cider luckily overpowered the dank, musty smell off the Willamette River.

Julie stood behind the counter with Nora. Her tent was a solid red and the color cast a mysterious glow to the cookies, cakes and tarts Nora had readied for the event. The jack-o'-lantern cinnamon rolls leered like evil sprites from their basket. No more happy faces for them. Bat cookies with equally evil smiles were propped up in rows and hung from orange ribbons overhead. When a particularly strong bit of wind rushed in, they swung madly and one had actually landed on Nora's wig. Yes, she was wearing a new wig this day, while Julie had contented herself with an orange-and-black apron covered with witches, owls and skeletons.

Nora fussed with more orange ribbon while Julie sold a box of cinnamon rolls to a little girl who was pulling a reluctant black cat along on a leash. The cat hissed and tangled itself in the leash twice before the girl scooped it up, tucked it under one arm, a box of cinnamon rolls under the other.

"Tell me again what you're doing on Tuesday?" Nora suggested, wielding a pair of scissors on the ribbon until the poor thing howled and curled beneath her ministrations.

"I never got the hang of that," Julie said with admiration.

"Smokescreen. You can curl ribbon with the best of them. Come on. Are you seeing him or not?"

"Not. He wanted a therapy session and for me to lead him around the dating scene. Or something like that. I'm not really sure. I almost fell for it, but then I caught myself at the last minute. I turned him down."

"Why?"

"I didn't want to hear about his divorce and how much he's suffered, blah, blah, blah. It's just so much bull—" She cut herself off at the arrival of a new customer.

As soon as they'd left with several loaves of apple bread, Nora pointed out, "Correct me if I'm wrong, but isn't that what you do? Counsel the newly divorced."

"Sometimes. Or, try to keep a marriage together."

"Well, by the sounds of it, this one's long over. So, what's the problem?"

"The problem is, I'm not a dating advisor. And that's I think what he really wanted. Or, I don't know. I just don't want anything to do with him."

"You said he offered you twice your hourly rate, and you still turned him down."

"Aren't you listening? It's not about money."

"Then what's it about?"

Julie narrowed her eyes at her best friend. "It wasn't so long ago that we were plotting his murder."

"That's before he offered cold, hard cash. Let's be realistic."

"You're a shameless opportunist," Julie accused.

"Card-carrying," she admitted with a wide smile. "Would it really be so bad? Hey, you could learn his innermost secrets. That would be worth something.''

''Yeah, but I wouldn't get to tell anybody about them,'' she said.

''You said he asked you back on his program.''

''To talk about *dating!* Like I know thing one about that process. The idea makes me break out in hives. I still wouldn't get to share Jake Danforth's secrets.''

Nora cocked her head thoughtfully. ''Maybe you could sing them to me.''

''Sing what to you? What are you talking about?'' Julie frowned at her.

''His secrets. That wouldn't be telling, in the strictest sense. Then we could both know.''

''Devious, but it would still be disclosure. No, if I learned any of Jake Danforth's deep, dark secrets I'd just have to keep them to myself, more's the pity.''

''But you would still know....'' she pointed out.

Julie sighed. ''He did offer up to three times the rate.''

Nora pretended to stagger. ''What are you waiting for? The man's obsessed! We could retire to the Bahamas!''

''He just wants a date,'' she said darkly.

''So give him one!''

''You're not listening,'' Julie snapped as she lifted a new pan of bats from the back and placed them in the window. ''These things are flying out of here,'' she said. ''No pun intended.''

''I'm listening. He wants a date. He wants you to counsel him and go on the air and talk all about it.

It doesn't sound that objectionable. And there's a lot of money involved.''

"Nora!" Julie gazed at her in exasperation. "I can't trust him. Can't you see it? He'll tell me all about himself and his *date* and then we'll go the air and he'll score points off me to boost ratings. 'My session with the psycho, mumbo jumbo therapist, Julie Sommerfield.' The listeners will be in orbit. No, make that *Juliet* Sommerfield. He keeps calling me that and it drives me wild."

"It's your name."

"Was. Past tense. And I never liked it. And then the listeners will call in and oh, I just can't face it…" She grabbed the scissors and ribbon and began curling shiny, orange coils. She wasn't as adept as Nora but what she lacked in finesse she made up in energy.

"I'm not going to risk having him go on the air and dissect my therapeutic tactics, all the while using me as a scapegoat for his marital failings!" Julie continued heatedly. "It's just not worth it. And that's what he'll do. That's the way he is."

"Make him sign a confidence agreement."

"Oh, sure, that'll work."

"If he wants you that bad, he'll do it, and I—" Nora sucked in a sharp breath, freezing as if suddenly turned to stone.

Julie glanced around. Irving and Clarice St. Cloud and a beautiful young blond woman were strolling through the booths. St. Cloud Bakeries' bright blue booth stood directly across from Nora's, hidden from view only by the crowd. As soon as they'd arrived Nora had leveled a glare at their enemy camp, but had thus far managed to keep her lip buttoned on her feelings. Now, however, she looked ready to explode.

At that moment Clarice looked up. Today she wore a Kelly green pantsuit and a matching felt hat. Spying Nora she waved as if they were old friends. Tugging on Irving's sleeve, she pointed at them, urging him forward. Nora made a sound low in her throat, which sounded suspiciously like a growl.

"They're coming this way," Julie said.

"I have eyes."

"Be nice."

"I'm always nice."

"Just remember all the advice you've been giving me. Keep things in perspective. Don't overemotionalize this."

"No problem." The smile on her lips was a great facsimile of the Joker's from *Batman.*

And she thought Julie was having problems!

"Hello, again," Irving said politely. He wore casual clothes today. Pressed blue jeans and a tan sweater, the sleeves pushed up very tanned arms. The young blonde hovered nearby and eyed Nora suspiciously.

"Darling, what a lovely booth!" Clarice said to Nora, eyeing the bats swinging on ribbons above their heads.

"Would you like to try one?" Nora reached for a plate of sneering bats.

Clarice's hand hovered delicately over the plate. She shot her grandson an impish look and said, "Irving, we've got to get more immediate, don't you think?" His look said he wasn't following her line of thinking. Julie wondered what she meant as well. "All of our baked goods are so," she gently nibbled on a corner of bat wing, "…so…the same. There's no sense of the now. Not like Nora's little bats. They're so clever. And they seem like they've just popped from the oven into your mouth."

The blond girl scooped up a bat and bit off a chunk, her eyes on Nora as she chewed. "They're just a sugar cookie," she complained.

Irving St. Cloud dropped a hand on her shoulder and said ironically, "You'll have to forgive my sister. She's always rude."

"Donna, stop being a problem," Clarice said on a sigh, to which Donna flounced away.

"She's still eating the bat cookie," Julie observed.

"She's rude. She's not stupid," said Irving.

Nora gave him a head-to-toe look that could scour a dirty floor to lily-white. He, in turn, gazed mildly back at her. Julie sucked in a breath, prepared for all-out war, when Clarice, a sneaky little smile crossing her lips, said, "Come on, Irving. We've got a booth of our own to check on."

As soon as they were gone, Nora set the plate down with a *whump* so that momentarily the bats took flight. Julie arranged them back in place, then turned to her friend, who was standing in the shadows at the back of the booth, arms folded across her chest.

"That wasn't bad," Julie said. "Almost nice. Mute works for you."

"What are they up to?" Nora demanded.

"What do you mean?"

"Are they stealing my recipes?"

"By just *tasting* them? Oh, come on."

"'Just a sugar cookie,'" Nora mimicked in a high falsetto.

"Okay, she was rude, but her family knew it."

Julie slid her friend a knowing look. "So, what's going on?"

Nora was still glaring after them. "What do you mean?"

"This isn't all about cookies and baked goods." Nora turned her glare on Julie, who held up her hands in surrender. "I was just saying…"

"What?" she demanded.

"That Irving St. Cloud is on the plus side of attractive and he seemed to be thinking the same thing of you."

"You're delusionary," she growled beneath her breath.

Nora picked up a metal spatula and shoved it beneath a pile of jack-o'-lantern cinnamon rolls with rather more force than necessary. Looking up, she started to say something to Julie, but then her expression changed at something she witnessed behind Julie's right shoulder. Turning, Julie gazed directly into Jake Danforth's blue eyes. Her lips parted in surprise and his brows lifted as he registered who she was.

"Juliet," he said, a bit cautiously. She could hardly blame him as she'd practically tossed him out of her office after his outrageous suggestions.

"Well, hello, Jake Danforth," Nora greeted him warmly. She slid Julie a look. An evil look. *Oh, God,* Julie thought. *She's planning something.*

He gave her a long look and said, "Nora?"

"That's right. It's old home week, isn't it? What a treat!"

And that's when Jake's "date" snuggled up to his elbow. She was practically a clone of Irving St.

Cloud's sister: blond, thin, petite and possessed of "attitude." A living nightmare.

She tossed a distant smile in their direction and kept her attention on the drifting crowds. One languid hand reached up and brushed her bangs from her eyes.

"Is this your booth?" Jake asked in discovery, reading the sign. "I've seen your shop on Twenty-third. I didn't realize it was you."

"Yes, well. Life's just full of interesting twists."

Jake turned his attention to Julie. "Yes, it is."

The blonde yawned and said, "I'm going to get a Perrier. You want anything?"

"No, thanks."

The three of them watched her saunter away. Jake added mildly, "Pammy's an intern at the station. I don't think she's going to last long."

"Why not?" Julie asked curiously.

"Because she doesn't do anything besides look good. She bedazzled the owner, but he's getting out of his daze pretty fast."

"Did Beryl have anything to do with it?" Julie asked.

"Everything," he admitted with a sideways smile.

Julie looked away. *Oh, you're too attractive, you devil! And you know it!*

"Who's Beryl?" Nora asked. "Oh. The lady you insulted in the elevator?"

"Yep," Julie said, annoyed by Jake's huge grin. She turned to him and said lightly, "At least Pammy helped you get back into the dating game."

"True," Jake admitted. "I wouldn't have thought of her as a date, but she told me that she looked into

a crystal ball and saw that we were meant to be together. It was fated.''

"Fated," Julie echoed.

"Fated to end after one afternoon." He added
charmingly, "I'm still hoping you'll change your
mind about Tuesday."

He was so smug. So sure of his drop-dead-
gorgeous appeal to women. She wanted to accuse
him of all kinds of things, but he'd done nothing
wrong. At least nothing she could put her finger on.

Feeling both Jake's and Nora's eyes on her, she
asked, "Want a bat? We seem to be giving them
away for free."

Nora pushed the plate his way. "Take one. Tell
me what you think."

"They're smiling," he said, accepting one of the
bats.

Nora swivelled the plate to stare down at her little
black critters. "I tried to make them sneer."

"They *are* sneering," Julie insisted.

"I guess that could be a sneer," Jake said, biting
into his cookie.

Julie couldn't think of one more thing to say after
that, which was just fine with Jake and Nora, as it
turned out, since they began chatting away like long-
lost buddies. By the time Pammy returned to tug at
Jake's arm, it looked as if he and Nora had become
fast friends. "Stop by later," Nora invited in a rush
as Jake was being dragged away. "Did Julie give
you the address to our apartment? No? Hold on a
minute there, Pammy." Quickly Nora scribbled
down the address and phone number on a paper plate
and handed the information to Jake as Pammy glared
at both of them.

Julie watched Nora hand the plate with their address to Jake, who folded it into a pie shape and stuffed it into the inner pocket of his black leather jacket. Pammy looked fit to kill. She clamped her lips together, stuck out her chin and made a *humphing* noise.

As she bore Jake away from Nora's booth, Jake called back, "I'll come and trick-or-treat you. That okay with you, Juliet?"

"It's Julie, Jake. Not Juliet. No *T* on the end. Got it?"

"I don't know if I can break the habit," he countered as Pammy held his arm at full length. One tug and she would overbalance him in her direction.

"Try," Julie encouraged.

"Nice seeing you again, Nora. The bats are great."

"Wait till you try a cinnamon roll. The jack-o'-lanterns are sneering, too." She swept an arm to encompass the tray of cinnamon rolls with their orange jack-o'-lantern faces.

"That's a smile," he said as Pammy rolled her eyes. "See you later."

As soon as they had turned the corner Julie picked up a towel and snapped it at Nora, who jumped and howled. "Well, you deserve it!" Julie declared in a harsh stage whisper as a group of children in costumes and harried parents headed their way.

"Do I?" Nora snorted. "How about you? I am not interested in Irving St. Cloud!"

"Is that what this is all about?"

"Actually, no. I like Jake. I always have."

"You *have?*"

"Not the way you like him, though."

''What—what—do you mean by that?'' she sputtered.

''He's your Romeo, Juliet.''

''Oh, Lord. Please stop with that. He was the school's Romeo, not mine.''

''You're in love. It's written all over you.'' Nora turned and smiled beatifically at the approaching newcomers.

Julie nearly had an apoplectic fit. ''I don't even like the man!''

''Love. *L-O-V-E.* Love, love, love, love, love.''

And she grinned—or sneered—at Julie in the same manner as her dastardly little bats.

6

FOUR HOURS LATER they were back at the apartment, the empty trays still in the trunk of Nora's car, the baked goods consumed, the bazaar a success from start to finish. "Now, we have to get ready for trick-or-treaters," Nora moaned. She was sprawled in one of the chairs. Julie had collapsed on the couch.

"All we have to do is throw the candy in a bowl and answer the door. We can do it."

Nora grimaced. "My feet hurt."

"Yeah, well, you deserve it. You invited Jake Danforth over here."

Yawning, Nora said, "You should be kissing my hurting feet." At Julie's incredulous look, she said, "When he shows up, offer him a drink. You can throw some poison in and see if it works."

"Well, that's just great. I haven't had time to get any poison," Julie grumbled.

"What a shame. You might just have to be nice to him."

Julie thought about sticking her tongue out at her friend, decided it was too childish, considered flipping her off, then finally internalized the whole thing and simply glowered across the room. Nora started laughing. Julie held out for a while, but then she started laughing, too. She threw a cushion at Nora and they both laughed harder.

By the time of the first ring of the doorbell, they'd munched down a couple of tuna sandwiches and diet cola, donned black wigs and blackened their front teeth and were poised to offer a huge bowl of candy to the gremlins tromping door to door. It was early, but even so Julie held her breath as Nora swung the door open; she couldn't help but expect Jake. Instead of his six feet of male swagger, however, there stood a short group of four toddlers on the top step sporting moptops, guitars and name tags: John, George, Paul and Ringo.

"The Fab Four as they've never been seen before," Julie greeted them. She held out the bowl and they blinked and shoved their hands inside as their parents admonished them to not take too much.

As soon as the last hand had been pulled out of the bowl by a helpful parent, Nora closed the door. Julie sensed her own disappointment, and that really bugged her. She didn't want him here. She certainly didn't want Jake Danforth anywhere near her. Isn't that why she refused to take him on as a client? Oh, sure. She'd had a moment or two of weakness, but luckily, sanity had prevailed.

Until Nora decided to invite him over and send her into this state of panicked excitement that had no place in her ordered, little life.

"He wouldn't show up this early," Nora said as if they were in the middle of a conversation. "The kiddies will all be tucked in bed before Jake decides to stop by."

"I don't want him to show up at all."

"That why you put on your 'Check me out, baby' black slacks and boots?"

"What?" Julie glanced down at her pants. "These old things?"

"Lie to yourself if you want, but if you weren't thinking about having some special company arrive, you'd be in your jeans and sneakers."

"My jeans are in the wash."

"Since when do you only have one pair?"

"I just wanted to wear something black."

"Yeah. Okay. You win. You're not thinking about Jake Danforth."

Julie got up and headed to the kitchen. Nora could be so blasted irritating sometimes! Pouring herself a glass of water, she gulped it down in one, long draft. As she did so, her eye fell on the mug with Jake's image. She kept shoving it to the back of the cupboard but Nora kept bringing it out and placing it on the shelf above the sink. Irritating? Nora was downright diabolical sometimes.

Sighing, Julie tore her gaze from the mug and glanced toward the cupboard above the refrigerator: the liquor cabinet. She really wanted something with more kick, but she didn't trust herself. A little bit of alcohol and she tended to get way, way too chatty. She could just see herself, her inhibitions slipping away, her tongue flapping as she admitted her ambivalent feelings about Jake to Nora, and then worse, blabbing to the man himself, should he deign to cross their threshold. She could picture herself becoming way too familiar with her old buddy, Jake. Reminiscing. Laughing. Maybe even giving each other a hug. Or…

Nope. Julie slammed the door on her brain. She didn't like thinking about Jake in these terms. It was much, much easier to loathe him.

By the time Jake did arrive it was half-past eight when the doorbell rang and Julie had practically forgotten he was coming. Practically... She'd slowly relaxed over the course of the past couple of hours, realizing that Nora was right about the trick-or-treaters. They came early so their parents could gather them up and get them into bed before they ate all their candy at once and stayed up all night on a sugar high. By eight they were pretty much off the streets, but when the doorbell rang and Julie twisted the knob, she still half expected to see them on her doorstep. So that's why her heart lurched so uncomfortably when she saw Jake standing in the soft glow of the porch light. Not because she *wanted* to see him, because she hadn't quite *expected* to....

Liar! she accused herself.

"What?" he asked, holding a bottle of red wine in one hand, a bottle of white in the other.

"Did I say something?"

"It sounded like you said, 'liar.'"

"Well, that wouldn't be a polite way to greet a guest." She stepped back to allow him inside.

His black leather jacket and jeans were his chosen Halloween costume, and he looked so fantastic that Julie had to struggle to drag up her long-nursed animosity. Faced with her nemesis bearing gifts, she felt somehow disarmed, her own feelings naked and raw. It wasn't fair that he had to try too little! It wasn't fair that she couldn't completely tamp down that cursed puppy love that never, ever seemed to vanish.

"I didn't really think you'd show," she said now, ignoring the little voice in her head that called her a liar once more.

"And give up an opportunity to wear you down?" She frowned at him.

"I want to meet with you. If not Tuesday, some other time."

"Like I said, it looks like you're doing fine on the dating scene."

"I want to have a therapy session with you," he said, and something about his tone sent a little shiver down her back. How could he make it sound so sexy? "As I recall, the bidding left off at triple your going rate."

"She'll take it," Nora called from somewhere near the kitchen.

"No, I won't," Julie yelled back.

Jake glanced around their living room. She saw the place through his eyes: the tan chenille slipcover bunched over the sofa, the wrought-iron and dark, stained-wood coffee table, the magazines jumbled in a corner wicker basket, the floor lamp that listed to one side. It was like a scene out of a home decor catalog that had somehow gone awry, as if a brisk wind had breezed through, disturbing everything.

"And I want you to come back on the show, of course," he said, handing the bottles of wine over to Nora, who appeared from the kitchen like a maid. A maid with blackened teeth and limp, dull hair. "You really stirred up the listeners."

"*You* really stirred up the listeners. I just sat back and took the abuse."

"You didn't just sit back. I have some scars." His lips curved faintly. "And I want to talk about the coincidence of our past together."

Julie had trouble holding his gaze. She wanted to look away, to hide, but she knew better than to give in to all those telltale signs of nervousness. "You mean you want to exploit the fact that we've known each other since grade school? And that I hid my identity from you? And that it just proves I'm a member of that pseudo-psychologist, wacko ilk?"

Nora hurried back with two glasses of red wine, practically sloshing the liquid onto the floor in her haste. "Now, now," she admonished.

"Maybe we could clear up a few points in your favor," Jake suggested, taking his glass.

Julie eyed his drink as he lifted it to his lips. She envisioned him falling over, clutching his throat, foiled by a little bit of garden arsenic. Feeling Nora's gaze on her, she lifted her own glass and raised one brow in her friend's direction. The look on Nora's face said she was reading Julie's mind.

"It's just a shame I can't hand out some of my baked goods on Halloween," Nora said, looking at Julie. "But all the goodies have to be wrapped up, factory-direct in case some really sick psycho should try to poison someone."

"Hard to imagine that kind of mind," Jake said.

"Yes…" Julie slogged down a gulp of wine, then realized Jake had brought something far better than her usual convenience store brand. She momentarily felt really bad, and she took a second, more delicate sip. She might have changed her opinion of him right then and there except for the amusement written all over his face.

"What is it, exactly, that you want from me?" she demanded.

"Were you listening the day that Teri, my ex-wife, called in?"

Julie hated to admit the truth, but yes, she listened

to his show every day. Country western station be damned; she'd switched the buttons back as soon as Jake's show started up the next morning. "Yes..." she said cautiously.

"Well, she called me at home that night and we talked about you, and I said—"

"You talked to Teri about me?"

"We do converse now and again," he admitted with a wry smile. "And I asked her about what you two had talked about."

"What did she say?"

Nora, who had poured herself a glass of red wine as well, slid into the room and perched on another chair, all ears. Julie waited with baited breath.

"She told me where to go and what to do when I got there. It was rather graphic."

"I'm liking her better and better," Julie murmured, forgetting her own rule and gulping her drink once more.

"She wasn't going to tell me what went on between her and her marriage counselor. I pointed out that since a) we were now divorced and b) she wasn't seeing you any longer, that confidentiality was hardly the issue."

"What did she say to that?" Julie set down her empty glass, her head spinning a bit.

"She told me where to go and what to do when I got there."

Julie laughed. She couldn't help herself. So did Nora. Even Jake grinned. Immediately Julie pulled herself together. Oh, no. She wasn't going to fall for him again. She'd been down that road in her youth and she had no interest in traveling it again.

"I wouldn't feel comfortable in a therapy session with you," she admitted.

He considered that for a moment. "I feel the opposite," he said in a way that could only be described as earnest. "I'm glad it's you. It hit me in the gut to think Teri was baring all our private marital moments to some stranger, but now that I know it was you, I don't know..." He shook his head. "I want to explore the whole thing myself. So, I want to come to your office and talk. See what develops."

Julie didn't know what to think.

"I'd like to have you back on the show as well, sometime in the future. I'm not planning to rake over the coals of my relationship with Teri on the air, believe me. But maybe you could reveal some of your techniques and I could reveal how I felt...?"

"You show me yours, I'll show you mine?"

"Something like that."

"And that therapy would be at triple the rate?" Nora reminded him.

"No." Julie held up a hand. "Regular rates."

"So, you'll do it?" He sounded pleased. Too pleased, Julie thought, wondering what she'd gotten herself into.

"Tuesday."

"Tuesday it is," he said, setting down his glass with a clink, settling back in his chair, hands behind his head and stretching out like a relaxed panther.

Julie wondered if there was enough red wine left to get her drunk, because she suffered from the distinct feeling that she'd just been coaxed, coerced and *had*.

JAKE STRODE rapidly through the studio, lifting a hand in greeting at all his co-workers, not eager to engage in idle chitchat. He was a tad late this morning, having been detained by his dearest and oldest friend—Seltzer, his golden Lab-mutt mix. Seltzer was failing. It was age more than anything else, but it nearly killed Jake to recognize that his dog was on his last legs. He couldn't conceive of life without Seltzer and though he was loath to admit it, he'd consoled himself through the worst of his divorce with the aid of his truest and noblest friend.

Okay, he hadn't been that brokenhearted over losing Teri. Scratch that. He'd been relieved when she'd finally thrown in the towel. Just shy of ecstatic, as a matter of fact. But it was the idea of being alone, of having no one in the world to truly trust and share with that dug into his psyche. Seltzer had filled that void admirably. The thought of his empty town house was enough to send him to a therapist's couch.

A therapist like Juliet Adams Sommerfield.

Jake grimaced as he let himself inside the glassed-in booth, sank into his swivel chair and reached for his headphones. DeeAnn was already inside but she recognized the "Don't talk to me right now" syndrome that sometimes plagued him and kept her thoughts to herself. Okay. In the interest of self-honesty, therapy wasn't the real reason he wanted to see Juliet again. The truth was: he liked her. Plain and simple. He always had. Even when she'd pelted him with cherries and the like. Even when she snubbed him after their post-prom encounter. Even now....

Especially now.

Halloween night came back to him. He and Nora had finished the bottle of wine while Julie, after guzzling her first glass, had simply sat in a chair, her fingers entwined so fiercely it looked as if she were clutching her own hands for support. She'd agreed to see him on Tuesday—tomorrow afternoon—but after that she'd grown dismally quiet, as if in fear her lips might betray her again. Jake had been ready to settle in for the evening. He had nowhere to go and nothing to do, and it had been a pleasure to be with Juliet and Nora. Still, he'd had to content himself in talking with Nora about her business and fears over the expansion of St. Cloud Bakeries. Juliet had sat and listened, but he'd been certain her thoughts were far away. Only when he'd reluctantly gotten to his feet and said, thinking of Seltzer, "I'd better go. There's someone waiting for me at home," had he elicited any kind of reaction. Juliet's head had jerked up and she'd eyed him with that "Aha!" look, a sort of self-satisfied smirk that said she'd known he was going to pull something like that. Jake had let her think what she wanted. It had just been nice to get a rise out of her.

DeeAnn was staring at him, waiting a bit nervously for him to kick in. Jake gave her a thumbs-up and she relaxed. A song was ending and his morning theme music came up a moment later.

"Hello, Portland," Jake said into the microphone. "Hope you're more awake than I am this morning. I had an interesting Halloween with several people from my past and I haven't quite recovered yet."

"Oh?" DeeAnn broke in. "Friends?"

"Kind of. Acquaintances from elementary school and on."

"Really?" DeeAnn's face brightened. She'd been afraid he was going to rant and rave about something, which he liked to do on Monday mornings. He was known as the Monday morning grouch.

"Let me say this. You know the other day when we had Julie Sommerfield on, the marriage counselor my ex-wife saw who wore the wig and psychedelic glasses? It turns out her real name is Juliet Adams. Or, at least it was, when we were in school together."

"You were in school together?"

"Yup."

"And she wore the disguise so you wouldn't recognize her!" DeeAnn practically crowed in delight. "How did you find out?"

"I went to see her."

The phones lit up, blinking furiously—every single line. Jake shook his head when DeeAnn poised her finger above one of the lights, silently asking if he was ready for a listener's point of view. "So, what happened?" she asked instead.

"We were both a little surprised, but I've decided to seek therapy on her couch, so to speak."

"No kidding." DeeAnn shook her head and smiled at him. Switching off her microphone temporarily, she whispered, "You dog!" Switching it back on, she said, "And how does she feel about that?"

"Reluctant. It took some convincing. But I've got an appointment tomorrow afternoon." He wondered if Juliet were listening, decided she had to be, and added, "I also invited her back on the show."

DeeAnn lowered her voice and asked insinuatingly, "Will she reveal your little tête-à-tête in her office?"

"Nope…patient-therapist confidentiality and all that."

"Oh, I see…. You can talk about her, but she can't talk about you. Well, that's kind of cheating, Jake!"

In his mind's eye he could see Juliet's death grip around the steering wheel of her car and the maniacal look in her eye as she heard and processed DeeAnn's words. "I'll let her talk about me if she wants to," he said. "Do you hear that, Juliet? You might get the last word after all!"

JULIE CAREENED into the parking lot, bouncing like a rubber ball as the little car leapt over the parking curb, which was meant to keep cars from ramming into the wall. No such luck today. Though she stood on the brake, the nose of her Bug tapped the building in front of her. She climbed out, was glad to see the damage was no worse than a little ding, released a pent-up breath, then got back in the car and threw it into reverse. It took three tries where the poor machine revved to a high-pitched whine before she managed to bump back over the curb. A couple of men in suits turned and grinned as they walked across the lot. Once again she felt like making a rude gesture, and she shook her head at herself.

Jake's turned me into a junior high rebel.

She entered her office in a blue funk, slapped her briefcase onto her desk and collapsed in her chair. Hanging her head over the back of the chair, she stared at the ceiling. There were a couple of marks in the overhead acoustical tiles where she'd attempted to shoot a pencil up there like a dart. She hadn't had the strength to make them stick, however, as her attempts thus far were conspicuously unsuccessful. Still, there was certainly a first time for everything. With Jake's smarmy voice goading her, she snatched up a good old number two pencil and hurled it upward with all her strength. It stuck for a moment and Julie brightened. But then it dropped with a clatter on her desk, rolled to the edge and onto and across the hardwood floor where it lodged itself against the far wall.

Growling beneath her breath she punched into her voice mail, astonished to learn she had twelve calls. Listening through them, she realized Jake's comments this morning had elicited a horde of new would-be clients. The prevailing thought seemed to be that if Jake Danforth deigned to see her as a therapist, the rest of Portland might traipse in his wake. His prediction had come true: her career would improve with the added publicity of being on his morning show and becoming his therapist.

Depressing. She didn't want to owe him anything. She didn't want to like him! He'd sure as hell ticked her off on his show this morning. Now the whole world knew about her relationship with Jake. If she'd felt bare before, she felt absolutely naked now! No armor. No shield!

Grabbing another pencil, she hurled it upward like a javelin. It stuck in the ceiling with a soft *thwanggg*. She blinked. "Fabulous," she said in true satisfaction when it looked as if it were going to stay there. As she returned her phone calls and sorted through her mail, she kept one eye checking the pencil. It held.

It took her an hour and a half to get through the callbacks and organize her bills. At this rate she might actually need a receptionist/office helper.

And she had Jake Danforth to thank for everything.

She was in the process of aiming another pencil when Carolyn Mathers appeared in her doorway. "Oh, good. You're alone."

"I'm busy," Julie said.

"I can see that," Carolyn said, ignoring Julie's new hobby as she curled into one of the chairs.

Julie set the pencil carefully onto her desk. "Carolyn, we need to talk about our professional relationship. It's been veering into another category, largely owing to your efforts, and I don't feel comfortable with the way things have progressed."

"You're the talk of the town. Jake Danforth has made you a household name. You can't buy that kind of publicity."

"I feel it's at the cost of my professional reputation," Julie said evenly. "But let's get back to the matter at hand."

"This is working for you, sweetie. Professional reputation! Good grief! I've been singing your praises to anyone who'll listen, and right now, *everybody* wants to listen. It's like my marriage counselor is a celebrity. Honest to God!"

"Carolyn—" Julie began, pained.

"You know I'm right. You've been right about my relationship with Floyd all along. And I haven't given you the credit you deserve."

"How do you mean?" Julie asked, aware that she was once again being sucked into Carolyn's loopy and self-involved conversation outside of her regular appointment, but certain there was trouble in there somewhere. Might as well hear where that trouble stemmed from.

"I'm giving Floyd up. The divorce is in the works. And my divorce lawyer is enough to make me want to weep, he's so gorgeous. But back to you. Julie—"

"Divorce? Carolyn, stop!" she cut her off. "Why are you getting a divorce? You love Floyd. At least that's what you've told me ever since you started coming to see me. Every time. You've just had problems. And what about the bear rug? And something about a trip to the moon? I thought you'd reached a new—appreciation—of your husband. When did this divorce talk start?"

"Is this on my dime?" Carolyn asked. "Or, are we talking as friends?"

"Our relationship is a counselor/patient one."

"Darn." She made a face and thought for a moment. "Since this is going to cost me, I get to say what's on my mind. You just listen, okay?"

"Carolyn—"

"Would you like another cigarette? I'm dying for one myself."

"No...smoking!"

"Okay, then, shhhh...." She lifted a finger to her lips. "You're on the verge of something really huge here. Maybe you *should* consult tarot cards, or see a visionary, or something. I sense you're on a real positive upswing, and you know the man to thank for it. And how well do you know him, anyway? He made it sound like there was something secret between you. Something beyond elementary school."

Julie, who had risen to her feet during this exchange, sank back into her chair. She didn't have any clients scheduled for another hour. She had no intention of charging Carolyn Mathers for this im-

promptu session, but neither did she want to delve
into her history with Jake.

"So, when you see him tomorrow, I think I should
be here," Carolyn went on. "I could be just getting
ready to leave and—"

"No!"

"—we could be discussing him. I don't mean private kind of things, just stuff like how good-looking
he is, how his radio show is your favorite, how much
it means to you to reconnect with an old friend
who's—"

"No! No!"

"—like a touchstone for you, y'know? A soul
mate. A part of what makes you, you."

"Oh, Carolyn, if you don't shut up I am going to
scream!"

Carolyn blinked at her for a moment. Then a slow
smile crossed her lips and she dug in her purse for
her cigarettes. "Well, my, my, my. This man's really
gotten under your skin...."

"You don't know the half of it," Julie conceded
on a sigh. "But you're not going to be here tomorrow when Jake arrives and no, thank you, I don't
want a cigarette."

"Maybe you do need a therapist," Carolyn suggested.

Julie regarded her silently. It was scary to think
that Carolyn Mathers might be starting to make
sense.

"C'MON MAN," Zipper whined, his teeth drawn back
in a perpetual skeleton smile, a smile that was his
trademark. He was just a few degrees above sleazy,
but his voice and "been there, done that, and who

cares'' attitude brought in the post-morning show listeners in droves. ''Tell me about the chick.''

''The 'chick' wouldn't appreciate me saying anything about her,'' Jake pointed out as he tried to leave the room, making way for Zipper. If he had another name, Jake didn't know what it was. Zipper was Zipper, for better or worse. Mostly for worse, and though he had a face made for radio, the women flocked to him. Zipper was way cool. Way, way cool.

''Y'knew her when, and now she's back. What's the old lady think about that?''

''You mean, Teri? My ex?''

''Ain't that far ex, my man. I know that look she gives you. It's a woman playin' games with what's hers, or at least what she thinks is hers.''

''Teri and I have been over for years. We've just finished the final act.''

''Uh-uh.'' Zipper wagged his long finger in front of Jake's nose. ''Mighta been that way if you'd let it alone, but now you brought this new chick in. And she's been listenin' to your ex givin' her an earful about you. Then you jump in and pretend to tell everybody how incompetent she is, and she's on the show and you're all twitchin' and jivin' and the next y'know, she's the mystery woman from your past. Mmm-mmm, it's delicious. And your ex is not gonna go for this. Women don't let other women win.''

Jake gazed at the man with the long braid and couldn't think of anything to say.

''You talked to her lately? Your ex?''

''Some.''

Zipper nodded. ''She'll come a-runnin'. You wait.''

That's all he needed, for Teri to ''come a-running.'' Jake was almost through the exterior doors when he ran into Colin, one of the producers of his show. Jake inwardly groaned. Zipper was bad enough, but at least he was into his own Zen thing. Colin was a workout from start to finish.

"Jake!" he bellowed. "How's it going with the therapist? Got her in bed yet?"

His voice echoed through the two-story lobby. Heads turned. Jake, having learned long ago not to engage in Colin's game, simply smiled and said, "Not trying."

"Oh, come on. With those legs? Bet she could wrap them around a man and make him weep!"

It was all Jake could do to keep himself from strangling the man. "How did you see her legs?"

"Just a guess, my man. And she's got Pammy all in a snit over you. And she's got Beryl upset, too. All your women are threatened. Ain't it great?"

Jake fought back a tide of fury. Instead, dragging out acting skills he hadn't known he possessed, he said, sotto voce, "I have a question for you, Colin."

Colin responded to Jake's lowered voice by moving in closer. "Shoot."

"This is just between you and me, you understand."

"The boy's club." He winked and clucked his tongue.

"How did you get the job of producer when you're a complete jackass who treats women as sex objects?"

Colin frowned, thought it over a moment, and said, "Talent. Now, let me give you a little advice in return. Stop pussyfootin' around and make a move. I usually resort to alcohol and lots of greenbacks if she keeps saying no. I've found the combination of the two is lethal to women. Trust me. She'll change her answer pretty quick."

"I'm meeting with her tomorrow afternoon. Mind if I tell her your theory? Think that'll work?"

Colin patted him on the back as he turned away. "You're such a putz, Jake."

"Yeah...."

At his house, Jake shrugged off his annoyance and called to Seltzer. The old dog hobbled up to him, nosed his hand and wagged his tail. Jake scratched his ears and Seltzer exhaled a contented doggy sigh. After a few moments Jake checked to see that his food and water dishes were full, then headed for the kitchen.

He leaned on the refrigerator door, then asked himself what he was doing. There was no food of any kind around; he had never grasped the finer points of cooking.

Actually, he'd hoped for a beer, but there was none. And the bottle of wine with its half inch of unconsumed liquid had been sitting in his refrigerator, forgotten, for too many days to recall. Damn. He shut the door and gazed at his cabinets, knowing that to open one was a waste of energy. Nothing.

What he could really use was straight gin. He could see himself pouring undiluted liquor down his throat. He felt the need to burn himself from the inside out.

Juliet....

He groaned. This wasn't good. His thoughts circled around and around, a whirlpool of desire. He wanted her like he hadn't wanted anyone, or anything, in a long time, and the worst of it was it ran deeper than a night of alcohol and greenbacks.

And she did have nice legs.

The phone rang. He picked up the receiver absently. "Hello."

"Jake?"

It was Teri. His ex. A *Twilight Zone* feeling swept through him, sending the hairs on his arms standing at attention. Damn that Zipper! "Oh, hi, Teri."

"I heard your show this morning."

"Oh, yeah?" Cradling the receiver, he did a quick search of the cabinets. Gin. Where was the gin?

"Julie Sommerfield is a friend of yours?" Teri asked in an aggrieved tone. "She never told me that!"

"She's an acquaintance. If you'd told her who you were right off the bat, she probably would have suggested someone else as your therapist."

"You knew her in *elementary* school? You've known her *that* long?"

"It's a coincidence."

"But now you're going to see her?"

"Well, you're the one who first suggested it," Jake reminded her, losing patience. "And you're the one who brought out the tarot cards, aren't you? She doesn't know the first thing about 'em. I should report you for practicing sorcery without a license."

"I really hate you," she said, sounding teary.

Zipper's warning ran through his head. Maybe Teri wasn't as over him as he'd thought. The knowledge filled him with anxiety. He didn't want her anywhere near him. And he realized with a start that it was mainly because of Juliet. Not that he'd ever wanted Teri back, but he hadn't felt this need to separate himself so completely before—like he wanted to push her into another county!

"What are you doing?" she demanded, hearing him opening and slamming cupboards.

"Looking for alcohol. I gotta go."

"Jake, I haven't told you why I called yet!"

"I thought it was to denigrate Juliet Sommerfield."

"Juliet?" she repeated.

"Julie," he corrected himself. "It used to be Juliet."

"Well, isn't that just too cute. Jake, I'm not going to appreciate it if you take up with my therapist. That can't happen."

"Goodbye, Teri."

She made a choking sound. "I was going to ask why we got a divorce. I couldn't remember this morning when I woke up. Now, I remember it's because you're such an incredible bastard!"

I wonder if that's better than being a plain bastard, Jake thought as he finally found the bottle of gin. Empty!

"Well?" Teri demanded.

Jake tried to remember what the point of their conversation was. He was inured to Teri and her games. He could have told her he'd grown tired of her consulting her astrological chart and reading tea leaves and meeting with an array of psychics. Once upon a time he'd believed he loved her, but it wasn't long after the wedding that he'd realized what she was all about. Then he'd limped through the five years of marriage, staying more out of guilt than any real feeling. The Tae Bo instructor incident had helped galvanize him into divorce proceedings, but Teri had blocked him at every opportunity. Just when he'd thought things were going to get really ugly the stars told her that her marriage was poisonous to her. When she hit him with divorce papers he practically shouted with joy. Hashing and rehashing the whole proceeding on the air hadn't been fun, but he'd managed to weather the storm and now he realized how truly glad he was now that it was all behind him. Especially with Juliet in his future.

"Well?" he repeated cautiously.

"Haven't you heard a word I've said?"

"I heard you say I was an incredible bastard."

She made some spitting sounds, very reminiscent of an infuriated cat, then slammed down the phone. Jake replaced his own receiver more quietly. A moment later he realized he no longer had the slightest interest in a drink. Talking to his ex had been like taking the cure—and of her, he was entirely cured.

Seltzer hobbled into the room and sank down with a sigh at Jake's feet. "That phase of life is over and done with," Jake said to him, rubbing his ears. "Got any advice on how to proceed with Juliet Adams Sommerfield?"

Laying his chin on Jake's lap, Seltzer moved his eyebrows up and down. He looked as if he were terribly worried.

"You're not exactly inspiring me with confidence," Jake said, to which Seltzer closed his eyes and stuck out his tongue in a huge, doggy yawn.

7

JULIE SAT IN HER OFFICE CHAIR, arms outstretched, palms flat on the desk. She'd tried sitting and appearing relaxed, but that hadn't worked. A strange little jumpiness had invaded her right below the skin, quivering, stealing her poise and hard-won confidence. It was Tuesday afternoon. Time for Jake Danforth to appear.

"Some therapist," she muttered aloud. She would maintain this position until she heard Jake come through the outer door. Isometric exercise. A way to tone and release tension.

At least that was the theory.

Her inner door was open, so her ears were attuned to the slightest nuance outside her office. The furnace kicked on and blew some air, then kicked off. It was that kind of day: warm when the sun broke through the clouds; frigid when it hid behind a thick gray cover.

Her arms were actually starting to ache when she heard the door open. Immediately she snatched them back and folded her hands in her lap. No good. She needed to look busy. Quickly, she grabbed a pen and pad, staring down at the white square of paper for inspiration.

The phone rang and she leapt from her chair as if shot. Jake strolled into the room at that precise moment that Julie scrambled for the receiver. He stopped short and she motioned for him to take the chair snuggled up to the opposite side of her desk.

"Hello?"

"Juliet? It's Mom. How are you doing?"

"Fine, Mom.... I'm, uh, with a client."

"I'm sorry. I thought you always turned your voice mail on when you were busy."

"I do. I will. I just forgot."

"I heard that nice Jake Danforth on the air yesterday morning. He said you might be on his program again."

She wondered if Jake could hear every word. It felt as if her mother's voice was echoing loudly. "I don't know about that."

"You'll let me know, won't you? I want to tell Aunty Doris and your cousins in Silverton."

"I'll call you later."

"Tell him how much I like his program. It really perks up my morning."

"I'll remember. Bye."

She practically slammed the receiver down, then switched off her phone so that future calls would go directly to her voice mail.

"I'm glad your Mom likes my program," Jake said, answering the question about whether he could hear her or not.

"Yeah, well, she likes reality TV and trash television, too."

He grinned. "You just can't stand letting a chance go by to twist the knife, can you?"

Julie made a face directed more at herself than him. "Sorry," she mumbled, glancing away from him. He looked good enough to taste. Casual jeans, a khaki shirt, his ubiquitous black leather jacket. His hair waved just so, and his smile threw out enough wattage to light three square blocks. Add those blue eyes and a hard-looking physique, well, it was just flat-out unfair. Lady-killer came to mind. He'd graduated from a mere Romeo...

"So, what do you do here?" he asked, looking around.

"Counsel people," Julie said deliberately.

"I mean, what's your routine? Give me an opening question. I'm here and I'm ready to go." He lifted his palms and smiled at her, a willing guinea pig.

Julie cleared her throat and forced herself to forget who was sitting in the chair. Drawing a breath, she said, "I generally like to explore backgrounds first, then let the person feel their way through their own history, so to speak."

"Okay," he agreed willingly. "Explore away."

"If you were asked who you are most like in your family as a personality, whom would you say?"

He considered for a moment and even that was attractive. How could someone improve so much with age? Julie was afraid, looks-wise, that she'd peaked just out of high school. Not true of Jake Danforth, however.

"People say I look like my mother, but I act like my grandfather," he finally supplied.

"How's that?"

"Determined. Maybe stubborn. Single-minded."

"Hmmm...."

"Are you going to make notes about me on that blank pad of paper?" he asked.

"These traits you just mentioned, they can be positive or negative, depending on how you implement them.''

"In my marriage, they were pretty negative. Teri told me I was a true Taurus. All that horoscope stuff always ticked me off, but now I'm changing my mind. I checked in today's *Oregonian,* as a matter of fact, and I was warned to beware of a treacherous old acquaintance.''

"Untrue. Your horoscope said to 'expect the un-expected in romance.'''

"Did it?'' His brows lifted.

Trapped! Damn the man. She should know better. "I'm a Taurus,'' she explained. "And yes, once in a while I check my horoscope.''

"Romance…'' he repeated, drawing the word out thoughtfully. "I like that.''

Julie felt her heart thump hard. She rearranged the papers on her desk. "I assume you're still interested in dating again. Any thoughts on that?''

"You mean since you turned me down?'' He lifted a challenging brow.

She'd known they were going to be discussing this issue, so why was she feeling so breathless? She didn't want to like him. She really didn't. She wished to high heaven she could get her feelings under con-trol. "I didn't turn you down. I—I knew you were kidding about that.''

"Was I?''

"Yes.'' She was firm. "You were. So, let's move on,'' she added quickly, when he looked as if he were about to argue. "What kind of woman are you looking for?''

Jake let the moment pass. "Someone intelligent. Attractive. Gotta have a good sense of humor. I've done some of the bar scene with co-workers and I don't think that's going to work for me.''

"How about a health club?"

Jake looked interested. "I belong to the one on Nineteenth Street. Around the corner. Actually…"

"Yes?" she asked politely, not liking the idea at all that he might actually take her advice and find some female hard-body at his health club!

"You know there's this one woman," he said slowly, as if turning the idea over in his mind for the first time. "She's blond and really into working out. I've seen her at the club a lot, but I've never said anything to her." He gazed at Julie with those blue, blue eyes and asked innocently, "Do you think I should say something to her?"

"That's entirely up to you." Green poison flooded through Julie's veins. Jealousy. She recognized it for what it was and was appalled at herself. The only thing positive about his words meant that whoever had been waiting for him at home Halloween night didn't seem to hold his heart. "Do you want to?"

"Every guy in the place has hit on her. If she turned me down, it could seriously wound my ego." The corner of his mouth twitched.

Like, oh, sure. "Maybe you should start up a conversation and just see," Julie told him stiffly.

"All right." He was more than congenial. "I'll go over there tonight. Why don't you come with me?"

"Me? Why?"

"As my guest…and therapist. If I fall flat on my face, I'll have you there to help pick up the pieces," he said lightly.

"Sorry. I'm busy tonight."

"Uh-huh." He placed his hands on the desk and

leaned toward her. Julie felt the change in air pressure as if she were on a plane that had just gone into a nosedive. "I think you're lying."

"Oh, really!" She leaned back, away from him, as much as she dared without completely scooting her chair out of range.

"I think you're afraid to spend any time with me. I think I scare you."

"Oh…for Pete's sake!… No one scares me! I'm just—not free tonight."

"Why not?"

"That's my business."

"Convince me you're not just giving me a story."

"I'm not! I'm—meeting—someone else."

"Bring them along."

"I can't."

"You—are—a—liar." He grinned like a satyr, enjoying the moment way, way too much.

Romeo. She wanted to scream. Shakespeare had it right. "…my only love sprung from my only hate…" Or something like that. Why did it have to be Jake Danforth that caused her heart to jump into triple-time? Why couldn't she find a good solid man like…like Miles Charleston. Okay, no. Bad example. Miles was a doormat under Candy's feet.

But couldn't it be someone else beside Jake? she asked her overheated senses. *Couldn't it?*

He was staring at her in that way of all conquering males. He had her on the ropes and he knew it. Time to go on the offense. With that in mind, Julie leaned forward as well, until her forehead was nearly touching his, her own palms flat on the desk. "I don't lie. Lying is bad." She inhaled a deep breath and added tautly, "If I'm lying, let the earth open up and swallow me down."

They stared at each other hard for a total of three seconds. The earth didn't open up. But the pencil fell from the ceiling and bounced onto Julie's head.

"See you at the club," he said. "Six o'clock."

And then he sauntered out of her office in a thoroughly irritating way. Pencil in hand, Julie had to restrain herself from hurling it after him.

"THE CHANGING ROOMS are right down the hall!" the toothy receptionist told Julie brightly, then practically jumped across the desk in her delight upon seeing Jake. "Hi, there, Mr. Danforth! How are you this evening?"

"Fine, Carrie. And yourself."

"Hunky-dory!" She giggled and jiggled. Julie did an inner mantra and pretended she was on another planet as Jake signed her in as a guest. Twisting on her heel, Julie headed down to the women's locker room, feeling as if she were about to face a firing squad.

In a corner area, divided by a set of lockers from the main room, Julie stripped off her sweats and stared at herself in the full-length mirror tacked on the opposite wall. She wore running shorts, a jog bra with a loose tank overtop and a pair of white socks and running shoes. Sucking in her stomach, she tried to imagine herself working out on the equipment next to Jake. She groaned aloud, slouched her shoulders and pooched out her stomach.

"What am I doing here?" she murmured.

"This your first time?"

Julie glanced around reluctantly. A short woman

in nauseatingly good shape smiled at her. "Well...
yes."

"Just stand up and pull your shoulders back." She
did as she suggested to Julie, thrusting out her breasts
and inhaling a deep breath. Lifting her arms over her
head she did a couple of deep knee bends. In a light
purple leotard, which displayed every defined muscle, she looked like a cover model for *Self* magazine.

Taking another look at herself in the mirror, Julie
inhaled a deep breath, but inside her brain reminded
her that it was useless effort because she could make
two of the pint-sized workout enthusiast just by vir-
tue of height alone. She exhaled in defeat. So, this
was hell. She'd wondered what it looked like.

Throwing her sweats in a locker, she clipped on a
combination lock, tossed a towel over her shoulder
and headed to the body beautiful arena. Why had she
accepted Jake's invitation? Why hadn't she been able
to back down from the challenge?

Because you're a Taurus...a stubborn bull.

Inside the weight room people were lifting and
grunting and sweating and straining. Jake Danforth
lay on a bench, pushing a bar over his head and
bringing it down again. She watched for several moments, noticing the sinewy muscles of his upper
arms. They moved beneath his skin in a sensuous
way that sent mysterious messages to her insides,
turning them to jelly.

Jake dropped the bar into its slot and sat up, spying
her before she could flee, which was what she really
wanted to do. "Hey," he said, motioning her over.
On leaden feet she approached his station.

"That's her," he said, inclining his head toward
another body beautiful: blond, tanned, seriously in

shape with a narrow waist, trim, muscular thighs and an unfair amount of cleavage. Pretty much what Julie had anticipated.

"I see," Julie said. She swallowed hard. Jake was watching her closely. For a moment it seemed as if he were going to reach out and touch her and Julie shrank back instinctively. But then she realized it was her overactive imagination when he simply shifted his weight and asked, "How do you think I should approach her?"

"I don't know."

"Well, how about a suggestion?"

"I'm a marriage counselor, not a lonely hearts club member. Figure it out for yourself."

He laughed, which really ticked her off. "Okay, I'll just go over and talk to her, but first, I want to see you working with weights."

"Did hell freeze over when I wasn't looking? I'm not a weight lifter."

"Come here..."

"No, Jake. You can be a health wacko if you want. I'm just here because you bullied me into it. I don't even know why you want me here."

"You don't?"

He slid her a look and the silky tone of his voice sent a thrill down her nerves. Was he *flirting* with her? No! She was, as ever, making too much of the whole thing. "No, I don't," she said through her teeth. "Go on over there and ask her out and get it over with. I do have a date still pending."

Jake ignored that. They'd established that she'd been lying, but she kept hoping he would believe her anyway. "Here. Sit down." He pointed to some contraption with bars and black vinyl cushions and various other pieces of machinery that looked as if they were meant for torture. Julie thought about protesting, but her truculence was wearing thin—even for herself. She never should have come. Never. She'd just let him coerce her because she'd wanted to be coerced and her whole attitude just really ticked her off all the more.

She sat down. Jake took her right hand and slid it through a handle. She ignored the tingle of sensation as she let him slip her left hand through the opposite handle.

"Now pull those paddles toward your chest."

"Paddles?"

"That's what they are. They work your triceps and forearms."

She pulled the paddles several times and quit. Jake gave her a look, so with a sigh she got into a rhythmic movement, feeling the strain. Maybe if she kept this up she could eventually look like the other women in the room. Well, sort of. Maybe…

Maybe you're just looking for a way to spend time with Jake….

"Well, hello, there," a male voice said with a drawl.

The paddles snapped back and Julie gazed into a stranger's face. He wasn't half-bad, if you liked men who oozed fake charm with every breath. "Hi," she said cautiously.

"So, you came with my buddy, Jake, eh? What do you think of him?"

Julie glanced at Jake, who was talking to one of the club trainers. "Jake Danforth's your friend?"

"We work together."

"Really."

"How do you know him?" he asked curiously, then snapped his fingers in sudden discovery. "You're the one with the witch's outfit. The marriage counselor his ex went to."

"Well…yes…." Julie admitted reluctantly.

"I knew you had great legs!" he crowed. Julie frowned down at her legs, wondering where that non sequitur came from as he rambled on, "Oh, yes. Our boy Jake loves a conquest and you were pretty good. Held out for quite a while, didn't you?"

"I was a guest on his show," she reminded him coolly. "Not a girlfriend."

"But you're here now, aren't you? Pretty damning!" He laughed loudly, as if he'd just told a real knee-slapper. "Hey, no offense, I'm just warning you. He knocks the women cold, y'know what I mean? Even when he was married they just threw themselves at him at every opportunity. Drove his ex crazy."

"I wouldn't know," Julie murmured, unwilling to hear another word, unable to keep herself from hanging on every word. Jake Danforth, the womanizer? She felt slightly ill.

The man laughed again and held out his hand. "Colin McNary. And you would be…? Besides the best-looking woman in this place?"

"Julie Sommerfield." She shook his hand and asked dryly, "Flattery, huh? Does it generally work for you?"

"Pretty much."

"I'll bet." She smiled in spite of herself.

He added in a whisper, cupping his hand to her ear, "And if you want to make Jake jealous, I'm your man."

ACROSS THE ROOM Jake got an unpleasant jolt. Colin! Talking to Juliet! He cut short his conversation with the trainer, who really wanted Jake to plug the health club on the air, something Jake couldn't and wouldn't do, and hurried back to Juliet. Colin looked like he was laying it on pretty thick. Jake's only consolation was that Juliet would see right through him.

Except that Juliet seemed to have brightened under the sleazy producer's attention. Why did women find the man irresistible, when he was such a slime? "Could I talk to you a moment?" Jake asked Colin, not waiting for a reply as he practically dragged him out of earshot. "What are you doing?"

"Hitting on your date," he said, unrepentant. "Watch and learn, my man. Watch and learn…."

When he would have turned back to Juliet, Jake grabbed his arm. "With alcohol and greenbacks?"

"That's the plan. Now unhand me so I can get back to the pleasant task of asking her out for drinks and…whatever…."

Powerless to stop Colin except by physical force, which wouldn't go over too well with dozens of people around, Jake followed him back to where Juliet had moved to another machine.

"Ah, leg lifts," Colin said. "Love a woman who does leg lifts. And with those legs…."

To Jake's consternation Juliet shook her head, smiled, and said, "Oh, you silver-tongued devil," to which Colin crowed in appreciation. Jake stood by in impotent annoyance and felt like a fool. What *did* women see in McNary?

The more they chattered and flirted, the quieter Jake became. Hiding his feelings was getting to be

an effort. His head actually hurt. When Colin helped
tip Juliet onto her back onto another piece of the
weight room apparatus, Jake reached the last point
of tolerance. He turned and stumbled toward the
blond woman whom he'd described to Juliet earlier.
She was working her thighs and mentally counting
how many times she'd pushed her knees together
against the resistance. He could see how much effort
it cost for her to keep up the count. Her lips moved
and she nodded slightly.

Not the sharpest tool in the shed, but she certainly
had a face and body.

"Hi," he greeted her, then cleared his throat, realizing he sounded dour and grumpy. "I'm Jake."

The knee paddles slapped back and her eyes widened. "I know!"

"We've seen each other here and I've meant to
say hello, but—"

"Oh, I know! I know! I'm so glad you came
over!"

"Yes…well…" He glanced over at Juliet. Colin
actually had his hand under her knee, showing her
some move that he didn't even want to think about!
"Care to go for a drink after your workout?" Jake
blurted out.

"Oh, my God! Yes! Oh, my God!" Her hand flew
to her lips. Probably screwed up the counting once
and for all. "I've just been hoping you would ask
me out. I mean, you're Jake Danforth, from the radio,
right?"

"Right," he said reluctantly.

"Oh, I'd love to! Oh, my God! I can't believe this.
I'll just be a minute."

"Neither can I," he said a trifle lamely.

JULIE PRETENDED not to notice Jake's interaction with the blonde. She kept her gaze on Colin and her smile fixed on her face. *Why did I come here with him again?* she asked herself. *Why?*

"So, why don't I take you out for a drink and help you replenish some of the fluids you've been sweating out?" Colin suggested.

"No, thanks," Julie said firmly. Now that Jake was out of earshot she had no reason to flatter Colin's ego. The guy thought he was God's gift to women but in truth he was a real loser.

Jake appeared a moment later, the blonde trotting eagerly at his heels. She was all hair and teeth and bouncy energy. As soon as Julie climbed off the inner thigh machine, she jumped on, squeezing her legs together and out again. The rhythmic movement was almost sexual—at least to Julie's way of thinking—and she turned abruptly away and headed for the showers.

"Juliet…" Jake tried to catch her attention as she brushed by him.

"It's Julie," she snapped back in a harsh whisper. "Do you think you could get that right, just once?"

He gazed at her, his face very close to hers. Julie could see the darker striations in the blue of his irises. She wondered if her own skin was as shiny with sweat as she expected it to be. She'd worked those machines like it was a job—like she was working every inch of muscle just so Jake Danforth would notice her.

Well, that was what she'd been doing, wasn't it? Struggling every way she knew how to prove she was the woman he should desire? Believing she was doing it just so she could discard him later, after he was well and truly smitten with her? What a crock! Nora had been right all along. She was fighting so hard and acting so stupidly because she *wanted* him.

"I like Juliet better than Julie," he told her softly.

She gazed at his lips, woefully certain that she was doomed to more unrequited yearning over him. "Right now, I don't like either one of them," she said, then slipped past him to the showers and her gym bag of clothes.

She reappeared twenty minutes later, wet tendrils of hair that she'd been unable to keep from the shower spray flattened against her temples, clad in a pair of black jeans, black turtleneck sweater and black leather jacket.

"You look hot," Colin said admiringly. "Kinda like a biker babe."

Blondie hadn't returned as yet, but Jake was there, also looking a tad moist around the temples.

"I've gotta go. Big day tomorrow," Julie murmured. "Lots to do."

"Oh, come on, baby," Colin coaxed, pulling a face. "One drink."

She leveled him with a cold look. "Anyone who calls me 'baby' isn't someone I would share a drink with."

"She's kind of testy about her name," Jake supplied helpfully.

"Sorry. We're heading to the Blue Moon. I'd like to buy you a beer."

"We?"

"Babbs and I are going, too," Jake said.

"Babbs?" Julie repeated. "That's her name? Babbs?"

"Jakey scores again!" Colin laughed, trying to

high-five Jake, whose hands were thrust deep within his pockets and whose face reflected his deep irritation with his so-called friend.

The Blue Moon was a local pub with several local microbrews. It was a popular spot in Northwest Portland. Julie hesitated. "I've heard more about moons the past few weeks than I have in a lifetime," she said.

"One drink?" Colin wheedled.

Julie looked at Jake, whose gaze reached around her to find Babbs. It was the long-suffering look on his face that caused her to relent and say, "Sure, why not? What can one drink hurt?"

THREE DRINKS LATER Julie still sat squeezed into the booth at the Blue Moon beside Colin, her escape blocked by his solid form. Once he'd got her there, he was reluctant to let her go. Jake sat directly across from her, and Babbs was on the outside edge of their seat. Though Julie had started on plain soda water with a slice of lime after her one and only beer, she was concerned about the amount of time that was passing.

And she didn't like being trapped so close to Jake Danforth.

Jake, too, was basically being a teetotaler. "I've got a 6:00 a.m. call," he explained. It warmed Julie a bit to think he was as dedicated to his job as she was. Colin sure as heck didn't seem to have any qualms about drinking and partying on a Tuesday night. Babbs wasn't exactly minding her p's and q's, either. The way she kept bumping up against Jake and giggling, apologizing for the fact that vodka went straight to her head—duh!—made Julie suspect she was angling for a ride home. Jake, however, didn't look all that excited about the prospect; Julie suspected he wanted to leave as much as she did.

In its curious way, the evening was turning out to be a success. Jake wasn't having fun with Babbs, and Julie was certainly not interested in Colin. Still, what that meant was rather frightening in itself. No good could come of a "crush" on Jake Danforth.

Jake caught her glancing at her watch. "I really have to go," she insisted.

"Not exactly the evening I'd hoped for," he murmured as Babbs and Colin consulted the cocktail waitress about another drink.

"What had you hoped for?" Julie asked quietly.

For an answer, the tip of his shoe touched the tip of hers. It was like an electric shock, its meaning sizzling into her brain. She had to look away from his stare.

Good God, was that a blush? *She was blushing.* Just when she thought things couldn't get worse— *bam!*—catastrophe!

His deep chuckle said he knew it, too, the scoundrel. Oh, she hated being so transparent!

"That's it," she muttered, practically toppling Colin out of the booth as she shoved her way to freedom.

"Hey!" he protested.

"Gotta go. It's been great, guys. And Babbs…" She shook the blonde's limp hand. "A real pleasure. I'll try to catch your show tomorrow, Jake. No, don't get up," she insisted as he tried to struggle past his loose-limbed "date." "I'm outta here."

She was gone before he could catch her. Jake half lifted Babbs from the booth but instead of making his escape, Babbs wrapped herself around him like an octopus, cooing in his ear, "Wanna dance—and make romance—"

He tried to peel her off. "Some other time."

"Just one dance?" She gazed at him appealingly, batting her lashes, the effect spoiled by the fact that when she turned toward the dance floor she stumbled out of one of her platform heels and tumbled into Colin.

"I'll dance," Colin murmured suggestively, and Jake was gone before either of them could say another word.

8

JULIE WRAPPED HERSELF in her quilt and willed sleep to come to her. She'd wanted to talk to Nora but her friend had been immersed in a rented video and Julie really hadn't known what to say anyway. Julie had perched on the couch and watched the rest of the film with Nora in silence and now could not remember one single frame, one word of dialogue.

Her mind kept drifting back to the events of the evening. Seeing Jake with Babbs. Feeling his toe pressed against her own. Recognizing that he was more interested in her than his blond date. It reminded her of their prom night, so long ago, yet so sharp in her memory. How many times had she recalled the way Jake looked that night, the things he said? Especially now, since he'd reentered her life? It was unfair how certain memories were so powerful, they were etched on one's brain, while millions of others—possibly more important memories!—were lost forever. It was *even more* unfair that she could recall every whisper, every nuance of making love to Jake Danforth that night, whereas whole months of her married life seemed to meld together into a bland sameness.

And now, once again, those memories ran around inside her head. Nothing she'd done to date, and apparently nothing she could do in the future, had the power to eradicate them. With a sigh, she closed her eyes and let them have full play.

She'd been standing outside the dance, which had been held in a building off Fourteenth Street in Northwest Portland. Her date—a goofy-acting guy named Tom, who was more friend than romantic interest—had hired a limo with so many other students, there had hardly been a place for Julie to sit. She hadn't liked her dress, she'd only accepted Tom's invitation because he'd been so eager for her to say yes and she'd suspected she might regret her decision because she was pretty certain proms in general were overrated and underwhelming. She'd been proved right on all counts, so as the evening wound down she found herself standing outside on the sidewalk, her white beaded shawl wrapped around her shoulders, wondering how she was going to get home as she had no intention of waiting around for Tom, who was three sheets to the wind and just getting started.

She'd passed the time by concentrating on where she would go to college. Somewhere exotic, perhaps. Why not the University of Hawaii? She could eat coconut and pineapple all the time and slather herself in banana-scented tanning oil and lie in the sun and bodysurf and maybe get a few classes in there somewhere. Sure, her family didn't have the money to send her and she certainly couldn't afford it herself, but it was a nice dream and it kept a smile on her face as she breathed in the soft night air.

She'd sensed someone come up beside her, but she hadn't immediately turned to see who it was. She didn't care. High school already felt distant. She wanted to dream about college and sun and sand and forget this period of adolescence completely.

"Are you cold?"

His voice brought her up short. She glanced over, certain she was wrong about who had spoken those words. But no, it was Jake Danforth. The most sought-after male in the senior class. Mr. Romeo himself.

"It's too warm tonight to be cold."

"It's just that your shawl is full of holes," he observed with one of his patented Jake Danforth smiles. To illustrate, he poked his finger through one of the crocheted loops and touched her bare shoulder.

She gave him a long look. "My date's drunk and I'm trying to figure out if I want to get in the limo with him, his drunken friends and their drunken girlfriends."

"My date's crying in the bathroom."

She hadn't expected him to respond in kind and it disarmed her. "What did you do to her?" she asked, mock serious.

He smiled crookedly. "Well, I didn't throw anything at her, like cherries or apples or anything, if that's what you mean."

She'd been surprised he remembered. "Did you twist her arm behind her back and make her cry uncle?"

"No." He frowned. "At least I don't think so."

"So, you've given up that particular form of torture?"

"Did I do that to you? Really?"

He sounded so worried that she had to fight back laughter. "Oh, yes. I've got the stretched tendons to prove it." He gazed at her, guilt-stricken, and her laughter bubbled over. "Just kidding. You were more the kind to launch an attack from afar. I think there was a fir cone or two thrown at me as well, and you were pretty good about hitting the target!"

Relieved, he returned the compliment. "You weren't a bad aim, yourself."

"So, what happened to make your date cry?" Julie asked curiously.

Jake grimaced. "I told her I was thinking about going to college on the east coast and that I couldn't wait for high school to end so I could get on with the rest of my life."

"Brutal words. Reality. People hate that."

"No kidding." He studied her, as if seeing her for the first time. "So, now she's a crying mess and I just want to go home. Maybe I should," he said a moment later. "She told me to leave. Said she would get a ride from someone else. And I've got my car...."

"What? No limo?"

"Trying to save up a few bucks," he admitted, surprising Julie with his candor. "I think that's why she's crying, too."

"I don't suppose you'd give me a lift?"

He gazed at her. In the semi-darkness, his eyes were hooded. "I'd love to."

She'd located Tom, who was hanging all over some other girl, told him she was leaving and he'd waved his fingers at her in goodbye. Jake was waiting for her outside when she appeared again and they walked to his car, which was parked in a nearby lot. They drove in relative silence to his house above the city. She didn't protest when he didn't take her directly home. It was as if by mutual, unspoken consent they stood on the balcony and looked out over the city lights. The softest of breezes lifted her hair and teased the skirt of her white dress. Jake ripped off his bow tie, jacket and cummerbund and opened the top button of his shirt. He rolled up the sleeves and leaned his arms on the railing next to where Julie's bare arms already lay.

They still didn't talk. Years later, looking back on it, Julie always wondered why she hadn't said anything. It was as if she'd been swept into some romantic fantasy from which she could not escape. Or, more accurately, didn't want to escape from. So, she simply stood beside him looking over the city and when he finally turned and cupped her chin and kissed her she melted like wax.

Boy, oh, boy. Julie shuddered. That memory still had the power to attack her physically. Burrowing deeper into the quilt, she let herself open the locked door inside her mind a little further. It was a delicious torture, one she rarely allowed herself because it was just so damn, plain counterproductive. How could she still feel this way? It defied all logic and it made her want to scream and thrash around and pull out her hair.

He'd taken her hand and they'd walked down the stone steps that led off the balcony and to the guest house. He opened the door and she stepped into the dimly lit one-room building. The place smelled dusty and dry, but the scent of cherry blossoms wafted in through the open window and moonlight streaked across the bed. Jake pulled off the dusty sheets and stretched across the bed, not in any predatory manner, more in the way one does when the bed is the only available seat, which it was.

She could see the shadows of his dark slacks and white shirt. She could make out his face and hair but not his expression. She perched on the edge of the bed in a rustle of white satin.

"So, where have you decided to go for college?" she asked him.

"I don't know. Maybe nowhere." The low timbre of his voice sent a shiver down her spine. "I just want to do something else.

"Anything but what I'm doing now. Well, not *right* now...." he admitted slowly.

The heady scent of the blossoms, the shadows, Jake's lean form stretched out on the bed...all of it went straight to Julie's head. She felt intoxicated. She, who prided herself on her levelheadedness, wanted to rip off her gown and stretch out beside him, stripping off his own clothes and pressing her body against his, flesh to flesh.

The image shocked her. She swallowed and looked away. "Sometimes I feel like I'm just treading water," she said, inwardly groaning at the sound of her squeaky voice. Did her body always have to give her away?

"Exactly." He sighed and she heard him adjust position. Daring a glance backward she saw that he'd flipped onto his back, staring at the ceiling. "I feel like I'm always asking myself, 'What the hell are you doing?' And I don't have an answer." He shot her a curious look. "Do you ask yourself that question?"

"I'm asking it now," she admitted, the words passing her lips before she really thought them through.

He held her gaze. "You mean, being here with me?"

"I should really go home."

She couldn't take her eyes off him. Her words were at war with her feelings and her feelings showed on her face. "You probably should," he agreed, his voice lowering even further until she felt that thrum inside her, her body's early warning system warning: *Danger, Will Robinson. Danger.*

But when he reached a hand out to hers she didn't pull away. Moreover she squeezed her fingers around his and when he drew her toward him she simply went. One moment they were talking, the next they were kissing, the next they were stripping off each other's clothes with eager fingers, the next she was lying beneath him and they were breathing hard and fast, and the next...well...

Julie jumped from the bed, throwing off the quilt that suddenly felt way, way too hot. She walked to the open bedroom window and turned her overheated face to the crisp November air. Her mind was evil. It wouldn't let go. She remembered the feel of Jake's mouth on her flesh, the sight of his body moving rhythmically above hers, the heat of him inside her.

"That does it!" she declared, her voice so loud in the quiet evening that she jumped at the sound of it.

A moment later, she heard footsteps in the hall and Nora knocked lightly before sticking her head inside Julie's room. "What?" she demanded, yawning, half-annoyed, her hair sticking out in strange ways.

"I'm through fantasizing about Jake Danforth," she stated defiantly. "It's over."

"Uh-huh." Nora turned back toward the hall.

"I mean it. I've been letting him get to me for too long, but I'm over it now."

"Then you won't tune into his program tomorrow, right?"

"Absolutely not!"

Nora's chuckle made Julie gnash her teeth in impotent fury. "I won't!" she called after her. "I won't! Nothing can make me turn the dial to his morning program. I swear it!"

JULIE DEFTLY WOVE through the early morning traffic, one hand on the radio dial. Okay. She'd lied. She'd lasted about a minute and a half listening to some other morning channel, one that blared music that was just too damn cheery for this hour. Unfortunately, she'd erased Jake's station from her preset buttons again, so now she was frantically dialing in search of his familiar voice.

Damn, but she hated being so predictable!

Suddenly, there was his voice, sounding lazy and full of himself. Ten seconds of listening to him banter with DeeAnn and Julie felt the sting of tears. Shocked, she touched a hand to the corner of her eye.

What the hell is wrong with me?

Staring at the congested traffic battling it out on the road in front of her, she moaned in defeat, "Oh, God. I think I need therapy."

"IT SOUNDS LIKE your evening was pretty nice," DeeAnn observed into her microphone, smiling widely. "A date, huh? Who's the lucky girl?"

"Who said I was on a date? Zipper? You can't trust anything he says."

"Colin, actually."

"For those of you who don't know, Colin's one of our show's producers," Jake said conversationally, making an ugly face at DeeAnn for putting him on the spot. That was a job solely reserved for his listeners. DeeAnn was supposed to sit back, regulate and defuse. She was not supposed to add fuel to the fire. Jake went on, "Colin's a notorious liar, and he dates a new woman every night, so beware, Portland. Sure, he's got a comb over and he favors polyester leisure suits, but the man gets the babes, oh, yes...."

Lies, lies, lies. Colin would kill him for that one. But he was still bugged at him for usurping Juliet, even if she did walk out on him in the end.

The phones were blinking madly, as ever. DeeAnn pointed to one of the buttons. Jake punched in. "Hello, there," he greeted the voice, knowing DeeAnn had already prescreened the caller.

"Oh! Hi, Jake!" The girl's voice made her sound as if she were about twelve. Jake lifted his brows at DeeAnn, who just shrugged. "This is Paisley!"

"Paisley? Ummm...how old are you?"

"Thirteen. Almost. Well, in a few months. But I'm calling to talk about my mom. She's crazy about you! And she's really pretty, and if you're dating, I want you to give her a call! Please! Pretty please!"

"Well, Paisley, I'm sure your mom is terrific, but I'm not really dating."

"Isn't that why you went to the shrink?"

Jake shot another look at DeeAnn. What had she been saying? "You mean, Julie Sommerfield?" he asked tentatively, knowing Juliet was probably listening.

DeeAnn was grinning. Hearing the door to the booth open, Jake swung around to see Zipper grinning as well. Since Zipper was at the station about two hours earlier than normal, Jake surmised something was definitely afoot. They'd set out to make his life a living hell.

The following series of calls were either about his therapy session or his interest in dating. Many listeners wanted to know when he was going to have Juliet back on the show. He was just finishing up his second hour when Colin stopped outside the glass booth, hands on his hips, glowering at Jake.

It was the comb-over line, Jake decided. Colin was really touchy about his hair. Or lack thereof.

Just before sign-off, DeeAnn shook her head to suggest he stop taking calls. He lifted his brows in a silent question. Why? Her answer was, "Looks like we've got a theme going here."

"Uh-huh...." As Jake waited for her to explain herself, his mind spun ahead. How many hours were there left before Juliet got off work? Too many. A full day. It felt like an eternity.

"You've been talking around it, but it's clear what's on your mind."

Jake tuned in, gave DeeAnn a hard look. "Oh, yeah? What's on my mind?"

"Sex."

Jake hesitated a half a beat. This was Zipper's doing. No. Probably Colin's. Or both of them. And DeeAnn, the turncoat, was the instrument they were using to get back at him.

"Sex seems to be a topic on most people's mind, at least some of the time," he said lightly, checking the clock. Lots of time left for his "friends" to do him in.

"Everyone's been asking you about Julie Sommerfield. You had a therapy session with her, and you won't say how that went apart from an allusion to pencils being thrown around. And you haven't really talked about your date with her apart from saying you went to a health club.''

"It was a double date. Ask Colin. He was the one with Juliet.''

"And you keep calling her Juliet…. That's kind of Freudian, don't you think?''

"It's her name.''

"The way I see it, and I think I speak for the bulk of your listeners, you, Jake Danforth, are suffering from a severe case of sexual frustration and its name is Julie—no, *Juliet*—Sommerfield.''

Jake knew he should say something. Negate her words. Outside the booth Zipper and Colin were slapping each other on the back and grinning like Nora's jack-o'-lantern faces, pointing at him through the window as if he were a sideshow freak. Very funny, he though dryly. A real pair of jokers.

He glanced at DeeAnn, who had the grace to look slightly sheepish. With a faint smile, he checked the clock. Ten seconds to sign off. "Well, DeeAnn, I think you might be right,'' he drawled, shocking both Colin and DeeAnn, and getting the usual unflappable Zipper to look intrigued. Colin's jaw dropped. Literally. He stared at Jake through the glass, dumbfounded that he would reveal something so utterly personal on air. DeeAnn was also surprised, but she regarded him warily. She knew his talent for turning things around.

Only this time he simply spoke the truth. "I've got a bad case of Juliet Sommerfield and I'm sinking fast. I don't know if there's any cure, and I'm afraid I may never recover. See you later, Portland. I'll keep you posted on my prognosis,'' Jake signed off cheerily, wondering what in the world Juliet would make of that!

Through the window Zipper, the Zen master, grinned and pointed both index fingers at Jake, then he placed his palms together and bowed his head over his hands, beaten at his own game and loving it.

"I CAN'T PAY YOU," Miles said for the fifth time. "I feel terrible, but Candy doesn't understand. I just had to come and see you, though. I'm sorry. I should have told you I couldn't pay when I asked for the appointment. Should I leave now?"

"No, Miles," Julie answered for the fifth time. "Just tell me what's going on. Don't worry about the money. I see that you're in a—crisis—financially speaking. How's your marriage going?"

He wrung his hands and paced the floor. Normally Miles just sat in the chair with a hangdog expression and Julie had to drag words out of him. But since Candy had swept back into his life—scooping up his checkbook and savings account and probably his Roth IRA along the way as well—Miles was in a state of great agitation. He was also pulling at his hair and now it stuck up in tufts all over his head. In fact, he bore more than a passing resemblance to the Statue of Liberty, the spikes of hair like Lady Liberty's crown.

"Love sucks," he said suddenly. And as if he'd sworn a blue streak, his face suffused with color.

Julie could sympathize. "Yes, Miles. Sometimes it sure does."

But her heart had been beating a little faster and she'd been in a perpetual state of bemusement ever since she'd heard Jake's incredible sign-off this morning. She'd been fighting off calls from her mother and Carolyn Mathers as well, and it hadn't helped that most of her other clients had heard Jake's show as well. There was definitely a collective buzz going on about her relationship with him. And though she'd tried to negate all the speculation, no amount of saying there was no relationship, there never had been a relationship and there was never going to be a relationship seemed to compute. Besides, what the heck did she know anyway? Was Jake serious, for crying out loud?

As if on cue, Miles surfaced from his own self-absorption. "Are you really seeing that radio guy?"

"No."

"Do you want to?"

He was so earnest, so hopeful, as if Julie's rocky road to romance would make his own problems seem less all-important. Julie wanted to lie to him; she really did. She could hardly bear to expose her feelings so completely. But then again she couldn't be untruthful to Miles, who was so charmingly innocent and candid about his own feelings. Not even to salvage her own pride. "Yes," she admitted, slumping into her chair.

Miles nodded, commiserating. "Have you told him how you feel?"

"Good God, no!"

"Maybe you should. Maybe he feels the same way and you just haven't had the right form of communication." Miles was earnest.

"You don't understand," Julie disabused. "Jake and I have this history, and it's in the way."

"Sometimes a shared history is binding between

two people. I read somewhere that most marriages that stay together a long time are between people who've known each other in their past. Grade school, high school, college... The longer that history, the better chance of the marriage surviving. Statistically speaking, that is.''

Julie was getting an odd vibe about this. ''I've heard that, too, and it's often true. But in our case...'' She shook her head. ''And Jake also has that—that show where everything is thrown out for his listeners! There are no secrets. None! No privacy. It isn't any wonder his first marriage broke up.''

''I don't think he'd say something damaging about you on his program.''

''Are you kidding? He already has!''

''That was before he knew it was you,'' Miles reminded her. ''He was just reacting to his ex-wife and all the pain over their divorce.''

''You're scaring me, Miles. You really are. Am I going to have to pay you for this session?''

He blushed again. ''Heck, no, Julie. This one's on the house.'' Stiffening, as if he'd suddenly remembered himself, he said in a stage whisper, ''Just don't tell Candy.''

BY THE TIME Julie pulled her Volkswagen to a stop in her apartment parking space and yanked on the brake, she felt tired all over. When Miles Charleston proved to be a better therapist than herself, it was definitely time for serious self-assessment.

And he wasn't the only one. Oh, no. The rest of the afternoon she'd been besieged with advice from all of her other clients, as well. Couples who would barely speak to one another during sessions suddenly put their heads together and worked toward helping Julie in her new romance with the estimable Jake Danforth. And the questions they asked! When did she first meet him? Did she have a crush on him in grade school? High school? Did they know each other in college? What did she really think of his ex-wife? When was she going back on the show? What was he like in person? Had she kissed him yet? Or…anything more?

That last was from Sue Frenzel, whose husband had left on a trip to Africa and never returned. Three years since his disappearance she still remained ever hopeful that her intrepid explorer would cross the threshold of their home, sweep her into his arms and—in Sue's words, not Julie's—bear her into the dark, steamy environs of their once shared boudoir. Sue lived in a romantic daydream and Julie's sudden catapulsion into a real life romantic drama had turned Sue's eyes bright with excitement and her heart full of hope.

It killed Julie to dash those hopes, but she'd had to be truthful. She'd worked hard to get Sue to recognize there were some really serious flaws in her marriage; she didn't want to undo the progress she'd made.

"There's really nothing between Jake and me but some old memories," Julie had tried to point out. But Sue was having none of it.

"That's really all it takes!" she answered in a breathy tone, swept away by her own vision of what Julie's relationship with Jake might be like. "Old memories are like sparks. Once recalled, they can burst into flames!" With that she flung her arms into the air and cried, "I'm keeping my sparks alive!"

So much for trying to keep things based on reality.

"Nora?" Julie called, stepping inside the apartment. The only sound she heard was the faint humming from the refrigerator and the rattle of sheet metal as the heat cycled on and off. She was alone.

Depressing.

Sinking onto the couch, Julie tried not to think too much about what Jake had said on the air that morning. *A bad case of Juliet Sommerfield...afraid I may never recover....* A smile crept across her lips. Could he possibly mean it? Or, was he just playing with her emotions? For ratings?

No. She didn't believe that for a minute...did she?

The doorbell rang. Pulling herself together, Julie got up from the chair, walked to the door and twisted the handle, her head still full of Jake Danforth and his unexpected announcement.

Her mouth dropped open. The object of her fantasies stood on the stoop.

"Jake," she said, dry-mouthed.

"I wanted to see you," he said. "I've been waiting for you to get home."

Julie swallowed, feeling the heat of excitement spread through her.

Sparks, apparently, were bursting into flames.

9

JULIE STOOD in the doorway. *Won't you come in?* The antiquated invitation hovered on her tongue. But it was so corny! Why had her brain just stalled like an overheated engine. She couldn't think of one single, solitary thing to say. After what felt like light-years, she stepped aside to allow him entry and said, "What's a nice boy like you doing in a place like this?"

He smiled, showing those incredibly white teeth. She felt blinded by their brilliance. *Careful, Julie,* she warned as Jake said, "I thought I'd better explain myself. Did you listen to the show today?"

"Mmm-hmm." Her heart sank. Was he here *to explain it all away?* She should have known! She should have known! And in that distant part of her mind she recalled him saying as he left her apartment the last time, "…there's someone waiting for me at home…."

"I was getting a lot of pressure from DeeAnn and Colin, and also Zipper."

"Zipper? Oh. Your 9:00 a.m. replacement."

"It's been kind of a three-ring circus at work since this whole thing started."

"What whole thing?" Julie asked, knowing exactly what he meant.

"You and me."

"Nothing's happening between you and me," she responded quickly, too quickly, involuntarily. Knee-jerk reaction at its worst.

"Well…okay…." Jake was now standing in the middle of the living room. The place looked worse than last time he was here. She tried to ignore it, but she couldn't stop herself from smoothing the couch cover and plumping some pillows. Motioning for him to sit down, she continued to stand in the center of the room. So, then, of course, did Jake.

"Let's talk about what's not happening between us, then," he suggested.

"Great idea. Ought to be a short conversation."

"First of all, can I get you back on the show? Say, Friday?"

"I'm kinda busy Friday," Julie demurred.

"The show starts at six in the morning," he reminded her. "What are you busy doing so early in the day?"

She looked at him. Her heart was skipping about every fourth beat. She was certain she was hyperventilating. Couldn't he tell? "It takes me a while to brush my teeth."

"How about Thursday, then?"

"Still have to give the pearly whites a shine."

"So, you're saying you don't want to come back on the show?"

Avoidance tactics. Her clients lived for them. And now she was one of the worst perpetrators. "I don't know." She hesitated. "I'm afraid."

"Afraid of—me?"

"Maybe. I'm not sure." She paused, thought about it, and finally admitted, "Afraid of sticking my neck out."

"Juliet Adams? Afraid?" he mocked lightly.

"Julie Sommerfield," she repeated deliberately. "Terrified."

"I don't believe it for a minute!"

"Okay, skip that for now," she said, uncomfortable. "What else were you going to say?"

At that moment Julie heard the slam of a car door. Moments later light footsteps sounded on the exterior steps, then the sound of a key threading into the lock. Nora.

"Could we go somewhere?" Jake asked suddenly, moving closer to practically whisper in her ear.

"I don't know. Maybe. You're in my personal space." Julie tried not to let him affect her so much, but she was fighting a losing battle. "Where do you want to go?" she asked suspiciously.

As Nora entered through the door, he said softly, "My place...."

Oh, holy mama, Julie thought, her heart lurching as her mind skipped back to the prom and the last time she'd been invited to his place.

"Hello, Jake," Nora said, seeming inordinately amused to find him at their apartment again.

"Hi, Nora."

"So, what's up?" she asked, gazing at Julie.

"Not too much," Julie heard herself say too brightly. Her smile, fake as fake could be, was just as wildly bright. "Jake and I were just heading out for—for—"

Nora lifted her brows, waiting. Julie's mind numbed. What would they be doing together that made any kind of sense?

"For cigarettes," Jake supplied, and then steered Julie out the door before she could put up any resistance.

"CIGARETTES?" she repeated, clapping her hand to her forehead. "For *cigarettes?*"

She sat in the passenger seat of his black SUV. There was a metal gate separating the far back space of the vehicle from the seats. For Seltzer, she determined. Jake's place was not all that far away, so he'd said, but it was still definitely a drive, and it felt like it was straight up as the engine whined and they wound into the west hills above the city.

"I thought it was inspired," he stated with the glimmer of a smile, "you being a smoker and all."

She narrowed her eyes at him. "You're a regular laugh a minute."

"Why didn't you just tell her we were going to my place?" he asked with a shrug. "What's wrong with speaking the truth? Isn't that kind of what your line of business is all about?"

"I'm a therapist, not an interrogator." She gazed out the window, piqued. It really bugged her when other people pointed out her flaws.

"And a sometime tarot reader."

"I don't read the tarot," she said through her teeth. "How many times do I have to say it?"

"Just once," he responded, maddeningly. "I always knew it was Teri's doing. Just wanted to hear you admit it."

"I've admitted it and admitted it."

"And I made the mistake of listening to my ex-wife when I should have known better. I'm sorry."

"That's right." Julie had to fight herself from crossing her arms over her chest and saying, "Humph!"

Perversely, now that he didn't seem to want to fight, she felt like lifting her dukes and going another round. Looking around, she suddenly asked, "Where are we?"

"My home," he said, giving her a long look.

"*Your* home!" They'd pulled into the long, circular driveway of his parents' house. The same house he'd taken her to the night of the prom. Unable to stop herself, she stole a look toward the guest house but it was locked up tight.

"I live here now. My parents moved to Palm Springs. They come back and visit in the summer when it gets too hot."

"Was this—was this where you and—Teri lived?"

He shook his head and Julie was relieved enough to sigh aloud. For reasons she didn't want to examine too closely she couldn't bear the thought of Teri being on these grounds with Jake. With a start she saw how possessive and nostalgic those thoughts were. A bad sign.

"No, I left Teri at the town house. Gave it to her during the divorce. But I held on to my parents' place."

"Good idea," Julie murmured. "Much more valuable, I'm sure."

He slid her another meaningful look. "Lots more memories...."

They walked together up the walk but didn't hold hands. Dampness hung in the air, a thick cloud cover. A few last, errant leaves danced across the path in front of them as Jake pulled out his key and opened the door. Julie stepped across the threshold with trepidation.

She'd never really been inside the main house. Yes, she'd leaned her elbows on the back deck and gazed over the city lights, and yes, she'd tripped lightly down the stone steps that ran along the north side and crossed the flagstone steps that led to the guest house. But she hadn't walked across the marble entry, nor gazed at the massive crystal chandelier that sent colored prisms of light scattering in all directions, nor had she noticed the curving stairway with its mahogany banister.

Even so, her thoughts crept back to the guest house with its one room that doubled as bedroom and living room, the windows with their jalousie blinds, the sweet scent of spring blossoms…

She had to shake herself back to the present as Jake led the way to the kitchen and pulled out a bottle of wine.

"Coffee?" she heard herself ask on a dry throat.

"Sure."

He put down the wine and opened a cupboard where she spied rows of Jake Danforth coffee cups. He followed her gaze and sighed. "I know. It's hell being an egomaniac."

"Must have been cheaper by the carton."

"Crate, actually." He shook coffee into a white filter and started up the drip coffeemaker. "My producers' idea. Freebie giveaways. Embarrassing as hell."

"Really?"

He nodded and gestured to the rows of cups as he pulled two down. "Need any extras?"

She smiled. "I just might."

Jake was just handing her a cup when Seltzer wobbled into the kitchen. She hadn't realized how old he was, even though she'd known he would have to be fourteen plus years. It made her feel awful, the way she'd been thinking of him as a terror all this time. "Hey, boy," she said, and he lifted his chin for her to scratch, curling up at her feet at the same time.

"He hasn't been feeling the best lately," Jake said. "I keep checking on him constantly. He's always waiting for me."

Someone waiting for me at home....

"So, it was Seltzer you came home to," she murmured. He gave her a swift smile and a nod. Julie felt like a heel. She'd misjudged Jake yet again. Nora always told her Jake was her blind spot and she had to admit that it was true.

They walked onto the deck and gazed over the city but this time the weather was cool, heading for downright cold, and Julie started shivering almost immediately. Ever so casually Jake took off his leather jacket and draped it over her shoulders. Jake's own particular scent wafted upward to Julie's nose, filling her head with its musky and male and utterly sensual odor. She inhaled deeply, involuntarily, as if it were her last saving breath. Vaguely she remembered that this had been her downfall—the smells and closeness of being with him. *Danger, Will Robinson! Danger!*

Once again she found herself unable to think of conversation, and once again she didn't much care. Jake, too, seemed affected in the same way. When he said, "Let's go inside," she didn't know how to feel. Yes, she was freezing to death, but entering the house meant giving up his jacket and she was beginning to feel very possessive about it.

He led her toward a den at the back of the house

and she immediately saw that this was his retreat. Two brown leather chairs and a matching couch were clustered in a semicircle around a massive television set. The set, in turn, sat in front of a cherry bookcase, which was filled with books and electronic gear. Jake flipped a switch and glowing blue LCDs rose and fell in vertical lines with the music that suddenly emanated from the speakers. The music was soft and seductive. A choice he'd made specifically? Julie swallowed and tentatively settled herself in one of the chairs.

"So, your parents moved to Palm Springs, huh?" she asked.

"Yep. What about yours?"

"Still in Beaverton. Nothing new there."

"The old neighborhood?" he asked, liking the idea, to which Julie nodded. A moment later, he added casually, "What about the ex?"

"Kurt?" Julie blinked. She opened her mouth to say something, but nothing came out. A moment later, she pressed her lips back together and shook her head.

"What?" Jake asked.

"If you can't say anything nice about someone, don't say anything at all."

He laughed. "Like you follow that advice!"

"Okay, okay..." She smiled. "I take everything back that I said about you. But it works both ways."

He touched his cup to hers in a toast. "Deal."

They sat in the two chairs. There was no clock in the room, so Julie stole a surreptitious look at her watch. Not that she wanted to leave. She just needed to keep some kind of reality check going. She felt— strange. Feeling as if he were still waiting for some kind of answer to his question, she finally admitted, "Kurt and I were just wrong for each other and when he went to 'find himself,' it was a relief." She made a face. "Even though he found himself with someone else pretty quick."

"I wish Teri would find herself with someone else," he admitted.

"I thought..." He glanced up at her, but she hardly knew how to go on. "Never mind."

"No, go on," he insisted. "You've met Teri. I'd like your opinion on what's going on with her right now."

"I met her just once," she reminded him. "It was just...you mentioned a Tae Bo instructor, I believe."

"Oh, him...." He shrugged. "I think that was just to get at me. And it did, at the time. Not anymore, though. I would really like her to find someone else and get out of my life once and for all."

"How is she in your life?"

"She's...been calling. And she was fairly specific about you, too."

"Me?"

"Didn't want me to see you, professionally or otherwise. Like she has any control over my life anymore!"

Julie gazed at him, aware of undercurrents here she hadn't recognized before. Clearing her throat, she asked lightly, "Is that why you're doing this?"

"Doing what?" A pause. "Seeing you? No!" He gazed at her in a way that made her knees go weak. Luckily, she was sitting down. "Juliet," he said in that soft, urgent way of his that got her so much, "I've wanted to get closer to you since you showed up in that witch's costume. Even before, but I didn't know where you were.''

''Now, that's a lie.''

''You just won't believe I'm interested in you, will you?''

Julie squeezed her hands together until her fingers ached. ''Not when there are the Babbs and Pammys out there, fighting over you. And, well, you were the high school Romeo.''

''Nope. Whoever called me that didn't know me at all.''

She wanted to laugh in his face but the laughter died in her throat at the intense way he looked at her. Julie's internal radar went wild. *Uh-oh. Bad sign. No, no, no. Turn those baby blues off right now!* When he rose to his feet and pulled her out of her chair, standing in front of her so closely that she could feel the heat emanating from his skin, his fingers lingering along the curve of her chin, his gaze dropping to her lips, she swallowed hard. Uh-oh, uh-oh!

''Ummm…Jake?''

Was he listening? She didn't think so. She watched as his head bent, then gave a slight gasp as he dropped a light kiss on her lips. Butterfly soft. Guaranteed to undo her completely. Calculated to break down resistance. Completely effective. She was doomed. Doomed! Tentatively, she kissed him back, rubbing her lips gently against his, afraid, excited and ready to run if he were suddenly to pull back with some kind of grade school–type, ''Gotcha!'', which was what she thoroughly expected him to do.

He did pull back. She braced herself. Here it comes, she thought, waiting. It was like watching a cobra about to strike; she couldn't leave because she was caught in the hold of its fascination.

"Juliet," he murmured, and bent his head for another kiss. Her eyes fluttered closed and she sighed. Complete capitulation. She was doomed.

The kiss grew deeper. His hands slid down her back. Her own hands ran over his chest. As much as she'd loved his jacket earlier, now she shrugged out of it as if its very presence offended her. His fingers pulled her blouse away from her slacks and she mimicked him, her hands tugging his shirt from his jeans and sliding onto the firm skin of his back, traveling up the shallow valley of his spine.

She felt his tongue parting her lips, touched the tip of hers to his. Moments later their kiss grew deeper, tongues thrusting, hands clutching their bodies close, feet shuffling as they shimmied backward and tumbled onto the couch.

Just a taste, she told herself. Not the whole enchilada. Not like last time!

But oh, what a taste! A part of her brain was saying, To hell with it! Go for it! Don't stop, don't stop, don't stop! Another part asked cautiously if she were out of her ever-lovin' mind.

"Juliet," he muttered again, on a groan, as their bodies melded together on the couch. She felt his fingers unbutton her blouse, her breasts straining against her bra as if they had minds of their own and were desperate to be set free.

"It's Julie," she said breathlessly in his ear. "No *T*. Is that so hard to remember?"

"Impossible," he said on a deep growl, and when his fingers found the tab of her zipper and slowly pulled it down she thought, oh, what the hell.

She was fully naked with Jake in the same position

when a cold nose pressed into her midriff and Seltzer whined so loudly she nearly levitated from the couch.

WHAT WAS I THINKING? she asked herself for the hundredth time as she walked up the steps to her front door on leaden feet. What was I thinking? Okay, that was the hundredth and one time. But she'd practically made love to Jake Danforth. Again! And only Seltzer's intervention had saved her.

Julie shook her head. She had to pull herself together and get over it. Enough! No more thinking about romance and sex. It was detrimental to her health. She needed to put her mind in a different place. Nora, she thought, relieved. Nora could help. Nora was sanity itself.

Except when she stepped into the apartment she found Nora and Irving St. Cloud jumping apart from a deep embrace as if they were high school kids, interrupted when the parents came home. And was that her lipstick all over his white collar?

"Hi, kids," Julie said with an edge to her voice. Now, this was just all she needed!

"I'd better go," Irving said, reluctantly, as he straightened his red-smeared collar. He reached for his jacket and smiled a hello at Julie. She smiled one back, but her lips felt tight. Nora and Irving both climbed to their feet, and there was an awkward moment as they stared at Julie.

"How about if I find something to do in the kitchen?" Julie murmured, turning on her heel.

Ten excruciating minutes later, while she suffered through the smacks of kisses and murmurs of loving goodbyes, Julie watched Nora enter the room. Julie glanced down at her friend's feet. Yep. She was walking on air, all right.

"Talk about getting in bed with the enemy," Julie pointed out.

"Oh...." Nora's distracted smile was downright irritating. "Irv just came by to talk about some things."

"Irv?"

"Clarice came into the shop again and we got to talking. She's kind of a matchmaker, you know."

"No, I didn't know." Actually, she probably did. Clarice's interest in Nora's Nut Rolls, Etc. had been suspicious from the start, Julie decided.

"And Irv came in and we were laughing about it, and then one thing led to another—"

"As it often does," Julie put in dryly.

"—and the next thing you know he called me up and asked if he could stop by, and well, we're talking merger."

"Merger?"

"Businesswise," she clarified. "It makes a lot of sense and I would still get to keep my name. In fact, St. Cloud's would sell a different selection than what I would offer at Nora's Nut Rolls, Etc. It's kind of that way already. But I would get to expand into lots more locations."

"Businesswise," Julie repeated. "Well, it looked like you had a lot more than hot-cross buns on your mind when you and *Irv* were on the couch just now!"

"What are you so steamed about?"

"You! And Irving St. Cloud! You of all people, Nora. You're selling out!"

"I'm making a smart business decision. This will benefit both Irv and me," she insisted. "And who's the sellout, here? The last I heard you were planning to murder Jake Danforth, and I come home to find you going out for *cigarettes?* What kind of euphemism is that?''

Julie's eyes narrowed. ''Euphemism?''

''You and Jake were being awfully coy about what you were doing together.'' She paused, peering at Julie intently. ''What *were* you doing?''

''Nothing.'' Julie answered too quickly. Now it was her turn to feel like the guilty teenager. ''We just went—out—for a while.''

''Where did you go?''

''Hey, don't turn this around on me.''

''Where—did—you—go?'' Nora demanded, stressing each word.

''His place, okay! We went to his place.'' She just stopped herself from asking, ''Happy now?''

''Aha....'' Nora was smug.

''I don't even want to know what that means. And believe me, nothing happened that can compare to whatever was going on with you and Irv.''

''Did you make love with Jake?''

''No! I just told you, I—''

''Did you want to?''

''No!'' Julie lied. ''Of course not.''

Nora lifted one knowing brow. ''You wanted to, didn't you? Oh, for pete's sake, Julie, stop fighting it. You love him. You always have, and throwing tantrums about it doesn't make it any less real!''

''Oh, now you're a psychologist, too? Well, take a number! All my clients have turned on me as well!''

''What do you want, Julie?'' Nora asked, more gently. ''I mean, really. Do you want Jake Danforth? Do you?''

''No.''

''Julie...'' Nora reproached.

She wanted to clap her hands over her ears and have that tantrum Nora had just accused her of. But memories of the evening with Jake assailed her. She couldn't deny the truth no matter how much she might want to. "Okay, yes. Yes, I want him! All right? I want him!"

"There...was that so bad?"

"Yes! It just kills me to admit it! But, Nora, he scares the daylights out of me. And that's just—too much power for one person to have over me. I can't bear it!"

"The reason you married Kurt was because deep inside you really didn't care that much, so you always knew you could walk away unscathed, and that didn't really work. Maybe it's time to follow your heart."

"What a terrible idea!" Julie said, feeling the conversation slipping away from her like water over stones.

"I'm following mine," Nora admitted softly.

Julie just managed to stop herself from saying, "Well, goody for you," but when she abandoned that retort she also lost the heat of her convictions. Nora was right and she was wrong and she had no idea what to do about it.

"So, how can you be so sure that Irv's the one for you?" she asked her friend.

Nora smiled enigmatically. "I make his dough rise."

"Tell me you didn't just say that."

"I did."

And that pretty much ended that conversation.

10

"SO LONG, PORTLAND." Jake clicked off his microphone and removed his headset, his expression grim. DeeAnn, who'd suffered through his mood all morning, gave him a hard look.

"Still mad at us?" she asked.

"Huh?" Jake regarded her blankly.

"What's going on with you?"

"Oh." In lieu of answering he drew a long breath, hooked the back of his leather jacket with one finger and headed for the door.

Zipper stood by the door, just inside the booth, arms folded over his chest. He shared a look with DeeAnn and asked, "You okay, man?" as Jake passed by.

"Couldn't be better."

Jake punched the elevator button. The doors opened and Beryl Hoffman stepped back to allow him entry. Jake inwardly groaned. For a split second he asked himself if it would be too rude if he were to suddenly break for the stairs. He actually glanced in that direction…but Pammy was heading his way.

The lesser of two evils. He stepped into the elevator car.

"I heard your show," Beryl said primly, repressively.

"Pretty much a one-note theme," he said.

''This city is inordinately interested in your personal relationship with that—*therapist*.'' Her lips curled around the word as if it tasted bad.

Jake had nothing to say and so he stood in silence, waiting for the bell to ding and signal the lobby floor. All day long he'd tried to change the subject. He'd even turned off the phones for an hour while he interviewed today's guest: a soap opera heartthrob who normally brought in a deluge of calls from devoted fans. But nothing had diverted the city's rabid attention, and the problem was Jake had never felt more like keeping his feelings to himself.

His memory tripped back to those moments on the couch with Juliet: the tenor of her breathing, the soft quiver of her skin, the curve of her lips. He'd played the events over and over in his mind, thinking he might be going slightly mad, till the wee hours of the morning. Somewhere around two Seltzer had nudged his arm—the one flopped over the edge of the bed from a restless night of tossing and turning—and Jake had absentmindedly scratched the dog's ears, only half-surfacing. Then this morning, as he was dragging himself around the apartment, trying to shake off the drugging effects of a sleepless night, wishing for even a glimmer of morning light to aid in his awakening, he'd noticed that Seltzer hadn't eaten a morsel of last night's dog food.

They'd stared at each other in the harsh kitchen light—Jake and his faithful friend. Fear knotted Jake's stomach. The water bowl was half-empty and he refreshed it. Seltzer headed for the bowl and lapped up some water, easing Jake's worry just a bit. Jake then tossed out last night's bowl of dog food and replaced it with new. "Have something to eat. I'll be back straight after work," he told the dog.

His worry hadn't completely abated, however; it had colored his whole morning. Seltzer was old. Ancient, really. But it didn't matter to Jake. He knew grief waited like a knife hanging over his head should Seltzer die.

He drove home as fast as the traffic would allow. Seltzer was waiting inside on the mat by the garage door. Jake stroked his head. The dog didn't move. Walking inside, Jake realized the food bowl had still not been touched.

"C'mon, boy," he said, helping Seltzer to his feet. For once in his life Seltzer, who always sensed when he was being taken to the vet rather than just a jaunt in the car, didn't object.

JULIE KNEW something strange was happening when Sue Frenzel burst in on her session with Carolyn Mathers. Never had Sue shown up at Julie's office except at the precise moment of her appointment, not a minute before, not a minute after. And her face was flushed. And her eyes were wild. And she absolutely sparkled with life.

And was that a hickey on her neck?

"He came back?" Julie asked, in disbelief. *The intrepid explorer had actually returned?*

"His brother did. I always had a thing for him, you know, but they went off to Africa together...but then he came back and told me he couldn't live without me and so I'm divorcing Tom and marrying Dick!"

"What happened to Harry?" Carolyn asked with interest.

Sue blinked at her in confusion. Then she turned back to Julie. "We're heading to the Ivory Coast. Just wanted you to know I won't be making my next appointment. Thank you so much!"

And then she was gone.

There was a moment of silence, then Julie remarked, "My patients appear to be curing themselves."

Carolyn took immediate offense. "What? Are you kidding? I'm in for the long haul, honey. I need years of therapy." And with that she pulled out her pack of cigarettes, silently asking Julie if she wanted one. Julie shook her head, pointed to the No Smoking sign, to which Carolyn paid no attention at all as she proceeded to light up. Julie, in turn, paid no attention as her own thoughts were traveling down different paths.

"What were you saying?" she asked, distracted.

Carolyn regarded her keenly behind her narrow lenses. It was clear Julie's thoughts were a million miles away. "Actually, I was thinking about joining you in your practice. You could use a partner. And I've been taking lessons from my masseuse. Sure, he doesn't have the credentials but he's so practiced in the art of head-shrinking that I thought I could skip the college courses and just jump on board. What do you think?"

"Maybe...." Julie checked the clock on her desk. Should she go over to Jake's when she finished today, or would that be too forward? She'd had an epiphany of sorts. She wasn't going to get over him. Ever. *So, if you can't beat 'em, might as well join 'em.*

"Aren't you supposed to listen to me?" Carolyn

demanded. "I mean, isn't that the point of why I write you checks? Money for therapy and vice versa."

Julie snapped out of her reverie. "I'm listening."

"Did you hear a word I said?"

Julie shook her head, tried to recall. "Something about getting a massage?"

Carolyn shot a puff of smoke from the corner of her mouth and smiled.

THE PHONE RANG just as Julie was locking up. She still hadn't figured out what was going on with Carolyn. They'd talked in circles for a while, Carolyn doing her best to be querulous and difficult, in Julie's opinion, then Carolyn had mysteriously said something about it being time to get a shingle and she was out the door.

Recognizing her own near worthlessness today, Julie was glad Carolyn was her last appointment. If she'd had to see Miles today, she wasn't sure she could have coped. Of all her clients, Miles and Carolyn were the most attuned to Julie's personal life, a situation that was fast getting out of control. As soon as she'd settled things with Jake she would have to do something to restore the client/therapist balance. If she didn't get herself together, she was going to have to take down her shingle and find other work as well!

Shingle? Julie nearly stopped short, but then the phone started ringing and her heart twisted. She snatched up the receiver. "Hello?" she asked a bit breathlessly.

"Juliet?"

Her heart sank. Not Jake. "Hi, Mom."

"I haven't heard from you for a few days. How's everything going with Jake? He didn't seem to want to talk about you on his show. When are you going back on? I've been telling everyone to listen, but they're getting impatient."

"I don't want Jake to talk about me on the show, Mom. He knows that, and I think he's trying to protect me."

"Protect you from what, dear?"

"All the speculation. That's why I'm not going back on the show. At least not now."

"When, then?" she persisted.

"Just...later."

"That's not very helpful."

"I know!" Julie tried to hide her growing exasperation. "Mom, can I call you back? I'm on the way out."

"Well, I suppose so.... Have you told Jake about Kurt, yet?"

"Told him about Kurt?" Nonplused, Julie responded before she remembered her rule not to get sucked into her mother's circular trap. It was like a whirlpool, dragging you under.

"That you never really loved him. That you still had that crush on Jake ever since prom night."

Julie yanked the phone from her ear and gazed at it as if it were a slithering reptile. She'd never told her mom about prom night. Never! Not even when everything came down on her so hard the following week. The woman was psychic. Either that, or....

"Have you been doubling up on your heart medication again, Mom?"

"Get a grip," her mother answered with asperity. "You've always thought everyone was blind but you! If you want that man, go get him. Marital counseling, my eye!'' She sniffed. ''You've got to land the man first, dear. Now, go do it before he slips the hook and swims away.''

She heard her mother's receiver snap into its cradle—a sharp dismissal. Certain she'd slipped into some extra dimension, or that she was on *Candid Camera,* or that she was heading for a nervous breakdown, Julie locked the office and headed for her car. Once the Bug was on the road she pointed its nose in the direction of Jake's house. Everyone seemed to know something that she didn't. Did Jake know it, too?

When she cruised into his driveway she suddenly realized she'd been running on automatic pilot. What was she thinking? Showing up at his home without calling? And here, of all places.... Involuntarily she stole another glance at the guest house. There was something about its two windows on either side of the door and the flower boxes running the length of its front wall, the boxes on the outer edges a bit higher than the ones in the center.

Was it *smiling,* for God's sake?

She would have turned around and sped away right then except that Jake stepped onto the porch. Something about the way he was standing there, his shoulders slumped, his hands in his back pockets, caught her attention.

She coasted to a stop and climbed out, her hair caught by a shivery little breeze. ''I should have called,'' she said.

''No, come in. I'm glad you're here.''

''You are?'' She brightened, trying to hide the reaction, failing miserably. But Jake was on some track of his own and she couldn't quite penetrate it. "When we left off last night, I just didn't know what to think. You know?" She peered up at him as they entered the house together.

"I couldn't sleep," he said.

"Neither could I," she said with relief, glad they were on the same page.

"I haven't eaten yet today," he said, then, on a note of discovery. "I could make some sandwiches."

"Perfect."

She wondered at his distraction but since it didn't appear to have anything to do with her, she let it slip away. For a moment her mind wondered about Seltzer and she glanced around for the dog. But then Jake, who'd led the way to the kitchen, suddenly stopped short. She nearly ran into his muscular back, and only managed to stop herself by placing her hands on his shoulders.

The touch seemed to ignite something. He turned around and pulled her to him and before she could think his mouth found hers, devouring hers, a kind of desperate kissing that made her heart sing. They were suddenly making out like the teenagers they'd once been and it was absolutely wonderful!

And like that time before, she found herself falling under his spell. No resistance whatever. Even when he lowered her to the floor, even when she felt the cool, maple planks beneath her shoulders and even when his tongue traveled downward from her lips, blazing a trail across her throat while his fingers removed her blouse and bra—she simply sighed and clutched him tightly. It happened so fast she had no time to catch her breath, and though she opened one eye for a quick look for Seltzer, that was all she could handle before Jake's fingers distracted her, moving downward, tugging gently but insistently on her zipper.

I should say something, she thought, faintly, her thoughts splintering as his tongue began exploring other parts of her. *I definitely should say something.*

She answered with her own hands. Hands that, impatient with his slow removal of her slacks, swept his fingers away and made short work of the job. Quickly she wriggled to remove the last remaining scraps of clothing. When she was naked she felt a flame of embarrassment, quickly doused, as desire took over and her own fingers nimbly worked on the buttons of his shirt, the tab of his zipper.

"Juliet...." he breathed into her mouth, his body lowering itself to hers.

I really should say something about this venue, she reminded herself. But the only word that came to her lips was, "Romeo," and they both collapsed into laughter until the rhythm of lovemaking took over and they forgot who they were completely.

"WHAT'S THAT?" Jake asked sleepily, two minutes after their explosive lovemaking. Not enough time for Julie to catch her breath. She was curled into him, still breathing hard, liking the feel of his leg thrown protectively over hers. He propped himself on one elbow and gazed down at her. "I thought I heard something."

"Probably Seltzer." She idly tugged at his ear with her teeth.

Her comment froze him and she searched his suddenly taut face. "I took Seltzer to the veterinary hospital today. He wasn't eating."

"Oh, Jake." Her heart squeezed in sympathy.

"It's been a hellish day. I just called over there but there's been no change. He's still not eating, but I'm thinking about going and getting him. I was heading that way when you drove up, and then, well—" He smiled faintly. "I got distracted."

"Who would've thought the kitchen floor would be such a fine place to get distracted." Jake grinned and Julie added more soberly, "Do you want to go alone, or would you like some com—"

Baamm! Baamm! Baamm!

The pounding at the front door shot them apart. Quick as a wink Jake was yanking on his boxers and trousers. Julie scrambled around and snatched at her clothes: pants, blouse, panties, but her bra was nowhere to be found. A glance showed it had been slingshot across the room and currently dangled from a barstool.

And suddenly the front door slammed open, bouncing off the wall and sending the chandelier tinkling. Julie choked on a gasp and scuttled around the kitchen island, trying to stick both legs in her slacks and peek over the top of the countertop simultaneously.

"Jake!" a female voice demanded.

Teri Danforth.

Julie eased down and peeked around the side of the counter. Teri's legs moved into view, striding toward them like the apocalypse in a pair of black, killer stiletto heels. Julie shrank back, out of view.

"Why, hello, darling," Jake drawled. "Home for dinner?"

"Where is she? I know her car. Where is she?"

As noiselessly as she could manage, Julie wriggled

one leg into her slacks. Her heart pounded like a hammer inside her ears. *Hurry, hurry, hurry!*

"I didn't know you had a key to this house," Jake said, unruffled but deadly furious. "When did that happen, Teri?"

"Goddamn it, Jake! Where is that little two-timing witch!"

Hey! Julie thought, stopped in action in spite of herself.

"Standing in front of me," Jake answered without a pause.

Teri inhaled in shock, absorbing the barb. She moved forward again, the tat-a-tat-tat of her heels sharp and angry.

Jake said quietly, "Teri, you weren't invited. So, drop the key, turn around and get the hell out."

A moment later, on a high-pitched shriek, she demanded, "Is that a bra!"

Julie wanted to die. She wanted to fall in on herself and turn to pixie dust. Poof!

All gone!

"I didn't mean for you to find out this way," Jake deadpanned. "I'm checking styles and sizes. Here...."

Julie heard a squeak as he leaned over to apparently grab her flimsy undergarment. She used the time to thrust one arm in her blouse. Rustling noises sounded. A snort from Teri. She strained her ears but couldn't tell what was happening. One arm was in. Good. She started on the second. Where was the armhole? Damn it! *Where was it?*

"Tell the truth, now," Jake said in a "just girls dishing" kind of voice. "Do you think it makes me look fat?"

Julie had a mental image of Jake wearing her bra over his bare chest. She clapped a hand to her mouth.

"Damn you, Jake," Teri said through her teeth, showing no sense of humor at all.

At that precise moment Teri leaned over the bar and caught her in her struggles. Julie gave her a sheepish smile, hugging her knees to her chest. Teri let out a banshee shriek that nearly broke her eardrums.

"The cards told me something was up!" she cried out in fury. "Now I know what that 'up' was!"

And that's when Jake grabbed his ex by the arm and marched her back outside. At least that was what Julie surmised from the sounds. Hurriedly buttoning up her blouse, she popped her head up in time to see Jake disappear into the entry hall, dragging a flailing Teri along with him, the unhooked ends of Julie's bra flapping behind his back.

Jake returned moments later, peeling off her bra and handing it to her, his eyes gazing deeply into hers, his face full of concern.

Julie swallowed. "Some days it just doesn't pay to start an affair."

"I'm sorry. She's gone now."

And so was the mood. Julie stuffed her bra in her pocket and couldn't help feeling like a complete idiot. She gave him a little shrug and turned toward the door.

"You don't have to leave."

"Somehow, I think I should."

He didn't try to stop her. He just kind of nodded. She knew his thoughts were turning from Teri's wild entrance back to Seltzer. Though she desperately wanted to share his pain and worry, Teri had irretrievably blown the tender moment between them. Their closeness, at least for now, was over.

"I'll call you later," he said, and Julie nodded, a lump in her throat. He remembered to kiss her on the stoop and she felt marginally better. *I love you* popped into her head.

"Jake...." He hesitated and she let those three little words chase around her brain, hovering on her tongue, aching to be said. But good sense prevailed and she said instead, "It didn't make you look fat. I just don't think tangerine is your color."

STUPID, STUPID, STUPID!

Why had she made a joke? Why? All night long she tossed and turned and restlessly flung the comforter on and off herself, as waves of remembered embarrassment attacked her like hot flashes every time she thought of the evening's events. She would have talked to Nora about the whole thing but Nora had been wrapped in Irving St. Cloud's arms—literally—when Julie had dragged her sorry self into the apartment, and this time neither Nora nor Irv bothered unlocking just because they weren't alone.

Love is hell, she thought. Loving Jake Danforth is hell. I'm in hell. And it's damn hot!

She flung the covers off one last time and glared up at the ceiling. It's déjà vu, she thought in despair. The prom, and now *this!*

Remembering Teri's dark face was enough to give her the chills. Except she was too hot with shame and embarrassment to make much difference.

Sleep, she begged her overheated brain. Sleep. Relaxation. Peace.

Nothing.

When her alarm went off at five forty-five, her hand was already poised above it. She slammed down the button before the first, faint beginnings of its buzz. Tired, miserable and certain history was about to replay itself, she ran through the shower, brushed her teeth with vigor, threw on some makeup and blew-dry her wet hair. Staring at herself in the mirror she made a strangled sound, rubbing blush into her wan cheeks and trying on a smile.

"It looks like Richter has set it," she said through her teeth, pretty sure she could get a role as the Batman's Joker if she tried. She'd certainly be in the top five.

Nora was humming and buttering a bagel as Julie entered the kitchen. "Good morning," she sang out. Julie glanced down at Nora's feet. Yep. Still walking on air.

"What's wrong?" Nora asked, giving Julie a curious look.

"Why? Does something look wrong?"

"I don't know. You just look kind of..."

"Kind of...?" Julie pressed.

"Ungood."

"Well, that's just great," Julie muttered, throwing her hands in the air. "Because you look absolutely fabulous and I'm sure it has everything to do with the oven-warming you've got going on with Irving St. Cloud!"

"Uh-oh. Problems with Jake?"

"More like extinction level catastrophes." She related the events of the evening before with all the emotion of a newscast.

For once Nora looked suitably alarmed although all she said was, "Bad scene."

Julie drove to the office with Jake's program blasting away. He sounded awfully distracted this morning, which she could hardly blame him. Distraction was the order of the day. He was so out of it, apparently, that DeeAnn started fielding calls in a desperate effort to keep things going. The callers wanted to know if Jake's current distraction was because he was lovesick over that hocus-pocus marriage counselor.

"He sounds like he's sinking fast," one female caller worried to DeeAnn. "Maybe he needs a stimulant, you know? There's a shop on Burnside. They've got tons of stuff that I'm sure—"

DeeAnn cut her off and grabbed another line.

"Tell him to just kiss the microphone," the next woman purred and then she must have tongued the telephone receiver from her end with absolute relish by the noise coming from Julie's speaker.

Julie groaned, switched off the dial, then turned it back on half a second later.

Just in time to hear Teri Danforth's strident voice yelling, "Yes, they were together!" she declared. "On the kitchen floor, no less! Jake, are you there? That's the last time you cheat on me!" she yelled, apparently forgetting completely that their marriage was long over and that Jake was completely happy with the arrangement. "You can have her, okay? You can just have her! You deserve each other. You're both lying, cheating—"

And then Teri was cut off as well. Julie held her breath, counting nearly five seconds before the dead space was filled with Jake's drawling voice. "Divorce," he said dryly. "A thing of beauty."

When Julie got to her office, she switched the radio back on, desperate to listen, yet afraid to hear more. Nothing much happened after that until right before sign-off and then Jake admitted the real truth of his somber mood. "My dog, Seltzer, died last night," he said. "It's been—not a lot of fun. Thanks for putting up with me this morning, Portland. See ya tomorrow."

Tears sprang to Julie's eyes. She fumbled for the phone. Called the office, but no one would put her through, even when she stated her name. "Stand in line," was the blunt answer from the receptionist. "There are ten Julie Sommerfields ahead of you."

"There are?"

"They thought her name could get them access, too. Nice try."

Julie hung up, lost. Miles came in and she gazed at him helplessly. "We don't have an appointment," he said, "but I heard a bunch of Jake Danforth's show this morning and I thought you might need me."

And then she broke down and cried and Miles sympathetically handed her a clean handkerchief out of his breast pocket. Julie ignored the little M♥C stamped on the corner and blew her nose with gusto.

"I've got to go see him," she said.

"Yes, you do." He nodded soberly.

"I feel terrible."

"He needs you."

"Miles," she said, a faint smile touching her lips, "how'd you get so smart?"

He cleared his throat. "Years of therapy. And thanks," he added, as she reached for her coat and walked with him to the door.

"Thanks?"

"I've left Candy for good. I always knew she never really loved me, but I just didn't want to be alone. But it was time to let go. Just like it's time for you to grab on, now. But maybe…'' He touched a finger to his nose, pausing for a moment. "Ahhmm, maybe you should go home first and freshen up.''

Julie gave him a look, pulled open her purse and flipped open her mirrored compact. She snapped it shut a moment later. "Good advice,'' she said tersely.

BY THE TIME she fought traffic, spent a good amount of time on herself—things had definitely taken a nosedive from this morning's "ungood''—stopped at the store, picked up a card, and agonized over what to get him as a gift, over an hour had elapsed. And by the time she'd driven to Jake's house only to realize that he wasn't home and then cruised back toward the station, not expecting to find him and happily surprised to spy his car still parked in the lot, another half hour had gone by as well.

She hurried into the lobby, waved to the coffee station attendant who looked worried that she might actually order something from him, then ran smack into Beryl Hoffman, whose sneer reminded Julie that not only had her disposition not improved since the last time she'd seen her, neither had her looks. Beryl was still a "witch'' while Julie hoped that she, at least, had moved up a couple ranks, especially given all the time she'd just spent on her appearance!

Beryl gave her a hard look. "You're Jake Danforth's witch guest, aren't you? Well, Jake is upstairs with two women.'' She breezed past Julie and pushed through the revolving door to the parking lot.

So much for congratulating herself on her appearance, Julie thought, stepping into the elevator. Given Jake's state of mind, Beryl's words didn't have much punch. Two women? So what. Still, she wasn't exactly sure what she would encounter as she got off on Jake's floor.

And that's when she saw the puppies. Two of them. One of them bore a striking resemblance to Seltzer—or at least what Seltzer would have been if he'd been a purebred: a golden Lab. The other was some kind of black mutt with a tongue that darted out and happily licked everything in sight.

They were in the arms of Pammy and Babbs, respectively, with Jake standing beside them, looking poleaxed. Julie realized the women had brought Jake the dogs to take Seltzer's place, and she was astounded by their insensitivity. How presumptuous! she thought, irritated beyond bearing. Jake was clearly bowled over by the women's gifts, and not necessarily in a good way.

"Juliet!" Jake greeted her, his voice full of relief.

"Is this a meeting of the Kennel Club?" Julie asked dryly, coming to his rescue, her gaze sweeping over Pammy and Babbs. With a snort Pammy unceremoniously dumped the golden Lab puppy in Jake's arms.

"If you don't like her, I can always take her back," she declared, scooting past Julie but not before scalding her with a "look."

Babbs was nicer. "My friend's dog just had puppies and this one was so cute, I just heard you talking about your dog today, Jake, and I thought…" She trailed off, looking after Pammy in confusion. "I can take him back, too."

Julie reached out her arms to the squirming creature with its pink, sloppy tongue. Babbs dropped the
black mutt in Julie's arms. After an awkward moment, she gave Julie a head-to-toe look and said admiringly, "Lucky girl," before she stepped into the
open elevator car and descended.

And then Jake and Julie were alone again. They
gazed at each other. "I'm sorry about Seltzer," Julie
told him softly.

"Thanks. Me, too." He glanced down at his
puppy, who lay sweet and placid in his arms while
Julie's whirling dervish couldn't settle down.

"They gave you dogs," Julie said in disbelief.

"Hard to believe," he agreed, but he didn't sound
as put off as she might have expected. That was a
certainly a good sign. And the puppies were too cute
for words.

"What have you got in the bag there?" Jake asked
her.

She'd nearly forgotten her own gift, gripped by the
ends of her fingers in a tight clamp as she attempted
to hold on to her dog, the card and the gift all at
once.

"Kind of an 'I'm sorry' gift."

"Not a dog, though, huh?" He lifted one brow
and she could see that, as bad as this day had been,
he was glad to see her. As if to emphasize that point,
he leaned forward and kissed her lightly on the
mouth while Julie's pup nipped and mauled the
golden Lab lying in Jake's arms.

"Not exactly," she murmured.

"Let's take these guys home and you can show
me what you brought," he suggested.

"You're keeping them?"

"Got any better suggestions?" As if hearing him, the golden Lab pup leaned its head into the crook of Jake's arm, nuzzled and yawned. Julie's dog yipped and struggled and tried to jump from her arms into Jake's.

Julie and Jake left together in Jake's car, the puppies loose and wriggly. Julie corralled them as best she could, and when they finally got to Jake's house it took a while to get them settled in the kitchen, the area blocked off by boxes and a coffee table turned on its side. Finally, when they were finished and had washed and brushed the dog hair from their hands and shirts, Jake clasped Julie's hand and led the way to the balcony, where he opened up her card. It read:

Wanna fight? Love, Juliet.

"Wanna fight?" he repeated, baffled.

"Look in the bag."

Jake reached inside. He withdrew a jar of cherries. He started laughing almost immediately. "Don't tempt me. It's been a bad day."

"Hey, I wore my jeans and black shirt because they can take the abuse," she said, smiling. "So, if you feel like working off some tension, I'm ready. Take your best shot, Jake Danforth!"

He opened the jar and plucked one of the red cherries out with his fingers. A moment later, he moved in close to Julie and she braced herself, half expecting him to smash it into her hair or against her face or something. Instead he held it up to her lips and she delicately took it from his fingers with her tongue.

"Good dog," Jake said, patting her head and she yanked the jar of cherries from his hand, pulled out one and smashed it against his laughing mouth.

Love at first fight.

Epilogue

JULIE GAZED WITH DISMAY at the bridesmaid's gown. It was a basic sack. Straight from the shoulders and down to the floor in a frightening shade of lavender satin that was matched in a pair of satin pumps.

"Nora doesn't really expect me to wear this, does she?" Julie moaned. "I may have to kill her."

Jake handed her a glass of guava-pineapple juice, her current favorite drink of choice. "Another murder plot, huh?" he said. He'd heard—from Nora, not Julie—about the planned attempt on his life.

"I will look like a whale. I already do."

She took the glass and glanced down at her bulging stomach. Seven months pregnant and Nora's wedding was still three weeks away!

Jake kissed his wife on the cheek. "But you're such a lovely, little orca."

"Funny. Comments like that could send us directly to a marriage counselor. Someone besides myself."

"Carolyn Mathers?"

Julie gave a mock shudder. Carolyn had actually tried to join Julie in her practice. Failing that, she'd installed herself as Julie's receptionist, insisting that Julie needed someone to organize her growing caseload. Julie's resistance had been but a minor inconvenience to the implacable wave that was Carolyn

Mathers. She'd simply run right over her and in the end had proved to be excellent at her job. She'd also quit smoking. Just up and quit one day and then became a rabid non-smoking advocate all in the same week.

Julie's office was now completely smoke-free and Carolyn glared at anyone who even gave off a whiff of the "I've been smoking" scent.

"I hate to admit that I needed her," Julie said, wrinkling her nose. "And now that she's got a job and is staying busy, she seems to have settled into her marriage. I haven't heard a Floyd-sex story in ages."

"What a shame," Jake said dryly.

Bing lifted his head and barked, as if in agreement. Jake patted the black dog's head. Seeing the attention, Cherry, the golden Lab, nudged his hand.

Looking fondly at the dogs, Julie said, "I refuse to let you have any say in the naming of our child. Look what you did to our pets."

"I got a few more suggestions from my listeners yesterday," he said.

"I heard. Romeo and Juliet again." She pretended to yawn.

"No. You've got it backward. Romy if it's a girl, Jules if it's a boy."

"Variations on the same theme. No thanks," she stressed, just in case he might be actually listening to this stuff.

"Well, I think Nora and Irving should name their first child Angel."

"Angel St. Cloud. What a lovely idea." Julie pretended to stick her finger down her throat and gag.

Jake laughed, plucked the glass from her hands,

set it on the counter and pulled his loving wife into his arms. Well, as far as his arms would allow since there was a lot of Julie sticking out.

"All right, you can name him or her whatever you want. I love you, Mrs. Danforth."

"And I love you, Mr. Danforth."

Jake suddenly stepped away from her and gazed down at her stomach in wonder. "Somebody just kicked me," he said in delight.

"Uh-huh." She grinned. "If you like that sort of thing, we could head to the guest house and I could try out some new moves on you...."

"You have a twisted mind, Juliet, my dear." He kissed her tenderly.

Julie melted in the warmth of his love. She was so lucky they'd found each other. So lucky. "Have I told you lately that I love you?" she asked. At his nod and mutter, "A few times, yes, but keep saying it," as he nuzzled her neck, she added, "But there's no *T*. It's just Julie. You think you could ever learn that?"

"Not a chance," Jake laughed. Then he stopped the protest forming on her lips with a long, deep kiss that told her how much he loved her.

PLAY

LUCKY HEARTS
GAME

AND YOU GET

FREE BOOKS!
A FREE GIFT!
YOURS TO KEEP!

TURN THE PAGE AND DEAL YOURSELF IN...

Play **LUCKY HEARTS** for this..

exciting FREE gift!
This surprise mystery gift could be yours free

when you play **LUCKY HEARTS!**
...then continue your lucky streak with a sweetheart of a deal!

1. Play Lucky Hearts as instructed on the opposite page.

2. Send back this card and you'll receive 2 brand-new Harlequin Duets™ books. These books have a cover price of $5.99 each in the U.S., and $6.99 each in Canada, but they are yours to keep absolutely free.

3. There's no catch! You're under no obligation to buy anything. We charge nothing— ZERO—for your first shipment. And you don't have to make any minimum number of purchases—not even one!

4. The fact is thousands of readers enjoy receiving their books by mail from the Harlequin Reader Service®. They enjoy the convenience of home delivery...they like getting the best new novels at discount prices, BEFORE they're available in stores...and they love their *Heart to Heart* subscriber newsletter featuring author news, horoscopes, recipes, book reviews and much more!

5. We hope that after receiving your free books you'll want to remain a subscriber. But the choice is yours—to continue or cancel, any time at all! So why not take us up on our invitation, with no risk of any kind. You'll be glad you did!

Visit us online at
www.eHarlequin.com

Not Precisely Pregnant

Holly Jacobs

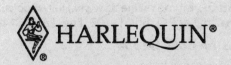

HARLEQUIN®

TORONTO • NEW YORK • LONDON
AMSTERDAM • PARIS • SYDNEY • HAMBURG
STOCKHOLM • ATHENS • TOKYO • MILAN • MADRID
PRAGUE • WARSAW • BUDAPEST • AUCKLAND

Dear Reader,

I've been pregnant four times, but let me tell you, never quite like *Not Precisely Pregnant*'s heroine, Paige Montgomery. We do share the sensation of rushing to the hospital, though. When I was in labor with my youngest daughter, I figured I had hours left to go and sent my older daughters off to basketball practices, telling them I was sure I'd be there when they got back. But shortly after they left, I noticed my contractions, while not precisely painful, were coming fierce and fast. So I called my husband home from work and we went down to the hospital. The faster my contractions came, the faster he drove. I walked up to the maternity ward and…ten minutes later, we had my fourth child, a beautiful baby girl. Talk about fast. (And this particular child hasn't slowed down since.)

But when Paige arrives at the hospital she doesn't get a baby, but a… Well, I refuse to give it away! You'll just have to read and see for yourself. Paige and Riley are two of my favorite characters. People who appear to be polar opposites, but in actuality are simply halves of a whole. I hope you enjoy watching them try to fit those halves together.

Enjoy!

Holly Jacobs

P.S. Please visit me online at www.HollysBooks.com, or snailmail me at P.O. Box 11102, Erie, PA 16514-1102.

Books by Holly Jacobs

HARLEQUIN DUETS
43—I WAXED MY LEGS FOR *THIS*?
67—READY, WILLING AND…ABEL
67—RAISING CAIN
84—HOW TO CATCH A GROOM

For Donald Jacob Fuhrmann, Sr.
A man whose tough act
merely covered a very soft heart.
Don, you are sorely missed.

Special thanks to Lisa Adams, WICU12 News;
Eda Burhenn, R.N., M.S.N, CRNP;
Anna Gehringer, hairstyling goddess

Any mistakes, or embellishments, intentional or not,
are completely the author's.

1

BEWARE OF THE BEACHED WHALE!

That's the warning Paige Montgomery wanted to call out as she jostled her way through the crowded shuttle. Instead, she offered a series of prim and proper "Excuse me's."

The small shuttles moved up and down Peach Street, transporting shoppers from one mall complex to another. They were built for Twiggy types, not for women who were wide as Mack trucks—Paige looked down at her humongous belly—maybe even wider.

"Take my seat," said a boy who couldn't have been out of his teens. Thankfully he was toward the front of the shuttle, saving her the effort of trying to get to an empty seat in the rear.

"Thank you." She smiled at him, sank gratefully into the seat and rubbed her distended belly beneath the thin jacket. Her back ached from lugging the extra weight around.

How on earth did women do this for nine months?

"When's the baby due?" the older woman next to her asked.

"Soon. Very soon," Paige said.

Sooner than this lady could know. At the shuttle's next stop Paige was ready to head back to the studio. She had her footage, thanks to the small hidden camera in her purse. She'd add a brief interview when she got off the shuttle, and she'd be done.

The shuttle slid in front of Wal-Mart and Paige rose with difficulty. There wasn't much to recommend pregnancy, in her opinion. Although she'd only been *pregnant* for the past three hours, enough was enough. She wanted nothing more than to rid herself of this pregnancy belly she'd borrowed from the hospital's birthing program and slip on her jeans.

Nice, tight, formfitting jeans.

She rubbed at the fake belly again as the shuttle reached its next stop and she slowly climbed down the steps. She'd had a nagging pain in her right side all day. Psychosomatic labor pains maybe? Even her subconscious knew it was time to de-pregnate herself.

A sharp jab made her wince. Psychosomatic, she told herself. That had to be it. As soon as she got rid of this humongous belly she'd feel right as rain.

She waddled after the boy, afraid she'd lose him.

"Pardon me," she called.

He turned, saw it was her and, with the concern in his dark brown eyes echoing in his tone, asked, "You okay?"

The look endeared him to her as much as his giving up his seat. "I'm just fine. I wanted to know if you'd consent to be interviewed."

Suddenly concern was replaced by suspicion. "For what?"

"I'm Paige Montgomery, from WMAC news." She lowered her voice. "And I'm not precisely pregnant. I'm doing one of my *About Town* pieces and I'd like to use you. Do you mind if I ask you a few questions?"

"What for?"

"You offered me your seat. It might seem like a small thing, but let me tell you, after hauling this belly around all day, it's bigger than you know."

"It was nothing," he insisted.

"It was kind and I'd like to let people know that there are still people who are kind. So would you mind answering a few questions?"

Continuing to look unsure, he nodded. "Okay, I guess."

She opened her giant purse and took out her camcorder. Most of her reports required a cameraman, but it wasn't always easy to get one when you needed one. The *About Town* segments weren't exactly earth-shattering news, but just brief stories the station was using in its promotion, *WMAC, Where Nice News Matters* campaign. So she'd forgone a cameraman. The fact that they were shot by an obviously less than professional camcorder was part of their charm.

Erie liked to think of itself as a big city with a small-town heart. It was the fourth largest city in Pennsylvania, having just lost its third-place rank to Allentown, much to the entire community's chagrin. But whether it was third or fourth, it still hadn't lost its small-town flavor. It was nothing to walk through the mall and bump into friends or acquaintances. And Paige's job with her *About Town* segments was to capture that small town-ness in the heart of the city.

"What's your name?" she asked the boy.

"Danny."

"Danny, you let me take your seat on the shuttle. Why?"

"'Cause you needed it." His eyes narrowed. "But you didn't really, did you?"

"No, not really. But it was still nice that you did it." Wanting to put him at ease, she switched to some easy questions. "What school do you go to?"

"Mercyhurst Prep…"

She led him through the rest of her questions, only a small portion of which she'd use on the air. She'd spend part of her afternoon editing the piece and probably doing a voice-over for part of it.

"Well, thanks again, Danny," she said. "I'll contact your mom to make sure it's okay to air this story. But I imagine she'll be as proud of you as I am, and she will want the world to know what a fantastic kid you are."

The boy walked into Wal-Mart with a small wave.

Paige was thankful this was his stop. Her car was across the parking lot, near Media Play. Rather than walk along the sidewalk, she took the most direct path diagonally through the parking lot. She just wanted to get home and out of this huge belly.

She pulled the thin jacket tighter around her. It was cold, and getting colder. Last week they'd had a brief taste of Indian summer, and now snow couldn't be far behind. Late October was a little early though, and Paige hoped that the snow held off until at least November—

Another stab of pain hit her and she doubled over with the severity of it. This was no psychosomatic pain. Something was wrong.

The pain ebbed slightly and she unbent herself as much as she could. The pain left her feeling too weak to make it to the car. She was going to die out here in a parking lot, strapped in her pregnancy belly.

Things couldn't get any worse.

"Is there a problem, ma'am?" asked a male voice.

Paige craned her neck upward so she could see the man through the screen of her fake red hair. As she saw the sinfully sexy, dark-haired man peering at her, she knew not only was she going to die, but that things could indeed get worse, because she was going to die at Riley Calhoon's feet.

Another wave of pain made her forget all about everything else, even dying at this man's feet. The only thing she wanted was for the pain to stop.

"I need to get to a hospital," she gasped. Whatever was wrong wasn't going away. It was getting worse. What she wanted to say was *Hi, Riley, long time no see,* but she couldn't spare the energy. Breathing was about all she could manage.

"Don't you worry. I've got my cab right here and we'll get you there pronto. Just don't go having the baby in the back seat." There was more than a little concern in his voice.

He didn't recognize her, she realized. The wig of red hair and the pregnancy belly obviously were a better disguise than she'd imagined. Paige wanted to ask what Riley was doing driving a cab. She wanted to explain she wasn't pregnant, so there was no danger of a baby. But she couldn't make the words come out around the all-consuming pain.

The pain intensified, and she groaned as he helped her into the back seat.

"You just hang on," he said.

Hang on. That was about all Paige could do.

RILEY CALHOON GLANCED at the redhead doubled over with pain in the back of his cab. "You okay?"

She groaned her response.

Stupid question, Calhoon, he thought. Of course she wasn't okay. She was about to have a baby. "Don't you worry. We'll be at the hospital in just a few minutes."

Riley didn't have to be a real cabbie to drive like

one. He wove in and out of the busy Peach Street weekend traffic. Of course the woman had to be shopping as far away from the hospital as she possibly could. There were stores right across the street from it, but shopping there would have made Riley's life far too easy.

And Riley's life was never easy.

"You okay back there?"

She groaned again.

This was just what he needed—some lady having a baby in the back seat of his borrowed taxi. He'd seen enough of those medical re-creations on television to know that having a baby was a messy business. If she gave birth in the cab he'd have to pay to clean the goo up. Chet might be enough of a pal to let him spend a day playing cabbie, but Riley doubted he'd be feeling very friendly when he found the back of his cab trashed with post-baby slime.

"You just hold on, lady. Don't you do anything back there."

She groaned again.

"Can I do anything for you?"

"Hospital, quick," she gasped.

"I'm going quick. Any quicker and we'll both be dead. Did you know that they don't call this Peach Street anymore? No, they call it Peach Jam, especially on the weekends." Traffic was at a standstill, so he laid on the horn a moment. It didn't get the traffic moving, but it made him feel a bit better.

"First, there was the Millcreek Mall," he explained, "and now they've added all these other malls and plazas. No matter how much they expand the street, they just can't keep up with the traffic demands. It's great news for the local economy, but frustrating for the drivers."

Riley—the man known for being stingy with words—was prattling. Riley Calhoon didn't prattle.

Another groan.

Prattling forgotten, he started again, anxious to fill the cab with any sound other than the woman's groaning. "It used to be I could have driven you from up here near the Interstate to Millcreek Community Hospital in five or ten minutes, tops. Now, it's a good fifteen-minute drive on a weekend with all the lights and traffic. But we'll make it, so you just hold on, okay?"

Another groan.

Riley, who liked to think of himself as calm, cool and collected, started to sweat and desperately tried to think of something else to say.

The traffic started moving again, and Riley eased forward, looking for a chance to move to a faster lane. But all there seemed to be was molasses and slower-than-molasses lanes of traffic.

"You're not much of a conversationalist, are you?" He realized what he'd said and wanted to groan himself. "What a dumb thing to say. I don't normally say dumb things. Actually, I don't normally say much. People say I let my pen do the talking, and they're right. I like it that way. I can really think about what I'm going to say and not make a fool of myself like I'm doing now. Not that you'd notice, eh?''

Groan.

''Did you see that green car? Of course you didn't. He just totally cut me off. Here I am, running my four-way flashers and speeding down the road with a lady ready to give birth and he cuts me off. Why am I not surprised?''

Groan.

Talking about cars didn't seem to be helping. Maybe she wanted to talk about babies? ''My boss's wife just had a kid. He claims it's kind of nice, but I don't know. The time I saw it he just cried. I mean, what's so nice about that?''

''Babies are nice,'' she gritted out mid-groan. The exertion left her panting and groaning.

He'd annoyed her. Annoying people was Riley's specialty, but this one time he wished he wasn't so good at it. ''Maybe they are.''

He tried to think of something comforting, and added, ''I'm sure yours will be. But most of the babies I've met haven't been all that great. I mean, they just make a lot of noise, take up all your time, grow up and start taking all your money. Go ahead and have all the kids you want, but I'll pass. Thank you very much.''

He glanced in the rearview mirror. The lady's long red hair had fallen forward, shielding her face, but he didn't need to see her face to know the pain was worse. And if the pain was worse, the baby had to be on its way.

"Hold on. Look, there it is. I can see the hospital. Once we're through this red light we're there. You can hold on that long, can't you?"

"I'll try," she said softly, punctuating the statement with another groan.

"That's my girl. You just go ahead and have that baby in the hospital, not in this cab."

"I'm not—"

"You're not having it in here." He swung on the sidewalk and flew past the cars.

"This is what I get for following an impulse," he said, more to himself than to her. "I should have just left you there in the parking lot. Someone could have called for an ambulance."

Her groaning seemed weaker. Did that mean the kid was almost here? "Don't you have that baby in this taxi, lady. I'm not cleaning up your mess. I'll bill you for the cleaning. That's what I'll do. I'm that kind of a guy. I'd do it. I mean it. So cross your legs if you have to, but don't have that kid in my cab."

She didn't say anything. Didn't even groan. Riley glanced back. She was slumped against the seat.

"Lady?" Silence was her only reply. "Look, I'm pulling into the hospital now. There's the sign for the emergency room. You just hold on one more minute.''

He pulled the cab right up to the door and honked on the horn. He was out of the taxi and opening the back door when an orderly ran out. ''You can't park here.''

''This lady's having a baby, but I think there's something wrong. She's not making any noise anymore. She was making noise, groaning and all, but now she's not. That can't be good can it?''

Gently he slid her out of the back seat and into his arms. She dangled over. He bet she was on the tallish side when she was standing. Even with her enormous purse resting on top of her, the lady still was an awfully light burden for as round as she looked. Weighing so little couldn't be good for her or the baby.

He had an impulse to brush the long red hair off her face and take a good look at the woman he'd just rescued.

What was he doing?

He was wondering how this pain-in-the-butt lady looked, and whether or not she'd put on enough weight, that's what. It was absurd. He didn't care how she looked. And how much she weighed was her worry. He just wanted her gone.

Riley quickly—as if she had a case of childhood cooties—handed her off to the orderly. ''She's all yours now.''

A nurse was coming out of the hospital with a gurney.

That was one burden Riley was glad to be rid of. He slammed the back door and walked around the car to the driver's side.

"Hey, you can't just leave her. You've got papers to sign." The orderly was setting her down onto a gurney as he spoke.

Riley almost yelled at the guy to be careful moving her, but caught himself just in time. "She's not my problem now, she's yours."

He needed to remember that. *This lady wasn't his problem.* He didn't even know why he involved himself in the first place. Someone else would have called an ambulance, or driven her down Peach Street to the hospital. It wasn't as if they were in some isolated place or anything. There was no place in Erie busier than the Peach Street shopping centers and malls.

Riley got into the cab and slammed the door. What had he been thinking, playing the hero for some knocked-up woman who was about to unknock in the back of Chet's cab?

That was some wild hair he'd got up his butt, but it was over now. He wouldn't be doing something that stupid ever again.

He glanced over his shoulder and spotted the orderly and nurse wheeling the lady into the hospital. Having a baby was certainly more painful than he'd ever imagined, not that he spent time imagining what having a baby would be like.

His passenger didn't look up to it. She looked sick. But then, you had to be a little sick to bring a new life into such a crazy world.

It was a good thing he got out of there before anyone found out who he was.

Playing the hero? No. He wasn't the type to rescue a damsel in distress. Distressing a damsel was more his style.

Riley Calhoon cruised down Peach Street and tried to put the pregnant lady out of his head. He proved just how *not* concerned about her he was to himself by hollering expletives at another driver who tried to cut him off.

He felt more like himself when the driver made a hand gesture.

Yeah, whatever that brief lapse in character was, he was over it. Riley Calhoon was back to being himself.

Though later that afternoon he called the hospital; they would only tell him the lady was fine.

Fine?

That didn't tell him anything at all.

As he slunk into a local florist to send the woman some flowers, he wondered just what on earth was wrong with him?

He comforted himself by hassling the salesclerk, insisting on seeing the flowers they were going to send. They'd gone through three different bouquets before he'd settled on the daisies because they were cheap, not because they were the cheeriest of the lot.

And of course the hospital hadn't released the lady's name so he simply addressed it to the emergency room pregnant lady. And he didn't sign the card, so no one would ever know he'd had a second aberration in his character in one day.

Yeah, this was just a small hiccup in his surliness. He was over it now. He wasn't going to waste any more of his time or thoughts on the redhead and her baby. He was back to being himself.

SLOWLY PAIGE CAME BACK to herself in a fuzzy sort of stage where she knew she was Paige Montgomery. Or maybe she only knew because someone kept calling her name as if to remind her. She wished they'd just shut up and let her rest.

The voice became more insistent. "Paige, open your eyes for me."

She wanted to shout *No,* but couldn't seem to find the energy. The voice kept calling her until finally it seemed easier to just give in and open her eyes. The light was blinding, so she squinted. She could make out a very chipper-looking female face.

Awareness brought with it an acute sense of pain. As she looked at the very cheerful, smiling woman, Paige wanted to wipe her chipperness away and—

Even in her foggy state, she cut off the thought. It

wasn't like her. Paige worked hard at keeping all her thoughts positive. Pollyanna Paige, people called her. She liked her nickname. Smacking the chipper lady wasn't positive in the least. Not one bit Pollyannaish. To make up for the surly thought, she tried to concentrate on what Miss Chipper was saying.

"Good. I thought you were about to wake up. That was some scare you gave us."

Not only was the face chipper, the voice attached to it was, as well. Though it grated, Paige forced herself to offer the woman a small smile.

"What happened?" It took all her energy to ask the question. The woman was listening to her heart and held up a finger, indicating she'd answer when she was done.

So Paige tried to dig through her clouded memory and answer her own question. The last thing she remembered was wearing that pregnancy belly and feeling as if she was really going to have a baby.

No, that wasn't right.

There was more.

She remembered a man's voice talking to her. She'd wanted to answer him but couldn't. Then he was yelling at her not to have her baby in his cab. And then he was holding her. Despite the blinding pain, Paige remembered it felt good in his arms.

Suddenly, she remembered more than his voice. She remembered him.

Riley Calhoon.

Riley was her hero?

The pain must have made her hallucinate. Riley was no one's hero. She couldn't decide if she should laugh at the absurd notion, or cry because he wasn't.

The nurse removed the stethoscope. "You're at Millcreek Community Hospital. It was your appendix. The doctor said it was a good thing you got here when you did. If it had burst you might have…well, as it was, you made it here in time and you'll be fine."

Her appendix? That explained the pain. But Paige found she had something more pressing on her mind than a useless organ that was now gone.

"Riley Calhoon, the man who brought me in, is he still here?"

The nurse looked past Paige. Out of the corners of her eyes she could see machines. The woman eyed them then scribbled notes onto a chart.

"The man who brought me?" Paige prompted, surprised at how weak her voice sounded to her own ears.

"I don't know." The nurse stopped her scribbling and really looked at Paige. "I could check for you, if you like."

How had she thought this lady was annoying? It must have been the drugs, and they must be wearing off, because Paige now thought the nurse was very nice.

"Would you mind?" she asked.

"Sure. As soon as someone comes in and relieves me, I'll check." She set down the chart and straightened imaginary wrinkles in Paige's blanket. "Now, you just lie back and rest."

"How long am I going to be in here?"

"At least a few days. You had a close call, you know." She gave the blanket another little tuck.

No one tucked in Paige's blanket anymore. Not since she was little. It was kind of nice. Despite her pain, this time her smile was genuine. "Thank you."

"You're welcome. I'm Stella, by the way. I was on break when they brought you in, and I ran outside with the gurney, so I've been with you since you arrived. I'll be watching out for you. You just call me if you need anything. Here's your bell." She placed the small buzzer in Paige's hand. "You're not to try to get up yourself. The doctor will be in to talk to you soon."

"You'll check on Riley...I mean, the man, right?" she asked.

"I'll check on it first thing."

Paige felt as if the taxi had run over her, but despite her pain, she lay back in bed, her thoughts centered on a certain cabbie with dark hair and a sexy-as-sin scowl. She wondered if he was always as crabby as he'd like everyone to believe, or if beneath that glower there was more than most people suspected.

Already a half dozen questions were spinning in

her mind. What was Riley doing driving a cab? And what was Erie's self-proclaimed biggest cynic doing rescuing a pregnant lady?

He hadn't recognized her. Of that, she was pretty sure. If he had, he'd probably have left her on the street, pregnant or not. He still bore a grudge toward their mishap-ridden past.

The door opened, and instead of the nurse, Aunt Annabelle rushed into the room. "Oh, honey, the hospital called your parents, and since they're so far away, they called me. They're trying to get the first flight out of Florida. The doctor finally said I could come in, but I can only stay a moment. I was so worried."

Aunt Annabelle was a five-foot-nothing mass of energy, and just seeing her made Paige feel better. "I'm sorry I worried you all. I'm all right. Tell Mom and Dad to just stay put. They're settled into their condo for the winter, and there's no reason to come home."

"But it was a close thing, they say."

The nurse came back into the room. "I'm sorry," she said. "The man simply handed you off to the E.R. orderly and left."

"Thank you."

"What man?" Aunt Annabelle asked.

"I brought a shot for the pain." The nurse had Paige's covers pulled back, her thigh exposed and wiped, and had plunged the needle in before Paige could respond.

''What man?'' Aunt Annabelle asked again.

The medication was starting to tug at Paige, take her drifting beyond the pain, but even as she floated in her drug-induced haze, Riley Calhoon's face floated along with her. ''Riley,'' she murmured.

''What about Riley?''

''He's a hero.'' As soon as she was able, Paige intended to let the world know it.

2

"MY HERO!"

Two weeks after his uncharacteristic bout of heroism, Riley had almost put the incident behind him. But that *H* word gave him a terrible feeling in the pit of his stomach, not that anyone could know. He just had to play it cool.

Pasting his annoyed-to-be-interrupted expression on his face, he looked up from his surprisingly good turkey sub and he immediately patted his pocket to make sure he'd brought his antacids. He was pretty sure he was going to need them.

The last time he'd seen this woman he'd needed more than antacids, he'd needed his head examined… literally.

Riley knocked on the pink front door. Pink? Who had a pink front door? Obviously Annabelle's niece, Paige, that's who. And the fact that she did didn't bode well for the rest of the evening. After all, a pink door?

The pink monstrosity opened and Riley's blind date smiled at him. She was about five-six and had short brunette hair, and brown eyes that were almost black. She looked familiar, and it wasn't any resemblance to her aunt. There was something about her....

"You must be Riley. Come on in. I'm so glad to meet you finally. Aunt Annabelle has been trying to get us together for months. But I've been so busy, and obviously you have been as well. She fell in love with you when you did that series on the retirement community and interviewed her, you know. She said if she were fifty years younger she'd date you herself. Since she's not, she figured setting us up on a blind date was the next best thing."

She stopped talking and stared at him expectantly, as if she was waiting for some response, but after that breathless gush of words, Riley wasn't sure how to respond.

"Annabelle's a nice lady," he tried.

Where did he know this woman from? It was going to drive him nuts until he figured it out. He hated puzzles.

She smiled, as if he was a student who'd just passed some test. "Yes. She is nice. Why don't you have a seat."

Now that she was done talking, Riley had a chance to really look at the room. It was chaos. A mishmash of bright, loud colors and...well, stuff was the best way to describe the stacks of books and piles of papers that littered almost every possible surface. He didn't know where he'd manage to find a seat. To be honest he didn't really want to try. He'd promised Annabelle he'd take her niece out, simply because it seemed to mean so much to her. But he planned on making it the quickest date in history.

"We really should go, if you're ready?"

"I'll be ready in a— Oh, watch out!"

As she spoke, it hit him where he knew her from— Paige Montgomery from WMAC. Pollyanna Paige. Gag. Right after that realization, something else hit him...literally this time. It hit him right in the back of the knees. As they buckled, Riley fell to the floor, whacked his head on the coffee table and felt a huge weight on his back.

Something was moving.

"Oh, Cuddles, what did you do?" Paige hollered, and suddenly the weight was removed.

Cautiously Riley rose, rubbing his aching head. He probably had a concussion. Didn't people slip into comas with those?

"I'm so sorry, Riley," Paige said.

He stood slowly, and looked at the mass of disreputable-looking fur in her arms. "What is that?"

"This is Cuddles. I just rescued him last week, and he doesn't have any manners yet. He, uh, tends to attack strangers. The poor FedEx guy was his first casualty. Luckily, Cuddles doesn't have any claws. And given time I'm sure he'll be a well-mannered, nice cat. He just needs a chance."

Cat? The mangy gray-furred beast was smirking at Riley with its one good eye.

"Are you ready to go?" Paige asked.

Resigned to his fate, Riley simply nodded, and immediately regretted it when the tempo of the throbbing in his head sped up.

Riley rubbed his head at the memory of that horrible introduction to Paige Montgomery.

What was *she* doing here now? More important, what was this business about him being a hero?

Paige slid into the chair opposite him, without waiting to be invited, and any hope Riley had of a simple cursory hello vanished.

Resigned to his fate, he asked, "What brings you here today?"

"I thought about calling you and thanking you," she said in the breathlessly fast way of hers, "but I didn't know quite how to say it, so I thought I'd say it in person. I went to your office, but they said you were at lunch, so I asked where, and they said here, and…well, here I am to tell you in person. Thank you. I wish I could have thought of a more eloquent way to say it, but sometimes the less said the better. Short and to the point, that's my motto. And my point is, thank you."

It had been six months since he'd seen Paige—well, except on the news, but that didn't count—and he could easily have gone another six without the pleasure.

"Thank you for what?" he asked cautiously. He'd learned on their one date from hell that being this close to Paige Montgomery was dangerous for not only his sanity, but for his safety.

"For saving my life."

"It's been a long time since our date, and if you've decided that I saved your life by not asking you out a second time, then you're welcome. Actually it was more self-preservation than anything, but maybe in saving myself, I saved us both." As a hopeful afterthought, he added, "Thanks for thanking me though. It was nice seeing you."

She didn't take the hint and leave. He'd strung together that entire breath of words and she was still here. Paige might be the most optimistically happy person he'd ever met, but she wasn't the sharpest marker in the box.

His waitress interrupted them, speaking to Paige, "Can I get you something?"

"Oh, how about a—"

"No," Riley interrupted. "She's not staying."

The waitress shrugged and walked away.

"You were rather rude to her, don't you think?" Paige asked. There was censure in her tone.

Riley shrugged. "No, I wasn't rude to her. Abrupt maybe, but not rude. I *am* about to be rude to you, since my subtle attempt to get you to leave failed. You're not ordering because you're not staying. I prefer eating alone."

"And I'm sure you have plenty of opportunities," Paige said, then took a deep breath. "Sparring with you wasn't why I came today. And I didn't want to thank you for not asking me out a second time. After all, if I had wanted a second date—which I didn't— but if I had, I would have asked you. It's not as if I was waiting by the phone for you to call and ask me. After that first date, a second one would have been tempting fate. I know I'm optimistic by nature—I know people say I live in a Pollyanna world—but even I didn't see the point of going on another date with you."

"If you're not talking about our date, what are you talking about? Not that your explanation is going to clear things up. I didn't learn much on that date, but I did learn that when you're around, people had better beware, and I also learned that you don't make a lot of sense. You know that, don't you?"

"I make plenty of sense. You just don't pay attention. I hollered at you to watch out for Cuddles, but did you listen? No. Just like a man. You think you know everything and would never admit that you don't. But I'll admit it when I need to. I don't know everything about anything, and obviously not everything about you. I underestimated you. There's more to you than a pessimistic reporter. You're a hero. A true-blue, ride-to-the-rescue, white-knight hero. I want an interview with you so I can tell the world about it.

Heroes are rare these days, and deserve all the acclamation we can give them.''

The term *white knight* started acid churning around the part of the turkey sub in his stomach. He should have known that he wouldn't get to enjoy the perfect sub without something, or someone, spoiling it.

Riley opened his pocket, took out his antacids and popped two in his mouth before he said, ''Hero? I don't know what you're talking about.'' And he didn't want to know, but he was sure she'd tell him.

''Yes, you do. You might not drive cabs for a living, but that was one crazy ride to the hospital.''

Of all the things he expected her to say—though he'd learned Paige rarely said what was expected—this wasn't even in the running. He choked more on the fact that she knew about his one small character aberration in the taxi than on the antacid tablet that had lodged itself in the back of his throat.

''How did you find out about that?'' he asked between coughing spasms.

''It was me.''

Mentally he tried to picture the scene when he'd dropped off the pregnant woman at the hospital, but he couldn't remember anyone other than the orderly and a blond nurse when he'd left. ''Where were you? At the hospital doing another one of your crazy, nonnews stories?''

Instead of telling him where she was at the hospital, she asked, "What do you mean, non-news?" Her tone sounded dangerous.

Or at least it would have been dangerous if it had been anyone other than Erie's sweetheart, Pollyanna Paige. Dangerous for her was rather like watching a kitten show its claws, which wasn't intimidating in the least. Not like Cuddles, the killer attack-cat.

As a matter of fact, Paige was sort of cute, all ruffled and riled.

"Paige Montgomery, with WMAC, where nice new matters," he mimicked. "Gross. That's not news. That's saccharine designed to sweeten up and warm the hearts of your viewers, not inform them about what's going on in the world."

"I do inform. And educate. And—"

Suddenly remembering where this conversation had started—and positive he didn't actually think Paige was cute—he interrupted her and said, "You still haven't told me how you found out about the pregnant woman."

"I was the pregnant woman."

"Listen, it doesn't take a reporter to see that you didn't just give birth." No. Paige Montgomery might be a walking health hazard, but she was packaged right. Oh, so very right. Long, lean and—

"I was in disguise. It's part of my *About Town* series. I disguise myself and find random acts of kindness throughout the city. You weren't just kind, you were a hero rescuing me like that. The doctor said if my appendix had ruptured, my prognosis would not have been good. It didn't rupture because you acted promptly, and that saved my life.''

Riley felt his cheeks heat up, almost as if he was blushing. Only he didn't blush. Real men didn't blush. His father had made a point of seeing to it Riley Calhoon was as real as a man came.

The only explanation for the heat in his cheeks was that Paige was simply raising his blood pressure. His blood was being forced into his head, where it was going to back up and cause a blood vessel in his brain to rupture and give him a world-class stroke.

First acid indigestion, now a stroke. And that was just today. If he counted their one and only date, the evidence would show that for someone who had a reputation for being nice, Paige was certainly not very nice to him. She was out to do him in. Her and that horrible beast she called a cat.

She gave him a soft little smile, obviously not the least bit concerned that she was giving him a stroke, and said in a soft, warm, sighy sort of voice, ''You saved my life.''

''I did no such thing.''

''Oh, yes, you did. You know it, I know it, and I want the entire city to know it. That's why I want to interview you. 'Erie's Hero,' I'll call it.''

''You've got to be out of your mind. I'm not doing an interview with you. I didn't save your life.''

''Riley, I might have been out of my mind with

the pain, but I wasn't so out of it I didn't recognize you. You're a hero.''

"Stop saying that. I'm no one's hero and I'm not doing the interview. I don't perform in front of cameras.''

"Erie's tough columnist, Riley Calhoon, has performance anxiety? Maybe you're afraid of freezing in front of the camera? Don't worry, we won't do the interview live. We'll tape it, and I swear if you sound stupid or freeze up, I'll edit that part out. See, no worries!''

"I have never had performance anxiety in my life. I can always perform. You can ask anyone.''

"Well, if you're not afraid, do you mind telling me why you won't do an interview?''

"Because…''

"Because?'' she prompted gently.

"Because I don't want to. And don't think you can just do a report on that *alleged* taxi ride. You can't prove it was me. So if you get on the air and try to tell anyone about it, I'll sue you for slander.''

He'd worked hard to build a name for himself. Tough. Opinionated. Always ready for a fight. Those were terms people associated with Riley Calhoon and his *Get Real* column.

White knight wasn't one of them, and if he had his way, it never would be. Being seen as a hero wouldn't be good for his acerbic, hard-hitting image.

And being a hero to Erie's Pollyanna reporter would just add insult to injury.

No way was he going to let this happen.

"You can't sue me for slander for telling the truth and saying nice things about you."

"Since I'm not nice, saying I am would be slander and I won't take it. I don't want to see a word about this on your news. Do you understand?"

"I won't breathe a word about it without your permission. It might not be station policy, but it's mine. Plus, you did save my life, so I guess I owe you that much. But I am going to do everything I can to change your mind and have you agree to an interview. It would be good for both of us."

"I won't change my mind."

"That's what Donny McMann said in fifth grade when I said I wanted him to be the first boy to kiss me. But within a week he'd changed his mind, and I had my first kiss in the coat closet on a rainy Monday morning. Of course, I had to pay him a dollar, but it was worth it."

"You had to pay a boy to kiss you?" Riley asked, despite himself. He wished he could suck the question back in because he was sure she'd feel as if she had to answer. And he wasn't disappointed.

Paige smiled, seemingly lost in the past, and said, "Well, Donny was the cutest boy in the whole fifth grade, and could have kissed any of the girls. So it was money well spent. Not that I have to pay for kisses now. I mean, it's not that I do all that much kissing, but what I do is free and easy. Not that I'm free and easy. That's not what I mean, I—"

"Paige, thank you for the history lesson, but it doesn't alter the fact that I'm not changing my mind. I'm no hero. I didn't save your life, and I'm not doing the interview."

"Okay." Paige rose and Riley breathed a sigh of relief, glad she was leaving before any disaster could strike. She took two steps and turned. "Oh, and Riley, I wanted to thank you for the daisies. They're my favorite flowers, you know."

"I didn't send—"

She cut him off. "Okay, you didn't send them. But thanks anyway." She turned back and almost tripped over a waiter, but skittered out of the way before they actually connected.

She laughed and said, "Look. We've had our second date and no one got injured. Maybe we broke our bad-luck streak?"

She gave another wave and left the deli.

Broke their bad-luck streak?

Somehow Riley didn't believe that. Just like he didn't believe he'd seen the last of Paige. She'd given up almost too easily.

He looked at the sub that had tasted so good before Paige, the walking disaster, had sat at his table.

Hero?

He was no one's hero. He was a hard-bitten, cynical newspaper columnist.

"Is something wrong with your sub?" the waitress asked.

"I've lost my taste for it."

"If there's something wrong with it, I can take it back and get you another one."

"Yes, there's something wrong."

The waitress just stood, waiting expectantly, a worried expression on her face.

Riley sighed. It wasn't her fault. "There was nothing wrong with the food or the service. I..." He paused and the waitress waited, expectantly. "I have to go."

"But you only took a couple bites. Do you want me to wrap it up for you?"

"If I wanted you to, I'd ask. But I don't. I'm done."

"I'll get your check," she said. It wasn't what she'd said but the look in her eyes that made Riley feel like a heel. He'd been abrupt with her when Paige was here, and now he'd been even more abrupt.

He slid a hefty tip under his plate. It wasn't that he felt guilty for his curtness—he lived to make people annoyed—it was just that making ends meet on a waitress's salary must be tough.

He took the bill from her and paid it at the register.

He wouldn't have admitted it to anyone, but he

was nervous because he was pretty sure he hadn't seen the last of Paige Montgomery. She had hinted as much.

What did she have up her sleeve?

THE NEXT AFTERNOON, Paige tugged at her sleeve as she scanned the crowd. Her cameraman, Kip, was setting up in the corner and all she had to do was wait. She generally hated covering *news* stories and preferred to stay with human-interest stories. But she wasn't here for just the press conference.

No. She had bigger fish to fry.

And speaking of fish, there he was. Like a large trout waiting to gobble up her bait.

She angled over his way.

He was arguing in hushed tones with the man next to him. "...and it doesn't take an accountant to see the benefits to the public."

With a throw of his hands, the man said, "There's no arguing with you, Calhoon," and stalked away.

Paige felt a spurt of sympathy for the stranger. She didn't even need to know what they were talking about to know that Riley had annoyed the man. Not that that was unusual. Riley annoyed everyone.

"Psst," she said from behind him.

He turned. "Oh, it's you."

"Yes. Glad to see you, too. Just wanted to check and see if you'd changed your mind about that interview."

"No," he flatly responded.

The mayor's assistant came to the microphone. "I'd like to welcome everyone here today…"

Since the assistant wasn't the story, she continued in a hushed whisper, "That was an awful quick answer there, Calhoon. Are you sure you don't want to think about doing the interview? It could be great promotion for your paper and for your column."

"There's nothing to think about. No." He paused a moment and then added in an equally quiet voice, "And what are you doing here?"

"Covering the mayor's press conference."

"Why? I thought you only covered the *nice news?*"

"Well, the mayor is nice, and rumor has it his news is as well, so here I am."

Paige didn't tell him that she'd begged Stephanie, her assignment editor, for the story. Or that Steph had been as surprised by her request as Riley obviously was. The look he shot her said he wasn't buying her story. But that didn't matter. What mattered was that he would decide to do the interview.

She wasn't sure why it was so important to her that she tell the world there was more to Riley Calhoon than his columns indicated, that beneath the cynic, there beat the heart of a hero. Annoying, maybe. But a hero.

"It's a free country, Calhoon. I can cover any story I want."

"You know, I haven't seen you in six months, and suddenly I see you twice in two days? That's a bit of a coincidence, isn't it?"

"Is it?" she asked sweetly.

"You're not following me in some misguided hope I'll change my mind, are you? Because I won't."

"...and here's Mayor Aggers," the mayoral assistant said.

Riley pulled out his notebook and pen, poised to take notes about the press conference.

Paige stayed where she was. The cameraman would film the announcement, and then film her doing a little sound bite when it was finished. She'd spend her afternoon editing the piece.

"Well," Paige said, "in order to change your mind you'd have to have one, so let's just say I'm not overly hopeful, but I am persistent."

Riley stopped fiddling with his notebook and shot her a stern look. "That wasn't a very Pollyanna-ish comment. I thought you lived in Polly World, a place where rose-colored hues were the only colors permitted. That crack about my being brainless wasn't very rosy. You made a crack at lunch yesterday, too. What would your viewers say if they knew you weren't as sweet as they thought?"

"Let's just say that you bring out the worst in me. Even my rose-colored, Polly World view of things dims when you're around. And if my viewers knew you, they'd understand completely," she said with a small smile.

"I bring out the worst in everyone, but I thought not even I could change your view."

"Oh, you haven't. It's only my view of you that's not so rosy."

"I thought you said I was a hero," he said.

"You are. But you're stubborn, opinionated and annoying, too. And wrong."

"...and it's time to address what's wrong with downtown..." the mayor said.

"Wrong?" Riley whispered to Paige.

"This interview would be good for you," she pressed quietly, "good for your career."

"I make my living as a columnist and reporter. How could being seen as a—" He stopped short and frowned, as if whatever he'd been about to say left a bad taste in his mouth.

"White knight...hero?" Paige filled in the words Riley was obviously hesitant to use.

"Neither. I'm not either. That's my point. Your saying I am wouldn't be good for anything but a laugh. Though I'm afraid the laugh would be at my expense, so I pass," he hissed.

"...and I think you'll all agree that this project is worth the expense and will forward our efforts to revitalize the downtown area. I'll take questions now."

Riley stared at the podium. "Questions?" He

turned to Paige. "It's over? How can the mayor be done speaking? I missed it because of your incessant chatter. You did that on purpose. You distracted me so that I missed what he said, and now I can't even ask a question."

"The mayor said that the city is going to receive that big state grant for revitalizing Parade Street. They plan on bringing it back to its old glory."

Riley scribbled notes and then looked up at her. "How do you know? You were busy arguing with me."

"I don't argue. You argue. I'm just sort of the wall you toss your shots at. They tend to bounce back at you without my even trying. That's not arguing, that's volleying. And I heard what he said because I'm a woman. We multitask. It all comes from being genetically programmed as the foragers and gatherers. We're forced to concentrate on many things at once. Men are genetically predisposed to be the hunters. They concentrate on one thing and blot out everything else. I'm flattered you chose to focus on me and not the mayor."

"I didn't choose that," he said quickly. Maybe too quickly.

Maybe she was getting to him? The thought made Paige grin. "Of course you chose to, or else you would have heard the mayor's announcement. And you're still so focused on me that you missed Marcy, from WJTC, ask how the money was going to be allotted, and the mayor saying he was forming a committee, and then Martin, from your paper, asking if the mayor really thought we needed another committee.''

Riley again scribbled wildly, then glared at Paige. ''You think you've proved something?''

''I think I just stopped by to see if you'd changed your mind, and you started fighting, which is what you do best. And can I ask why you're here if Martin is covering this for your paper?''

''I'm not writing the article, I'm writing a commentary in my column and wanted to hear the speech myself.''

''But you didn't hear it, did you?'' she asked as sweetly as she could.

''Because of you.''

''Hey, don't blame me. Now that you've given me your answer, I'll just go catch up with my cameraman and get some footage of me here, then head back to the studio to edit the piece. Great seeing you, Riley. I'm sure I'll be seeing you again soon.''

''It's no use,'' he said. ''I won't do the interview.''

''Okay,'' she said, shrugging her shoulders. ''Whatever you say.''

Paige raised her hand. Mayor Aggers pointed in her direction. ''Paige?''

Riley glared in her direction, which for some perverse reason, made Paige want to smile. But as she

was noticing Riley's annoyance, she was already for-
mulating a question for the mayor.

Chalk another one up for multitasking females.

"Assuming this economic windfall does breathe
new life into Parade Street, what sort of impact do
you see it having on the downtown district?"

"I think innovative ideas like the Parade Street
project, or the new conference center and the rebirth
of the Boston Store, are what the downtown…"

"YOU HAVE AN INNOVATIVE IDEA? You mean, more
innovative than traipsing around town in your disguises?" Stephanie asked Paige that same afternoon.

Stephanie Cooper had been assignment editor at
WMAC for almost a year now. She'd joined the staff
just after Paul Hartly, the news director, had. It had
been their combined effort that changed the direction
yof the station's news programs. Oh, they presented
the headlines, both local and national, but the station
really worked to present a show that appealed to
women.

The new, gentler news had pushed the station's
ratings up three points all ready. Steph's willingness
to let her staff have freedom in their reports had
made her a popular boss.

Paige was counting on that freedom to pursue this
new series.

She leaned forward in her seat and propped her
arms on Steph's desk. "Well, maybe not as inno-

vative as my disguises. But new. I want to do a weeklong series on heroes. If it goes well, I thought we could make it a weekly segment.''

Steph tilted back in her chair. ''This is about Riley Calhoon, isn't it?''

''No,'' Paige denied, and then felt a stab of guilt because that was a lie.

It was about Riley. She wasn't sure why doing this interview was so important to her. Maybe it was just gratitude? Letting the world know that he was a hero was a great way to thank him for saving her life. But that explanation didn't ring quite true and she didn't feel inclined to delve for a deeper reason.

''I thought Riley said if you told about this incident, he'd sue,'' Stephanie pointed out.

''I won't say his name. Not even once.'' Paige made a little cross-your-heart gesture. ''I won't even mention him obliquely, like 'the cabbie who saved my life.' No, I won't mention him at all.''

''And you're sure that this has nothing to do with the fact he dated and dumped you all in one evening?''

''He didn't dump me. I have no idea where that nasty rumor got started. In actuality, I realized that we were a horrible match and have never figured out why my Aunt Annabelle thought we'd get along. He sees the glass as half-empty and—''

''And our resident Pollyanna Paige sees it as half-full,'' Stephanie finished for her with a small chuckle.

''Right. And even someone as optimistic as I am couldn't see any point in going out with Riley Calhoon again. End of story. And speaking of stories, I'm almost insulted that you would think I'd use my job—a job I take tremendous pride in—to get even with a man you think dumped me.''

Stephanie massaged her temples and Paige felt a momentary stab of sympathy for her boss.

''Do you want some aspirin?'' she asked.

''No. I'm fine. And you don't have time to play my nurse. You have some fieldwork to do for our 'Erie's Heroes' pieces.''

''Thanks, Steph. You won't regret your decision.'' Rather than sprinting from Stephanie's office, Paige opened her huge purse and dug around for a moment. She set a bottle of aspirin on the desk.

''Indulge me, take something for that headache,'' she said before she left.

She was grinning like some crazed lunatic by the time she was a few steps down the hall.

Riley accused her of not reporting real news? Well, his rescue was real, at least to her. And Paige was about to show him what a real reporter she was. She was going to do this series on heroes, and eventually she'd do Riley's story.

And like any good reporter, she was going to begin with some research, and Paige had the perfect source.

3

─────────

ANNABELLE MYERS WAS the undisputed queen of the retirement community, at least in her mind. Actually, Paige's great-aunt thought she was pretty much the queen wherever she went, and acted accordingly. Maybe it came from being one of the first female news anchors in Erie. Or maybe that type of confidence was simply bred within her. Either way, the small gray-haired woman was center stage wherever she was.

It was Aunt Annabelle who had inspired Paige to pursue a career in journalism.

Paige found her dealing cards in the west solarium the next day. Her smile lit up the room as Paige walked in.

"Aunt Annabelle. Ladies," Paige said by way of a greeting to the entire group.

"Okay, everyone, get. Take your chips, and we'll finish the poker game tonight. And Ruth," Aunt Annabelle said to the woman seated next to her, "don't you dare add your personal chips to that pile. I know, chip for chip, what you've won in this game."

''Annabelle,'' the elderly woman gasped, ''you know I'd never—''

''Not if you think you'll be caught you wouldn't cheat. So I'm just letting you know you'll be caught.''

Ruth and three other women gathered up their chips and walked away, Ruth still muttering about her innocence.

''She cheats terribly,'' Annabelle said. ''And you know what I always say?''

Paige kissed her aunt's wrinkled cheek and took the seat the poor wanna-be-cheater Ruth had just vacated. ''You always say, if you're going to cheat, don't get caught.''

''And she's terrible enough at it to get caught every time. No sense of imagination there. Now, when I cheat, no one is ever the wiser. But I don't think you're here to talk about cards, or cheating.''

Annabelle studied Paige a minute and said, ''Okay, spit it out. You look like you're ready to burst. So what did you do now?''

Paige tried to look innocent. ''I don't know what you mean.''

''Pshaw. Don't try lying to me, girl. I can see it in your eyes. Those dark brown eyes don't hide a thing, you know. You did something you're so proud of that you're dying to tell. You know you want to, and you know I won't stop pestering until you do, so you might as well tell me now and save us the hassle of my whining. Although you know I'm good at whining, and it's important to use our talents—that's one of the things they stress here, use it or lose it—so maybe I'll just whine for a few minutes on the principle of the thing."

Annabelle's pitch climbed a couple octaves, and there was a tiny tremble in her voice for effect as she said, "Please, Paige, tell your old auntie what you did."

"Old auntie my—"

Annabelle interrupted with a chuckle, "Don't be vulgar, girl. You wouldn't want to offend my delicate ears."

Paige couldn't resist joining her laughter. "There's not a delicate bone in your body, and I'm sure your ears are no exception."

Annabelle assumed an injured expression, though Paige knew her aunt well enough to know that she'd consider Paige's non-delicate comment a compliment.

"Now, you're insulting me," Annabelle said. "Keeping secrets is just adding insult to injury, and you know I—"

"Okay, okay, your whining wins." Paige knew when she was beaten. Truth be told, she'd never wanted to win—she needed Annabelle's help. She'd merely kept up the fight for appearances. "I got Steph to agree to let me do a weeklong series on Erie's heroes."

Annabelle's eyes widened. "And you got Riley to agree to an interview?"

"No." Paige shook her head. "Though I haven't given up trying."

"You're not going to air the story without his permission, are you? I mean, I know things didn't work out between the two of you the way I'd hoped, though I don't think either of you gave it much of a chance. Anyone can have a bad date—"

Paige corrected her, "The worst date in the history of dating."

Annabelle continued, ignoring Paige's comments, "—bad date, but that's no reason to betray your journalistic integrity. In forty years of working in the news game, I never betrayed a confidence. And Riley asked you not to—"

"It's okay, Aunt Annabelle. I'm not going to mention his name, not even obliquely. You and Steph are the only two people I've told about his rescuing me, and both of you are sworn to silence, so there's no worry about the news leaking out. And you can bet when I talk about Riley's heroism on the air, it will be with his permission."

Paige picked up the cards and started absentmindedly shuffling them. "I did my first story this afternoon for 'Erie's Heroes.' A police officer who talks to school kids about peer pressure and drugs. There was nothing about cabbies saving quasi-pregnant women."

"But you're doing the series to egg him on, aren't you?" Annabelle asked with a knowing smile.

Paige stopped mid-shuffle. "I can't believe you'd think I was that unprofessional. I would never use my position to torment someone, not even Riley Calhoon—though if ever a man deserved a little tormenting, it's him. He's annoying, opinionated—and those opinions are generally wrong—and...I never did figure out why you set us up."

"I like him. I like you. I thought you'd be good for each other. I still do."

"How can you say that, especially after that date from hell? I mean, I've had bad dates before, but that was beyond my worst nightmare. I should have known when Cuddles attacked him that the evening was going to be a disaster. This was one instance when I should have forgotten about being optimistic and just bowed to the inevitable."

"Well, you gave it a try. And speaking of being optimistic, just what have you been up to with this interview business?"

Suddenly remembering the cards in her hands, Paige started shuffling again. She looked at them instead of her aunt. "Well, that's where you come in. I need to know everything you know about Riley Calhoon."

"You swore me to secrecy about his role in saving you. I haven't even told him I know, though I'd like to thank him. But I know how to keep a secret. Do you think I'd betray his confidence?''

Paige looked up and met Annabelle's piercing look. "Of course not. But unless he said 'This is off the record,' you have to assume whatever he told you is fair game.''

"Paige, I'm ashamed of you.'' Annabelle grabbed the deck of cards from her and started to set them down with a thump. "Thinking that you can manipulate an old woman into dishing the dirt on a man who has been nothing but kind to her. Tsk, tsk, tsk. Why, just last week he came in with Zac and brought me Greek burgers, and you know how much I love Greek burgers.''

"Zac?'' Paige asked.

"His Little Brother. Oh, not little brother, as in his sibling, but Little Brother, as in part of that Big Brothers program. The boy's about twelve and has been with Riley for, oh, what did he say? Maybe two years. He—''

Annabelle didn't get to finish her sentence. Paige was on her feet kissing her aunt's forehead. "Thanks, Aunt Annabelle. You've been a big help. I've got to go, but I'll stop by again soon.''

"Where are you going?''

"To do some research on my next installment of Erie's Heroes. The Big Brothers program here in Erie,'' Paige called as she sprinted from the room.

"Oh, you're a sly one, getting me to help you even

though I swore I wouldn't,'' Annabelle called after her. ''And I'll…''

Paige was out of hearing range before Annabelle finished her threat, but she really wasn't worried about Aunt Annabelle's revenge. She was too caught up in digesting this newest fact about Riley.

He was a Big Brother? That certainly didn't fit the image she had of him.

If asked right after their horrendous date she'd have simply described him as tough, cynical and abrasive. Now? Well, in all fairness, she'd have to add heroic. And how would you describe someone who donated time to a cause like the Big Brothers program? Kind? Maybe.

Heroic and kind.

No, that's not what she'd thought when she'd first met Riley.

THE NEXT DAY Paige entered the Erie Civic Center just as they started to play the national anthem. She stopped and placed her hand over her heart, though she didn't try to sing along. The notes in the song weren't meant for mere mortals to hit.

She scanned the crowd and couldn't help feeling a bit smug. He was out there somewhere.

Not a real reporter?

Ha!

She not only had a great story on the Big Brothers program here in Erie, she'd found out that the group had sponsored a hockey night tonight. And she knew the group was seated down below her, as close as they could get to the ice.

She scanned the back of a sea of heads, confident she could identify Riley, even from behind.

There he was. She spotted him right next to a boy, on the end of the first row. They were practically sitting on the ice. That was great.

Trying to seem nonchalant, she started with the first pair she saw. Camcorder in hand, she said, "Hi, I'm Paige Montgomery with WMAC. And I'm here this evening interviewing some of the adults who volunteer with the Big Brothers program. Would you mind answering a few questions?"

The very nice-looking gentleman agreed, but even as she chatted with him, Paige kept an eye on Riley. Because she was behind him, he hadn't spotted her. He was engrossed in something the boy was saying.

The man she was interviewing wound down. She thanked him and decided to forget about subtlety—she couldn't wait any longer. Her excitement didn't have anything to do with seeing Riley. No, she was excited merely because she'd bested him.

She made her way down toward Riley, her heart beating a rapid rhythm.

"Riley Calhoon," she said in a voice filled with blatantly fake surprise. "Imagine seeing you here to-night."

Riley kept a smile pasted on his face, but she could

see the annoyance in his eyes as he said, "Paige Montgomery. What brings you out?"

"Why, I'm doing a story on the Big Brothers program and thought tonight's event was the perfect way to speak to some of the adults who volunteer their time to the program. And since you're sitting in this section, why you must be one of them. And this is…?" She knelt so that she was eye level with the boy sporting a blond crew cut and a smudge of something on his cheek.

"I'm Zac."

"Hi, Zac. I'm Paige. I—"

"I know who you are," the boy said excitedly. "Mom watches you every night. You and Rosie O'Donnell are her two favorite TV people. She says you're both nice. And after a long day at work she doesn't have time for doom and gloom. She just wants nice."

"Well, you tell your mother I said thank-you. That's a huge compliment," Paige said.

The boy paused a moment, then hesitantly asked, "Do you think you'd give me your autograph for her?"

"Sure thing. What's your mother's name?"

He held out his program. "Phylis. With just one *l*. She says her mother wasn't much of a speller, because most of the time Phylis has two *l*'s, but hers is just one, so she has to tell everyone. So it's Phylis with just one *l*."

Paige dug into her bag for a pen, then signed the program with a flourish. "Phylis, with just one *l*." She looked past the boy to Riley and asked, "Now, about that interview?"

"No. I told you, I keep telling you, I'm not doing it. And stalking me isn't going to change my mind."

"Not that one—though you'll change your mind eventually—but just a few words about why you're a Big Brother and a question or two for Zac about what the program's done for him."

She held up her camera. "I brought my trusty camcorder so I can capture it all for posterity and for the evening news. So how about? A few words about Big Brothers?"

"No."

Zac looked up at Riley and said, "You mean I can't be on the news? My mom would think it was totally rad if I was talking to Ms. Montgomery on the television."

Paige was all for needling Riley Calhoon, but upsetting a little boy wasn't in her plans. "Riley, if you won't agree to talk to me, even about a program as great as Big Brothers, then how about I just talk to Zac?" She sent him a pleading look, then smiled at the boy. "I'd have to clear it with your mom before I put you on the air, but I think she'd be proud to see you on the news."

"Could I, Riley?" Zac asked.

Riley's expression said that letting Zac talk to

Paige was the last thing he wanted to do, but as he looked at the boy his expression softened and Paige knew he was going to agree.

She added another Riley fact to her growing list…he was a pushover for kids, at least for this kid.

"Just don't say my name," he warned. "I want to remain anonymous. I do this because I want to, because you and I are buddies. I don't do it because I want everyone to know."

Paige turned on her camera and focused on the boy. But not before she caught a quick glimpse of Riley from behind the lens. She'd keep her promise and edit it out before she put the piece on the air. But she lingered half a second, hoping that looking at him through a lens might give her some perspective, offer some new insight.

Nothing. He was still dark-haired, dark-view-of-the-world Riley Calhoon, a mass of contradictions. Cantankerous. Stubborn. Cynical. Heroic. Kind. A pushover.

She purposely focused on Zac. Figuring out the complexities of someone like Riley Calhoon would have to wait for another time.

The boy chattered happily about things he'd done with Riley. There'd been season tickets to the Erie Sea Wolves baseball team, trips to the beach and to see the Monster Trucks and…

"He's even taking me to see some musical next week. Riley says a man should know more about the world than sports. He said he never had a little brother of his own, and asked me if I'd mind helping him out and…''

The boy was a font of information, but eventually he stopped.

''Thanks, Zac.''

''Paige, do you mind if I talk to you a minute?'' Riley's voice was tight as he stood.

She shut off the camcorder, surprised Riley had let Zac run on for as long as he had. ''Sure thing. Would you mind holding this a minute, Zac?'' She handed the camera to the boy before Riley practically dragged her into the aisle. They stood in the small walkway where the stairs ended at the ice.

''This has got to stop,'' Riley said.

''I don't know what you mean.''

''Do you honestly believe that I don't know you're following me?''

''You know, I discovered your overinflated ego on our date, and I see that the past six months haven't done a thing to deflate it. My world does not revolve around you, Calhoon.''

''No? You could have fooled me. Thursday you ruin a surprisingly good turkey sub and give me acid indigestion. Friday you're covering the mayor's press conference—not your normal kind of story—and set out to try to keep me from hearing what was said. And now, on Sunday, you're at a hockey game. I don't think spending an afternoon with the Erie Otters is part of your normal schedule, is it?''

''Coincidence. Other than that first day, it's just

coincidence. I'm here for a segment of 'Erie's He-roes' and—''

"Aha, you admit you're still following that absurd hero angle.''

"Yes. I'm just not following you." It was a blatant lie, so she crossed her fingers behind her back to salve her conscience. "I'll admit you gave me the idea, but since you're not interested, I'm following other stories. Like I said, you've got an overinflated eee—Riley, watch out!'' Paige cried even as she ducked.

He had his back to the rink and didn't even see it coming. She ducked and pulled him down to safety with her. She heard the *thwack* of a hockey puck contacting with the back of a chair even as he was falling toward her...no, not just toward her—on her.

His head knocked against hers and Paige found herself sandwiched between Riley and the floor. "Ri-ley? Are you okay?''

"Hey, I got the puck!'' Zac cried.

"And there's another fan with a lucky puck! Bring the puck to the Fan Assistance Center and claim your prize!'' the voice on the loudspeaker announced.

"Riley?'' she asked.

He moved slowly and sat upright.

"Hey, cool, can I take the puck up?'' Zac asked.

Riley swayed back and forth as he got to his feet. "Sure. Go see what they give to spectators they maim.''

As soon as Zac was out of earshot, he said, "You are trying to kill me."

"What?" Paige asked. He might have said, *Thank you, Paige, for trying to save me,* or, *Thank you for cushioning my fall.* She was definitely going to have a few bruises from having him land on her. Instead, he was blaming her for getting his fat head out of the way of a hockey puck? "This is my fault?"

He gave a half nod, then winced, obviously thought better of it and settled for simply glaring at her as he said, "First that date…you almost did me in on three separate occasions that night. And then the heartburn, and the stroke—"

"What stroke?"

Riley didn't answer, but talked right over her question. "And now this. I'm sure its a concussion. And actually if you count the concussion your cat gave me on our date, then this is the second concussion you're responsible for."

"Maybe Cuddles was my fault. I should have controlled him. But if you think you're going to blame me for saving you from a hockey puck, well, I take offense."

"If I hadn't been talking to you—"

"Yelling at me," she corrected.

"You're here, causing me grief again. You're a dangerous woman. Everyone says you're sweet, but you're not really. You're out to do me in."

"Oh, I'd like to do you in, all right."

"There you go again, saying those un-Pollyanna-ish things. Polly World isn't all it's cracked up to be, is it?''

"Not when you're around. You can dim even the rosiest view of the world."

"You know," he said, "everyone might think you're sweet, but I know the truth. You just pretend to be sweet. I, on the other hand, am honest about my non-sweetness. I want you to stay away from me."

"Fine," Paige said as she climbed to her feet. "I'll stay away—as far away as I can. I might be a health hazard for you, but you're starting to affect my sunny disposition. Around you I feel…well, as sour-natured as you are."

With that, Paige grabbed her camera from Zac's vacant seat and walked, head held high, up the stairs, out of the civic center and out of Riley Calhoon's life.

RILEY HAD DROPPED OFF a very excited Zac after the hockey game. It turned out that the team gave away autographed hockey sticks to their maimed spectators. The boy was bubbling over winning one, and about being on the news. Riley wasn't sure how his mother was ever going to settle Zac down for the night.

But Zac wasn't his worry. Actually, now that he'd gotten rid of Paige, he had no worries at all. And he was thrilled at the thought.

Totally thrilled.

Yet, there was some other feeling there when he thought about not seeing Paige anymore. Something other than being thrilled. Something...

No. Thrilled. That was all he was feeling.

He rubbed his head and flicked on the television, using the remote to mindlessly scan through the channels as he thought about Paige.

Riley was glad to have seen the last of her.

Even as he had the thought, he saw her face on the screen. Of course, he didn't mean to end up on WMAC just in time for the late-night news. It was a total accident.

It was an accident that had happened over and over again the past six months.

He knew the station tended to run her spots on all three newscasts unless they were bumped by some big late-breaking news.

"This is Paige Montgomery, and I'm here with Adam Bartlett. Adam, why don't you tell me what happened."

The boy launched into a story about saving a dog that couldn't swim, from the small pond near his farm.

"I think Hercules here was lucky to have a hero like Adam Bartlett around. Life is full of heroes. Sometimes they do big things that everyone notices, and sometimes, like Adam, they perform a small heroic gesture that should be noticed. This is Paige Montgomery with *WMAC, Where Nice News Mat-*

ters, and 'Erie's Heroes' get the notice they deserve.''

Okay, maybe Paige was better than he thought, Riley mused. She'd taken his talk of a lawsuit to heart and hadn't used his name. Hadn't even mentioned the cab. Though she'd given him another little jab on the air, clearly hoping to make him as miserable as she must feel about not getting her interview. Well, she deserved to be miserable about not interviewing him. It was only fair. She'd made his life miserable all week.

Maybe it wasn't enough that she'd simply lost the interview, though. Maybe she deserved a lesson on how it felt to be stalked. Maybe he was the one to teach it to her.

After all, how would she feel about having someone dog her every step? He doubted she'd like it.

He could follow her around for a change. Turn it into a column. ''A Day in the Life of the Terminally Optimistic,'' or ''Peeving Polly,'' or something along those lines...something guaranteed to annoy her and cause those rose-colored glasses to teeter.

A lesson.

He'd teach Paige a lesson, and get a column out of it.

Yeah, tailing Paige. It was a good idea.

And it was all about revenge, and didn't have a thing to do with not liking the idea of not seeing her.

Not a thing at all.

4

―――――

"SHE'S A MENACE, that's what she is," Riley muttered as he tossed a queen of hearts on the discard pile.

Annabelle eyed the pile of cards. "I'd ask who, but I know who. You two seem to be at odds."

"Odd is the word. Your niece is odd."

Annabelle scooped up the queen and laid out an ace, king, queen and jack of hearts, then discarded an ace of spades. She gave a happy little cackle. "I believe I'm out, which means I won this hand. Do the math, boy."

"I think you cheat," Riley said. He didn't just think it, he was almost positive.

It was one of the things he liked about the older woman.

"First you insult my beloved great-niece, then you insult me by calling me a cheat. Riley, you've always had an abrasive personality, but it's getting worse by the minute. Why, just last week you scared poor Bertha."

"She was talking to you as if you were a child, not a responsible adult."

"It's just her way. She's very kindhearted. You just take offense much too quickly."

He refused to discuss Bertha any further. When she'd come in and started asking Annabelle how "we" felt today, he'd simply seen red. Annabelle might be slowing down physically, but she was sharp as a tack, and could think circles around the Berthas of this world any day of the week.

Instead of commenting, he slid the tablet toward her and Annabelle glanced at his figures.

"Only fifty-three more points and I've won the match," she said gleefully. She scooped up the cards and shuffled them.

Riley watched her carefully, trying to see if she was stacking the deck. Though he couldn't catch her, and wouldn't be able to prove it in a court of law, it was a pretty sure thing that she was.

She dealt out seven cards apiece. "Play."

Riley picked up his hand and studied it carefully before drawing a card from the pile and discarding a seven of spades.

"You're a sweet lady until you get cards in your hand, and then you're a barracuda," he grumbled.

Annabelle looked as pleased as if he had told her she'd just won the lottery. "Barracuda. I like that almost as much as I like to win. You know, Paige likes to win, too, though she's much nicer about it than I am."

Annabelle drew from the pile and then discarded a nine of spades.

Riley took the nine and laid down a nine, ten, jack of spades set. He discarded an ace of hearts. "I don't know that Paige is nicer. She was at the mayor's news conference and distracted me on purpose."

Annabelle picked up Riley's ace. "Oh, you find Paige distracting, do you? Maybe fixing you two up was a better idea than either of you thought."

"Not distracting in the way you mean. She sidetracked me on purpose. I mean, she kept yammering at me, until I missed most of what the mayor was saying. And then she almost got me hit by a hockey puck. She's distracting in the worst way."

"Rummy!" Annabelle cried, laying her entire hand on the table. "I'm playing the queen and king on your set. And I have the ace, two and three of hearts. I'll just discard this little four of diamonds and I think that puts me over the top, and I won the match and game."

Riley did the math and gave her a little nod. "You're right. You won."

"Paige was correct, distracting you is an effective tool." She studied Riley a moment, and then said, "But that technique only works on men. A game of cards isn't going to make me ignore the fact that you want something. What is it?"

"You don't think it's possible I just wanted to play a game of five-hundred rummy with you?"

"No."

It was time to lay his cards on the table, figuratively this time. He got straight to the point. "I want some information about Paige."

Annabelle gave him a stern look. "I'll tell you what I told her—I'm not getting in the middle of whatever it is you two are doing."

"She's stalking me." He didn't mention that he hadn't seen hide nor hair of Paige for two whole days. He didn't really expect to see her today. But it didn't keep him from constantly looking over his shoulder. And maybe, just maybe, he was a little disappointed.

He'd watched the news that night and seen her segment on the Big Brothers program. There was a long clip of Zac, talking about all the things they'd done together. And there was no mention of Riley at all.

He'd called and talked to the boy. Zac was beyond excited to have been on television, and couldn't stop talking about Phylis's delight.

Riley had worked on Monday, fully expecting to bump into Paige at any given moment all day. But he hadn't seen her. Obviously, she'd meant what she'd said. She was giving up on the interview idea.

He couldn't believe she'd admitted defeat so easily.

That night there was no segment on heroes, just

Paige interviewing a local woman about Erie's Warner Theater's new renovation and extension plans.

Paige Montgomery was out of his hair.

Riley was relieved to be rid of her. But there was still the little matter of teaching her a lesson.

Of course, he wouldn't be doing it because he missed her. It was just that he couldn't let her get off so easy. She'd made his life miserable for days, and now it was his turn to do the same to her.

So the fact that he was here, playing cards with Annabelle and milking her for information had nothing to do with missing Paige. It was just that Annabelle was the key to Paige's lesson.

"I mean," he continued, "first she ruined my lunch, then the press conference, and then—well, feel this…." He took Annabelle's hand and rubbed it over a tiny bump on his forehead. "She knocked her head against mine and almost got me seriously injured at that hockey game. I just want to turn the tables on her."

"Well, turn them on your own time, because I'm not going to tell you anything." Annabelle picked up the cards and started shuffling. "She's not doing anything that would interest you anyway. I mean, you certainly wouldn't lower yourself to covering the financial problems of the pound, would you?"

"The pound?" Riley asked, as nonchalantly as he could.

"Yes. Paige got a letter from the director explaining that it was running in the red, and that they're hoping this new fund-raiser will—''

''So when is she doing this piece?''

Annabelle glanced at her watch. ''Why, she was taking her cameraman over this morning. I talked to her right before you came. She was so excited about filling in for the anchor, and was going to do this piece, then get her hair done and—''

Riley was out of his seat before she finished her sentence. ''Thanks. I'll bring Zac over next week.''

''Oh, you and Paige both think you can just harass me for information whenever...''

Riley was halfway down the hall before Annabelle finished her sentence.

It was time to teach Paige a lesson. Little rays of sunshine should stay out of storm clouds' way before they got completely blotted out.

ERIE'S DOG POUND WAS a small cinder-block building on the west side of town. Riley parked across the street, then watched and waited until he saw the WMAC news van pull into the parking lot.

He felt like whistling, though he didn't, because Riley Calhoon didn't whistle any more than he made a habit out of saving damsels in distress. Instead, he allowed himself one little smirk as he got out of his car, zipped his jacket against the brisk October wind and walked across the street.

Paige and the cameraman were taking equipment

out of the back of the van when he nonchalantly walked up behind her.

"Why, Paige Montgomery, what on earth are you doing here?"

She turned around. "Riley?"

Riley wished he could take a picture of Paige's expression. She was shocked to see him and it showed.

"Now, isn't this a coincidence?" he said.

"I'm not following you," Paige said hurriedly. "After that little hockey game injury, I thought maybe you were right. Maybe I am hazardous to your health. And you're certainly hazardous to—what did you call it?—Polly World? Well, I like my Pollyanna outlook, and you're ruining it, so I've given up on following you. No more talk of interviews. Plus, I was here first, so I can't be following you."

"If you say so," he said with just enough sarcasm to cause her to frown.

He wasn't about to tell her that he enjoyed annoying her. When she gave him the look that said she'd like to stomp on him, she got the cutest little dimple in her cheek.

No. No. He took that back. There was nothing about Paige Montgomery that he enjoyed. This was about teaching her a lesson, not about dimpled cheeks.

"So, what are you covering today?" he asked. "Let's see, you like witty little titles such as 'Erie's

Heroes.' I'm sure you've got something great in store for your viewers. How about 'Tail Tales,' or 'Rover's Report,' or 'The Flea Files,' or some such non-news caption to attract the attention of your non-news seeking viewers?''

He was pleased to see she looked even more annoyed than she had a minute ago. Oh, yeah, he was getting even with her.

''I'm here to talk to the director about the pound's financial instability and what the community can do to help,'' she said in a tight voice.

''Oh, that's so much more newsworthy than fleas. I apologize.'' He gave a small bow of his head.

''I realize it's not *we interrupt your scheduled programming* sort of news, but it's still news. It's current. It's relevant. And it is important to the people here and the animals they work with. It's important to Erie as well. Without the pound we'd be overrun by stray pets. Now if you'll excuse me, I have work to do.'' She turned her back to Riley and started walking into the pound.

''I'm sure, since you're so good at multitasking, you won't mind if I just tag along and see you on the job.''

Paige didn't reply. She just kept walking.

Riley trailed after her, which meant he got a great view of Paige's tight little behind.

Darn. She might be a walking disaster, a woman whose sunny nature annoyed him, but that didn't stop him from admiring her ass…ets. And, oh, what an asset it was.

Paige Montgomery was a looker, the kind of woman he found attractive, and—

Riley cut off the thought.

Attracted to Paige? Maybe in the most base, physical way, but that was it. She was too upbeat, too focused on feeding the public pap rather than real news. A woman like Paige didn't interest him at all, at least not in more than the most elemental way.

She was his total, diametrical opposite. They had nothing in common. Not even the fact they were both reporters. She didn't have a clue what it was to be a real reporter. After all, her idea of a hot story was a dog pound.

Riley followed Paige into the building, lost in the view, when suddenly he felt his foot sink into…he didn't even have to look to know what his foot had sunk into.

"Oh, I'm so sorry," a woman said. "I meant to get that, and just hadn't—"

"This was a new pair of shoes," he grumbled. "When I put them on this morning I knew I'd step in something disgusting today. If it hadn't been dog excrement, it probably would have been bubble gum, or something. It was only a matter of time. Don't worry."

Riley stopped. Suddenly he was the one who was worried.

Was that him, trying to make the woman feel better? He should have said something more along the lines of *If you'd done your job, I wouldn't have ruined a brand-new pair of shoes.* Or maybe something like *I'll be sure to send you a bill for the new pair.*

Maybe he'd caught a sweetness gene from Paige. Was sick and pathetic cheerfulness contagious?

Next thing he knew, he was going to start to look on the brighter side of things. He'd be...optimistic! The shudder that ran up the length of his body had more to do with the thought than the excrement on his shoe.

He caught Paige smirking in his direction as he walked on his right full-foot and left toe toward the door. He didn't want to track the goo all over the pound, though if he had, he'd be teaching another lesson to that woman who ran the place. But he just wasn't up for any lessons except the one he was planning to teach Paige.

When he reached the grassy area outside, he started wiping his shoe off with gusto.

Annoying Paige. He was supposed to be annoying Paige. Instead, she looked almost amused at his predicament and he had ruined a pair of new shoes.

Satisfied he'd gotten most of the mess off the bottom of his shoe, he walked back inside just as Paige began her interview. He moved quietly against the wall and watched. At first the woman being interviewed was nervous and fidgety, but under Paige's careful guidance, she was soon answering questions like a pro and seemed to forget that the camera was even present.

They discussed pet overpopulation, the pound's role in controlling it, and the need for money to fund their operations, but even more so their need for people to adopt pets before they had to be euthanized.

"Take Pugsley here, for instance," the woman said, holding up a small, pug-nosed bulldog. "He's a wonderful dog...a wonderful dog who's scheduled to be killed tonight if no one adopts him..."

Paige wrapped up the piece, but Riley was no longer listening. He was watching the dog. The dog on doggie death row.

Only there would be no pardon from the governor for Pugsley.

"So what do you think?" Paige asked, after she finished. "Still think it was non-news?"

Instead of answering, Riley simply continued to stare at the dog that the director had held up as an example. He was sitting morosely in his pen, as if he knew his end was near. "They're going to kill that dog tonight."

"He looks like such a nice dog, it's a shame. It's too bad this piece won't air until tomorrow when it will be too late for Pugsley. But hopefully people will come in and other dogs will find a home."

The dog stared at him with soulful black eyes. It was as if he were accusing Riley of letting him die.

Well, it wasn't Riley's fault the dog was about to be executed. He didn't have anything to feel guilty about.

And yet those dark soulful eyes sent a shot of something through Riley's system.

"They couldn't give him one more night?" he asked.

"They have rules, just like everyone does. If you'd listened to the piece, you'd know they don't like that part of their job any more than you do."

She gave the dog a small pat on the head and murmured, "Poor thing," then started to put her files back in her briefcase. The cameraman had already taken the equipment out to the van.

Tentatively, Riley reached into the pen and stroked the dog's head.

Pugsley licked his hand.

Normally he would object to dog saliva on his hand, but since the poor dog was going to bite the doggie bullet in a few hours, he didn't complain.

"He seems like a nice dog," he murmured, more to himself than to Paige. He withdrew his hand and felt as if he were abandoning an old friend.

"He's an old dog," Paige pointed out gently. "I'm sure he lived a good life."

"I used to have a bulldog when I was a kid." Riley wished he could take the words back the minute he saw the softening of Paige's expression.

No dimples now, just concern, and maybe even

empathy. He wasn't sure why he'd brought it up. He stood by Pugsley's cage, hands in his pocket, staring at the dog.

Well, he certainly wasn't going to mention that he'd only had his bulldog for two days until his father found he'd hidden it in his room and took it to the pound.

The Major—that's how he always mentally thought of his father—had claimed that with all the moving around they did in the military, a pet was inconvenient, that they couldn't afford to feed it and, mainly, that Riley wasn't responsible enough to care for one.

"You did?" Paige asked.

"It was a long time ago," he muttered. He always wondered what had happened to Pete. He hoped the dog had been rescued before it met the same fate as Pugsley.

Paige moved closer to the cage. "Hey, Pugsley."

The small dog's tail twitched in response to her voice.

"He likes me," she said.

Of course the dog liked her, Riley thought. Everyone liked Paige. Everyone except him, he reminded himself sternly. Her upbeatness annoyed him. At least it did when he reminded himself it annoyed him.

Needing that reminder, he said, "Oh, don't act all surprised that he likes you. You work hard at making yourself likable, but I've caught glimpses of the real you, and you're not as sweet as you'd like people to think. Why, you pushed me in that puddle on our date. That wasn't exactly nice…''

THE DATE.

For six months Paige had thought of it as the date from hell.

Why did Riley keep bringing it up? All Paige wanted to do was forget it. Just like she planned to forget Riley himself. Of course, she couldn't help that he seemed to be creeping into her thoughts, and even her dreams, lately. That wasn't her fault. She was doing her best to forget him. She'd given up on the interview idea, hadn't she?

Let him wallow in his surliness. Why should she care? Let him remember the date as inaccurately as he wanted. It didn't matter to her that he remembered it wrong…

It rained while they ate their dinner in the restaurant. The rain seemed appropriate to Paige, after all, this date had been all wet. No, not the date, the man.

What on earth had made her aunt think that she had anything in common with Riley Calhoon? He was annoying, opinionated and cantankerous. He'd sent his steak back twice, claiming the cook didn't understand the term well-done. *After the second trip back to the kitchen the waiter brought back what looked like a charcoal briquet, and Riley had actu-*

ally looked almost pleased. He ate the entire charred piece of meat.

Thank goodness, this date was almost over. Paige was relieved to be out of the restaurant and away from their stilted conversations. Just the quick couple blocks back to the parking garage and he'd take her home. She'd go back to her nice, quiet apartment and never have to worry about Riley Calhoon again.

He was still at it, prattling on about some new tax plan and how the cuts were going to cause economic hardships, as they crossed the street.

"But working families need that money in their pocket, not—" She cut off her argument as a truck came barreling down the street, heading right toward them.

"Look out," she cried, and gave Riley a hefty shove toward the sidewalk, then jumped out of the way herself.

He landed face first in a huge puddle of water and came up sputtering. "Why did you do that?"

"There was a truck heading…and you…I mean, I didn't want it to hit you and…"

He stood and shook his hands, as if that would be enough to free himself of the muddy water. All it did was splatter Paige. "I didn't see a truck," he muttered. He looked up the street. "And I don't see one now."

"It was obvious you didn't see it, prattling on about taxes when it was coming right at us. And you

don't see it now because it turned that corner." She gestured up the block.

"I think you just pushed me into the puddle because you know your argument about taxes didn't hold water. And you're mad that I said I didn't think we should do this date again. You don't like being dumped. You were angry, so you pushed me."

"I was winning our debate, so there was no need to push you to distract you from the fight I was winning. Let's face it, you were already wet. Right after the waiter spilled the water on you, you said, this evening wasn't going the way you planned and hoped you never had to go through another one like this, and I said, even as optimistic as I was by nature, I couldn't see the point of another date. Not dating again was my idea. I dumped you."

"You really feel you have to rewrite history? Fine. Let's just take you home."

It wasn't the decision to not go out again that bothered Paige, she assured herself. It was that Riley thought she'd actually pushed him in a fit of annoyance. Oh, he might annoy her, but she'd never push someone into a puddle for that. "Riley, I pushed you so you wouldn't be hit by a truck."

"Rewrite history however you like, just don't try to get me to agree."

"Ha! As if I believed you could agree with anything. You're belligerent and rude. You're the type of man only a mother can like..."

"Pugsley likes you, too," Paige said as the dog stared morosely at Riley.

She pushed thoughts of that awful date out of her mind and concentrated on what was at hand.

"It's time to go," he said, casting an uncomfortable glance at the dog.

"Are we really going to leave this dog here to be killed?"

"What do you suggest?"

"You could adopt him."

"Why don't you adopt him?" he asked. "You said he liked you."

"Cuddles is the jealous sort. He'd eat Pugsley alive." She didn't tell Riley that Cuddles had mellowed over the past few months. He even liked the FedEx guy now. She was sure the cat could get used to Pugsley. But Paige could see that Riley wanted the dog, even if he wouldn't admit it to himself.

She was beginning to be able to read him and wasn't sure if the thought made her pleased or uncomfortable. Maybe she felt a little bit of both.

"I don't want a dog."

Paige noticed that he look at Pugsley again. Sad doggy eyes stared at him.

"Maybe you could just take him home until we find someone else to adopt him?" Paige offered. "I could mention him in my piece. And wouldn't mention you, I swear. I'll just have people interested in adopting him contact me."

"What if no one does? I'd be stuck with him."

Pugsley flopped onto the floor of his solitary pen and dropped his big jowly head onto his paws, as if admitting defeat.

"Never mind. You're right. What was I thinking? You couldn't handle a dog." She patted Pugsley's head and picked up her bag.

"What do you mean by that?" Riley asked.

"I mean that a dog requires work. You have to pay attention to him. Walk him. Feed him. You're so self-absorbed you'd forget about him after a day or two, and that would be it for poor Pugsley." She started toward the door.

"I can handle a dog," he muttered. "That's just what the Major said, that I couldn't, but he was wrong and so are you."

She turned and forced a small laugh. She wondered who the major was but didn't ask. It was just one more Riley mystery. Right now, she was concentrating on Pugsley. "No. I don't think so."

"Paige, I can handle one small, old dog."

"Prove it," Paige challenged him.

"Fine. I will." He looked at the dog and said, "I'll be right back for you, Pugsley. Just let me fill out the paperwork." With that, Riley stormed into the office.

When the kennel door slammed shut, Paige leaned over and patted the dog's head. He stared at the door.

"So, what do you think of that, Pugsley?"

The dog sat on his haunches looking rather shell-shocked. That's how Paige felt, shocked that Riley was adopting a dog.

It didn't seem like a Riley thing to do, not that she'd know what a Riley thing to do really was.

Oh, he was a bit of a curmudgeon, but was never mean-spirited. Opinionated but not obstinate…at least not very obstinate.

Pugsley licked her hand.

"So what should I do now, Pugsley? He likes to think he's tough, but I'm beginning to suspect it's just a facade. After all, he rescues pregnant women, he has a little brother, he visits older ladies in retirement homes and now he's giving a stay of execution to a death-sentenced dog."

Pugsley gave a tired *wroof.*

"You don't know either? Some help you are."

The door to the kennel opened and Riley strode back into the room. A cacophony of barking started.

"You did it?"

"Yeah. But it's only temporary." He lifted the dog out of the pen. "We'll find someone to adopt you. Someone who's good with dogs," he said to Pugsley.

Riley talked to dogs.

It wasn't a goo-goo sort of voice that some people used when speaking to animals and babies, but it was a softer, huskier tone than he normally used.

Paige liked the sound of it. It sent a little shiver climbing up her spine.

And she liked the way he looked, cradling Pugsley in his arms. She knew he'd be insulted if she told him how cute he was. As a matter of fact, she didn't want to think Riley Calhoon was cute so instead she said, "Well, I've got to go."

"You mean, you're going to abandon me with the dog?"

"Riley, you said you could handle a dog." Again, she started toward the door.

"And where are you hurrying off to?"

"I have a hair appointment. Our regular evening anchor is off tonight, so I'm filling in."

"But—"

"See you later, Riley."

5

PAIGE SANK a little deeper into the chair at Snips and Snaps Beauty Salon and sighed. There was something about being utterly pampered for an hour that seemed to make tension melt away. Why, she wasn't even near finished and she could almost forget about stubborn newspaper men like Ri—

Nope, she wasn't going to think his name. She was going to simply sit here and let Pearly Gates entertain her as the stylist fed small sections of her hair through a cap for highlights.

Pampered and entertained, and not thinking about what's-his-name. That was her plan.

"So tell me about Libby," Paige said, prompting Pearly, who truly didn't need much in the way of prompting.

"Well," said the gray-haired woman, whose voice whispered a hint of the South. "They're expecting, you know. We've hired a new girl named Merry. She was here this morning. Maybe you'll meet her next time. Anyway, Libby and Josh took Meggie to Disney World. Between you and me, I think Josh was as excited about the trip as Meg was. I'll bet he comes home with a pair of ears.''

Paige chuckled. ''I'd like a picture of that.''

''I'll see what I can do,'' Pearly promised. ''I'm glad they got away. Everyone needs to now and again. And speaking of getting away, maybe you should think about a vacation, too. We were all worried about you when you were in the hospital. And I'm not happy to see you back at work after only a couple weeks off. You can downplay what happened, but it was serious.''

Without thinking, Paige ran a finger over her incision. Even covered with a layer of cloth, it was still tender.

''But it wasn't serious. It could have been, but it wasn't. And I was ready to come back the next week, but Steph wouldn't hear of it. The last thing I need now is another vacation. What I need is to work.''

''Did I ever tell you about my Uncle Bucky?'' Pearly asked.

Paige couldn't help but smile. She wasn't sure how many of Pearly's relatives were real and how many were fictional characters, but it didn't matter, they were always interesting. ''No, I don't think you did.''

''Oh, don't get her started,'' Josie, the redheaded, gum-chewing, bubble-blowing manicurist said as she walked out of the back room. ''Wow, it's getting cold out there. What happened to Indian summer?''

Josie hung up her coat and continued, "Hey, Paige. You're looking good. But I think that surgery affected your brain. You know better than getting Pearly started on one of her stories. I could turn on the radio for you, nice and loud, if you like. That will drown her out."

"Now, you just hush, Josie. If I can make the girl's life a little easier by sharing some of my wisdom, then I will. You see, my Uncle Buck—"

The chime on the door jingled. Everyone turned to see Riley and Pugsley walk in.

"What are you doing here?" Paige asked. So much for peace and pampering.

She resisted the urge to pat the little plastic cap on her head with the tufts of hair poking out of it every which way. She must look horrible. She refused to pat her head.

Why on earth did she care how she looked for Riley Calhoon?

She didn't.

"Now, Paige, that was not a very inviting greeting, and a woman should always be inviting to a man who looks that good. Want to introduce us?" Pearly asked.

"And, while you're at it, introduce us to his friend. How are you doing, sweetheart?" Josie asked the dog, whose stubby little tail wagged.

"I think he likes me," Josie said, scooping the dog

out of Riley's arms and sitting down in her chair with Pugsley cushioned on her lap.

"The dog is Pugsley. And the other dog, I mean person, with him doesn't need to be introduced. He's just the burr on the backside of my life, and that's all you need to know."

"I'm Riley, and it's a pleasure to meet such lovely ladies," Paige's personal burr said, flashing Pearly and Josie a toothy smile. He was acting as if being suave and gallant were the mainstay of his existence, instead of being annoying and toadish. "I'm here following a story."

"Oh, sweetums, I could tell you a story or two," Pearly said.

"Tell him a story?" Josie said, popping a large, pink bubble for emphasis. The dog jumped at the sound, and Josie patted his head soothingly. "Why I'd help the boy create a story that would shock and amaze everyone."

Paige could see that Pearly and Josie were completely taken in by Riley's little cute-guy charade. Oh, he might be cute, if you liked his sort of looks—which she didn't—but he was devious.

Riley might have fooled Pearly and Josie, but she wasn't fooled at all.

"So, what's your story on, handsome?" Josie asked him.

"I write a commentary piece in the paper, and I

thought I'd base a whole series on the incurably optimistic."

"That, ladies," Paige said through clenched teeth, "was supposed to be a shot at me, but it missed the mark, because I'm not optimistic at all about our chances of having Riley leave anytime soon."

"You're right," he said, settling into the chair across from Josie and Pugsley. "I heard that this was the best place in town for haircuts, and here I am, if you can squeeze me in. A column and a great cut. Who could ask for more?"

"Well, you'll have to wait until I'm done with Paige, but then I'd be happy to squeeze you," Pearly said, reaching for the bottle of developer.

Paige felt the cold gush of liquid as Pearly worked it into the exposed strands.

"I think there are some health regulations about bringing a dog in here," Paige said.

"Not that I've heard of," Josie said. "He's such a pretty boy."

"Paige here is going to be the news anchor person tonight. That's why she came in," Pearly said. "She wants to look her best for her first time in the big chair. She'll be a while yet."

"You don't worry about that," Josie said. "I'll help you pass the time while you're waiting. I'd like to buff and polish you."

"Pardon?" Riley asked, sounding a little nervous.

Paige couldn't help smirking—Riley was out of

his league with these two—but she didn't say anything. She simply sank back into the chair to watch the show.

"I'm Josie. I'm the manicurist." She snapped a huge bubble.

"Oh. Buff and polish my nails?" There was more than a hint of relief in Riley's voice.

"Yeah, but I'd be happy to buff and—"

"Josie," Pearly scolded. "You know Libby would have a conniption hearing you talk like that to a new customer." To Riley, she added, "I'm Pearly, by the way. Pearly Gates."

"Ma'am," Riley said with a nod.

"Oh, you do know how to wound a woman's heart, don't you. *Ma'am?* Why, I never. If you weren't Paige's friend—"

"He's not my friend," Paige felt compelled to assure them "He's the burr on my—"

"On your backside…at least that's what you say," Pearly finished for her. "But I don't believe it. A good-looking man like that?"

"Why, thank you," Riley said.

"Listen, Calhoon, I'm not sure what you're trying to prove, but how about you do it elsewhere?" Paige said.

"I don't think so." He swiveled in his chair so he was facing her. "And let me tell you why. Someone was telling me just the other day that women multitask, that they are genetically programmed to do many different things at once. But men? Well, we focus on one thing to the exclusion of all else. And right now, I'm focused on you, Paige. You were flattered last time that happened. Are you feeling flattered now?''

''Riley, do you really want to know what I'm feeling? I'm—''

Pearly interrupted. ''Now, where was I before your admirer came in, Paige?''

''He's not my anything,'' Paige said at the same time Riley said, ''I don't admire Paige at all.''

Point for Riley. That was a direct hit. She knew, of course, that he didn't think much of her or her reporting, but to hear him verbalize it so succinctly hurt.

''Well, thanks, Calhoon,'' she said, trying to assume a nonchalant attitude. ''You do know how to cut to the very heart of the matter, don't you? I might not want to date you, and I might think you overemphasize the bleak and morose side of the news, but I've never said I didn't admire your way with words.''

''You read my column?'' he asked.

''On occasion. And though I don't always agree, you are well-spoken and I can admire that.''

''I didn't mean I don't admire your work. I mean, for people that want to be fed sweetness and happily-ever-afters, you're a perfect reporter.''

''Wow, Calhoon. I was right, you do have quite a

way with words. Why, you can word a description in such a way that it's hard to tell if it was a compliment or another gibe. Of course, I know you well enough to realize it wasn't a compliment. But I bet Pearly and Josie weren't sure."

"I—" he started.

Paige interrupted, snapping, "Oh, be quiet. Pearly, you were telling me about your uncle?"

Pearly climbed into the chair next to Paige and began. "Uncle Bucky. That's right. Well, he got out of jail and Aunt Fred said he couldn't come home—"

"Aunt Fred?" Paige interrupted.

"Fredricka Mae. With a name like Fredricka Mae you can understand why she preferred being called Fred. Anyway, she said Uncle Bucky could take his moonshining butt someplace else because he wasn't coming home when his time in the hoosegow—"

"Hoosegow?" Paige asked.

"Jail. And if you keep interrupting, I'll never get this story told." Pearly's Southern accent became more pronounced by the second.

"Don't listen to her—she'll never finish even without interruptions," Josie said. "Pearly's long-winded."

"Why, Josie, have you been sniffing your nail polish remover again? Because you and I know I'm the soul of brevity," Pearly said. As if to prove it, she continued, "Well, Uncle Bucky ended up living with us for two weeks, but he said all the kids gave him a headache. So he moved back in with Aunt Fred and laid off the moonshine.''

''Oh.'' Paige wasn't sure what to make of Pearly's story, and hesitated to ask, because she wasn't sure an explanation would clear it up.

Obviously Josie wasn't afraid. She said, ''What the hell does that have to do with anything, Pearly Mae Gates? And what's with all the relatives with the middle name Mae?''

''Mae is a perfectly good middle name. I was named after Aunt Fred and am pleased as punch to carry that legacy. And, the story has to do with when I was telling Paige here she needed to take a vacation. You see, Uncle Bucky got a six-month vacation in the hoosegow because of his moonshining, and then another two weeks with us before he could go home. And do you know why?''

''Why?'' Paige asked, totally confused by Pearly's story. She'd been coming to Snips and Snaps long enough to realize that reaction wasn't unusual. Pearly's stories tended to have oblique morals attached to them.

''Well, Uncle Bucky said he drank because Aunt Fred wasn't putting out. But once he stopped with the moonshine and moved home, she was inclined again, and they lived happily ever after.''

''Pearly, I still don't think I get it,'' Paige said.

Pearly sighed a put-upon sigh. ''Sex, girl. If you

can't get away for a vacation, then sex is the next best thing.''

''Actually, Pearly,'' Josie said, ''sex is the first best thing, and a vacation is just a sad replacement for old maids like you and me.'' She popped a huge pink bubble for emphasis.

''Who are you calling an old maid?'' Pearly asked. She got up and toyed with Paige's hair.

Paige felt the older woman's fingers still as Pearly said, ''Uh-oh.'' The gray-haired beautician picked up the bottle of developer she'd squirted on the hair.

''Uh-oh, what?'' Paige asked.

''Um, honey, how soon do you have to be to the station?'' Pearly asked.

''Why?'' Paige had a sinking feeling that she wasn't going to like the answer.

Pearly picked up a bottle and looked at it. ''Because your beau walked in just as I picked up the developer for your highlights, and maybe I was a bit distracted, because I used forty-volume developer instead of twenty volume.''

''What does that mean to us non-beauticians?'' Riley asked.

''Well, let's just say Paige's highlights aren't quite the subtle blond we were going for,'' Pearly said.

''What are they?'' Paige asked, not quite sure she wanted to hear. ''Because I have to be back at the station in half an hour.

Pearly shook her head as she toyed with the high-lighted strands.

"What are they?" Paige asked again.

"Orange," Riley said.

"HI, I'M PAIGE MONTGOMERY, filling in for Dana Marcus tonight…"

Somehow she made it through the show with her slightly orange highlights. Pearly swore she'd fix them tomorrow, but there just hadn't been time to-night if Paige was going to make it to the station in thirty minutes.

Paige's choices had narrowed down to being late, or doing the news with orangeish hair.

She chose orange.

Pearly and Josie had tried to convince her it wasn't as bad as she thought, but Paige wasn't buying it. Riley, the cause of her hair disaster, didn't say a thing.

The fink.

When the show was over, she stormed toward her cubicle.

Riley Calhoon was responsible for her hair. He'd come into the salon and distracted Pearly, resulting in her stunningly orange highlights.

He'd wanted to get even, and he had. He'd gotten even and then some.

"Paige," called Penny, the receptionist. "You have a message from Riley—"

"Don't use that name around me ever again. If he calls again, tell him I said..." Paige drew in a big breath. "Never mind. Just take a message and toss it in the garbage."

"But—"

"Thanks."

Riley Calhoon had had his revenge. He blamed her for all sorts of things, from pushing him into a puddle that saved him from a rampaging truck, to a near miss at a hockey game, which was in no way her fault.

But he'd revenged himself.

She ran her fingers through her orange-streaked hair. He'd revenged himself in a very public way.

RILEY HAD CALLED the studio. He'd called Paige's house and all he got was an answering machine and no return call. He'd spent the entire evening trying to contact her. Finally, this morning he'd given up. He was going to have to corner her, face-to-face.

She was never going to believe how bad he felt...bad enough to apologize.

He almost didn't believe he was about to say the words. *I'm sorry.* They were two words Riley Calhoon tended to avoid. The Major used to say, *Never apologize, never explain.* It had been part of the Major's parenting guide.

Never apologize, never explain. Riley had adopted it as his motto as well—until now.

He couldn't believe he was standing here in the WMAC lobby, waiting to apologize to Paige Montgomery.

"Mr. Calhoon," the receptionist said, "Paige asked me to show you to her office." She got up and held the door open for him, and Riley followed her down the hall.

"It's not really an office," the woman explained. "It's more of a cubby, a hole in the wall. WMAC spares no expense for its staff, let me tell you," she added with a soft laugh.

It was a laugh designed to make a man sit up and take notice, but the only thing Riley noticed was that the woman kept talking. He barely even noticed that she was a knockout and that the view she presented, leading him down the hall, was one that should make him thank God he was a man.

That he'd only noted the woman's attributes, and certainly hadn't appreciated them with the depth of devotion they deserved, was Paige's fault. Normally he'd not only have noticed, but he'd have made a move to see if the woman was available. Now he really didn't care if she was available. He just wished she'd shut up. He wanted to concentrate on what he was going to say to Paige.

I'm sorry.

How hard could it be to say those two little words? Actually, *I am sorry* was three words, but if he made the *I* and *am* into a contraction, it was two. And he figured two words would have to be easier to say than three.

"...and we won the award last year for..." the woman continued.

Riley barely registered her existence. His thoughts were on how to apologize.

He wasn't quite sure why he felt the need to say the words. After all, he was getting even with Paige. She'd pushed him into puddles, let her attack cat have its way with him, ruined a perfect sub, given him heartburn, made him miss a press conference, and got him an almost-concussion from basically falling on top of her.

All he'd done was distract a beautician and given Paige a few orange streaks in the process. They hadn't even been all that noticeable on television. He knew because he'd watched, just like he watched most nights.

Who had been injured the most?

Him. That's who.

"...her office is back here..."

And yet, he'd seen the glow on Paige's face when Pearly was bragging about her filling in for the anchor, and then watched as her expression changed to horror when she looked in the mirror, he'd felt...bad.

Guilty.

Responsible.

So here he was, ready to venture into unknown territory and offer a heartfelt apology.

"Here you are, Mr. Calhoon."

It took him a moment to register that the receptionist had finally said something he wanted to hear. They stood outside a cubbyhole-ish cubicle.

"Thanks." He knocked on the side of the cubby. "Paige, can I come in?"

She was sitting at a cluttered desk—her hair once again a light brown with slightly blond highlights— glaring at him. "No. I had Penny show you here just so I could have the pleasure of kicking you out."

"Come on, Paige. I have something to say to you." He didn't wait for the invitation that obviously wasn't going to come. He stepped into the cubicle and looked around. "Nice place."

"Go away, Calhoon. I'm not interested in interviews or you. And I certainly apologize for ever thinking you were a hero." She paused a moment and sighed. "Just go away and leave me alone."

He moved a pile of papers from the small metal chair against the wall and dragged it in front of Paige's desk. "You know, you're not being very nice. I thought you prided yourself on being nice? *WMAC, Where Nice News Matters.* What would your news director say?"

"You seem to bring out the worst in me. Right now, I'm not feeling nice at all. People who know you would understand and support my less than nice attitude toward you. Just go away, Calhoon." She took the piece of paper she'd been writing on, crumpled it and threw it toward the wastepaper basket. Unfortunately, she wasn't a very good shot, and missed.

Riley absently noted that the paper had landed on the floor at his feet. Wondering what she had thrown away was easier than contemplating what he was about to do. But finally he looked up and forced himself to meet her eyes. A man could get lost in those dark brown depths, though Riley couldn't afford to lose himself. He had something to say—words that were choking him. "Listen, I wanted to say—"

"Save it. I've heard everything from you that I want to. Oh, maybe you could add a new refrain, something about having orange hair being my just reward. Well, maybe it is. Maybe I deserved to be humiliated on television yesterday because I thought there was something more to you than most people see. Maybe all the e-mails and phone calls from people asking what I did to my hair was what I deserved for being an optimist."

She sighed and ran her fingers through her short hair. "Listen, when I said you were a hero I was wrong. You were right. Rescuing me was just an irregular blip in your surliness. So you don't need to follow me, don't need to try to prove that I was wrong. I admit it."

For some reason, hearing Paige repeat what he'd been saying all along bothered him. After all, why would he care if she saw him as a hero? He wasn't anyone's hero. He was simply a journalist doing a job. Having her acknowledge that was what he'd always wanted, and now he'd accomplished it. He should just turn around and leave. He should just...

Damn. He wasn't going anywhere, at least not until he said the words, so he took a deep breath and blurted out, "I wanted to apologize."

"What?" Paige stared at him. If he'd had to describe her expression, he'd have called it *surprised.*

No. Scratch that. *Shocked.*

"I wanted to say I'm sorry." There they were. Those two words. He'd said them and he lived to tell the tale.

On a roll, he continued, "I know I didn't actually turn your hair orange, but my tailing you to the beauty salon distracted Pearly and, well, I did instigate the situation. And I know you were excited about filling in as anchor, and I ruined the experience. I'm sorry about that, too."

"Wow." She looked bemused. "Wow," she repeated.

"If you tell anyone I apologized, I'll deny it," he said, but he smiled as he said it, and could see that Paige recognized the joke.

She shook her head and he thought he could hear the hint of a small laugh in her voice as she said, "Don't worry. I won't. They'd never believe me."

"I thought maybe..." Riley played with the collar of his shirt for a moment. It suddenly seemed tight and restrictive. Had someone moved the buttons in? That would be the kind of joke that would appeal to his colleagues.

"Well," he tried again. "Listen, I think we've both behaved like kids, trailing each other around town, trying to get the best of each other. What if we went to dinner and really talked this whole interview thing out?"

"Dinner? Talking? You do remember our last dinner, don't you?"

"Yeah." He was feeling hot and flushed. He took off his jacket and set it on his lap, hoping he didn't have sweat stains in the armpits of his dress shirt.

He was disgusting, sweating and stammering like some high school kid asking a girl on a first date.

Riley was no kid. He'd asked thousands of women out.

Okay, maybe hundreds.

Okay, maybe less than a hundred, but more than a few.

No matter what the amount, he'd never felt this nervous before. What was wrong with him? This wasn't a date as much as a business meeting.

"Are you the *real* Riley Calhoon?" Paige asked. "I mean, either you're a pod person, or the fumes in the beauty salon yesterday have affected you. Amnesia. That's the explanation. Because I can't imagine the real Riley remembering our first date and asking me out again, unless he'd in some way been altered or had his memory wiped."

"Listen, this was a mistake. Forget it." He stood and his jacket fell to the floor. He picked it up and, without even thinking, scooped up Paige's crumpled paper as well, then started toward the door.

"Riley, stop. Now *I'm* sorry. Don't go."

He turned back around, facing Paige.

"Really," she said, "I'm sorry. That wasn't like me. Except around you, I guess it is. Whenever we're together I get sarcastic and mean. And I'd like to apologize for that. That's not the kind of person I want to be."

She took a deep breath. "I'd love to have dinner with you and discuss whether an interview would work for either of us."

"When? I'll pick you up." His heart was beating so hard he wondered if Paige could hear it. And his palms were sweating.

"Can we do it tomorrow, about seven?" she asked. "You can pick me up at my place."

"That works for me. I remember where it is. See you then."

Riley hurried out of her cubbyhole before either of them said anything else that they shouldn't. He waited until he was outside the building to look at the paper Paige had tossed away.

It was his column. The one about renovating the Warner. The story was big here in Erie. The old theater had received a lot of television and print time. His column had nothing to do with Paige's report. Nothing at all.

Sections of the column were highlighted, but that's not what grabbed his attention. It was the picture the paper had run next to the column that caught his eye. He was standing in front of the Warner Theater.

Someone had drawn a dozen arrows throughout his body. One of the arrows hit a very intimate spot of Riley's anatomy that made the real Riley wince. But he noticed that it was the biggest arrow of them all and if you looked at it just right it looked like…

He grinned. Well, well, well. Pollyanna Paige wasn't as innocent or sweet as her viewers believed.

And for some reason, the thought made Riley extremely hot…not in his normal bad-tempered way, but in a hot-and-bothered, need-a-cold-shower way.

Pollyanna Paige was neither sweet nor innocent.

6

RILEY STOOD at Paige's neon-pink door and hesitated. What on earth was he doing here?

First he apologized, and now he was risking life and limb to take her out again.

"I must be insane," he muttered.

Pugsley voiced his gurgly, growly agreement.

Riley looked down at the dog. "And I don't know where we're going to go with you. You'll probably spend your evening in the car. You know that, don't you?"

Pugsley simply stood looking doggy eyed at Riley.

"I'm going out with a woman who's tried to kill me on more than one occasion, and bringing along a dog I never really wanted just adds to the fun. I think there's something wrong with me. Something that probably requires medication. I can't believe I'm doing this."

Before he could change his mind, he knocked on the door. The sooner this dinner started, the sooner it could end. The sooner it ended, the sooner he could get back to himself.

No one answered.

Fortune was finally smiling on Riley Calhoon.

"Look, Pugsley, she's not here. I guess we'll have to go home and—"

The door flew open and a less than ready Paige stood there in holey jeans and a Temple University sweatshirt. "Riley, you're early."

Fortune was a fickle mistress. His perfect escape, foiled by Paige Montgomery. Bowing to the inevitable, he tried to think of something to say.

"I'm not early. I'm right on time." It came out more surly than he intended, but that obviously didn't faze Paige.

She smiled and said, "Then I'm late. That's not entirely unusual. Well, come in and I'll go change. I—"

She looked down and noticed Pugsley. "You brought the dog on our date?" She bent down and patted the dog's head, and his stub of a tail wagged vigorously.

"It's not really a date. It's just a dinner to discuss a potential interview. I never used the word *date*." He wanted to be very clear on that point.

"And," he continued, "I didn't plan to bring the dog. But he misses me when I'm at work all day, and came to me with his leash when I started to the door. You know, I didn't even have to teach him that. He just knew it. He might be an old dog, but he's smart. So, anyway, there he was with his leash and…well, I couldn't say no. He can wait in the car while we eat, I guess.''

He stopped talking, and in his mind replayed the words that had just tumbled out of his mouth. He'd been prattling. Running on and on at the mouth and not saying much of anything. Oh, maybe it wasn't as bad as that first day in the cab when he thought Paige was a pregnant woman about to give birth, but almost as bad.

Riley Calhoon didn't prattle…except, evidently, around Paige Montgomery.

Maybe she gave off some prattle-inducing pheromone?

"Or…" she said.

"Or?" What was she or-ing? What had he said? He couldn't remember. He had run on about such a large quantity of meaningless stuff all at once that he'd totally lost his train of thought and had no idea what he'd said.

"Or, rather than lock Pugsley up in the car…"

Pugsley.

Relief flooded through his system. Pugsley. That's what they'd been talking about. The dog. Phew. Something to hang on to. He could talk about a dog without any elocution elopements. Without any discordant discourse. Without any bumbling babbling. Without—

Damn. He was pathetic.

"…I could stay in my jeans, and simply order in

a pizza, or Chinese, or something and we could eat here,'' Paige finished.

"You wouldn't mind?'' he asked, surprised enough to rein in his rampaging thoughts and tongue.

Over the years he'd found most women wanted fancy restaurants and designer clothes.

"I don't mind at all. I prefer my jeans. If we eat in, I don't have to change. I had a long day, and probably would have canceled dinner with anyone else.''

She'd have canceled dinner with anyone else but hadn't canceled on him. What did that mean? Riley wasn't sure, but the warm rush that flowed through his body at the thought made him nervous. More nervous than having dinner with Paige made him. He wasn't going to talk, or else he'd probably prattle again.

She shut the door with an ominous thud and ushered him into her still cluttered, loudly colored living room. "So what sounds good?''

A question. He had to talk. Talk, yes. Prattle? No. "It doesn't matter.''

Doesn't. A contraction. He'd only said three words because he'd contracted does and not. Thank Webster's dictionary for contractions. He was learning to love them. You couldn't be prattling if you only said three words.

"Chinese then,'' Paige said. "What would you like?''

''Chicken and broccoli.''

Three words again. Riley was king of short, succinct sentences. No prattling here. He was doing so well he could probably be a monk and take a vow of silence.

''Well, have a seat and I'll make the call, and then we'll talk.''

She bent over and picked up a cordless phone from underneath a pile of newspapers on the table, exposing an excellent view of her backside and convincing Riley that there was no chance of monkhood in his future.

Desperately he tore his eyes away from her and concentrated on looking for a clean place to sit, while she dialed the number.

Paige's place wasn't dirty, just cluttered with stacks of newspaper, and books and magazines. And of course, her bright yellow walls and the deep red furniture only added to the frenzied feeling of the room. It was loud and nerve-racking. Riley preferred things more sedate and orderly.

''Sorry,'' she said, a hand over the phone, obviously noticing his seat dilemma. ''I've been working on some research and the living room is the most comfortable place to work. Just move something and—''

Obviously someone finally picked up on the other end of the line because she started giving their order.

Riley lifted a stack of newspapers from the chair,

set them on the floor and took the seat. Pugsley waddled up next to the chair and flopped at his feet.

Riley looked down at the dog, and the top section of the paper caught his eye. It was his column, and the paper was folded in such a way that he knew his column was up because Paige had been reading it.

Part of him wanted to ask what she thought about *Get Real,* but the bigger part of him wouldn't let that minority part do it. Other people's opinions didn't matter. He wouldn't let them. Not even Paige's opinion.

Especially not Paige's opinion.

Paige hung up, and pushed some magazines on the couch over to the side and sat down. "They said it would be here in a half hour, but it will probably be more like forty-five minutes or an hour. They're good, but they're not exactly fast."

Riley didn't respond since no response was necessary. He was going to just sit here, wait for the food and not prattle.

Silent or monosyllabic. That was the extent of his plan.

"So, about the interview," Paige said. "Why don't I tell you why you should do it, and then you tell me why you shouldn't. No interrupting, no fighting. Just clear logical reasoning."

"Sounds good." Two words. Two single-syllable words. Yep, he was back on track.

"Okay," Paige said. "Here goes. You are a hero.

I'm not sure why that term bothers you, but you are. And doing an interview won't jeopardize your tough-guy image. John Wayne was the epitome of a tough guy, and he was a hero in his movies. The interview would be good for you, give you a little more balance in a public way. I mean, you come off as such a tough guy in your columns that it would be good for your readers to see that you have more to you than just strong opinions.''

''Why does this mean so much to you?'' he asked. Crap. An entire string of words. All single syllables, but still quite a lot of them. But worrying about syllables was suddenly fading as he thought about what she'd asked.

Why? This was the one question he needed an answer to. Why was she so intent on this interview?

It was also the one answer he wasn't sure he wanted to hear.

The conflicting emotions didn't make sense, but then nothing in Riley's life had made sense since he'd stumbled on Paige giving pseudo-birth in a parking lot. So he tried not to let the lack of sense bother him now.

''When we went out on that date,'' she said, ''I'm ashamed to admit, I saw just what you wanted me to see. I didn't look deeper. If asked, I would have said you were an acerbic, cynical man who was more than a little abrasive. But as I've followed you around, I've seen another side, one that you keep hidden.

Heroic and kind. You're a pushover for old ladies, kids and dogs. And I don't know why it matters to me that people know there's more to you than you let show, but it does. Maybe what I'm saying is, for some reason you matter to me.''

She opened her mouth, as if she was going to say more, then snapped it shut, gave a tiny, almost imperceptible shake of her head and sucked in a deep breath. Then she said, ''So, it's your turn. Why can't you let people see that side of you? A side you try to hide, but is so much a part of who you are.''

''My father was a hero,'' Riley blurted out. He couldn't believe he'd said those words.

''Pardon?'' Paige asked gently.

He wanted to shut up and not say another word, but there was something in Paige's eyes that didn't merely encourage him to continue, it insisted.

''The Major,'' he said. A mental image of his father, all spit and polish, regimented rules and pride. ''That's how I think of him. The Major. Never father, and certainly not Dad. He was in the army and we lived our lives with structure and discipline. And he was a hero.''

''In a war?''

He registered the question, but barely. He was suddenly plunged back into his childhood. Whenever he forayed into the past he was consumed by an almost overwhelming feeling of suffocation.

Forcing himself to breathe, he said, ''No, not a

war. That's what he always craved, but it never happened. His act of heroism happened at a burning house on the base. He saw it and got everyone out. He got a medal for it. He was a hero, they said. Not mine. That's not what I saw. I saw the Major. *Boys play football, son. They don't edit the school paper. Boys go into the military. You don't need to go to Boston University, even with that scholarship. With your grades you can go into West Point and come out with a degree and be an officer. Boys—*"

He cut himself off. He couldn't believe he'd said all that. "Sorry."

Why had he told Paige something he'd never told another living soul?

He wasn't sure. And that confused him even more.

"Anyway, I don't want to be like that. Like him. He was all show. The big hero. But he wasn't a hero, at least not at home. I always swore I'd be different from the Major. When I do something, I don't do it for the world to see, don't do it for pins and medals, I do it for me. Like Zac. I don't need recognition for hanging out with him. He's a great kid, and we get along really well, and that's enough for me."

He paused, a new thought hitting him. "But maybe I'm not as different from the Major as I think. You say I'm cynical? Maybe I am. Acerbic, abrasive? Yes. But I'm not going to paint over all that and call myself a hero because of one minor incident. I thought he was a hypocrite accepting all those accolades. And I won't do it. I might be a lot of things, but I'm never a hypocrite.''

"You see rescuing me as one small aberration?" Paige asked. "Don't you see, being a hero is as much a part of your nature as being acerbic. There's me. There's Zac. Being a Big Brother is heroic. You volunteer your time to be there for a kid who needs you. That's a hero. There's Pugsley there. You saved him.''

"You're misreading all—"

"No." She reached down and grabbed a small stack of newspapers. "Those all could be counted as minor blips. But then there's *Get Real.*"

"That proves my case, not yours. It's hard news. There's nothing heroic about it."

"You think?" She picked up a paper and read, "Slumlords, fluoridation, The New Academy High School: a chance for public school kids to shine, tourism in Erie, and how about Belinda Byers.''

Riley groaned. She would have to have read that particular column. "Now, wait a minute, I know what you're going to say, but that column doesn't make me a hero."

"Riley, the girl was accepted at Harvard and was going to have to say no because she didn't have the money—even with loans and her scholarship she couldn't have done it. Your column highlighted her plight, and the local donations and scholarships it generated got that girl to school. You're her hero.''

Softly she said, "Don't you see? Being a hero isn't a blip, it's a trend. It's a fact. Riley, you are a hero."

"With Belinda, I was talking about the inequities in life," he said, desperate to make her understand. "That some people have it all and throw it away, and some people work so hard and are so deserving, but that doesn't matter. I'm—"

"A hero. And there's something I've wanted to do for… I don't know when it started, but it's here and the wanting to do it is growing. I…" She let the sentence trail off and stared at him. "Oh, what the heck."

Paige got up, walked the two steps it took to reach his chair and leaned over, pausing, her face right in front of his.

"What?" he said. There was something in her dark brown eyes that made him feel hunted. If he could have gotten any words past his constricted throat he'd have happily prattled.

"What?" he said again, pleased that he'd managed even a monosyllabic question.

Paige didn't answer. She just leaned forward…and kissed him.

Riley saw it coming. He should have ducked. He could have pushed her away. Instead he simply waited. And when her lips reached him, it wasn't a slight peck on the cheek. Not even a platonic buss on the lips.

No. This was an all out, lip-locking, toe-curling kiss that rocked Riley's world.

PAIGE FOUND HERSELF tongue-tangled with Riley and couldn't help but wonder what she was doing. Her kiss was a hard, fast introduction that made her knees go weak and her blood pressure spike.

He smelled of something spicy.

Hot and spicy.

Her knees weren't just weak, they were giving out. So she let herself sink onto Riley's lap, feeling as if she could melt into him, become a part of him. She felt suddenly at home as she wrapped her arms around his neck and continued kissing him, learning every intimate contour of his mouth. Not wanting to stop—not ever.

Who would have guessed that Riley Calhoon was such a great kisser?

Well, Paige hadn't known until right now, but that hadn't stopped her from fantasizing about it for the past few nights. She'd thought those fantasies were hot, but the reality was hotter.

Much hotter.

"Wow," she said as she finally pulled back. She stared at him.

How had she missed so much last spring? She, who prided herself at seeing the best in the world around her, in the people who surrounded her, had only seen the facade Riley preferred the world to see.

Gently, she traced the curve of his jaw with her forefinger.

"Wow," she said again.

Riley didn't say anything. He just looked dazed.

"Riley? Are you all right?" she asked, staring into his gray eyes.

Gray eyes that narrowed as he asked, "What the hell did you do that for?"

Paige scrambled off his lap, readying for a fight.

Riley was going to be difficult. But that was okay, she suddenly realized. It was expected. It was part of who he was. It was part of why she wanted him.

She wanted him with a deep and growing ferocity that surprised her, that tilted her world off balance. Well, she was ready to tilt his as well.

She was ready to take him on in order to get what she wanted. Interview be damned. She didn't care about putting him on the air anymore. She wanted to put him in her bed…and keep him there for a long, long time.

She wanted to continue to delve behind his facade, eager to discover what other treasures he hid determinedly behind his mask.

The battle lines were marked.

She moved back to the couch, regrouping. Let him think she was retreating as she prepared for an all-out frontal attack.

"I don't know what I did that for," she admitted. "I was sitting here listening to you, and I started wondering again what it would be like to kiss you, and then next thing I knew, I *was* kissing you. And I have to tell you, I thought it would be good, but you surpassed my wildest imaginations.''

"*Again.* You said you started wondering again. So, you've been imagining kissing me? For how long?''

"Well, not after that date. I imagined many things about you after that date, and kissing wasn't one of them. Not even after you saved my life. I mean, I wanted to tell people about you, but I didn't wonder what it would be like to be with you. But lately, after I followed you around and got to know there was more to you than meets the eye, well, I'll confess, I've wondered. But optimistically, I never imagined it could be like this, I mean—''

She cut off her sentence as Riley stood, stepped over his dog and approached the couch.

"Riley?'' she asked, unable to gauge his mood and suddenly feeling more than a little nervous. "I'll apologize for kissing you, if you like. I won't do it again.''

That was a lie. But it was one she willingly made if only it would get that terribly intent expression off his face.

"Yes, you will,'' he said. His voice was a soft...

Could that be desire? She wondered about his tone and her heart was beating so fierce and fast she wondered that it didn't explode.

"I will?" she asked.

He kicked the rest of the papers off the couch and sat down next to her.

Right next to her.

He leaned close, and his breath caressed her neck as he practically whispered, "Oh, yeah, you will if I have my way."

"Oh."

He pulled her into his arms. Paige found herself completely wrapped in Riley. It was an amazingly good feeling. He slowly ran his fingers through her short hair and a small shiver ran down her spine.

She'd expected something hard and fast, instead he seemed content to just hold her, to simply touch her hair.

"Riley?" she asked, unsure what her question was.

"You know this is going to lead to more than just kissing, right?"

She nodded.

"I need to be sure we're clear that it's not...I mean, I like you."

She snorted. She wasn't sure *like* was the right description for their relationship, at least not Riley's end of it.

He laughed. "Yeah, it surprised me, too. But I do. I'm not the kind of man who is going to wax poetic and tell you that your eyes are dark pools that I could easily lose myself in. I won't tell you that. And though I might complain about your sweetness, I'm finding it addictive. I won't…''

He paused and finally said, ''I'll just tell you that I want to be with you. But I don't want to hurt you, Paige. I don't want you to put on those rose-colored glasses in your Pollyanna world and think this means more than two people who like each other, who are attracted to each other, being together this once.''

She concentrated on the thought of being with him, and refused to think about his *this once* disclaimer because the idea of him leaving cut at her in a totally unexpected way.

She forced herself to be as casual as he seemed to want. ''I wasn't looking for a proposal, Calhoon. And I'm not looking for talk. I understand what you're saying, and I think the time for talking is over.''

Her understanding was all he'd obviously been waiting for, because he kissed her then. It was as hard and hot as she'd expected. He was demanding, his tongue probing, joining hers in a preview of what was to come.

Kissing Riley went on forever. There was no time, just sensation. When his hand moved beneath her shirt and cupped her breast through her thin silk bra, Paige thought she'd died and this was her reward.

''Calhoon,'' she gasped. She wanted to strip off her clothes, strip off his. She didn't want any barriers to stand between them. She tugged at his shirt and was ready to pull it up over his head when there was a knock at the door.

"Who the hell could that be?" Riley asked breathlessly, as if he'd just finished part of a marathon.

She'd done that to him. She was affecting him.

The thought was a heady one. He might say differently, but she was getting to tough-guy Riley Calhoon, at least in this elemental, physical way.

"It's probably the food. Leave it to them to be prompt this once. More than prompt, early." She stood, adjusted her clothing and ran a finger through her rumpled hair. "I'll take care of it."

She grabbed a twenty from her purse on the coat tree and opened the door.

"Hi, Paige," said Les, the delivery boy.

"Hey. You were fast tonight." Too fast, darn it. Would Riley get cold feet and remember how much he didn't like her now that he'd had a chance to think?

The thought of the desire that was beating hot and furious in her blood going unfulfilled made her want to groan.

"It's a slow night," the boy said, handing her the bag. "It's cold enough to snow."

"Bite your tongue. It's way too early in the season to think about snow." She gave him the twenty. "Keep the change."

"You know Erie, snow in October isn't unheard-of. Thanks for the tip.'' He waved as he started down the hall.

Paige shut the door, turned and went back into the living room. She stood awkwardly, suddenly unsure of herself, waiting for Riley to make some move. ''Uh, dinner's here. Did you want to eat it now?''

''That's one option,'' he said.

''Or?'' Paige prompted, her voice little more than a whisper.

''Or, you could put it in the fridge, and you and I could go into the bedroom.''

''I think I like plan B better. I wasn't sure you'd want to…I mean, I know you don't like me most of the time, and I was afraid you'd remember and—''

He closed the distance between them, not quite touching her, but so close she could feel the heat radiating from his body, warming her, tempting her closer. He silenced her with a finger against her lips. ''Shh. You're wrong, you know.''

''Wrong?''

''I like you. I've always liked you. I watch WMAC news every night, just to watch you.''

''Because my segments annoy you.''

She annoyed him. He annoyed her. That's the way it worked, and it was important she remember that. Riley claimed his heroism was a blip in the surliness of his life, but this… She had to remember this attraction was a blip in the annoyance they tended to cause each other.

"What annoyed me," he said softly, "was that I only got to see you on TV. Just watching a two-dimensional you wasn't enough to satisfy me. I wanted more."

"But you never called after our date."

"We agreed it wouldn't work out, so I couldn't and…"

"You could have," she said softly. "No matter what I said, I…well, you could have."

They stood facing each other, looking, but not touching. The reality of what they were going to do—because there was no longer any doubt about what they were going to do—sank in.

Paige wanted this man with a force that took her breath away.

Primal. Fierce.

She wanted to touch him and yet didn't want to break the moment, this endless moment of exquisite anticipation. Of knowing that she would have him, would learn his every contour, would have his body.

But not his soul.

Where had that thought come from?

Having Riley's body was more than enough for her. She knew they were too different for more than this. And she was willing to take this.

"The food," Riley said. "Maybe we should start by putting it in the fridge?"

"Yes," Paige said, realizing she still held the bag of Chinese food in her hand, and thankful to have something to do, to break the moment. She wasn't sure what had just happened, but she didn't want to stop and analyze it. All she wanted was Riley.

She put the entire bag of food in the refrigerator, shut the door and turned—and bumped into him. "Sorry."

"I'm not." He took her into his arms and kissed her again, hard and probing. He broke off the kiss and asked, "Which way?"

"It's down the hall, first door on the left."

He swept her into his arms.

"Riley, you don't have to carry me," she protested.

"I want to."

"But I'm heavy."

"I've held you before. That day I thought you were delivering a baby. You aren't, and weren't too much for me to handle. As a matter of fact, I worried then that you didn't weigh enough."

"I don't think I've ever worried about not weighing enough."

"You're perfect."

"And this, this will be perfect," Paige said, as they entered her bedroom.

7

_____

RILEY WASN'T SURE what he expected Paige's bedroom to look like. Like her office or her living room, maybe. But as he entered her room, he was surprised to find something else entirely.

The walls were a warm sandy color and the carpet a shade or so darker. Warm, but neutral. A plain wooden chest of drawers almost faded into the walls. None of it made any particular visual impact.

No, it was the bed, pure and simple, that dominated the room. King-size, it swallowed most of the floor space. But even its size wasn't the eye-catching feature. What covered it was. A light canopy of some gauzy gold material was overhead, and a darker gold satin spread covered the mattress, that and a dozen or so pillows. Satin, velvet, silk and other fabrics he couldn't even begin to name in reds and golds littered the entire surface.

''Wow,'' he said.

''You like it?'' Paige asked, gazing up at him from his arms.

He looked down at the woman in his arms. ''I feel

like some prince or sheikh carrying you off to be ravaged.''

''Really, do tell,'' she prompted with a throaty laugh.

''I hate to mess it up.''

''And I can't wait to mess it up. This bed, it's my one vice. It makes me feel sensual. So many people see this Pollyanna image as the width and breadth of me. But this room, well, it's like my naughty little secret. It's a reminder that there's more to me than most people think.''

''How many people know this particular secret?'' he asked.

''Including you and me?'' she asked.

He nodded, afraid if he spoke she'd hear the jealousy in his voice. A jealousy that surprised him even as it ate at him.

''Uh, that's it. No one else has ever come here with me, Riley.''

''But—''

''Listen, I'm not saying there's never been anyone else, I'm just saying, I've never had anyone else in here. It's intimate and personal, and...''

He felt, rather than heard, her sigh, a long exhalation of air that warmed his chest. ''Just put me on the bed, Calhoon. I don't think it's time to think about anything except the way you make me feel.''

''And how is that?'' He set her on the bed, and looked at her. She was a holey-jeaned, sweatshirted, short-haired goddess. The incongruity of the girl-next-door lying in the middle of a bed that would make a courtesan blush made him physically ache.

"How do I feel?" she asked, her voice husky and soft. "I feel powerful, watching you look at me like that."

"Like what?"

"Like you could eat me alive and then come back for seconds. Like when we do this, once isn't going to be enough. Like you're touching me all over with just your eyes."

"Damn, Paige."

"Take off your clothes and come to bed, Riley." She sat up and stripped off her sweatshirt in one smooth, fluid motion.

The air hissed from his chest as her bra followed suit.

"Come on, Calhoon, your turn. You take off yours, and I'll take off mine."

"Is that a challenge?" he asked, surprised to hear himself chuckle.

"Maybe. You think you're *up* to it?"

"Oh, honey, I'm about to show you how up to it I can be."

"Really? I'm finding it *hard* to believe you're as *up* to it as you claim."

He laughed then. A wholehearted roar. "I don't think I've ever wanted a woman this much, and then found myself exchanging quips as we stripped."

He kicked off his shoes and started to tug his jeans down past his hips.

"You should laugh more often, Calhoon. It's a nice sound. And laughter should be a part of the wanting and the receiving."

"Yeah?"

"Oh, yeah. But there's a time for laughter, and a time for..." The sentence trailed off as she stared at him, drinking in the sight as he finished removing his clothes.

"Paige? You're not laughing now."

"No."

"So now that we've laughed, what's next?"

"You lie down on my bed, and let me have my way with you."

He gulped, trying to move a sudden lump in his throat. "Your way?" he croaked.

"I want to touch, taste, every piece of your body. I want to memorize each line. I've driven you crazy in the past, but this time, I want to make you crazy with desire."

"Honey, it won't take much. I think I'm already there."

"Oh, you're not even close. Just lie back and trust me."

Riley willingly turned himself over to Paige. He lay back on her bed, the cool, smooth fabric beneath him and the hot, willing woman above him.

She pressed her body against his as she started

with his face. She scattered featherlight kisses every-
where, then settled on his lips and kissed him
again—long, hot moments of eternity with her body
close to his and their mouths joined, a preview of
what was to come.

Slowly she worked her way from his lips down to
his neck, finding sensitive areas that had him jumping from the bed. But when he tried to join her ex-
ploration, she simply whispered, "Not yet."

So he lay back and let her continue, clutching the
smooth comforter to keep from putting his hands all
over her.

She moved lower, finding every sensitive area and
driving him wild as she teased each one.

Lower still. As her lips engulfed him, Riley knew
he'd reached the limits of his endurance.

"Would you think me forward if I…" she let the
sentence trail off as she reached for something in a
nightstand drawer. "I don't want you to think…well,
I bought these in case."

She tore open a foil packet, blushing. Embarrassed
and brazen at the same time.

She looked up, her eyes met his and then she
smiled, a small upturn of her lips that made him ache
with wanting her. With agonizing slowness she slid
the protection into place and Riley knew he couldn't
wait another minute.

"My turn," he said, his breath coming in short
gasps. He lifted her and rolled before she could pro-

test. Now it was Paige trapped beneath him, an uncharted territory for him to map.

"Riley, I wasn't done," she complained.

"But I would have been if you hadn't stopped. And that's not how I want it the first time."

Following her lead, he kissed her, silencing any further protests. He ran his fingers through her short hair, enjoying the soft feel of it as he moved downward from her mouth. He concentrated his kisses on the hollow of her neck for a time, before he moved lower still.

Her small breasts, which had pressed so insistently against his chest, begged for all his attention, and he happily obliged. Taking the hard nubs into his mouth, his hands moved lower yet, toying and teasing, trying to ignite the fire in her that burned so strongly within him.

Gently, he traced the five-inch scar on her abdomen.

"Does it hurt?" he whispered as he studied it.

"No. It itched for a while, but it doesn't hurt. It's ugly though."

"No. Not ugly at all." He carefully kissed the length of it. "You could have died without this surgery. That makes this scar beautiful."

"It wasn't the surgery that saved me, it was you." Paige writhed to and fro, and her hands clutched him tightly. Finally she cried out, "Now, Riley. Please."

"Not—" *Yet* he'd planned to say, but she arched against him. Bold and commanding.

"Now," she insisted.

No longer able to wait, he obliged her, pressing himself into her warmth. He plunged into her moist depths, over and over again, pounding his need and desire against hers. She matched his rhythm, taking in the whole of him. Tight and demanding, he could deny her nothing. He took her to the edge and, as he sensed the tightening of her body and knew that she'd reached the pinnacle, he allowed himself to follow suit. Together they climaxed, their cries mingling, joining, even as they themselves were joined.

It was eternity.

It was perfect.

When it was over, he lay next to her and pulled her into his arms.

She was his.

He wasn't sure where the thought had come from, but he couldn't fight the knowledge that what they shared had changed things, had changed him. He'd lied when he said it was just this once.

For the first time in his life, Riley was suddenly thinking in terms of forever.

Once with Paige could never be enough. He even had his doubts about a lifetime being enough. Holding her, he felt something new, something all-encompassing.

He felt whole.

PAIGE WATCHED THE MAN sleeping at her side. She ached to touch him, but didn't want to disturb his sleep. He looked peaceful lying there next to her.

She thought about what he'd told her of his father, and her heart bled for the little boy he'd been. But she stared at the man he'd become.

Riley was good-looking. As annoyed as she'd been that first date, she'd never denied that. But now, having glimpsed at least a part of what was behind his facade, he was absolutely gorgeous to her.

He'd touched her tonight. Oh, he'd touched her in quite a physical way, she thought as the memories heated her body. But he'd connected with her on a deeper level as well. He'd opened himself to her and shared something true and intimate.

She reached out and traced a line down the length of his arm, ready to wake him up and try to show him how much she was feeling—though she really couldn't sort out the feelings.

Maybe *couldn't* wasn't the right word. Wouldn't. She didn't want to delve any further than she'd already delved. She just wanted him and to at least show him physically that this meant something.

This time she gently ran her hand down his back and he turned to offer her a lazy, satisfied smile.

"I—" She started, but was interrupted.

A loud thump in the living room stopped her. Strange scuffling noises followed.

"What the heck?" she whispered as she slid out of the bed.

Riley tried to untangle himself from the sheet as he hollered, "Hey, don't open the door. You don't know what's out there. Let me—"

But it was too late. Paige opened the bedroom door, and it was as if a Tasmanian devil had been admitted. Or rather two Tasmanian devils.

"What the—" Riley exclaimed as the whirling mass of fur ran toward, then jumped on, the bed.

Pugsley and Cuddles had obviously met and the meeting was no more successful than Riley and Paige's first date. The big bruiser of a cat, who recently had become more gentle, wasn't very gentle at the moment. He was swiping his paw at the poor dog, who had crawled on Riley's lap for some measure of protection.

"Paige, get that killer cat out of here," Riley shouted, trying to protect the animal from the whacking cat.

She couldn't help laughing at Riley as she walked to the bed, and scooped up the still-hissing Cuddles. "Now, what's all this about? Where are your manners?"

She sat and held the cat up to the poor whimpering dog. "Cuddles, this is Pugsley. Pugsley, Cuddles. I want you two to play nice."

The dog sniffed at the cat, and the cat completely ignored the dog as Paige stroked his head. She set

Cuddles on the floor. "Now, go on and get to know each other."

Cuddles walked out of the room, his head and tail held high. Paige picked up Pugsley and scooted him toward the door as well. "Go lie down somewhere."

She shut the door. "Well, that will get the blood pumping. I thought someone was committing murder out there."

"I'm not thinking about murder now, though my blood is certainly pumping." Now that it was safe and he no longer had to protect himself from attack, Riley sprawled on the bed and wiggled his eyebrows at her.

"Why, Mr. Calhoon, what could you be thinking of?" Paige asked, laughter in her voice.

"Come back to bed and I'll show you."

She walked toward the bed and asked, "Is it a surprise?"

"Yeah."

"A big surprise? I do like *big* surprises."

"The biggest," he promised.

Paige launched herself onto the bed and pulled back the covers, studying her *surprise*. "Why, look at that, it is the biggest. Do you suppose you could help me with it?"

"Oh, I suppose that could be arranged," he said, as he willingly obliged her.

RILEY WOKE UP with Paige in his arms. She was still sound asleep, and so he had time to study her. She wasn't beautiful, at least not in a classic sense. Her features were rather ordinary at the moment—relaxed in sleep. But he knew that what was ordinary in her sleep was extraordinary when she smiled. And since she was always smiling, Riley doubted anyone ever noticed that she wasn't precisely beautiful.

Her short hair was sort of all pushed toward the top of her head in an almost Mohawk sort of look. Whatever little makeup she'd had on yesterday was reduced to dark smudges under her eyes.

No, maybe she wasn't exactly beautiful.

But right this moment, wrapped in his arms, her body pressed against his, Riley had never seen anything as lovely.

He wasn't sure how long he lay there, just watching her breathe in and out. But he saw her eyelids start to flutter and suddenly snap open.

"Riley, you're still here?"

He wasn't sure if it was a statement or a question, if she was happy or annoyed to find him in her bed. But as she snuggled even closer to his warmth, he figured she couldn't be too annoyed.

He wanted to tell her he'd never spent a night, an entire night, with anyone. That this was something special, though he wasn't sure quite what. He wanted to tell her that he thought he liked waking up next to her.

Instead of saying any of that, he said, "I've got to go home and change for work."

She backed away from his embrace and simply said, "Okay."

Riley sat up. "About last night—"

"Riley, please don't worry. I'm not some virginal woman waiting for you to offer some apology for ruining me. I rather enjoyed being ruined by you, truth be told. Really, really enjoyed. But I'm not reading anything more into it than a fluke. A fantastic fluke."

He shook his head. "That's not what I wanted to say. Paige, I know I said this was just a one-time thing…." He hesitated a moment, trying to think about how to continue. "Um, you know it occurs to me that we never did settle the interview business."

Slowly, a smile spread across her face. And for a moment, all the oxygen rushed from Riley's body. She was so absolutely beautiful at that moment.

"You're right," she said. "We didn't resolve any of our interview dilemmas."

"Right. The interview has caused so many problems. I hate to leave the question of do we or don't we hanging over us. So maybe…" Riley took a big breath and said, "Maybe I should come over tonight after work and we could discuss it again."

"Well, that might be best." She nodded solemnly, but the grin on her face spoiled the effect. "I mean, we can't really leave the question of an interview hanging, now can we?''

"What if I brought dinner. Pizza?''

"With mushrooms?'' she asked.

"With anything you want.''

"Anything?'' Her voice was tinged with suggestion.

He grinned, relief flooding his system. He was going to see her again tonight.

"Anything,'' he promised.

"I'll hold you to that tonight,'' she said, and shut the door.

Riley Calhoon whistled as he walked down the hall.

8

"YOU LOOK LIKE THE CAT that ate the canary," Aunt Annabelle said the following week as she and Paige played a cutthroat game of war.

"Do I?" Paige turned over a king and took Annabelle's queen.

It had been one glorious week of Riley.

Eating dinners together, walking Pugsley together, talking about their day at work, doing dishes, and then spending the night—the whole night—exploring each other's bodies. Learning what pleased and what thrilled.

In the past week Paige had experienced sensations that she'd never imagined existed. And maybe they couldn't…not without Riley.

Somehow over the last few days, he'd become part of her life. Just what part he'd play in the future she'd yet to discover, but for now, what they had was wonderful.

"More than a canary," Aunt Annabelle said as she scooped up Paige's ten with an ace.

She realized her aunt was studying her and she tried to wipe the thought of Riley out of her head.

"You look as if you've swallowed an ostrich, or something even bigger. So what did you do now? Land a regular anchor position?"

"No. Though the powers-that-be were pleased enough with my performance, despite the orange hair, to tell me they'd ask me to fill in again."

"So what else could have you looking so—" Annabelle suddenly grinned and gave a little whoop. "War!"

They'd both thrown down twos and then slapped cards on top of them.

"I won!" Annabelle announced as she scooped up the pile with another ace.

"What I'd like to know is how you always seem to have all the aces," Paige said.

"Not all," Annabelle said with a grin. "You've obviously been holding back a few aces of your own."

"What do you mean?" Paige asked.

"I mean, you've finally done it. You've found a man. Wait till I tell the girls. We've been worried about you. A career is all well and good, but a career and a *man* is even better."

Cards forgotten, Paige knew she was caught, and admitted with a grin, "Oh, he's better all right."

Remembering just last night and how much better each time got. And it wasn't so much the physical end of things, though that got better, too. It was the emotional side.

She thought Riley was really opening up to her.

He'd told her about his father, told her about his childhood. Just little snippets here and there, and she'd been able to piece together the rest. A smart, sensitive boy raised by a tough, suck-it-up sort of father.

Riley came by his tough-guy image honestly. But beneath that, the sensitive side still thrived. Quietly. Secretly. But if you knew where to look, it was there.

Every time he visited Aunt Annabelle. Every time he took Zac somewhere, patted Pugsley, rescued a damsel in distress—every time his veneer cracked and she could see the sensitive side that he tried so hard to hide.

"How long have you been seeing this man?" Annabelle asked.

Paige shook off her Riley ruminations and asked, "Seriously seeing him?"

Aunt Annabelle nodded without saying anything. She'd obviously forgotten so she just waited, studying Paige.

Feeling rather like a bug under a microscope, Paige said, "A week."

"And?" Annabelle prompted.

"And that's it. I've been seeing a guy in a rather serious manner for about a week."

"I assume *serious* can be equated with *sleeping with*."

Before Paige could sputter an embarrassed response, Annabelle continued, "Good for you. You've needed a man in your life, and more specifically, a man in your bed for a while now. You should have someone to put a blush on those cheeks."

Paige thought of the wonderful things Riley had done to her last night, of the things she'd done to him and knew there was more than a little bit of color staining her cheeks.

"So are you going to tell me who it is, or do I have to guess?" Annabelle asked.

Paige chuckled. "You'd never guess."

"Bet I can get it in three guesses."

"You're on. We'll play for ice cream. Loser treats."

"Deal." Annabelle paused a moment and said, "Jerry, that guy you interviewed a few weeks ago?"

"No."

Jerry? He was a nice enough guy, and maybe a hero in his own right. After all, he'd caught the guy that had stolen a lady's purse. Though he couldn't hold a candle to Riley.

No way was Annabelle going to guess.

"That Steve guy. You know, the waiter."

"He's not a waiter. He owns the restaurant, and no."

Steve was nice, too. He opened his downtown restaurant to the homeless in October every year. He said there were so many hungry people who were fed on Thanksgiving and at Christmas that he wanted to make the month of October his. The Saturday before Halloween every year, he served meals free of charge.

Yeah, Steve was a nice guy, but he wasn't Riley Calhoon.

As if she could read Paige's mind, Aunt Annabelle blurted out, "Riley."

"You knew all the time," Paige accused.

The look on her aunt's face answered the question before Annabelle could respond. "Of course I did. After all, have you ever known me to make a bet when I haven't first stacked the odds?"

"No. So what kind of ice cream do you want?"

"Forget the ice cream. I just want you to be happy. Be very, very happy."

"I hope to be. I don't know where this is going, but right now, I'm enjoying it immensely."

"I'M ENJOYING THIS," Paige said that evening, echoing Riley's thoughts.

He was enjoying this as well.

This was nothing special. They'd had a quiet, early dinner at Joe Roots, a popular restaurant at the base of the peninsula. And now they were bundled up against the cold October wind and walking along the beach.

At least it would be nothing special except for the woman at his side.

"Me too," he finally said. Oh, he was the king of articulate tonight.

There was so much he wanted to say to Paige, but he didn't quite know how to get all the words out. After worrying about saying too much, worries about not being able to say enough seemed incongruous. But the dark beach made the long silences easier. Quiet seemed expected here.

He reached out and took her hand.

There. He was having trouble getting the words out, but surely she'd understand that he was telling her how special tonight was, how special every night for the last week had been with her.

Because of her.

The fall moon was big, bright and full, casting enough light that they could see clearly. They stopped and stood quietly looking out on the lake.

"The moon sends a little ripple of light across the water," he said without thinking. "Almost like a bridge, daring you, begging you to walk across it."

"That's poetic, Riley."

Realizing she'd called him Riley rather than Calhoon, and that she was right, it was almost poetic, Riley got an odd feeling in the pit of his stomach.

When he was around Paige he found himself saying things, doing things, even thinking things that were disconcerting at the least.

"It's time to go," he said, hoping to cover the

confusion he was feeling. "We're not supposed to be on the beach after dark."

"Oh, we're such wild lawbreakers, aren't we? Well, if we're going to break the law, let's really break it. Let's go skinny-dipping." She laughed. It was like the sound of rain hitting the sun-warmed concrete in spring—warm and inviting. Contagious.

"You've got to be kidding," he said, trying to sound stern but suspecting his smile ruined the effect. "It's freezing out. I swear, it's cold enough to snow."

"Actually, it hit the sixties today. And the lake is still warm. The water won't be that bad. Come on, Calhoon. Let's go."

"You're insane."

"You're the one spouting off about ripples begging you to walk on them. Let's be daring."

"Oh, I can just see the headlines now. Prominent Reporters Bare All. Come on, Paige, let's go."

And yet, he knew if she pressed the issue, he'd jump in the lake even if it was frozen solid. All she had to do was ask and he'd try anything, just to see her smile, to hear that laugh.

She unzipped her jacket. "So what're you going to do, Calhoon, arrest me?"

"Paige," he said, trying to infuse a warning in his voice to hopefully cover the laughter that he could feel bubbling around.

"Handcuff me? Is that what you enjoy, Calhoon, handcuffing women?" She took off her jacket.

"No, that's not what I meant, and you know it. It's just time to go."

She shrugged her jacket back on and grinned. "You've got no sense of adventure, Calhoon. You're lucky I came along to liven things up or you'd start sinking into middle-aged stodginess and become so mired in it nothing could rescue you."

"Keep walking while you're talking, Paige. I want to get you off this beach before you start stripping again. Let's go."

"When you say go, do you mean both of us go home, as in our own personal spaces?"

"I'd hoped you'd invite me to your apartment."

"Nope."

He made out the little shake of her head.

"Not tonight. But I could come to your place. I mean, you've been to my place every night this week. You've never had me over to your house."

"Why do you want to come to my house?" he asked.

"Where you live reveals details about you. Maybe I just want to know everything about you that I possibly can."

"Why?"

"Because maybe I…"

"You what?" he prompted.

In the moonlight he could see a certain seriousness in her face as she said, "Maybe I lo—"

A floodlight hit her right in the face and seriousness was replaced by surprise. "This is a park ranger. What are you two doing on the beach? The park closes after sunset."

"We were just heading back," Riley said.

"He's taking me to his house to ravage me," Paige said, seriousness and surprise having given way to silliness.

"Paige," Riley warned.

"He's sort of dictorial, but he's good at ravaging." Paige patted his arm. "Only he's never ravaged me at his house. I've never seen it. He's been to my place a number of times. That's not right, is it? I mean we should alternate or something."

"I like my privacy," Riley grumbled.

"You know, she has a point," the ranger said.

"See, I have a point," she said with a grin.

"A pointy little head," he muttered. "Come on, we're going."

"If we're not going to your place, then I'm going on strike." She sat on the sand and folded her arms and legs.

"Paige, you're being childish," Riley said. The ranger safely watched the situation from behind his spotlight. Riley didn't have to see him to know he was probably laughing.

"Me?" Paige asked, the picture of innocence.

"I'm childish? You're the one who won't let me come over and play."

"You're not going to let this be, are you?" he asked.

"Nope."

"Fine. You can come to my house."

"Gee, Calhoon," she said, rising and brushing the sand off her behind. "That was such an elegant invitation. How's a girl supposed to refuse?"

"I take it you're both leaving now?"

"Yes, Officer. Thank you."

"THANK YOU," Paige said a couple hours later. "That was nice."

"Nice?"

Riley sounded insulted, and that made her want to laugh, but she tried to look serious while she nodded.

"Very nice. And speaking of very nice, your house is very nice. It's not what I expected."

"What did you expect?"

Paige didn't answer. She wasn't sure what she'd expected, but it wasn't the stately brick home in Erie's old neighborhood, Glenwood Hills; it wasn't a house full of antiques and warm colors. There was a richness and a texture in this house. Comfort.

She felt as warm and safe in the house as she felt in Riley's arms. Like everything else about him, his home had taken her by surprise, but when she thought about it, she wondered why. It suited him.

"I like it," she said, rather than offer up an explanation. "And I like you, you know."

He pulled her close. The soft mat of hair that covered his chest brushed against her cheek and tickled, but she didn't move away. She just drank in the scent of him—hot and spicy—even as she sank into the warm protected circle of his arms.

Wrapped in Riley, she felt brave enough to say what had been nagging at her for a long time. "More than like, I love you. Don't think you have to say anything back. I'm not asking. I just had to tell you."

She waited, sure that Riley would have something to say. Riley always had something to say.

But rather than words, she heard a deep breath.

He was asleep.

He'd missed her declaration. Paige didn't mind. She'd say it again, and again and again until he realized she meant it.

Until he said it back.

Because though he hadn't said the words, Paige suspected that he cared for her, too. As a matter of fact, she'd even begun to hope that he loved her.

With a Pollyanna certainty, she believed it was only a matter of time until he admitted it.

Paige Montgomery loved Riley Calhoon.

Now all she had to do was make him see he loved her, too.

9

RILEY WALKED ACROSS the parking lot toward the office building and realized he was humming.

He had experienced a lot of firsts since meeting Paige. He'd apologized; he'd shared things with her he never even realized himself; he'd prattled. But humming?

Now he was humming?

He realized something else—he was happy.

Deep down, bone deep, contentedly happy.

He could tack on a multitude of adjectives and still not completely describe the depths of his happiness.

Every now and then a niggling of worry, of his old cynical self appeared, telling him that this type of happiness couldn't last, but he ignored it.

He wasn't sure how long it would last, wasn't sure exactly what he felt for Paige, but he was sure that whatever it was, right now, at this precise moment in time, he was happy.

He did, however, stop humming. It wouldn't do to let the guys at the office hear him. The amount of ribbing he'd receive would be unbearable. He'd just hold on to the feeling and enjoy it privately.

He pasted a well-practiced scowl on his face and walked into the crowded office. There were no private offices for mere reporters and columnists. Instead, there was a huge room with a jumble of desks and file cabinets, ringing phones and the steady tapping on collective keyboards.

For Riley, the sights and sounds were comforting. They made his blood start to pump. They were familiar, like coming home. He slid into his chair and booted up the computer.

Maybe the reason he felt so comfortable at Paige's was that she was rather like the office—loud, slightly chaotic, and when he was with her, he felt his blood begin to jump, and he felt as if he was home.

"Hey, if it isn't Riley Calhoon, Erie's hero," said Todd Samuels, the paper's sportswriter.

He was standing next to Riley's desk, grinning in such a way that Riley knew the paper's resident joker was up to something.

"What are you talking about, Samuels?" Riley barked. A sinking feeling enveloped the happiness he'd felt just moments before.

From behind his back, the balding man with the potbelly and annoying sense of humor pulled a key dangling from the end of a string. "By the powers vested in me by the powers that be, I now present you with the keys to the city...well, at least the men's washroom here at the newspaper portion of the city."

Riley didn't touch the key. He simply glared at Samuels and waited, sure that there was more.

"Yes, the key to the city for Riley Calhoon, rescuer of pregnant mamas." Samuels paused and added, "Only she wasn't precisely pregnant, was she?"

"Samuels," Riley warned, and the sinking feeling in his stomach worsened.

Martin, who owned the desk separating Riley and Samuels, was all ears now, along with half the office staff.

"What he'd do?" Martin asked.

Samuels starting laughing and said, "About a month ago our own Riley Calhoon rushed a pregnant lady to the hospital thinking she was about to give birth, only she wasn't pregnant. She was that Paige Montgomery chick from WMAC, and she was in one of her crazy getups looking for a story."

"So why'd he rush her to the hospital?" Martin asked.

"It was her appendix. It was ready to burst, and Calhoon here basically saved her life."

"Samuels," Riley said, infusing as much warning as he could into his tone.

"Oh, did I embarrass you?" Samuels asked, innocence in his voice. "You don't want the office to know that you're a softie when all is said and done?"

The sinking feeling was replaced by dull, burning sensations. Paige had told. It wasn't that the office knew, although he was sure they were going to do their best to make his life a living hell. It was that he'd trusted her.

Actually, though she asked every day—and every night—if he'd do the interview, it had simply become part of their banter. A running joke.

No, it wasn't that the office knew.

It was that he thought Paige had understood. Though they joked about meeting to talk about an interview, he thought she realized he wasn't ever going to do one. That he was meeting her simply because...

He should have known better. He should have known that whatever he and Paige had couldn't last. He'd been stupid to think there was anything more than a momentary flare of passion. And even that spark had died the moment he realized she'd gone behind his back and told the story.

His very private story.

"Hey, Calhoon, where're you going?" Samuels called. "I didn't mean to make you mad. I was just joking."

"Come on, Calhoon," Martin called.

"I'll be back," Riley said simply as he stormed out of the office. There was no humming as he got into his car. The Major had been right—don't count on anyone but yourself.

He had begun to count on Paige, and she'd let him

down. The thought beat a steady tempo in his head as he drove from the paper to the news station.

He'd trusted her, maybe even cared about her more than he should. And she'd told. He'd explained his reasons, and still she'd told.

"I need to see Paige," he said to Penny, the receptionist, as he stormed into the WMAC office.

She'd obviously become used to seeing him, because she just smiled and waved her hand. "I guess you know the way by now."

Yeah, he thought as he opened the door and made his way through the office, he knew, but he was going to forget as soon as he had this one last meeting.

"Riley," Paige said, a warm smile on her face as he walked into her cubbyhole. "What's up?"

"You told."

She looked confused. Riley wasn't buying it. She was a good actress, she'd already proved that. She'd let him think she really cared, when all the time she was planning to get her interview, one way or another.

"Pardon?" she simply asked.

Willing to play along and explain, though he was sure she knew what he was talking about, he said, "I trusted you, and you told about that hero stuff. It's all over the office. You knew how I felt, and you told anyway, hoping to make me do the damned interview. Were you hoping that if my boss got wind of it, he'd agree with you that it was great press and try to pressure me into your interview? Well, it won't work."

"Riley, I didn't—"

"You told someone."

"Listen, in the hospital I told Aunt Annabelle and Stephanie, but neither of them breathed a word. I'd bet my life on it. Aunt Annabelle didn't even mention to you that she knew because I told her not to. Riley, I didn't tell anyone else."

"I don't believe you." Maybe there was a certain sincerity to her words that made Riley pause a moment. A small voice whispered that maybe she was telling the truth. He shoved the doubt away. He didn't believe, couldn't afford to believe, her story. This was a reminder that he'd become too dependent on Paige.

"What?" she gasped.

"I didn't come here for excuses. You told someone—someone in my office. Samuels and Martin both know now. I just came to tell you that this was a mistake."

"*This?*"

"You and me, and whatever it is we've been playing at. We knew it wouldn't last, and this just reinforces it for me. I won't be calling, and I won't be doing any interview."

"Fine."

Riley wasn't sure what he'd expected, but it was

more than her terse monosyllabic response. "That's all? All you have to say is fine?"

"I've already told you that I didn't tell anyone. You don't believe me. So why would I think you'd believe me when I say that I don't think what happened between us was as casual as you seem to feel it was? That I had thought we had something deeper going on. But you were right, and I was wrong. Because deeper would imply trust, and it's obvious you don't trust me. So, you're right, we need to end this—whatever *this* is—now. Goodbye, Riley. It's been, well, not exactly fun, but interesting. And thank you for saving my life. It might not mean much to you, but it meant everything to me."

"That's it?"

"What else did you want me to say?" She watched him and he thought there was a hint of something, maybe optimism, in her expression. But as time stretched and he remained silent, whatever that glimmer was faded.

The hell of it was, Riley didn't have a clue what he'd expected when he confronted her. He'd been out of his element since the moment Paige had reentered his life. All he knew was that who and why she told didn't matter. He should have called things off well before this. It was time to go.

"Goodbye, Paige."

"Goodbye," Paige whispered as she watched the man she loved walk out of her life.

Rose-colored glasses?

Everyone said she wore them, but right now, she couldn't seem to find them. Couldn't think of a silver lining for this entire situation. Couldn't feel the least bit optimistic.

What on earth had she been thinking? Trying to make herself believe that Riley was changing. That there was a chance for them.

There was nothing between them, and no future for them. She'd been a fool, reading what she wanted to see in their situation when all the time there'd just been a healthy sense of lust, and nothing more. Well, fine. She could live with that, or at least she would learn to live with it. But first she needed some time. Time to put whatever it was that had been growing between them behind her. She was going to give herself permission to wallow in the misery that racked her.

"Paul," she said as she walked into her boss's office. "I have to take some time off. Personal time."

"Is something wrong?"

"Wrong? No. It's that, listen, I just need some time off."

"How long?"

"A couple days. I have plenty of vacation time." She might have plenty, but she wasn't wasting more than a couple of those days on Riley. She'd give herself that much time to grieve over what they could have had, and then she'd come back to work and put the whole unfortunate incident behind her.

Riley's veneer might have cracked on occasion, but he was good at pasting it back together. There was no hope of reaching the man she knew was there. She could keep smashing her head against his wall, or admit defeat and move on.

She was admitting defeat.

She wasn't masochistic enough to keep chipping away his charade when it was clear he was comfortable with it.

She realized Paul, the news director, was talking. "You also have some personal time owed you. Just go. We'll cover things here. I'll talk to Steph. Don't worry."

Paige turned and left the office. She wasn't going to worry. She was going to get on with her life, maybe a little wiser, and a lot less Pollyanna-ish than she had started.

THAT AFTERNOON, Riley sat at his desk and typed, but it was simply a jumble of letters. He was moving his fingers, but nothing worthwhile was coming out.

He went over and over his conversation with Paige, and something didn't ring true. She'd denied leaking the information. But if she hadn't done it, who had.

"Hey, Samuels?"

"Calhoon. Listen, I'm sorry I upset you. When Stella told me about you saving Paige—"

"Stella? Who's Stella?"

"You know, the nurse from the hospital I've been seeing now for a few weeks. She was Paige's nurse and Paige was asking for you right after she woke up, sent Stella out looking for you, only you'd gone. I was talking about the office, and she mentioned it. I didn't mean to tick you off by mentioning it."

"You didn't. Not really."

"If that's you not really ticked off, I don't ever want to get on your real bad side."

Riley turned and simply walked away from Samuels, walked out of the office.

What had he done?

He'd accused Paige and broken things off with her. And she hadn't done a thing. He'd jumped to a conclusion. That wasn't like him. Why?

Because he was scared.

"Hey, Calhoon, where are you going now?"

"To take my foot out of my mouth."

He was terrified by the strength of his feelings for Paige.

She thought he was brave, thought he was a hero. But he was a coward. He'd figured that much out within minutes of walking out of WMAC's station.

He felt so much for her, it left him uncertain and afraid.

Well, it was time to get over his fear and win Paige back. He was going to have to grovel. He knew that.

What was it about Paige that made him willing to apologize? He cared about her.

More than cared.

The reason he'd been so mad that she'd told was he'd trusted her. That he...

Damn.

He loved her.

What on earth was he supposed to do about that?

Apologize. That was his first step. Thank goodness he was getting good at saying *I'm sorry*.

Once he was back in her good graces, he'd worry about the next step.

MEN.

Paige took a huge bite of ice cream.

Men. You couldn't live with them...you couldn't live with them.

The ice cream melted, trickling down her throat.

They were toads.

She stabbed another spoonful of the ice cream from her float.

No, men were the warts on toads.

They were the hemorrhoids on the backside of life.

No matter how cold the ice cream was, it wasn't cooling the heat of her ire.

She sat silently admonishing herself. No matter how mad she was, she didn't have the right to condemn an entire gender. It wasn't men who were the problem. It was *a* man. One single individual of the male species.

Riley Calhoon.

He was everything she originally thought he was.

His act of heroism was, just as he had claimed, a small blip in his surliness.

He'd rather believe the worst about people.

The worst about her.

That's what hurt.

She drank the dregs of her ice-cream float. It hadn't helped ease the ball of tightly wound anger, twisted with a good deal of hurt, that sat in the pit of her stomach.

Normally, ice-cream floats fixed almost anything, but not today. Despite three floats, as the day went on, her anger got tighter and tighter until right now, at this moment in time, it was all she could do not to combust.

She needed to do something.

What she'd like to do was kick Riley good and hard. But she didn't believe in violence. So, instead of tracking him down and kicking his butt, she threw on a pair of sweats and went running. And Paige hated running.

It was a cold and drizzling fall day. It was as miserable out as she felt inside. Every cold, wet step only made her madder. And the fact that she avoided physical exertion until it was absolutely necessary, made her madder still.

She hated to sweat. Hated exercise.

Each cold, wet, sweaty step infuriated her. By the time she ran back into her building, she was steaming. The cramp, caused by running on an ice-cream-float-filled stomach, only served to increase her anger.

She reveled in the heat of what she felt. It was so much easier to cope with than the pain she'd experienced when Riley had said goodbye.

Yeah, mad was good.

She turned down the hallway to her apartment and saw Riley standing there, and her anger burst into a full-fledged rage. "What are you doing here?"

"I had to see you."

She brushed by him, pulled her keys from the rope around her neck. "You've seen me, now leave."

"Why are you all wet?"

"I was out running." She fumbled trying to get the key into the keyhole. It didn't seem to fit. She must have grabbed the wrong key. That had to be the answer. It was much more palatable than the thought that Riley had flustered her so much she was trembling and couldn't stop long enough to get the key in the hole.

"You were running in this? You'll catch your death of pneumonia and I'll be hauling you back to the hospital."

"Don't worry, I think I'd prefer suffering to getting a ride with you." Finally the key slid in and she twisted it in the lock.

"I'm sorry about this afternoon."

"Okay." She opened the door a crack, holding on to the handle so that there was a narrow opening.

"I mean, I found out where Samuels got his information. Do you remember a nurse named Stella?"

"Stella was very nice." She gave Riley a meaningful look and added, "Unlike some people."

"She remembered you too and told Samuels that you were looking for the guy who had brought you in, Riley Calhoon. He took it from there."

"Okay." She shrugged her shoulders.

"What I'm saying is, I jumped to a conclusion and I'm sorry."

"So am I." Sorry that she'd been wrong thinking she was building something with Riley.

A relationship.

Yeah, that's what she'd imagined. But it hadn't been. A relationship required trust, mutual respect. He didn't feel either toward her.

"Then we're okay?" he asked.

"We're fine. Now, if you'll excuse me."

She started into the apartment, holding on to the door so Riley couldn't enter.

"Can I come in?" he asked.

"No."

"I thought you said we were fine."

"We are. I'm fine here, and you're fine wherever it is you want to be as long as it's not here."

"Paige, I'm sorry."

"So am I. I'm sorry that for a short time I forgot that your cup is always half-empty. I used to feel sorry for you, but now I'm rethinking it. You're right. I mean, there I was, thinking something was growing between us, something special. I'd put on those damned rose-colored glasses, moved into Polly World, lock, stock and barrel, and was convinced that things were going to work out between us. And look what's happened.''

"Things can work between us. I want them to."

"No, you don't. If you did, you would have offered me some measure of trust. But the first chance you had of convincing yourself I was out to get you, you grabbed it. If I had told your colleagues, then all your paranoid, cynical fears were confirmed. I think you were relieved that you had some tangible excuse to break things off with me."

"I wasn't. I'm not." He raked his hand through his hair. "I don't want to break things off."

"Doesn't matter. Because I'm done. You win. Life sucks. You suck. We're over. Pollyanna's glasses have just chipped and she's moved back into the real world. She's learned that life doesn't always have a fairy-tale ending. You're no hero, and I was never a princess that needed saving."

"But I—"

"Goodbye, Riley. I've got to change."

She shut the door in his face.

10

WHAT THE HELL had he done? And how was he going to undo it?

The questions pounded at Riley. He'd chased away the one woman who'd ever mattered to him. The one woman he loved.

Loved.

He'd spent a lot of time weighing the word, as if he was measuring its use for some column. And no matter how he twisted it, it was the best word to describe his feelings for Paige.

He loved her.

Riley Calhoon loved Paige Montgomery.

I love you. That's what he wanted to say to her. He couldn't contract any of the words, but it was a short enough sentence. He'd willingly turn it into a longer sentence though, if it would make her believe him. He'd feed her rhapsodizing, poetic proclamations of his love. He'd prattle on and on about the depths of his feelings, because even the prospect of prattling didn't faze him. He'd prattle away happily if only Paige would listen to him. But she wouldn't.

She was screening her calls at home, and told the

receptionist at the station not to put him through. Though he tried tailing her, she threatened to get a restraining order.

That was a very un-Paige-ish thing to say.

It was more something Riley would say. The thought that he'd driven her to taking on his dismal view of the world depressed him.

At wit's end, he decided to go to Annabelle. He found her in the solarium playing solitaire.

Solitaire.

That's how Riley was going to end up. Solitary. Alone for the rest of his life. Once upon a time that's how he'd thought he wanted it. Now? A life without Paige wouldn't be much of a life.

"Annabelle," he said as he took the seat opposite her.

"Thought you'd show up eventually. You certainly made a mess of things, boy."

"I didn't mean to."

"No, I don't suppose you did. You're a man, and men tend to be prone to mistakes. You'd think Paige was smart enough to know that. But the girl put you on a pedestal—"

Riley snorted. Pedestal?

"I don't think so," he said. "The thing about Paige was that she saw me as I was and liked me anyway. Obviously, she hadn't seen everything and when she dug a little deeper she didn't. This is hopeless."

"Oh, you're absolutely a boneheaded, thick sort of man, Riley Calhoon. You're just going to give up?"

"I don't know what else to do. I've called, I've followed her, hell, I even wrote her. It was a long, sappy tome of a letter. I got it back unopened, marked 'return to sender.'"

"So think of something bigger." Annabelle discreetly pulled a card out of mid-deck and laid it on the solitaire hand.

Riley was too depressed to call her on her cheating. "Bigger?"

"When you've dealt yourself a rotten hand, you simply have to stack the deck with something bigger and better. You hurt her feelings by not believing in her. Now you have to do something big, something out of character, to show her you were wrong. It just so happens that I've been thinking of ideas. There's always your column. I mean, rather than writing about what's wrong with the world, write about what's right. Write about love."

"Hell, Annabelle, what would people think if I started writing about love? I write about issues—stories that mean something. What would they think?"

She slapped the deck of cards on the table and looked him in the eye. "They'd think that you're in love."

"I'd look foolish."

"You're supposed to look foolish when you're in love. The bigger the fool, the bigger the love."

"Is that written down somewhere?"

She laughed. "I have an idea that would make you look like an even bigger fool. If you're brave enough. It's something that might just be big enough to make Paige sit up and take notice."

Looking foolish was something Riley tended to avoid, but he'd already looked about as foolish as he could in Paige's eyes. And he'd discovered those were the only eyes that mattered. So what if the rest of the world thought he was nuts? If he had Paige back, it didn't matter.

Annabelle's grin was unsettling, but Riley found himself saying "I'm listening," anyway.

"Well…"

Two hours later, Riley still couldn't believe he was taking Annabelle's advice. If Paige needed him to make a fool of himself to prove his love, then this one stunt was going to make her feel like the most loved woman in the world.

He sucked in a deep breath and pressed his case before he could talk himself out of it.

He faced WMAC's news director and assignment editor. "Paul and Stephanie, you've been trying to put a gentler spin on the news here at WMAC and, from the statistics, it seems to be working. What if I had an idea for something new and innovative? Something no one else in the market has ever done.

Something guaranteed to reach your target audience of women and keep them tuned into WMAC.''

"We're listening," Paul said.

"Well…"

"THIS IS DANA MARCUS here at WMAC news, where nice news matters. We're interrupting your program for this breaking news story." She paused a moment and said, "Riley?"

The camera panned to Riley Calhoon, who was seated behind the news desk. "I'm Riley Calhoon. Generally, you only see me in the paper, but today I'm branching out with a news flash. I'm in love. If you're a regular reader you might be surprised, but no more so than I. I'm in love. There it is."

He took a deep breath and tried to control his racing pulse. "I'm hopelessly, head over heels in love with WMAC's own Paige Montgomery. So in love, in fact, that I want to marry her. The problem is, I did something stupid and she won't talk to me. So I took this drastic measure to reach her. Paige. I love you. I'm sorry. Give me another chance."

The camera moved back to Dana. "We'll keep you updated on this emerging story, here at WMAC, where nice news matter and matters of the heart matter most. Now, we return you to your regularly scheduled broadcast."

THE PHONE RANG.

Paige glanced at the extension by her bed and saw three empty glasses and groaned.

She'd switched from regular floats to diet cola because she was on the television and had to watch her weight. But diet cola didn't negate her bloated stomach.

Floats might be her comfort food, but if she was any more comforted, she might explode.

The phone kept ringing. She'd turned off the answering machine last night. She didn't want to talk to or hear from anyone.

Whoever was calling was persistent.

Paige had been lying in bed, thinking about getting up, but not going much further than thinking about it. Oh, she'd got up and went to the bathroom once—after all those floats it was a necessity—but afterward had immediately crawled back into bed and pulled the covers over her head.

She was depressed.

Riley used to taunt her about seeing the glass half-full. Well, right now the glass was totally empty—she'd probably drunk it down along with all those floats—and she didn't know how to get it back.

The phone continued ringing, and Paige mustered up enough energy to answer it. "Hello?"

"Paige, how could you be so cruel?" came a voice she knew she should recognize but couldn't quite place.

"Who is this?"

"Pearly. Pearly Gates over here at Snips and

Snaps. We had to pull a television into the salon because everyone's been following the story all day. Even the new girl, Merry, is hooked. He was stupid, but honey, all men are stupid. If you hold that against them, you'll never hold a man against you. And like we said that day Riley came in here, he's definitely a holdable man. Make up.''

"Pearly, what are you talking about?" Paige asked, flipping back the covers and sitting up.

"Have you turned on the television today?"

"No."

"Turn on WMAC. You'll see. Then go find the boy and make nice." Pearly hung up.

Paige pulled herself out of bed and turned on the television in her room. What she saw was a soap opera. Pearly wanted her to watch a soap opera?

Paige crawled back in bed, pulled up the covers, closed her eyes and listened to the drone of voices. Some woman argued about who Diego really loved.

No one. That's who that Diego loved, Paige thought bitterly. Men were like that. They made you think they cared, and then they broke your heart.

Not that her heart was broken. No, not at all.

She wasn't in bed pining for Riley. She was simply...

"And now it's time for a Marry-Me-Paige-athon update, here on WMAC, where nice news matters and matters of the heart matter the most."

Paige sat up and stared at the television screen.

The camera focused on Riley. He was looking a little worse for wear. His face was stubbled, and he looked weary. He started talking about the hockey game and almost getting hit with a puck. "Maybe that's when it hit me, this is a woman I could love."

What woman was he talking about? Certainly not her. He didn't even like her. He thought she'd betrayed his confidence. But she knew that it wasn't the thought of her telling, as much as his way of backing out of their relationship. He didn't want to need her and that was just fine with her. She didn't need him.

"She was so warm, so giving. Maybe she'll be forgiving as well? Paige, if you're listening, I'm sorry. Call me."

The camera turned back to Dana, who said, "Stay tuned for our next Riley break at the top of the hour."

What was Riley up to? Better yet, why would WMAC think this was news?

Just then the doorbell rang.

Suddenly, very aware of her ratty sweats and bedhead hair, she peeked out the spy hole. The building's super stood, scowling, outside her door.

She cracked the door an inch, leaving the chain on, trying to hide behind it. "Yes?"

"You gotta do something, Paige."

"About what?" she asked.

"Have you looked out your window?"

"No."

"There are people out there with signs."

"Signs?"

"Saying things like Riley's Sorry and Marry Him, Paige. They're marching up and down the street out there, and the other residents are starting to complain. Three of the marchers have tried to get up here. I had to hire someone to watch the door. This is a quiet building. You know I like you. Everyone here does. But that doesn't mean we can put up with this."

"I'm sorry, Henry. I didn't ask these people here. It's all Riley's fault."

"Well, you have to do something."

Something. She had to do something.

She racked her float-addled mind for something she could do.

Her parents. They were in Florida.

Florida was a long way from Erie and Riley Calhoon.

"I'll do something. I'll leave town until this all dies down. I'll make sure everyone knows I'm gone, so maybe they'll leave you all alone." Her giant cat rubbed against the back of her leg. "Will you feed Cuddles while I'm gone?"

"You know that cat hates me," Henry grumbled.

"No, he's reformed. Remember, last time he didn't even try to claw you."

"No, he just hissed and sounded as if he was possessed.'' The big man paused a moment, and then added, ''But I'll do it, if you'll just leave till this blows over.''

''I will.''

Paige shut the door and looked out the window. There were half a dozen people out there, just as Henry had said.

Her fingers trembled with fury as she dialed the office and got put through to Stephanie.

''Hello. WMAC. Stephanie Cooper speaking.''

''Steph, what the hell are you doing?'' She realized she swore, but she was beyond caring. She wasn't sure what was going on, but she knew she didn't like it.

''What I'm doing is putting on one of the smartest marketing ploys of my career. The phones are ringing off the hook. And the e-mail…Paige I'm forwarding them all to you. They're all telling you to forgive him, to take him back.''

''I don't want them and I don't want him.''

''Paige, our viewers are seeing this as a true romance story. They're identifying. We've been working at making this station woman-friendly. Well, you can't get more woman-friendly than a good love story. Riley's looking like the hero. He's every woman's fantasy. Come on. It was one stupid mistake, Paige.''

''You're on his side, too?'' Paige couldn't believe it. She thought Steph was her friend, and yet, she'd allowed Riley to commandeer the station and now she was pressing his case.

"This is business. Good business. Our ratings are going way up," Stephanie said. Immediately her voice dropped and she added, "But that's not all it is. I'm not taking sides. Or if I am, I'm taking yours. I'm hoping you don't throw away a good thing because he hurt your feelings."

"Don't you see, if I stay with him, being hurt would become the norm. He's a pessimist—always willing to believe the worst. Do you really think he's going to change?"

"Yes," Steph said. There was a certainty in her tone. "Have you listened to him?"

"Just the last update."

"Well, you've missed a lot. He told about rescuing you and mistaking your appendicitis as labor. He told about your following him for an interview. He's being open and honest. How could you doubt his sincerity? Come on in and tell him you forgive him. Let me interrupt the show and tell everyone you're on the way down. The whole city will be tuned in."

"Forget it. Remember when I said I need a few personal days? Well, let's dock my vacation a few more days because I'm leaving town."

"What do you mean?" Steph asked.

"I mean, I'm going to take my vacation elsewhere. There are people marching outside my house. My super is complaining. And I've already had a call from my beautician, yelling at me. I'm not waiting around for any more. I'm leaving.''

"Paige you're being awfully hard-hearted about this.''

"I'll be back in the office next week. Riley had better be gone by then. Bye, Steph.''

"Paige—''

Paige hung up and immediately the phone rang. She picked it up without even thinking. "Hello?''

"Paige Montgomery, just what are you thinking?''

What had Riley done to her? One more torture, that's what. On top of everything else she had to deal with, she had an irate Aunt Annabelle. Her aunt could be tough enough to deal with, but when she was annoyed, watch out.

"I'm not going into this with you, Aunt Annabelle.''

"You're not too old for me to take you over my knee, young lady.''

"I'd pay to see you try that." Cuddles crawled onto her lap and she stroked him, comforted by his warmth.

"When are you going to put the boy out of his misery?''

"I'm not. I'm going to Florida to visit Mom and Dad. Maybe I'll even do Disney World.''

"Paige—''

"Goodbye, Aunt Annabelle. I'll see you when I get home.''

"Stubborn. You're pure and simply the most—"

Paige hung up and, before the phone could ring, she called the airlines and bought a ticket to Orlando.

RILEY STARED DISMALLY at the camera. It was off but would be back on shortly. He'd been sure this idea would work. Sure that it would touch Paige.

He remembered their first date, all those months ago. He'd mocked Paige when she'd commented about a couple in the restaurant...

"They look so happy. I wish I had my camera. I'd find a way to work them into a segment."

"You'd call them news? See, that just goes to prove my point, you're not a real reporter."

"And you, who claim to see the world in such cynical terms, can't see that two people who've found love is news? That finding love is something that should be honored and acclaimed?"

"I think you're incredibly naive. Have you looked at the statistics lately? Love doesn't last."

That's what he'd said then. But now? Now he believed that love could indeed be forever. If the two people involved were right for each other.

And he and Paige were as right as two people could be.

They complemented each other. They challenged each other.

Generally, he wrote his column on the computer.

He thought better when he was typing. But necessity could be compelling.

He grabbed a piece of paper and started writing a new column. A column about love.

PAIGE, HIDDEN BENEATH a scarf and the biggest, face-covering pair of sunglasses she could find, couldn't help but watch the television at the airport.

It wasn't as if she had anything else to do as she waited for her flight to board.

A television in the corner blared.

WMAC.

Darn.

Maybe they'd board her plane before another update came on.

As Dana announced another Marry-Me-Paige-athon update, Paige knew she shouldn't have been overly optimistic about her chances. After all, that's not how her life was working lately.

She just couldn't escape Riley.

''Paige, I know you're out there. Remember when you said that my columns spoke about my being a hero? Well, this next one is going to talk about love. True love. Couples whose names are forever linked. And right at the top of that list is Paige and Riley. Two names that are simply part of a whole.''

She studied him as he went on and on about true love. His face was a mess. His eyes looked…haggard. He looked as if he was almost in physical pain.

"I love you. Marry me, Paige, and put me out of my misery. We belong together."

That she'd done that to him suddenly hit home.

Riley, the man who valued his privacy, the man who swore he didn't want to be viewed as a hero, was on television, announcing to the entire city that he loved her, that he wanted to marry her.

What on earth *was* she doing?

So he'd had a momentary pessimistic lapse. She was running away because of that?

She sat in the hard plastic airport seat, watching him but not really listening. She was thinking.

Thinking about her feelings for Riley.

She accused him of not trusting her and had used that as an excuse to break things off. When actually, she wasn't breaking things off as much as running away. Why?

Because Riley scared her.

More than that, he terrified her. The depths of her feelings were so strong that it was almost overwhelming. She could lose herself in Riley with the greatest of ease.

She'd accused him of running, but it had really been her.

She loved him.

Paige Montgomery wasn't a runner. She was a fighter.

She loved Riley Calhoon, and she wasn't running to Florida. She was running back to the station where she was going to accept his marriage proposal—right there, on television. Then, if he tried to back out, she'd have proof and sue him for breach of contract.

Paige got up and whipped off her scarf and glasses as she strode from the airport, ready to take control of her future...ready to capture the man she loved.

"CALHOON, I WANT TO KNOW what you think you're doing?"

Paige heard Stephanie in the background whisper to the cameraman, "Are you getting this?"

Paige should have objected, but she didn't care. She was going to have this out with Riley here and now, and she didn't care if the entire city watched. She wanted them to see.

"What am I doing? I'm making an utter fool of myself. I've been on this television all day trying to prove to you that I'm different since you came into my life. Me, who never spoke of feelings, I'm here spewing them in front of the camera all day. What am I doing? I'm trying to tell you that I love you. I made a lot of mistakes, but loving you isn't one. We go together. I've been writing about it."

He picked up a piece of paper. "Calhoon and Montgomery. We're a pair. Like Romeo and Juliet. Like Héloïse and Abelard. Like Samson and Delilah. Like Tarzan and Jane. Like Donny and Marie."

He loved her? He'd been saying it on air, but it sounded oh so much sweeter to hear it in person.

Paige grinned and said, "Calhoon, don't they teach you about research at the paper? Romeo and Juliet died. Abelard was castrated and sent Héloïse into a nunnery. Samson lost his hair, and eventually his life. Tarzan was a real ape. And Calhoon, Donny and Marie were brother and sister."

"But the point is, all those couples are forever connected in people's minds. Just like Calhoon and Montgomery. Riley and Paige. We're a team. We're meant to be together."

"It's Paige and Riley. I get top billing." The joke fell flat and she realized she was hiding from what she really needed to say. "You accused me of leaking the hero story. I told you I didn't, but you didn't believe me."

"I'm sorry. I trust you. That's why I'm here. I'd trust you'd come save me from this." He smiled. "It took you long enough."

"I never said I was coming to save you."

"Don't you see, you've been saving me since the beginning. Like you saved me from a truck that first night."

"You didn't believe me then, either."

He ignored her protest. "And then you saved me from myself. You taught me how to love."

"Damn, Calhoon. That's not fair."

"Fair? What's fairness have to do with it? Love

isn't fair. It doesn't come when it's expected. It won't be commanded, won't be put aside. It sneaks up on you and changes your entire world. For years I didn't believe in anything, but you taught me to trust, to believe. Hell, Paige, I'm even optimistic. I know you're mad, but I believe that you'll get over it and realize you love me, too. You've proved it.''

"How on earth did I prove I loved you?''

"I couldn't have hurt you so deeply if you didn't love me. You wouldn't be here now if you didn't love me.''

She moved around the desk until she was standing next to him, close but not quite touching. ''You think you're pretty smart.''

"No. I know I am.''

"Okay, maybe this once you are, because you're right, your not trusting me cut so deep because I love you.''

"I trust you now to do this on the air.'' He reached into his pocket and held something out to her. It took Paige a moment to truly process what it was.

"A ring?'' she whispered. It was a small gold band encrusted with tiny rubies.

"Paige Montgomery, will you marry me? Will you let me back into your ever-optimistic Pollyanna world?''

"Yes. I don't know if anyone will ever call you Pollyanna-ish, but I'm sure willing to try to teach you how to see the glass half-full.''

"As long as you're around, my glass is completely full. I love you."

Wrapped in Riley, Paige simply said, "I love you, too."

Epilogue

THE SNOW WAS BLOWING, swirling around the mass of humanity that had headed to the Peach Street stores to do their Christmas shopping.

Riley glanced at the well-bundled woman next to him. They'd just celebrated their first anniversary. How on earth had he gotten so lucky? A year with Paige hadn't dimmed the strength of his feelings. If anything, it had intensified them.

He hoped his luck hadn't deserted him, because the streets certainly weren't deserted and he was going to need all the luck he could get to make it down Peach Street.

"Paige, I told you we shouldn't go shopping today. It's too close to Christmas. Just look at this traffic."

She blew out a long, audible breath and said, "Riley, calm down. Take a deep breath with me. We have plenty of time."

"I don't need a deep breath." He beeped the horn and forced his way into the right-hand lane because it appeared to be moving a little faster. "You're breathing enough deep breaths for both of us. And you're breathing them a lot more often. I told you. I warned you. You didn't listen, though. But you better listen now…don't you dare. Don't you do it. I won't have it. Think of the mess. Think of my nerves. I'm having a nervous breakdown."

"Calhoon, would you stop your incessant babbling? I'm fine. Everything's fine."

"I can't." His hands ached from gripping the steering wheel so tightly. "How could I relax now? It's your fault. You're sitting there breathing and I know what you're thinking. You're going to—" He glanced her way and saw the look of concentration on her face and knew what was going on.

"Look, there you go. You're doing it again. It's only been a minute since the last time. I told you not to do it until we got there. I won't have it. You're in pain. If you wait a few minutes we'll get to the hospital and they'll give you drugs."

"I don't want drugs," she gasped.

"Then *I* want drugs. Lots of drugs. For you. I can't stand seeing you in pain."

"I'm not taking drugs, but you don't have to worry about the pain much longer. I think I have to push."

He felt sick to his stomach. Paige seemed to thrive on keeping him off balance, but this was going to heck with the joke. "Oh, no you don't. There's the hospital. I'm turning now. So hold on. You said we had a lot of time. The midwife said first babies take a lot of time. Hours and hours. Days even. They don't come this fast.''

"The nurse lied. I lied. Someone lied. Maybe that nagging backache was more than just strain and I was actually in labor last night. I don't know, but Riley, I've got to push.''

"Hell no. No pushing in this car. No babies either. I can see the hospital. Don't you dare. Paige, don't you dare.''

He threw the car into park and raced around to the other side and opened her door. He scooped her into his arms, even as she protested. "Riley, don't. I weigh too much.''

"Shut up, Paige.''

The next few minutes were a blur. Paige found herself on a gurney being whisked up to labor and delivery.

"I have to push,'' she said again, as they got in the elevator.

"Paige, don't,'' Riley pleaded.

The nurse from the E.R. had taken one look at Paige and immediately rushed her toward the obstetric floor.

Paige let out a long groan.

"Paige,'' Riley cried helplessly as she panted and sweated.

The elevator stopped.

A small part of Paige wondered why she wasn't embarrassed about having a baby in a very public elevator, but all she could think of was Riley and this proof of their love.

She groaned. The urge to push was overriding any other thought.

She realized that they'd wheeled her someplace else, because when she opened her eyes, it wasn't the elevator ceiling she saw. Brighter lights, different ceiling tiles.

"I see the head," Meghan, their midwife, said. Part of Paige wondered how Meghan had got there, but the part didn't care. She simply focused on Meghan's words. "Easy now, Paige. Take a breath. There we go."

There was an intense pressure and suddenly, there was a feeling of relief.

"It's a girl," Meghan said.

"A girl, Riley. We have a girl," Paige gasped, and Meghan laid the wrinkled mass of baby on her stomach. "A girl."

Riley reached out and touched the small, dark-haired head. "You know, she's going to be just like her mama. Doing things her own way."

"And that's not so bad, is it?" Paige asked, awed by the small miracle she and Riley had created together. Created in love.

"Not at all," he murmured. "I'll even buy her her very first set of rose-colored glasses and do my best to see that nothing and no one ever makes them slip."

Vaguely Paige was aware of the fact that Meghan was bustling around her, but all she had eyes for was her husband and daughter.

"I have the perfect name for her," she murmured as she stroked the small head.

"What?"

"Polly. Polly Calhoon. It has a ring to it, doesn't it?"

Riley's laughter was his only response. "Polly Calhoon. It will do."

Love and laughter, Paige thought as she looked at her family. What more could any woman ask for?

* * * * *

*Look for Holly Jacobs's next
Duets in May 2003 when the
romantic comedy series celebrates
its 100th volume!!*

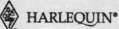
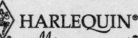

HARLEQUIN® *Blaze*™

From:	**Erin Thatcher**
To:	**Samantha Tyler;**
	Tess Norton
Subject:	**Men To Do**

Men to do!

Ladies, I'm talking about a hot fling with the type of man no girl in her right mind would settle down with. You know, a man to *do* before we say "I do." What do you think? Couldn't we use an uncomplicated sexfest? Why let men corner the market on fun when we girls have the same urges and needs? I've already picked mine out....

**Don't miss the steamy new Men To Do miniseries
from bestselling Blaze authors!**

THE SWEETEST TABOO by Alison Kent
December 2002

A DASH OF TEMPTATION by Jo Leigh
January 2003

A TASTE OF FANTASY by Isabel Sharpe
February 2003

Available wherever Harlequin books are sold.

HARLEQUIN®
Makes any time special ®

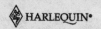
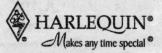

If you enjoyed what you just read,
then we've got an offer you can't resist!

Take 2 bestselling
love stories FREE!

Plus get a FREE surprise gift!

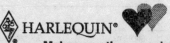

HARLEQUIN® *Blaze*™

Bestselling author Tori Carrington
delves into the very *private*
lives of two *public* defenders, in:

LEGAL BRIEFS

Don't miss:

#65 FIRE AND ICE
December 2002
&
#73 GOING TOO FAR
February 2003

Come feel the heat!

**Available wherever
Harlequin books are sold.**

HARLEQUIN®
Makes any time special ®

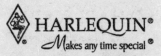